BY THE SAME AUTHOR

Special Relationship

Just Friends

Weekend in Paris

Summer in the City

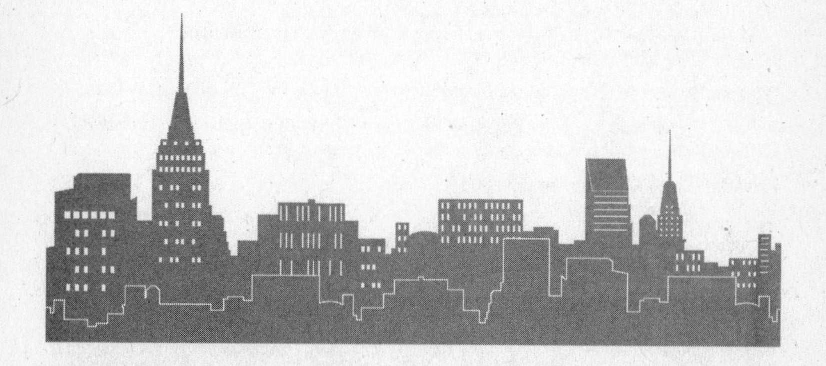

ROBYN SISMAN

A PLUME BOOK

PLUME
Published by the Penguin Group
Penguin Group (USA) Inc., 375 Hudson Street, New York, New York 10014, U.S.A.
Penguin Group (Canada), 10 Alcorn Avenue, Toronto, Ontario, Canada M4V 3B2 (a division of Pearson Penguin Canada Inc.)
Penguin Books Ltd, 80 Strand, London WC2R 0RL, England
Penguin Ireland, 25 St Stephen's Green, Dublin 2, Ireland
(a division of Penguin Books Ltd)
Penguin Group (Australia), 250 Camberwell Road, Camberwell, Victoria 3124, Australia (a division of Pearson Australia Group Pty Ltd)
Penguin Books India Pvt Ltd, 11 Community Centre, Panchsheel Park,
New Delhi – 110 017, India
Penguin Books (NZ), Cnr Airborne and Rosedale Roads, Albany, Auckland,
New Zealand (a division of Pearson New Zealand Ltd)
Penguin Books (South Africa) (Pty) Ltd, 24 Sturdee Avenue, Rosebank,
Johannesburg 2196, South Africa

Penguin Books Ltd, Registered Offices: 80 Strand, London WC2R 0RL, England

Published by Plume, a member of Penguin Group (USA) Inc. Previously published in a Michael Joseph edition, under the title *Perfect Strangers*, in Great Britain.

First American Printing, March 2005
10 9 8 7 6 5 4 3 2 1

LIBRARY OF CONGRESS CATALOGING-IN-PUBLICATION DATA

Sisman, Robyn.
Summer in the city / Robyn Sisman.
p. cm.
ISBN 0-452-28612-3 (trade pbk.)
1. British—New York (State)—New York—Fiction. 2. Women in the advertising industry—Fiction. 3. Exchange of persons programs—Fiction. 4. Americans—England—Fiction. 5. Advertising agencies—Fiction. 6. New York (N.Y.)—Fiction. 7. London (England)—Fiction. I. Title.

PS3569.I75S86 2005
813'.54—dc22

2004058374

Printed in the United States of America

PUBLISHER'S NOTE
This is a work of fiction. Names, characters, places, and incidents are either the product of the author's imagination or are used fictitiously, and any resemblance to actual persons, living or dead, business establishments, events, or locales is entirely coincidental.

For Adam

Chapter One

The rain had started during dinner, some time between the removal of the red snapper with herb polenta and the triumphant arrival of Bridget's homemade tiramisu. This was not the usual diffident English drizzle, but a drenching deluge that cascaded out of the sky, rat-tatted against curtained windows and gathered in splashy pools in basement wells. Two hours on, it was still spraying across the slick London pavements in fierce gusts. Standing on a street corner somewhere at the nastier end of Kensington, desperate for a taxi, Suze felt as if she had been hosed down like a horse. An animal tang rose from her ruined leather jacket. Wet crawled like spiders from her hairline. Only a blaze of indignation kept her warm.

I will never get married, she vowed. *Never will I be as smug, as patronizing, as boring*—she leaped away from the curb as a newspaper delivery van shot an arc of dirty puddle-water at her knees. The *Sun,* she read, in the rat-eyed glimmer of its taillights. How very appropriate. Cold water trickled down her tights and seeped into the new suede shoes she had worn to impress Bridget's spare man. Vanity, thy name is woman. Bridget, thy name is mud. Suze, thy brain is mush.

She should have known better. Bridget used to be a lark back in the good old days when they'd worked together in a publisher's publicity department, Suze as a design minion and Bridget as the youngest and prettiest of the "puffettes"—publicists prized more for their legs than their brains. The two of them had become best mates, flirting heartlessly with anything in trousers and spending their lunchtimes in designer shops trying on clothes worth a month's salary. They went clubbing together—sometimes all night, readying themselves for another day of toil with a double espresso in a Soho café and a quick facial repair in the office loo. But ever since Bridget had lured Toby to the altar—Suze had an image of him hacking his manly, deluded way like a portly Prince Charming through a fairy-tale thicket of posies and ribbons and swathes of ivory taffeta—Bridget had acquired an air of quiet condescension that drove Suze wild. In quick succession Bridget had given up work, cigarettes, alcohol and all power of original thought. Within a couple of years she had acquired a Madonna smile and a baby. Nowadays she regarded Suze's life with a mixture of matronly disapproval and drooling curiosity. Suze's career, she implied, was no substitute for a husband. Yet when Bridget had invited her to dinner, Suze had felt the tug of friendship and accepted. She had gone prepared to sparkle.

There had been eight of them: three married couples, one single man and herself. Subtle stuff. The single man was a work chum of Toby's, a mortgage broker called Charles. He was blond and well fed, confident in City suspenders and striped shirt. After the initial introduction he ignored her utterly, possibly out of the same embarrassment that made Suze feel like an exhibit in an ethnological museum. "Unmarried urban woman, late twentieth century," the label would read. "Note the mating-display rituals of scarlet lipstick and short skirt."

For the first ten minutes she had been marooned on the sofa between Katie and Victoria, while they discussed childbirth in chilling detail. The men stood at the other end of the room, doing important stuff with wine bottles. Toby's elder brother, Hugh, was a wine merchant, said to be awfully sound on claret. Suze had sipped her Pinot Noir and smiled brightly into the middle distance, trapped in the counterflow of alien jargon. *Epidural . . . tannin . . . blackberry nose . . . placenta . . . pethidine.* She drained her glass much too fast and, on the pretext of getting a refill, escaped to the kitchen, where she found Bridget peering anxiously into her wall oven.

"Can I do anything?"

"All under control," Bridget said, in a strangled falsetto. "At least—could you be an angel and reprogram the video machine? The timer's gone up the spout, and there's a football match Tobe wants to record. Machines aren't really his thing."

Suze loved gadgets. Returning to the living room, she parted the men like Moses at the Red Sea, and reset the controls under their silent, critical gaze.

"Not just a pretty face, eh?" Toby winked at Charles.

"They say a four-year-old can do that," Charles replied crushingly.

Suze just laughed. "Unfortunately, Toby's nearer forty."

Dinner was an elaborately grown-up affair, complete with candelabra, tablecloth, three sizes of glassware and matching bone china. Suze was placed between Charles and Toby. Conversation flitted over the usual topics: holidays, films, restaurants, whether it was pretentious to have a Jeep-style car in town, the ethics of private medicine, the price of Agas, how they would spend their lottery millions, the best place to buy fresh pasta. Nigel and Katie, who spoke in stereo, found a lot to say about their experience of attending childbirth classes. Charles explained to Suze, quite confidentially, that he could probably remortgage her flat at a lower rate. "I'd have to come and see it, of course," he hinted. He and Toby then spent the whole of dessert discussing office politics across her chest. Suze tried to open a line of communication with Katie by offering her some wine, but gave up when Katie placed her hand virtuously across the top of her glass and simpered, "The baby."

Suze was almost relieved when Toby turned his attention to her—until she heard his question. "So, young Susannah," he trumpeted, "how's your love life?"

Instantly the room went quiet. Seven pairs of eyes turned to stare at her.

"OK," she said lamely. What was it with married people? Was a tact lobotomy a compulsory part of the marriage vow?

"Still no one special?" Bridget asked sympathetically.

"Well—"

"Poor you." Katie's hand rested complacently on her pregnant stomach, which seemed to begin about three inches below her chin. "I honestly don't think I could bear to go back to those days of 'And what do you do?' and 'Ohmygod, is he going to ring?' "

The other women groaned.

"Don't remind me . . ."

"The agony . . ."

Suze rallied. "But that's the fun of it." She tossed back her hair and leaned her elbows on the table. "Who wants to know you're going to go home with the same man for the rest of your life? If you're single, every night's a magical mystery tour. Surely you can still remember? Parties, clubs, the excitement of the chase."

"Tally-ho!" Charles yelped excitedly. He was now looking at Suze with distinct approval.

"It's not the same, though. Is it, Hugh?" Victoria put a hand on her husband's plump thigh.

"Absolutely," he agreed, gazing at Suze's breasts. "I mean, no way. Ouch, Vicky, that hurt."

"The thing is," Nigel pontificated, "once a girl's past her prime, the best chaps have already been nabbed."

"Fact of life," Toby agreed smugly, smoothing his balding head. "Loads of females at work, over thirty and still single—little crackers, too, some of them. Eh, Charles?"

Charles said nothing for a moment. Then a sly grin spread across his features. "Karen Wiggins," he pronounced. Both men guffawed.

Suze flushed. "I'm not past my prime," she squawked. "Anyway, what's so great about washing socks and cooking dinner for someone who's just going to lose his hair and spend the rest of his life reading the sports pages?"

There was a silence. The others looked away, embarrassed for her.

Hugh cleared his throat. "What do we think of the wine?"

There was a burble of praise. Suze realized she had drunk about ninety-five glasses without tasting a thing. Still smarting, she sipped ostentatiously, then frowned. "Perhaps just a soupçon more pethidine for absolute perfection?"

"How's work?" Bridget asked quickly. "Suze is on the design side at Schneider Fox, the advertising agency," she explained to Charles. "What's your latest project, Suze?"

Suze pretended to think. "Weight Watchers," she said at last. "This week I had to supervise a photo shoot for the ad campaign—make sure it fits in with the new company profile and all that guff. Anyway, the idea is that there's this naked man lying on the floor. All you can see is his view looking down—just a vast dome of hairy stomach, then some feet sticking up. The copy line reads, 'Where has it gone?'" She giggled. "Then at the bottom it says, 'You can find it again with Weight Watchers.' What do you think?"

"Naughty, naughty." Charles leered. He had perked up considerably since the public discussion of Suze's love life.

"Bloody feminist propaganda," Toby protested. "It's normal for men to fill out a bit as they mature." He patted his middle-aged spread fondly.

"As Nigel said," Suze reminded him gravely, "once you're past your prime . . ."

Suze's recollection of this ignoble triumph was interrupted by a familiar throaty roar. Sure enough, a taxi was miraculously drawing to a halt about twenty yards away. She splashed toward it and wrested the open door from the hand of the previous occupant.

"Islington," she panted, then threw herself into the back before the driver could say he was going off duty.

"Blimey, love. Been swimming?"

Suze wiped the water from her eyelashes and eyebrows, wrung out her hair and leaned back stickily against the seat. Opposite her was a poster for a dating agency. "LONELY?" it asked in giant letters. She closed her eyes.

During coffee Bridget had stiffened, laid a warning hand on Toby's arm and shot out of the room. She returned, bearing what looked to Suze like a surprised pork sausage. "Timmy-wimmy's lonely," she crooned. "He wants to join the party."

The baby stared cross-eyed at the flickering candles for about two seconds, then burst into a head-banging wail. He was jiggled and juggled, held upside-down, thrown over shoulders and shown how the oven timer worked while the six parents and parents-to-be discussed infant sleep patterns, before moving on to brands of diapers and trainer cups.

In desperation Suze cleared the dishes from the table. As she rinsed and stacked them in the dishwasher, she was aware that Charles had followed her into the kitchen. He shut the door and leaned against it, lazily looking her up and down.

Suze wished she was not wearing her new hip-hugging leopard-skin skirt. "This is what we women call 'washing-up,'" she enunciated, as if to a foreigner.

He laughed easily, a self-satisfied, drunken chuckle. "So what are you doing this weekend, you wild unattached woman?" He sauntered toward her across Bridget's Provençal floor-tiling. "Fancy a couple of days in the country? Green fields, farmhouse breakfast, four-poster . . . me. No strings."

Suze stared at the swirling water in the sink. Did other women really say yes to invitations like this? For a moment she forgot she was a tough, modern career woman and felt like bursting into tears. Instead, she carefully turned off the tap, picked up a dish towel to dry her hands, then turned to look him in the eye. Charles smiled cockily back.

"I don't think so," she said coolly. "Thanks anyway."

"Oh, come on, have some fun for a change." He took one end of the towel and pulled her toward him. "Toby said you weren't seeing anyone."

"Then Toby is sadly misinformed," she answered, sounding hoity-toity even to her own ears. "I have plenty of fun, as it happens. And let go of my towel."

He held on to it long enough to show her who was boss, then chucked it back at her. "Your loss."

When Timmy-wimmy had at last been returned to his baby lair, they played the hat game. Everyone had to write down names of famous people on slips of paper, which were folded and placed in a hat.

"Help!" giggled Katie, casting moo-eyed glances at the men. "My mind's gone a complete blank. It must be all the pregnancy hormones."

Marie Stopes, scribbled Suze, *Germaine Greer*, *Herod.*

They split into teams of two, one taking a slip from the hat and firing clues at the other. Toby, who had the sensitivity of a double-decker bus, insisted that Suze was partnered with Charles.

"Here's at least one game we can play," she said, trying to make peace. "Stick with me. I always win this."

He raised his eyebrows at her. "I think I'm past the party-game stage, actually."

"Right, chaps." Toby unbuckled his watch and laid it on the dining table. "Suze and Charles to start. One minute to get as many answers as poss."

Suze drew her first piece of paper from the hat and unfolded it. She turned to Charles, trying to beam thought messages into his brain—if he had one.

"Prince of Denmark," she prompted.

"Er, Olaf?"

Try again. "Shakespeare."

"William."

"To be or not to be."

"That is the question." Charles snickered nervously.

"Failed to marry Ophelia."

Puzzled silence.

"Stabbed Polonius." Suze demonstrated with a fork. "Behind the arras."

"Hmmm. Tricky one, this."

"A very small joint of cured pork," Suze shouted in desperation.

"*Ping!*" went Toby. "Time's up."

On the dot of eleven Victoria jumped to her feet. "The babysitter," she moaned guiltily. They all began collecting their coats. Charles did not offer Suze a lift. At the front door Bridget peered out at the wild night from Toby's protective embrace. "Are you sure I can't call a cab to take you home, Suze?" she asked, in a low, social-worker's voice.

Suze flipped up the collar of her leather jacket. "Home?" She laughed incredulously. "Before midnight? Some of us have parties to go to, Bridge."

And off she had walked into the sheeting rain, as jauntily as if it were high noon.

Shivering in the back of the taxi, Suze winced at this pathetic line. She hadn't been to a party in months. No one had even asked her out for weeks—no one tempting, anyway. Besides, she didn't have time for a social life anymore. She regularly worked a twelve-hour day. Leaving the office at eight or nine, she was too exhausted to do more than pick up a frozen calorie-counter's dinner from the supermarket and eat it in front of the television before falling asleep. Maybe Toby was right: she would gradually turn into one of those briskly cheerful middle-aged women who ate microwaved pudding for one at Christmas and had to take a week's compassionate leave when their cat died.

But was the married state any better? Anger welled again. What gave Bridget and Co. the right to act so superior? Why would anyone think she wanted all that stuff—the granite countertops, the ruched blinds, the wedding-present cutlery, the Italian-designed baby buggy, the arguments over who took out the rubbish, the way Toby called Bridget "old girl" and allowed her to fetch and remove dishes all evening while he blahed about the office?

The cab radio was tuned to a golden-oldie station. *All the leaves are brown, and the sky is gray . . .* The Mamas and the Papas. Her parents' music, the music of her childhood, of magical parties that she had watched, dozing, from a makeshift bed of fun-fur coats. She remembered the smoke and noise, the texture of her mother's velvet skirt, the thrill of being picked up and whirled to the music. Her parents were married by then, yet there had been passion, friendship, energy, laughter. What was the secret?

I'd be safe and warm if I was in LA . . .

Ha. If only. Suze rubbed a circle on the steamy window, and cupped her hands around her face to look out. They had reached Liverpool Road, a dark procession of locked shop-fronts and piles of rubbish disintegrating in the wet. One of the shops was a florist's. She resolved to send Bridget a sumptuous bouquet first thing tomorrow, to compensate for her ungracious behavior. The food had been delicious, after all.

"Turn left here," she shouted at the taxi driver, unpeeling herself from the seat, "third lamppost on the right." As soon as he had stopped she cranked open the door, leaped on to the pavement and shoved a note through the window. Too cold to wait for her change, she fled up the steps to her front door.

Inside the flat, she took off all her clothes and dumped them in the bath, toweled her hair, then wrapped herself up in a man's dressing gown made of scarlet cashmere that she'd found in a market stall. She hugged it tightly around her, and bent to check herself out in the mirror, wondering if she looked like a tragic Tolstoyan heroine, too passionate and sensitive for this world. She didn't. Hair blackened with rain, hazel eyes leaking mascara, a potentially haughty nose completely undermined by the wide, curvy mouth so often misinterpreted as an invitation to pounce: same old Suze. The product did not match the image. She extinguished the bathroom light with a snap.

It was still not even midnight. The weekend stretched long and empty before her. She roamed the flat, looking for diversion. She ran her fingertips along the spines of her videos and CDs, eyed her freebie bottle from last month's vodka project, opened the fridge and contemplated an individual sticky toffee pudding, shut the door again, rattled the keys of her computer. If only it weren't Saturday, tomorrow she could go to work.

When the phone rang, she could have kissed it. An Australian voice at full throttle scorched down the line: Harry Fox, her boss. "Where the bloody hell have you been?"

"Out. But my machine—"

A small explosion interrupted her. "Machines are for wimps. Now listen, Suze, I have a problem. What do you say to four weeks in New York?"

Chapter Two

At 7:30 A.M. precisely, Lloyd Rockwell walked out of his apartment building on West Seventy-second Street and turned toward the subway. It was a morning of warm June sunshine, the air fresh, the sky bright, and he stepped out confidently, admiring the way the city's geometry was reflected in sharp, slanting shadows on the sidewalk. He smiled at Mrs. Grumbach and her dachshund, as he did every morning, said hello to the Korean woman setting out her buckets of flowers, as he did every morning, waited at Broadway until the street sign told him to walk, then crossed over by the corner fruit store.

Today there were piles of golden melons outside, flown in from Turkey or Morocco or the South of France to reassure New Yorkers of their God-given right to life, liberty and the pursuit of consumer goods. Breathing in their musky, exotic scent, Lloyd felt a wild impulse to buy a whole luscious bagful to take home to Betsy for a chin-dribbling feast. But the melons were five dollars apiece, and he and Betsy were supposed to be on an economy drive until she had finished with Jane Austen. Resisting temptation, Lloyd walked on to his usual newspaper stand, took the exact change from his raincoat pocket (the television weathergirl had predicted showers sweeping up from the south during the afternoon) and bought a *New York Times*, which he slotted carefully into the outer pouch of his briefcase. Then he descended into the steamy underworld of the subway.

Hell must be like this, he sometimes thought. The harsh light, the lung-stripping air, the sudden rank smells, the press of so many people with their anxious, shuttered faces—always together, never communicating. When he was fourteen Lloyd had been forced to study *The Aeneid* by a Latin teacher who later got himself dismissed for smoking dope on campus. Only two things had stuck in Lloyd's memory: the Latin word *quercus*, meaning a holm oak, a tree he had never come across before or since; and Virgil's bleak picture of souls in hell, tormented by having to do the same thing over and over again without hope of remission. It was an image that rose in his mind with alarming frequency these days.

The train was packed, but for once Lloyd managed to find a seat ahead of the crowd. He tried to fold his long legs out of the way as a woman dropped her briefcase at his feet and reached for the railing above his head. As the train started to roll, her coat swung open to reveal a swelling stomach inches from his nose. Pregnant, he wondered—or just fat? Lloyd pondered his dilemma. Should he offer her his seat? It was almost certainly the right thing to do, but what if she were not pregnant, after all? Would she find it offensive to be offered a seat on the grounds of gender alone? What if she realized that he had thought the unthinkable: this woman is fat? Even if she were pregnant, would she regard it as offensive that a man deemed her incapable of standing? Life seemed full of such pitfalls nowadays—Lloyd remembered the girl who had bounced her tennis racket on his head and growled, "After you, Sir fucking Galahad," when he had held open the clubhouse door for her. At the next station he solved his moral conundrum by surrendering his seat on the pretext of getting out, then reentered the next car.

Lloyd's mind began to focus on the pitch he was due to make later that morning. This was the moment he liked best in his work: when the research data was collected, the competition assessed, the brainstorming sessions completed, and it was Lloyd's job to distill the results into a single creative concept. "We try harder." "Come to Marlboro country." "*Ich bin ein Berliner.*" He was still a copywriter at heart, even if he had a fancier title these days. Whether you were selling politics, jeans, AIDS awareness or soap, it all came down to words in the end. Manipulating them was Lloyd's favorite game.

Today's presentation was to a Montana footwear company that had started up back in the seventies as a hippie-ish, eco-friendly commune called Sam & Martha. By a mysterious quirk of fashion it had suddenly become cool to be seen in their unbleached cotton running shoes. Kids in Harlem were playing basketball in them. Andie MacDowell had been photographed for *Vanity Fair* wearing a pair on her ranch. Sam & Martha had risen from their hash-and-lentil trance, cut their hair, taken a suite at the Pierre and were now talking about going head-to-head with Nike and Reebok. Privately Lloyd thought this a little ambitious. Instead, he wanted to make a virtue of their hey-let's-do-it-right-here-in-the-barn quality, and had plotted out a series of print and television ads featuring everyday domestic scenarios, using the slogan "the human race." People said advertising was a sophisticated form of lying, but Lloyd argued the exact opposite: that the most effective advertising was the most truthful. Lately he had begun to think that not all his colleagues shared his view.

Somebody must have told Sam & Martha that it was Lloyd who had dreamed up the campaigns for Passion. They said this was "something they could really relate to," and had insisted on interviewing him in person. Lloyd's colleagues had been teasing him all week about how he would have to wear sandals to the meeting and call everyone "man." Lloyd fingered the precise knot of his Brooks Brothers tie. Very funny.

If Sam & Martha liked his concept, the agency's reputation would rise another notch, Lloyd would be flavor of the month, and a whole team of designers, PR people, commercials directors, print buyers and assorted media clowns would be let loose on the project. If, on the other hand, the client was not convinced, then Lloyd would have presided over a colossal waste of time and money. It was a lottery he played several times a year. Normally on the morning of a presentation he woke early, mouth dry, head buzzing with ideas and anxieties. But not today.

Although today seemed just like every other Friday, it was not. Today was the last day for four weeks that the subway would spring its shadowy trap, that he would feel the twitch of an invisible leash drawing him to work every day and back home again every evening. This weekend, within forty-eight hours, Lloyd would be boarding a plane to London. For six weeks he was going to live in another man's apartment and do another man's job. Betsy wasn't coming—she had her dissertation to finish—but somehow going alone was part of the adventure. He would walk the same streets as Charles Dickens, take tea at the Ritz, watch the Thames slide under his feet from Westminster Bridge, ride on the top of a red double-decker bus, discover a marvelous pub with oak beams, find out what exactly Yorkshire pudding tasted like. The women would wear extraordinary hats. The men would wear tweed jackets and smoke pipes. Everyone would have a garden and a dog, and discuss the weather. They would be masters of irony, saying the exact opposite of what they meant. Lloyd sneaked a look around the train compartment, and a feeling of liberation swept through him. He might look like the rest of the commuter herd—sober suit, polished shoes, trophy briefcase—but in his heart was pure romance.

Next month he would be thirty-five, time to settle into the future he had mapped out for himself. The whole plan was clear in his head, and he was sure it was a good plan—grown-up, responsible, the right thing. But like the saint who prayed to be virtuous—but not yet—Lloyd relished the idea of one final fling.

This was the third year in a row that he had applied for the Schneider Fox exchange program. The first time he had been rejected on the grounds of inexperience; the second, because he had become too valuable to the company. This time the plum had simply plopped into his lap. Julian Jewel, his opposite number in England, had volunteered his flat as well as his office for Lloyd's use, though Jewel himself had elected to stay in a New York hotel. Jewel sounded pleasant enough, in his lofty English way. How much damage could anyone do in four weeks, after all? Lloyd was happy enough just to lie back and think of England.

Besides, he deserved this trip. For his junior year in high school Lloyd had been chosen to spend a year at Winchester School in England. During the spring semester he had spent weeks poring over the literature they had sent him, half suspecting it was a joke on dumb Americans but smitten by the alien glamour of it all nevertheless. There were fuzzy photographs of boys in high collars and tailcoats, strolling through ecclesiastical-looking buildings; a timetable that included ancient Greek, cricket and something called "prep"; a uniform list as weird as a pervert's wardrobe. The school alumni were known as Wykehamists—an exotic new word Lloyd had rolled around his tongue.

But that was the summer everything changed. The scandal broke in May. Lloyd had been withdrawn at once from his preppy New England school, lodged for a jittery period with his bewildered grandparents and then fled to California with his mother. At seventeen, the door had slammed shut on his childhood. He had avoided looking back. But the Winchester opportunity glimmered in his memory like a promise. Now it seemed that something was to be redeemed from those lost, innocent times.

At Christopher Street Lloyd stepped out of the train and was swept back up into daylight. He turned toward the Hudson River and tacked his way through the genial, leafy streets of the Village, suppressing a stab of nostalgia for its kooky boutiques, Zen bookstores and arty cafés, where NYU students flirted with each other over earnest discussions of Nietzsche and styrofoam cups of espresso—just as he had done a lifetime ago. The blare of traffic hit him as he reached Hudson Street. Wind whipped across from the river, carrying a chemical tang from the Jersey shore. The Schneider Fox building rose before him, a massive block of snowy granite with its grandiose chrome entrance flashing in the morning sunlight. Lloyd had dubbed it the Winter Palace, on account of its triumphalist architecture and mercilessly efficient air-conditioning. Schneider Fox occupied two floors somewhere in the middle of the building, the meager filling in a giant's sandwich. He wondered about the London office, indulging in a fantasy of wood paneling, sit-up-and-beg typewriters and buffoons in monocles yelping, "What? What?"

As Lloyd rode the sleek elevator, listening to its familiar whir, he reviewed the day ahead. There were photographs to pick up for this morning's presentation, hand-over briefings to be completed, clients to be reassured. He needed to bring Sheri up to speed on the projects she would be babysitting while he was away. Most important of all, he needed to ensure that nothing could go wrong with the Passion account. If it did, he wouldn't have a job to come back to.

The doors slid open straight on to the reception area, a chic confection of bluey-greeny grays designed to lead the eye through the far glass wall and out into the bay, where the Statue of Liberty rose like a pale-green goddess. The outsize reception desk, carved into a sinuous *S* for Schneider out of a single hunk of environmentally correct wood, was still untenanted, apart from a minimalist flower arrangement. Beside it crouched a postmodernist sculpture made of Perspex and animal hair that was supposed to represent a fox. Lloyd called it "Rover." There was no evidence whatever of Schneider Fox's trade—no campaign posters, no awards trophies, no brand-name logos, nothing more ostentatious than virgin copies of *The New Yorker*, *The Economist* and *Fortune*, arranged in a tasteful fan across a low, slate table. The subtext was clear. Schneider Fox was so famous that it didn't need to advertise.

It was still too early for most people to be at work. Lloyd punched his security code into the panel of the steel-framed inner door and made his way to his very own glass box, its square footage calibrated to match his status. As a small boy visiting the magnificence of his father's Wall Street office, with its thrilling swivel chair and attendant secretaries and masculine tang of cigar smoke, he used to wonder whether he would ever be that important. Now he knew. He dumped his briefcase, hung his jacket on the steel coatrack and tapped the entry key on his computer to release his e-mail. Most of it was junk of one sort or another, including the daily joke. Question: How many advertising people does it take to change a light-bulb? Answer: Twelve—one to fix the light and eleven to explain the concept. Lloyd saved a couple of messages to deal with later, deleted the rest, then went to see if Dee Dee had come in early as she had promised.

Dee Dee was a dumpy girl from Queens, with an invalid mother and a wardrobe so unfashionable it was spooky, whom Lloyd had picked out of twenty more-sparky-looking candidates. He had picked right. Dee Dee worked hard, thought ahead, remembered everything, laughed at his jokes and never, ever sulked. By now she did the job just about as well as it could be done. Pretty soon, Lloyd thought gloomily, they would have to think about promoting her.

He found her in the small conference room, collating photocopies and storyboards for Sam & Martha. "Last day, huh?" she said, squaring the edges of the photos and sliding them into a folder. "I brought you a present to celebrate." She nodded toward a brown paper bag. "Almond croissant—Balducci special."

"Oh." Lloyd took the bag and held it awkwardly, wondering if he was supposed to eat the damn thing now, even though he wasn't hungry.

Dee Dee scanned his face with amusement. "You don't have to eat it right this minute, Lloyd. You know how you get without regular fueling. I'll put it in your briefcase." Deftly, she slid all the presentation material into a portfolio, placed the bag on top and led the way back to Lloyd's office. "I love your Sam & Martha idea," she said.

Lloyd eyed her suspiciously. "You're very solicitous this morning. Don't tell me you're going to miss me. Not when you can have the great Joolian Jool."

They laughed together over the name.

"And Sheri," Dee Dee added, without enthusiasm.

"And Sheri," Lloyd agreed. "She's in charge while I'm away. I know you'll do everything to make that easy for her."

"Of course." With the tiniest of sighs Dee Dee packed everything into Lloyd's briefcase, while he put on his jacket, then stooped to catch his reflection in one of the posters on his wall.

"How do I look?"

Dee Dee rolled her eyes. "Like you always look. Clark Kent without the glasses." She put the briefcase into his arms. "Don't forget your Kryptonite."

Lloyd opened his mouth to explain that Kryptonite was just what Superman did not need, then told himself not to be a pedant. He was already branded a "pointy head" in the office, having once let slip that he had read a Henry James novel prior to its Hollywoodization on the big screen.

It took until lunchtime to reassure the shoe people. Lloyd was too busy to stop and eat, but Dee Dee had been right about the hunger pangs. He devoured the croissant in three huge bites as he rode down in the elevator, dusted himself off and hurried back downtown to Schneider Fox. Stuck to his computer screen was a note in Dee Dee's handwriting: *Bernie wants to see you a.s.a.p. No reason given.*

Lloyd felt a twinge of anxiety. Bernie never wanted to see anyone. Alone of all the Schneider Fox staff, he had a proper office to himself, with solid walls and a door that closed. He preferred to communicate with his employees by memo, which he recorded into a Dictaphone that he carried with him everywhere. It was just one weapon in his arsenal of power, reminding his staff that however long they lasted in the business they would never launch as many successful campaigns as he had, or call as many millionaires by their first names.

Bernie Schneider was a legend in the advertising world, the enfant terrible who had put the first naked woman in an American ad, the crazy guy who had stuck a real car onto a billboard to advertise glue. In the glory days of the 1970s he had done drugs, girls, motorbikes; moved on to houses, wives and his own company; graduated to alimony and corporation tax. Now he was nudging sixty and had discovered Himself in a big way.

At Bernie's door Lloyd took a breath, knocked, and entered a ballroom-size expanse of pale carpeting, with giddying views on two sides. The walls were studded with expensive contemporary art and posters from Bernie's design-guru days. In one corner a fountain tinkled, strategically positioned by his feng-shui adviser. In another, incongruously placed on a marble plinth, was a battered New York fire hydrant—"To remind me of my humble Brooklyn origins," Bernie liked to tell clients sententiously, though the word was he'd been born in Hoboken. Obliquely positioned in front of Lloyd was a giant mortuary slab of a desk. Behind it sat a big man in a suit, with restless eyes and gray curls beginning to slip backward. The desk was empty apart from a telephone and a white dinner-plate with an artistic arrangement of bite-sized pieces of fruit. Bernie had an ongoing love affair with his stomach. He had tried every diet invented, except the simple one of eating less.

"Bernie," said Lloyd, perhaps a little too heartily. "What can I do for you?"

Bernie gestured toward a black leather couch. He stabbed a piece of pineapple with a toothpick, eyed it suspiciously, then popped it in his mouth. He chewed slowly, making Lloyd wait. "Bad news," he said eventually. "London's fucked up. They lost Julian Jewel. Guy walked out this afternoon. No warning, no apology. Seems Sturm Drang made him an offer he couldn't refuse: double the salary and a red fucking Ferrari parked outside his fucking apartment." A frown of distaste creased his face. "Jeez, a Ferrari. It's so eighties."

Lloyd stared. "Julian's quit the company? But I just talked to him yesterday. We had a whole session about the job, the apartment, which day the garbage was collected. He said—"

"He lied," Schneider said succinctly, already bored. "You know what these Brits are like, especially the creatives. The guy walked. End of story."

Lloyd sat in silence while the implications sank in. "So does this mean the exchange is cancelled?"

"Looks that way, doesn't it? And, you know, maybe that's not such a bad thing." Bernie's gaze settled intently on Lloyd. "Four weeks is a long time out of the office. Maybe too long to take your eye off the ball." He speared a berry, gave it a little twirl and ate it.

"Any particular ball?" Lloyd asked.

"You tell me."

"Everything's looking good. Clients happy, budgets under control, billings on the up."

"Including Passion?"

"Especially Passion."

For several long seconds, Lloyd endured a hard, challenging stare.

"That's OK, then." Bernie wiped his mouth on a white napkin, leaving a red trail. He checked his watch. "Shit," he said, "I'm late for my astrologer."

Dismissed, Lloyd walked back through the open offices, feeling weightless, disoriented. It was as though a door had been slammed in his face. Back at his desk, he sat idly for a while, letting depression steal over him like paralysis, then reached for the phone. There was only one person who would understand.

After several rings a voice answered, "Chinese laundry."

Lloyd almost smiled. "How did you know it was me?"

"I didn't. I'm pissed off. Lousy day."

"Me too. You doing anything after work?"

There was a world-weary sigh. "Counting my billions. Auditioning Kristin Scott Thomas for my new picture. Same old stuff."

"Good. I'll meet you at Kiki's around six." Lloyd put down the phone, feeling better.

"Kiki's?" said an amused voice from the hallway. "I didn't know you led such a wild life."

"Ah, Sheri." Lloyd straightened in his chair. "Come in."

But she was already in, slotting a cassette into his VCR in that assertive way she had, filling the room with her perfume. As always, she was dressed for success, yet with a blatant femininity that was disquieting. It was impossible not to notice her legs or the snug fit of her skirt as she bent over the machine. Lloyd had never asked for a deputy, nor had he been asked if he wanted one. Bernie had just produced her one day, about three months ago, like a birthday present.

Sheri cleared some files from his desk, perched on the edge and started the tape. "Lloyd, the most terrible thing," she breathed. "Have you seen this?"

"I don't think so. Is it the latest Bertolucci?"

Sheri looked blank for a moment, gave a polite laugh and continued. "It's an ad for that horrible little bank. They premiered it last night. Isn't it just a total rip-off of our last campaign for Citybiz?"

Lloyd watched little animated dollar signs dance across the screen. "Our" campaign for Citybiz had been 99 percent Sheri's, and in his private opinion 100 percent cliché. That some other agency should have come up with something similar was hardly a big surprise.

Sheri was stabbing her finger at the screen, pointing out the offending details. "Can't we sue or something?" she asked.

"Well . . ." Lloyd began carefully. "You know what they say, imitation is the sincerest form of flattery. I think you should take it as a compliment, Sheri. If the client questions you, just say you got there first. Remind them that Schneider Fox is the best. That's why people copy us."

Sheri seemed delighted by this interpretation. Seamlessly, she moved on to outline a plan she wanted to implement while he was away, to analyze the effectiveness of their print-buying, agency wide. Lloyd's attention wandered. Sheri was the sort of person who read management books. Sometimes he felt that they had increased her word power to an unfortunate degree.

". . . so the way I figure it there will be significant financial implications above *and* below the line," Sheri concluded.

"Very impressive. Put it in writing, will you? Now, about the next few weeks—"

Sheri reached over and gave his shoulder a friendly rub. "Relax, Lloyd. Just because I'm a woman doesn't mean I can't run your clients."

"That's not what I meant. That is, I don't think of you as a woman," floundered Lloyd.

"Really?" She flashed him a smile.

"Sheri, read my lips. I'm trying to tell you something that has nothing to do with being a woman." He explained about Julian Jewel.

To his surprise, Sheri seemed genuinely upset. "But this is awful," she burst out. "You have to go. You were so looking forward to the trip."

Lloyd shrugged. He didn't want to talk about it.

"Can't London send someone else?"

"Most people have commitments—work deadlines, families, vacations."

"Well, did you at least ask?"

"Bernie was too busy to discuss it. He had an appointment."

"What was it this time? His inner child?" Impatiently, Sheri stood up and faced him across the desk, fists on hips. "You're not going to just leave it, are you? Did you fix to see him again later?"

Lloyd's temper rose. She was beginning to remind him of Betsy's mother. "Let's drop it, OK?" He reached for a pencil and opened a file at random. "I'm sure you've got work to do."

He heard a sigh of exasperation and the rustle of stockings, then the click of the glass door as it shut behind her.

Abruptly, Lloyd swung his chair around to face the window. Out behind the tangle of wire fencing and rubble, where they were widening the riverside highway, stretched the docks, their gigantic piers jutting into the water. Once everyone had gone to Europe by boat—Southampton, Rotterdam, Cherbourg. Lloyd pictured the majestic liners nosing into the Hudson, streamers fluttering, hands waving: the start of an adventure. He wondered if Sheri was right, if he should insist, if he should subject himself to another session on that clammy black couch.

No, he decided eventually. Julian had turned out to be a lying bastard, but Lloyd had felt comfortable with him. They had discussed the exchange in detail. Everything had been planned, organized, under control, the way Lloyd liked things to be.

It just wouldn't be the same with a perfect stranger.

Chapter Three

Kiki's was a tiny basement bar off Washington Square, where Jack Kerouac had once been sick over a female folk singer. An aura of 1950s Bohemia lingered in its sepulchral lighting and black leatherette furniture. It was one of the few places in Manhattan where smoking was positively encouraged. Tonight it was empty, except for a skinny waitress in vampire makeup and a figure slouched in a corner, camouflaged in sunglasses and black leather jacket. His blond Andy Warhol hair glimmered like a beacon through a haze of smoke. Lloyd stopped at his table. "Jean-Luc Godard, I presume."

Jay waved his cigarette in welcome, then uncoiled himself slowly to frown disapprovingly at Lloyd's suit and briefcase. "Jee-sus," he drawled. "Every time I see you, you look more like a banker. What is it you guys carry in those cases?"

Lloyd shrugged. "Emergency toilet paper. Baseball mitts. Grandma's ashes." He put his briefcase on the floor. "You want a beer or what?"

Jay started to laugh, a reluctant scratchy chuckle that turned into a cough. "They're going to love you in jolly old England."

"Actually, they're not." Lloyd waited until they had ordered their drinks, then settled himself moodily in his chair, hands in pockets, legs stretched out. "I'm not going," he pronounced.

Jay took off his sunglasses. "Don't tell me Little Miss Muffet put her foot down."

"I wish you wouldn't call her that." Lloyd scowled. He waited while the waitress set out their drinks, running his fingers irritably through his hair. "Betsy was happy for me to go. She has her dissertation to finish. Anyway," he went on more calmly, "she would never do a thing like that. She is loyal and supportive and thoughtful and—"

"And all the things I'll never be," Jay finished for him. He raised his glass. "Here's to us, Manhattan's very own Jekyll and Hyde. Now, speak. What's the story?"

Lloyd gave up. There was no point getting angry with Jay. He explained the whole messy situation.

Jay shook his head. "I'm sorry, pal. I know you have this crazy thing about England. Still," his eyebrows shot up, "a red Ferrari! Remember that old rust-bucket you got in California? You offered me a ride East, then stung me for the gas. Cheapskate."

"It was a 1969 Chevy," Lloyd protested. "The rust was an integral part of its mature charm. It was the Jeanne Moreau of the American car industry. I was in love with that car." He chuckled. "I probably could have married it under California law."

"On a cliff top, with a Buddhist priest . . ."

"Naked . . ."

". . . with a poodle for best man."

" 'With this hubcap I thee wed.' "

They laughed together at the fantasy. Then Lloyd sobered. He smoothed his tie down his shirt-front, neatly tucking in the tail end. "I've come a long way since then."

"Yep." Jay sipped his beer. "You certainly have."

"What's that supposed to mean?"

"Don't you ever miss the old life? Bombing down the highways, picking towns off the map just because you liked the name, everything you owned in a beat-up bag in the trunk."

"I was nineteen." Lloyd flicked his long fingers dismissively. "And screwed up. You can't spend your life playing piano bars at twenty bucks a night. Why would I want to go back to that stuff?"

"I didn't say you wanted to go back, I just asked if you ever missed the fun."

Lloyd hesitated. He didn't want to go back to the chaos and

shame of those times, but Jay was right: there was something he missed. What was it? Youth, probably—that feeling that any second something extraordinary might happen to change your life. "Four weeks in England would have been fun enough for me." Lloyd could hear the sourness in his voice. "How's the movie?" he asked, changing the subject. "Any takers?"

Jay's face twisted. "You want to hear the latest? It's 'too good.' Too smart, too ironic, too 'European.' Little Miss Gum Chewer in Lobotomy, Nebraska, won't get it." Jay waved his fists in the air with frustration. "What is it with the nineties? It's like everything *died.* No one wants anything that hasn't had all the life sanitized out of it. What happened to ambiguity, to originality, to ideas?"

Lloyd looked away, feeling uncomfortable. Was that what he did in his job—sanitizing, commercializing? A form of lying? "Maybe it's just us," he suggested. "We're getting old."

"Not me, buddy," Jay objected.

For a while they sat in silence, sipping their drinks. The bar had filled up. Over the ripple of conversation Lloyd could hear Thelonious Monk stumbling artfully over the piano keys. He cleared his throat. There was something he needed to raise with Jay.

"Speaking of Betsy," he began casually, "I was thinking we might get married."

Jay's expression did not change. He nodded consideringly. "Betsy must be happy."

"Well . . . I haven't actually told her yet. I was going to wait until I got back from London, but now—"

Jay let out a cackle of laughter. "*Told* her—I love it! What if she says no, you cocky bastard?"

"I just—" Lloyd stopped, abashed. "Look, we've been together almost two years. We're not twenty any more. It's about time."

"Marriage isn't about time, it's about love."

"We have a good, stable relationship. We like the same things—literature, the outdoors, traveling . . ."

"Very logical, Mr. Spock."

Lloyd suddenly felt furious. "Jesus, Jay, is that all you can say?"

Jay raised a conciliatory palm. "You don't need my approval, Lloyd, or my opinion. Look at me. What am I ever going to know about marriage? But love . . ." Jay reached for his matches and lit one. He held it up to his pale face, watching the flame flicker and dance as it scorched a black path toward his fingers. "Does it burn? Does it dazzle? Does it hurt?" He raised his eyes to Lloyd's and gave a sad little smile. "Love. It's the only thing." Then he blew out the flame.

By the time they left the bar, the predicted rain had arrived, snarling the streets with traffic and shrouding the city in a gray gloom. They parted at the subway station. Lloyd traveled home on autopilot, staring into space. The melons were still there at the corner store, but he didn't even notice them.

When the elevator opened at his floor, Lloyd could smell cooking, a rich concoction of onions and herbs. At least someone was having fun. He took out his keys, opened his front door and stopped in surprise. The antique table that Betsy's mother had given them was set for two. Candlelight flickered on their best silver and crystal. In the wine cooler was a bottle of champagne.

"Surprise!" The swinging doors to the kitchen flipped open and Betsy emerged, beaming as if it were somebody's birthday. She was all dressed up in a silk blouse and earrings, hair held back in a black velvet band.

Lloyd felt a stab of irritation. The last thing he needed was a farewell dinner when there was nothing to celebrate.

"Poor baby, you're all wet." Betsy hurried across to help him out of his raincoat. She wrinkled her nose. "Pooh, you smell of old ashtrays." But she smiled to show she forgave him.

Lloyd let her carry his coat off to the bathroom, watching her smooth brown legs. His heart cramped with guilt and affection. Why hadn't he called to tell her he wasn't going to London?

"I'm sorry, I should have called you," he said when she came back. "There's been a change of plan." He sat down heavily at the table, rattling the silver. "London's off."

Betsy's smile only widened. "No, it isn't," she trilled. She picked up a piece of paper from the telephone table and waved it in front of his eyes. "Look."

Bewildered, Lloyd took the note. On it there was a name—Susannah Wilding—and a London address.

"They're sending someone else," Betsy explained. "Sheri called here a couple of hours ago. No one knew where you were."

"Sheri?" Why Sheri?

"She told me about that awful man in London. I was so shocked, Lloyd. What a thing to do, just to leave everyone up in the air like that."

"But they're sending someone else?" Lloyd hardly dared to believe her. "I can still go?"

"Apparently this Susannah person leaped at the opportunity, which means her own apartment in London will be available. It's all working out beautifully."

Lloyd felt a balloon of happiness swell in his heart. He was going to London after all. Kensington, Chelsea, Westminster Abbey, St. Paul's—he checked the piece of paper—"Islington," wherever that was. He pictured a white stucco house, big old-fashioned windows with a view of trees, maybe a real fireplace. Suddenly he could hardly wait to get out of this boxy little prison, with its mean ration of sunlight.

"But wait a minute." Lloyd had spotted the fatal flaw. "If I'm staying in her apartment, where's she going to live over here?"

"Aha." Betsy's eyes sparkled. "That's the best news of all. I've been trying to fix this for weeks, but I didn't want to spoil the surprise." She came over and sat herself on Lloyd's lap. "You know what a mean old tightwad I've been recently?" she murmured, smoothing his hair. "Well, what do you think I've been saving up for?"

Before Lloyd could answer, Betsy jumped off his lap and flung out her arms triumphantly. "The English woman can stay right here!" Face glowing, she clasped her hands together. "Oh, Lloyd, isn't it wonderful? I'm coming with you!"

Chapter Four

Suze dragged her overweight suitcase out of the air-conditioned terminal and paused as the steamy air outside smacked her in the face: American air, heavy with heat and car fumes, peppered with city grime, rich with the sound of uninhibited American voices. She took a deep breath. It felt marvelous. America! Suze thrilled. Cadillacs, Badlands, Dorothy Parker, gangsters, motels, *Gone With the Wind*. Spellings like "nite" and "kleen." Tanned lifeguards who swept back their bleached hair, gave a knee-dissolving smile and drawled, "Coming to the beach party?"

Beyond the tangle of concrete ramps and fly-overs she glimpsed a strip of sulphurous sky, hazy with the afterglow of a hot summer weekend. Out there somewhere was New York City, waiting for her. She loaded herself up again and stumbled toward the queue of taxis. They were bright yellow, crouched low over scarred hubcaps, just as she had known they would be. She took her place in line behind a pair of fiftysomething women in sunglasses.

"I don't know what my shrink is going to say when I tell her about Venice," one confided nasally, at a decibel level that an English person might have used to address a conference.

"So don't tell her," retorted her friend. "What are you? A telephone-sex line? Let her find her own Latin lover, she should be so lucky."

When Suze's taxi rattled to a halt in front of her, no one got out to help her with her luggage. Perhaps customs were different here. Or there could be a dead body in the trunk. Awkwardly, Suze maneuvered everything into the backseat, climbed in and pulled the door shut with the piece of string provided. A rusting chrome plate showed where the handle had fallen off.

She shook back her hair imperiously. "Seventy-second Street," she commanded.

There was a silence. "What street?" the driver asked eventually. At least that's what it sounded like. The man was obviously a foreigner; perhaps he didn't understand English accents. Suze repeated the address.

The driver took his hands off the steering wheel and twisted to face her. Dark eyes glittered through the grille. She hoped he wasn't a serial killer. "Lady, I need avenue. I need East or West. Seventy-second, you know, this is very long street."

"Oh." Suze scrabbled in her capacious handbag—hairbrush, Evian face spray, trashy paperback, cigarettes, eye mask. At the bottom, among the sweepings of English change, she found Lloyd Rockwell's fraying fax and read out his detailed directions. She hadn't paid much attention to them when they arrived, thinking him over-fussy. Now she understood that they served a purpose. "I'm English," she apologized, as the taxi lurched forward. "This is my first time in New York. Where are you from?"

"Bosnia."

Suze felt her mind fog over with undigested geopolitical data. "Ah." She nodded, feeling it wisest to leave the subject there.

The cab sped onward, left the ramp with a terrific wallop that bounced Suze right out of her seat and cruised out to join the highway. Suze peered eagerly through the window, reading the overhead signs with their half-familiar names—Queens, Triboro, Flushing—printed white on green in a spiky, unfamiliar typeface. Small wooden houses painted gray or green or brick red lined the road, each with its own porch and unfenced patch of worn grass, some with a flagpole from which the Stars and Stripes drooped in humid folds.

Well, every city had to have suburbs. Come to think of it, visitors to London had Hounslow to contend with on the slow crawl into the center. Suze hugged herself at such an arresting thought. This was what her trip was all about: new experiences, new thoughts. She would return a new person—sophisticated, mature, nicer, smarter, suntanned.

Suze subsided happily into the ripped upholstery. Thank you, Julian Jewel. She had never much liked him, certainly not as much as he liked himself. He probably cried out his own name during lovemaking. For weeks Julian had been poncing on about "my secondment to the States," as if the president himself had found America impossible to govern without Jewel at his side. In fact, he was just another jumped-up copywriter with an ego bigger than his underpants. He was welcome to his car and his six-figure salary. Suze knew she had the best of the bargain.

Not that she was here to enjoy herself. Harry Fox had called her again this morning and given her a stern lecture. This was not a holiday, he had warned. Her job was to observe how the sister company worked, to get an overview of the New York advertising scene and most of all to soak up American culture and values so that she could contribute intelligently to the management of global accounts. He reminded her of the agency that had spent megabucks on the launch of a cosmetics brand in the Far East, only to discover that the product name meant "fart" in Japanese. She was to write a report on her return. Suze said yes to everything, too excited to be intimidated. She had already rung up practically everyone she knew, casually dropping news of "my New York business trip" into the conversation. The reactions had been intensely gratifying.

"So why did you choose me?" she had asked Fox coyly, pushing her luck.

"No one else was free."

The first person she had told was her father, whom she had dragged to the telephone from his darkroom to hear the news. The two of them were the "artists" in the family. It was from him that Suze had inherited her extraordinary hair—thick and heavy and the color of the very best vintage marmalade, and secretly Suze knew that she was her father's favorite. It wasn't fair, it wasn't something either of them would ever acknowledge in so many words, but there it was, a continuous source of warmth and confidence that glowed within her. It had been wonderful to hear him shouting his enthusiasm down the phone and making her write down the names of his favorite New York hot spots.

An irritated muttering from the front of the cab interrupted her thoughts. Suze saw that the traffic had become thick with weekenders trickling home to face another Monday morning. Curious, she stared into the cars that stop-started in the lane beside her. They were dusty and dented, crammed with dogs, golf clubs, tennis rackets, children, even small sailing boats that hung casually off open tailgates. Young men in baseball caps crooked tanned arms out of open windows. One woman with blond hair cascading over a skimpy T-shirt had folded up her legs to rest bare brown feet on the dashboard. Here, Suze felt, were people who knew how to have a good time. Hooray: no more excruciating dinner parties.

She patted the bloated suitcase beside her. If there was one thing she knew about New York it was that you had to be hipper than hip. In her case were outfits to knock them dead. Suze had spent all of Saturday shopping and getting her hair cut, intending to spend Sunday morning cleaning her flat. But friends had lured her out for a champagne-and-pizza send-off, and she hadn't woken up until midday. Such was her fragile state that it was as much as she could do to pack. Curiously, the flight had revived her. She had eaten and drunk everything offered, watched the action movie, then fallen asleep. When she awoke the plane was already circling over the ocean, ready to land, though miraculously it was still only seven in the evening. The cheering thought occurred to Suze that she was actually five hours *younger* than when she had set out from chilly London.

She glanced out the cab window and felt her heart leap. There at last, rearing out of nowhere, stretching as far as the eye could see, were the jutting towers of the Manhattan skyline, dark against a fiery sunset. No photograph or film clip or ad had prepared her for the magnificent reality, or for the almost religious exaltation it inspired. This was how an early desert traveler must have felt on seeing the Great Pyramids rise inexplicably from the empty sands. In the evening light, with its monolithic blocks cluttered against a bonfire sky, New York had the mythic quality of a necropolis built by a race of giants. Even as she watched, entranced, the road veered away from the view. Now the cab was stopping at some kind of tollbooth. Suze heard the jingle of coins, then the car sped down a slope between the criss-cross girders of the bridge, and she was plunged into the shadowed canyons of the city.

The taxi cruised down broad, straight avenues and shot across narrower side streets, progressing in sharp, angular movements like a knight across a chessboard—forward and across, across and forward—quite unlike the meandering motion of London travel. There were people out on the streets, walking, roller-skating, lounging at restaurant tables, their body language bold and expansive. Neon signs blazed brashly: *PSYCHIC READER. NAILS. FALAFEL. MUFFINS. LIQUOR. DRUGS. SOUVLAKI. VITAMINS.* The buzz was exhilarating. At length the taxi slowed, then came to stop outside an apartment building with an awning over the entrance. Suze paid off the driver, adding a gigantic tip to preclude abuse or knifing, and stacked her luggage on the pavement. Clammy air closed about her like a vise, gluing her clothes to her skin. For the first time she felt a qualm of anxiety, alone in a strange city as darkness fell.

"Ms. Wilding?" a voice inquired at her side.

Turning, she saw a powerfully built young man in uniform, with Prince Charles ears and a wide smile. "Yes," she acknowledged, with a rush of relief.

"My name's Raymond. Mr. Rockwell told me to look out for you," he said importantly, stowing all her possessions about his person as if they were toys. She followed him through a dark lobby, and together they crammed into the small metal lift. As it rose in a stately fashion, Suze began to worry about how much she should tip him, mentally doubled the amount, and finally quadrupled it. They stopped at the ninth floor, and Raymond led the way to a wooden door studded with locks. He opened it, carried her bags inside and turned on the light.

Suze's first impression was of a spanking, spotless tidiness that was faintly intimidating. To one side of the room was a large window screened by venetian blinds. Dumping her handbag, she walked over, pried the slats apart and found herself staring straight into an apartment in the block opposite. A couple were eating dinner at the window, framed in a little square of yellow light, like a miniature stage. She could even make out the pepper grinder on the table. Suze wondered who they were, what they were talking about, whether they were happy.

"All set?" Raymond asked.

"Yes. Sorry." Hurrying back to him, Suze found her plastic wallet of virgin dollar bills, extracted a twenty and handed it to him with a smile. "Thank you for looking after me so well."

"No problem." Raymond grinned, trousering the note. "Here are the keys. I'll be seeing you."

As soon as he had gone, Suze kicked off her shoes and explored. It didn't take long. The living room had white walls, parquet floors and pretty pastel fabrics that evoked the word "mumsy" in Suze's mind. One end had been turned into a study area, with bookshelves, a leather club-like sofa and a sleek, modern desk with a fax and a computer on it—a fancy new Mac, she noticed. Not bad. At the other end, by the window, on a large table covered with luxuriant potted plants, she found a plastic folder inscribed with her name. Suze opened it, saw the title, "Household Hints" and decided to save it for later.

A bite had been taken out of the living room to create a tiny kitchen, which one entered via swinging doors, like a saloon in a Western. Inside were orderly rows of jars, polished steel fixtures and work surfaces so clean you could have performed heart surgery on them. Suze opened the wardrobe-size refrigerator and found that someone had thoughtfully left her milk, eggs, butter and a squat carton of orange juice. Suppressing a guilty pang about the contents of her own fridge in London, she returned to the living room and followed a narrow corridor lined with books. At the end was a bedroom, small and neat, dominated by a double bed with one of those flouncy things around the bottom Suze could never remember the name for. The window had the same view as the living room, and Suze noted that the couple had now disappeared and the light in their apartment had faded to a blue TV flicker. Beyond the bedroom was a bathroom, a little haven of American-style luxury with a glassed-in shower and piles of thick towels. Suze resolved that she would unpack, wash her hair, check out the TV and go to bed early to beat the jet lag. She had to be at work in twelve hours' time.

A wave of fatigue rolled over her. She dragged off her jacket and lay down on the bed, staring into the semi-darkness. Around her, the room seemed to rise and fall, as if she were on a ship. She stroked the quilted material of the unfamiliar bedspread, soft under her fingertips. Her body pressed down into the contours of a stranger's bed. Lloyd Rockwell, creative director: what was he like, she wondered? Suze had been out whenever he called, so they had communicated in a flurry of e-mails. His were straightforward, practical, rather formal—probably typed by some secretary with a bun. She imagined a hand-shaking executive in his fifties, with an orthodontically perfect wife wearing one of those blazers with little gold buttons at the cuff. What was her name—Beth, Betty, Becky? Suze yawned. Her eyes closed. From the street below a medley of car horns and sirens drifted up. Beneath it were the bass notes of thrumming machinery and the roar and rumble of a city in full swing—the most exciting city in the world. She pictured poor old Bridget and Tobe, pacing the hall with a screaming baby draped over one shoulder, and smiled. Who said it was no fun being single?

Of course the credit-card killjoys would catch up with her eventually, demanding retribution for her shopping binge, but by then anything could have happened. She could have been talent-spotted and asked to redesign *Cosmo*. She could be living in a loft with a rich filmmaker. This was New York, after all, where people came to reinvent themselves. Nobody knew her here. She had no past, no connections, no responsibilities. She could do absolutely anything she liked.

Chapter Five

The small house was of dirty yellow brick, packed tight in a row of similar buildings—late Victorian, Lloyd guessed. Purple weeds rioted in the narrow front garden behind black iron railings. Above the slate roof a jumble of chimney-pots and television aerials showed dimly against the louring evening sky.

"Picturesque, huh?" Lloyd gave Betsy an encouraging smile.

Outside the front door a tumble of black plastic garbage sacks awaited collection.

"Positively Dickensian."

"Did I give you the keys?"

Betsy rolled her eyes. A soft rain began to fall.

"Just testing." Lloyd began to search through the zipped pockets of the small airline bag over his shoulder. The car service that had met them at the airport had brought the house keys in a sealed bag. Lloyd knew he had put them in a safe place. But which safe place? He began to empty out the bag onto the low pillar that supported a sagging gate, laying down his wallet and credit cards under Betsy's steely gaze.

"Try the raincoat," she suggested.

"You know I never carry things in my pockets." In fact, it was Betsy who had taught him that this spoiled the line of his clothes, and had broken him of the habit.

But she was right—as usual. Lloyd picked up the suitcases, climbed the short flight of stone steps to the front door and unlocked it. Inside was a small hallway with two farther doors. The left-hand one was theirs. It opened straight on to a steep flight of stairs that led to the upper flat.

"Goodness!" Betsy exclaimed, recoiling from the brilliant color of the stairway.

At the top, off a narrow landing, was a small, cluttered kitchen painted daffodil yellow, with a sycamore tree pressing against the tall window. A couple more steps led up to a corridor with three farther doors. Betsy opened the first one cautiously. The room was dark, the light barred by shutters. All Lloyd could make out was a high brass bed that seemed to allow little room for anything else. His heart sank. He knew Betsy would be wondering where she could hang her clothes.

The bathroom was worse. When Lloyd finally found the piece of string that turned on a noisy extractor fan as well as the light, it was to reveal a minute, windowless cubbyhole.

"I didn't know they made toilets like that anymore," Betsy said, in an awed whisper. "Still . . ." She went inside and shut the door. Lloyd could hear her fumbling with a catch that didn't seem to work.

Exploring further, he found himself in a large living room that ran the full width of the house, with two handsome, arched windows overlooking the street. This was better. Venetian red paint had been slapped exuberantly across the walls; the floors were of old pine, scattered with rugs; at one end was a large marble fireplace with a cast-iron grate sprouting dried artichoke flowers. Most of the furniture was cheap and modern: angular lamps, self-assembly shelves, simple canvas chairs. A spectacular exception was an enormous Empire-style sofa, piled high with cushions to hide its fraying velvet upholstery and resting on bulbous lion's-paw feet. Clearly this was the nerve-center of the room, positioned within effortless reach of a sleek sound system and a telephone answering-machine that was flashing red. Behind one of the woodwormy legs, Lloyd noticed a forgotten mug encrusted with old tea or coffee. Frowning a little, he bent down and picked it up to take it to the kitchen. First he circled the room, like Sherlock Holmes searching for clues.

On the wall above the mantelpiece a clever pencil drawing

showed Fred Astaire in mid–tap dance, coattails flying, while a 1930s busboy tried vainly to call him to the telephone. The caption underneath read: "I'm dancing and I can't be bothered now." By the window was a long wooden table set on curving steel legs. Right in the middle of it was an old milk bottle stuffed with two bunches of flowers, still tied with green sticky tape. Lloyd saw that the bottle had been used to secure a small sheet of lined paper, obviously ripped from a Filofax and scrawled in haste. He picked it up.

> *Welcome! Sorry the place is a bit of a tip, no time to tidy what with short notice. Please feel free to use everything, move stuff about, etc. Good Indian take-away around first corner to the left if you arrive starving. Could you very kindly forward any interesting-looking post, no brown envelopes or beastly bills? Thanx.*
>
> *P.S. Immersion heater sometimes clonks in night—just hit pipe with hammer.*
>
> *P.P.S. Hope you don't mind Mr. Kipling. He is old, but exceedingly friendly.*

It was signed with a big *S*.

Lloyd read the note once, turned it over to check there was nothing more, then read it again, savoring the unfamiliar idioms. He wondered what an immersion heater was, though if it "clonked" he would find out soon enough. Mr. Kipling must be some talkative neighbor, perhaps a companion for Betsy if she got lonely. She was good with old people.

Right on cue, there was a distant, despairing moan from the kitchen. Lloyd found Betsy looking unhappy, arms folded fiercely. "Lloyd, I can't believe this. There's no refrigerator."

"Nonsense." Handing her Suze's note and the dirty mug, he rooted around the jumble of cupboards, then triumphantly flicked open a door that had been painted over to match the cabinets. "Da-dah!"

It was the size of a hotel minibar. Inside were three milk cartons, all open, a jar of sun-dried tomatoes with mold on top and a wedge of cheese sweating malodorously into its supermarket wrapper. Betsy squatted down to pull out the vegetable drawer, revealing two wrinkled apples and a desiccated knob of ginger. Then she tried the tiny freezing compartment, but it was sealed tight with a thick coating of ice that had oozed out like some alien lifeforce. She stood up and closed the door without a word.

"She's single," Lloyd said defensively.

Betsy gave him a baleful look. "So am I." Brushing past him, she headed for the bedroom. "I'll start unpacking."

Lloyd let her go. He knew she would feel better when she had everything shipshape. Besides, he hated all that unfolding and fiddling around with hangers; if he stayed out of sight long enough Betsy would probably do it for him. Instead, he set himself the challenge of concocting a little supper for them both.

There was a radio on the kitchen counter. Turning it on, he heard: "This is Radio Four. And now, *The Power of Pursed Lips*, a short program on whistling." Lloyd waited to see if this was a joke, but no: it was a lighthearted but apparently perfectly normal British program. Lloyd felt a glow of optimism warm his soul as he listened to the crisp accents soberly discussing virtuoso whistlers, songbird imitations and the covert uses of whistling in the Second World War. *I like England*, he thought.

Susannah Wilding's cupboards were a mystery to him. How did the woman live? Saffron and cardamom pods, but no thyme; four opened bags of brown sugar in various stages of solidity, but no flour; two Italian coffee machines, but no colander—did she drain her spaghetti with a tennis racket, like Jack Lemmon in *The Apartment*? One cupboard was crammed with empty wine bottles, presumably destined for recycling on some distant day of ecological atonement. Another held a brand new mixing-machine with no plug. It didn't matter. While the late English twilight darkened slowly into night and the radio voices twittered gently, Lloyd assembled cans of tomatoes and haricot beans, unearthed a box of bay leaves, located some garlic cloves in the door of the despised refrigerator and let his creativity flow. Warmed by the gas stove, he tasted and stirred, and tasted again. *Cassoulet au Rockwell.* Not bad.

Suddenly Lloyd remembered the winking red light on the answering-machine. It could be an urgent message from the office, even from Harry Fox himself. Leaving the pot to simmer, he hurried into the living room, crouched on the floor beside the phone and pressed the PLAY button. A laid-back male voice filled the room.

"Sorry, sweetheart, only just got your message. If I've missed you, damn and blast. I rang to say I don't think I'll be in town after all while you're away. But don't worry, I'm sure the Yanks won't trash the place. An old married couple is probably a hell of a lot tidier than you are. I love you anyway. Call us when you arrive."

"Old married couple?" Lloyd felt a prickle of irritation. He was sure he had referred to Betsy as his partner. And why should anyone presume they were old? He wondered who the man was. He sounded too friendly for a lover: her father, perhaps. Lloyd rewound the machine, erasing the message. Whoever the man was, he was right about the tidiness. When he entered the bedroom, Lloyd felt a glow of proprietorial pride as he saw Betsy, neat as a pin after all that traveling, tucking his socks into a drawer. Now that she had turned on the lights and cleared the surfaces he realized that it was a pleasant room, small but well proportioned, with a decorative cornice around the ceiling. An artistic hand had been at work in here too, painting the walls in wide stripes of grey and ivory, and draping a swathe of crimson material around the window to give the effect of curtains.

On the chest of drawers a diptych of photographs caught his curiosity, and he went over to examine them. One was a faded snapshot of a hippie-ish young couple with their arms around each other. The other showed a girl in a bright pink dress, eyes laughing into the camera from beneath a tumble of dark caramel hair. Lloyd held it up to show Betsy. "Do you think this is her?"

Betsy pursed her lips. "Whoever she is, she should know better than to wear pink—especially with that hair."

"Oh." Lloyd replaced the photograph. Women were extraordinary in the way they noticed details about each other that completely escaped him. "You've done a terrific job on this room," he added, perhaps a little too enthusiastically. "Don't tell me you unpacked my stuff too?"

Betsy was sitting on the edge of the bed, rubbing her feet. She gave him a dry look. "Isn't that why you brought me?"

"Of course not. And I haven't 'brought' you. You wanted to come. I thought you needed background for your thesis. You said—" He fought down irritation. "I know it isn't exactly Julian Jewel's riverside penthouse, but hell—" He floundered, but only for a moment. "Jane Austen probably didn't even *have* a toilet."

"I know." Betsy caught his hand. "Stop pacing."

Lloyd stopped, still feeling ruffled, but allowing Betsy to keep his hand. She raised it to her cheek. It was warm and smooth. He sat down on the bed beside her and moved his arm around her shoulders. "You're here so that we can be together," he reminded them both, "so that we can share a new experience. If you never get the vacuum cleaner out of the closet, I wouldn't care. All I want is for you to enjoy yourself."

Betsy leaned into his shoulder and sighed. "It's just that London seems different from when Mother and I came over after graduation."

"No kidding. The last time you were staying in a four-star hotel in Mayfair. It's bound to feel different living in a stranger's apartment. But I know you." He gave her a squeeze. "Within a week you'll have transformed this place. You'll have found all kinds of little stores and galleries you like. You'll have Mr. Kipling—whoever he is—eating out of your hand, and carrying your groceries upstairs and probably inviting you to lunch while I slave in the office."

Betsy gave him a wavering smile.

"Meanwhile," Lloyd went on, "you are going to have a long hot bath, I am going to complete my culinary masterpiece, and we shall eat it in the living room with our bottle of duty-free Burgundy, while we feast our eyes on the lights of London. How does that sound?"

"Wonderful!" Betsy sagged against him, beginning to give a little stretch of pleasure, then stopped. "What in the world . . .?" One of her blazer buttons had snagged on something. Betsy disentangled herself, then slowly drew the object out from under the mattress. She dangled it in the air for Lloyd's inspection, holding it between finger and thumb as if it were a dead mouse.

It was a lacy black garter belt. Lloyd started to laugh. "Well, here's at least something we can use," he teased, making a grab for it and putting it playfully around Betsy's waist.

She giggled and pushed him away. "Stop being silly."

But Lloyd, suddenly frisky, started chasing her around the room, rattling the garter clips in her ear and growling like a predator. Eventually, Betsy whipped it out of his hand and pushed him onto his back on the bed.

"You're a cruel woman," Lloyd said, smiling at the ceiling.

Betsy dusted herself down. "If I were the sort of woman who felt it necessary to wear black underwear, I'd buy my own—"

"Great!" Lloyd rolled over to watch her, head propped on his hand. "You can ask Mr. Kipling tomorrow where to get some."

"—but I'm not," Betsy added conclusively. She folded the offending item and slipped it into a drawer. She lingered there for a moment, studying the picture of the woman in the pink dress. "I just hope this Susannah Wilding is going to behave responsibly in our apartment. I'm not sure she's a serious person." She turned to Lloyd with a worried expression. "Did you see? She's got the complete works of Jilly Cooper on her bookshelves."

"Not everyone can be an intellectual." Lloyd bounced himself gently on the bed. "She likes Fred Astaire."

"And did you see the bathroom floor?"

"The living room's nice."

"If you like red." Betsy stood for a while thoughtfully, as if compiling a silent inventory of every precious and immaculate item in their apartment. A spasm of alarm crossed her face. "I hope she'll remember to water my plants."

Chapter Six

"Plants," Suze read, as the subway train hurtled downtown. "Three drops of Plantogro in a pint of water twice a week. Take care not to spill water on the table, as this damages the veneer." Suze rolled her eyes. There were pages of this stuff. Instructions about garbage collection, the air-conditioning, uses and abuses of the basement laundry room, where to find guest soaps (what were guest soaps?). It was duller than the *Economist*. Suze had brought it only because her instructions for getting to work were on the back page. When her stop came she ripped the page out and left the rest of the "Household Hints" on her seat.

Outside it was hot and sunny in an exhilarating, un-English way. Down here the buildings were on a more human scale. There were children and dogs and small scruffy parks, and street-traders selling fresh fruit and bagels. The colors were pure Edward Hopper: sycamore-leaf green and the dark rust of brick houses zigzagged with fire escapes. She had only to turn her head to see the skyscrapers that marched at her heels: the Empire State Building, with its King Kong spire, and the Chrysler's silvery pinnacle, spinning like a top in the sunshine. Suze gave a deep sigh of satisfaction, adjusted her Audrey Hepburn–style sunglasses, and headed south, checking out her reflection in the shop fronts. She was wearing a white linen crop-top, shiny black cigar trousers and her new ultra-cool sandals with an Eiffel Tower snowstorm scene embedded in each Perspex heel. She thought she looked pretty divine.

The Schneider Fox building sat on the junction of two streets, like a great white corporate elephant. Suze tightened her hold on her portfolio, pushed through the revolving glass door and entered a lobby big enough to park a jumbo jet in. The sound of her heels tip-tapping over the stone floor echoed intimidatingly. She went up and down three times in the elevator, trying to get it to stop between the lobby and the twenty-fifth floor, before a kindly woman who called her "honey" explained that Suze should try another bank of elevators. Eventually she reached the right floor, only to be blocked by a Bambi-eyed receptionist, who seemed astounded by Suze's claim that she had come to work there. For half an hour Suze crouched on the edge of an absurdly low leather couch, pretending to be amused by cartoons in *The New Yorker,* while she listened to the receptionist make one phone call after another in pursuit of someone prepared to claim her. She felt like a lost dog.

Eventually the receptionist announced that Suze was to be taken to meet Quincy Taylor himself, head of design. A minion led her through an open-plan maze, marked off by bosom-high partitions behind which workers browsed at telephones and computers, like cattle in stalls. From time to time she caught tantalizing glimpses of the outside world. Inside, the air was cool and tasted of airplane. Suze's trepidation deepened. But the art department looked reassuringly familiar, with its plan chests, its black snakes of electronic cabling and the usual clutter of glue-guns, spray paint and acetate clippings. Girlie rock music played softly. At the door of one of the glass boxes that ringed the building, Suze's guide left her. Suze knocked and entered.

Quincy was in his late forties, dressed in black ankle boots, Armani jeans and a black collarless shirt, his artistically graying hair gathered into a neat ponytail. He was good-looking—narrow-eyed, with the kind of aloof charm that could bring women to their knees, begging for approval. Suze eyed him warily. The world was full of art directors like this. She should know. She had practically lived with one for three years.

He shook hands formally and gestured to her to sit down. For a while he sat twiddling a pencil and lazily surveying her body. "So.

I understand you will be joining my department for some weeks. What can you do?"

"Everything," Suze said firmly.

"Everything?" There went the eyebrows. Here came the inward, mocking smile.

"Quark, Photoshop, Illustrator," Suze chanted. "I can do color photocopies, I can access images on the Net. In advertising, I've done everything from concept to storyboards through to presentations. I've also worked on magazines, art-directed photoshoots, done a little mixed media, some film and TV, and I know my way around editing suites."

"*Suites?* How quaint. I'm afraid that here in America we have plain old editing rooms."

"I brought my portfolio," Suze persisted, making a move to open it for him.

"Maybe later." Quincy passed a hand over his face and rubbed his brow, as if he had had too little sleep, then shot her a secret, apologetic smile. Suze knew this trick too: the overworked genius who needs an adoring woman to look after him. She allowed her gaze to wander over his shoulder.

"OK." Quincy snapped into gear. "Let me take you over to Dino. He's working on an outdoor campaign for beer. We're just developing some preliminary ideas to show the client. Maybe you can find him some images to play with." He stood up and led her out into the main office and down a long aisle between banks of computers where the junior designers humbly toiled. "Basically, this is a crap beer for people who can't afford anything better. We're talking urban male, lower social class, tough but decent. You know, 'Drink this beer and you too can have an honest-to-God job on an American assembly line.' By the way," he added, "over here we start work at nine. Be on time tomorrow."

Suze felt as if she had been slapped. So many different retorts sparked in her brain that they blew a fuse and she remained silent. Her fantasies of stardom ebbed as she envisaged four weeks of being ordered about like one of Santa's elves.

Dino was unmistakably gay, well muscled in a tight white T-shirt and about nineteen. He gave her a tour of the department, introduced her to the staff, then very sweetly explained to Suze computer systems she had been using for years. Suze wouldn't have minded taking him home to play with, but watching him laboriously line up his image on the layout grid was like watching a three-year-old try to thread a needle.

"Listen," she said, after a decent interval, "why don't I scout around in the library for some more pictures?" The fact was she was dying for a cigarette, and had earlier earmarked the library as a good place for a quick puff. She made a detour via the coffee machine and was soon ensconced at one of the computer terminals, screened from view by a bookcase. Coffee cup, ciggie, solitude: bliss. She was on her second cigarette when some kind of alarm went off. Suze peeked around the bookcase to see if anyone was reacting, but it was just like England. No one ever took any notice of alarms unless there had been at least three specific memos about a drill. Suze continued with her work, surfing through the photo-library stock. None of the pictures seemed quite right, but she downloaded half a dozen images to show she was willing, and was just exiting from the program when she became aware of a commotion outside. There was the clamor of anxious voices, a deep masculine shout, then the pounding of footsteps. Suddenly the glass door to the library flew open and a terrifying figure in black, carrying an ax, thundered toward her. Suze rose from her seat, cigarette arrested halfway to her mouth, heart pounding. This was it. Her very first day in New York, and she was going to die at the hands of an ax murderer. *"Put that out!"* he roared.

"Whuh?"

"No smoking. Put out that cigarette!"

Suze opened her fingers and dropped the burning butt straight into her plastic coffee cup, where it died with a sizzle. She now saw that the man was dressed not in killer black but official navy: a security guard. From the street Suze could hear a siren, and prayed it wasn't the fire brigade called out to rescue her. The knot of curious spectators gaping at her through the glass was bad enough.

"OK, back off, everybody," the guard told them. "Emergency over."

"It's not my fault." Suze folded her arms defensively. "It's my first day here. I'm from England."

"I don't care if you're from Planet Zog," the man growled. "This is New York City. No smoking in public buildings, understand?"

Suze nodded meekly.

"No smoking in taxis, subways or buses."

She nodded again.

"No smoking in banks, hotel lobbies, sports stadia or public restrooms."

"How about hospitals? Only joking."

A faint smile of surrender lit his face. He laid down his ax and took off his cap to run a meaty hand over close-cropped hair. Underneath, his head was shaped and pitted like a root vegetable. He had small, deep-set eyes shaded by bristle-brush eyebrows and an aggressive chin. It was an interesting face, in a battered, roughneck way. In fact, he looked just like the sort of person who would drink crappy beer. Suze gave him a brilliant smile. "How would you like," she asked carefully, "to have your picture taken?"

They did the shoot in the rooftop canteen, using Coke cans instead of beer and a camera raided from the design department storeroom. The guard's name was Ivan. He loved it, posing ever more ferociously with his ax. Suze gave him some Polaroids to take home to his kids and returned to Dino with the best shots.

"These are great," he agreed, "but the quality's too poor. We can't use them."

"Why not? It's only for a dummy. We can run them through that thing." Suze pointed at the digital scanner in the corner of the department, a giant machine that looked like a futuristic photo booth.

Dino looked at her in surprise. "You know how to operate one of these babies?"

"I should think so," Suze said breezily. "I tried one out at a trade fair a couple of months ago. They're brilliant. You could put a Francis

Bacon in one end and get your passport photo out the other. Come on, I'll show you."

Suze installed him at the controls, and flicked switches experimentally over his shoulder. "You just feed the image in there," she pointed, handing him Ivan's picture, "and then . . . hmmm." She fiddled some more. "Try that white button." Dino obeyed. The machine hummed to life, swallowed the photograph and projected it onto the screen. Suze smiled smugly. "Warp factor number nine, Mr. Sulu."

They were having quite a lot of fun giving Ivan a moustache when a voice beside them said, "Don't tell me someone's gotten that thing to work."

Raising her head, Suze beheld a vision of executive womanhood. At the bottom was a pair of perfectly toned legs encased in sheeny tights, at the top a bounce of blonde hair. In between, a stunning pink suit skimmed every curve, the top button faultlessly positioned to guide the eye straight to her cleavage without revealing a millimeter more than was decent. Suze felt suddenly schoolgirlish in her funky outfit.

The woman gave Suze a poised, queenly smile. She had beautiful white teeth. "Won't you introduce me, Dino?"

The woman was called Sheri Crystal. Cutting short Dino's stumbling introductions, she reeled off a list of impressive titles. She seemed to be in charge of practically everything. More important, she knew who Suze was, and was the first person to welcome her properly. Glowing under this attention, Suze set out to impress. "I can make most things work," she boasted when Sheri asked her about the scanner. "The office always sends for me when the computer goes down or they lose a file. I could have made a fortune as a computer hacker."

"Really?" Sheri gave her a hard look.

"But, of course," Suze added hastily, "design is my first love."

"Glad to hear it." Sheri gave a full-blooded laugh. "I can see you're going to be a big asset. You must tell me more." She checked her watch with a neat turn of the wrist. "Drop by my office in half an hour."

What about Quincy? Suze wanted to ask, but Sheri had already turned on her stiletto heel and was gone in a vapor trail of musky perfume. Suze and Dino stared after her in silent appreciation.

"Whooh!" Dino gave an ecstatic little shiver and flexed his biceps. "Don't you just love those Hitchcock blondes?" He turned to Suze. "She likes you."

"Is that good?"

"Do bears shit in the woods?"

Sheri had her own office, naturally, furnished in soft grays and feminized by a vase of Casablanca lilies that trumpeted their heavy scent into the hallway. At the appointed hour, Suze presented herself, hair combed and confident smile in place. Sheri was on the telephone, and Suze hovered, observing the Georgia O'Keeffe prints on the wall, interspersed with small framed mottoes that she had to come close to to read: "Don't let the past get in the way of the future." "Success is 90 percent planning and 10 percent balls."

"You're right, I don't understand," Sheri was saying frigidly. "If the bill isn't settled by the end of the month we will be instituting legal proceedings." She cut the line with a manicured finger. "Excuse me, Suzanne," she said, with an apologetic smile. "So much work! I've been here since eight and I've hardly made a dent in it. And there's all Lloyd's stuff to take care of too." She sighed. "As if I wouldn't like a little spell in London. Piccadilly Circus and Harrods and—and all the rest of it. What do you say we get out of this madhouse?" She cocked her head in a friendly manner. "Come on, I'll take you to lunch."

They walked a couple of blocks to an Italian restaurant, where they could sit outside under a sunshade, screened from the street by a low hedge. Suze's spirits rose. Determined to make a good impression, she confined herself to pumpkin ravioli and a salad, with a single glass of red wine, only to be trumped by Sheri's order of grilled baby vegetables and mineral water. It didn't seem to matter. Away from the office, Sheri was wonderfully easy to talk to. She probably wasn't more than forty: old, of course, but not too old to be enthusiastic about shopping and films and tell Suze places to go in New York. It just showed that you could be successful *and* nice.

"And have you brought anyone with you to New York?" Sheri inquired. "Husband? Boyfriend?"

"God, no! I'm here to have fun. When I'm not working, I mean."

The waiter brought espresso for Suze and mint tea for Sheri, and a chocolate each, wrapped in gold foil. Suze, still starving, devoured hers in one bite. The other remained tantalizingly on the plate.

Sheri asked about her work and Suze found herself enthusing about the individual character of typefaces and the great designers she admired. "I'd so love, one day, to produce a piece of work and say, 'No one else in the world could have done that.'"

"The quest for excellence." Sheri nodded seriously. "I like that. Quincy must be thrilled to have someone so experienced to help him out."

Suze hesitated.

"Come on," Sheri laughed, "you can tell me."

"Well, he is rather patronizing. I can do a lot more than he seems to think."

"Can't we all? Don't you hate it when people feel they have to guard their own little empires instead of pulling together? It can happen in the best of companies, particularly if people want to stop a woman succeeding."

"Not you?" Suze was shocked.

"Tell me, when you look around any boardroom, what do you see?"

Suze cocked her head intelligently. "Power?"

"Men," Sheri corrected. "Take Schneider Fox. Who runs the office here in New York? A man. Who runs London? A man. Who runs our art department? A man. Who did they pick to go on the exchange program to London?"

"A man," Suze chipped in. She was getting the hang of this.

"Exactly." Sheri acted as if Suze had said something brilliant.

Suze felt warmed by a glow of sisterly solidarity. "It's just as bad in England," she confided. "Some of the men are so macho they've even got to leave the lid of the photocopier up. My first job in advertising was for a company that had some major sanpro accounts—you know, sanitary products?" Sheri nodded. "Another woman and I joined an all-male team at the same time, and when we arrived for our first day at work we found every surface of our workstations—desks, chairs, computers, everything—covered with tampons."

"Ugh." Sheri closed her eyes in horror. "That's just so degrading. I hope you sued for sexual harassment."

"Chah," scoffed Suze. "What we did was send off for some of those impotence kits that you see advertised in cheap newspapers—you know, a leaflet, a magic potion and a sort of plastic pump like one of those gadgets to keep wine from going off. One night we stayed late and put a kit on the chair of every man in the office." She laughed. "They said it was pathetic, but we kept finding them in odd corners reading the leaflet with a kind of haunted look in their eyes."

"Goodness. I had no idea things were quite so primitive in Britain." Sheri took a sip of mineral water. "You know, Bernie told me to fire whoever set off that alarm," she went on conversationally.

"But I—" Suze began. "I mean, it wasn't—"

"But I have a much better idea," Sheri continued smoothly. "Suzanne, I can tell that you are a very talented and creative person, and I would like this time in New York to be a fruitful period for you."

"Thanks. Um, are you going to eat your chocolate thing?"

"Have you any idea how long it takes to rid your body of all those toxins?" Sheri shuddered. "You go ahead." She looked around the restaurant, then leaned close across the table. "I'd like to take you into my confidence. There's a special project I'm working on, very important, very lucrative, very confidential, and I need someone to help me on the design side." She paused. "Someone discreet. Someone talented. Someone I can trust." Her blue, unblinking eyes bored into Suze's. Suze held the melting chocolate in her mouth, feeling that it would be unseemly to chew. "How would you like to spend these weeks in New York working with me?"

"Gosh!" Suze crunched Sheri's chocolate and swallowed it. "I'd love to."

Chapter Seven

Tony says thanks for the list. Lloyd swivelled his chair away from the desk, propped his feet on the low window-ledge and frowned out at the canal. *Tony who? Which list? List of what?*

It was one o'clock on Monday afternoon, the beginning of his second week at Schneider Fox, London, and the first sunny day since he had hit England. It was also his birthday.

Ten minutes ago Dee Dee had called to wish him a happy birthday. What a sweetheart. She must have gone in to work extra early to catch him before lunchtime. It had made him smile to hear her broad nasal vowels, already unfamiliar after only a week, as she updated him on office gossip. The photocopier had broken down again. Sheri had installed the English woman in Lloyd's office. Bernie had discovered a new diet. No, Lloyd responded, he hadn't met the queen yet, and yes, it had rained a lot. In among the chit-chat she had suddenly dropped the baffling message from "Tony." He had called on Friday. When Dee Dee explained that Lloyd was in England, Tony had left his enigmatic message and hung up.

Once again, Lloyd scanned his memory. The only Tony who came to mind was the computer salesman in San Francisco who had dated his mother for a while, in a sweaty, ingratiating way that had sped up Lloyd's decision to leave home. Lloyd gave a grunt of frustration and lowered his feet to the floor with a thump. He hated mysteries in the same way that he hated muddled thinking or an inept sentence. He toyed with the idea of calling Dee Dee back for clarification, but he knew it was pointless. Dee Dee had her Little Black Book in which she kept a written record of the date, time and content of every telephone message. She would have no more to add. Conceivably Sheri might be able to shed some light on the mystery, but Lloyd had already put in one call to her last week, to which she had so far failed to respond. He didn't want her to feel he was checking up.

What the hell. The sun was shining, he was in jolly old England and his stomach told him it was lunchtime. Lloyd stuffed his wallet in his back pocket and ran down the steel staircase, out across the cobbled courtyard and through the imposing wrought-iron gates that marked the entrance to Schneider Fox's London office. It was about as different as it could be from New York's corporate monolith; a handsome, four-story building of decorative brickwork that embodied the virtues of nineteenth-century industrial architecture. To the front it looked out on an unpromising area of inner-city wasteland awaiting development; its glory was the view from the tall windows at the back, across the canal and over a mosaic of slate roofs sloping up to the green fringe of Hampstead Heath. One hundred and fifty years ago, it had been a warehouse for goods shipped down the canal system from the north, or ferried up from the London docks. Wine, tea, wool, books, coal, everything traveled on barges, pulled by horses along the towpaths. To negotiate long tunnels, the bargemen had had to lie on their backs and walk their feet against the tunnel roof to push the boats through—or so Lloyd had been told. He was still grappling with the English sense of humor. When the railways came, such warehouses had either been demolished or had languished, like this one, for decades, awaiting transformation into chic offices and yuppie apartment blocks. The Schneider Fox building was a time machine: step inside and you were transported forward a century and a half. Behind the Victorian facade it was the epitome of cool, with smoked-glass panels and walls of bare brick. Sleek computers rested on elegant desks of pale wood. Clutter was kept to a minimum, and carefully coordinated in shades of gray.

Lloyd headed down toward King's Cross station, enjoying the sensation of the warm sun on his face. The neighborhood reminded him a little of the East Village in its combination of hip and semi-derelict. Italian delis, dance studios and seedy aromatherapy clinics jostled for space with pungent corner stores run by Asian men in robes and beaded caps, their lips stained red from chewing betel nut. There was a basement pool club frequented almost entirely by Chinese, and a kebab house where a wild-haired Greek grandmother used a hair dryer to keep the charcoal fire alight. By day, a throng of stylish young professionals with their briefcases and portfolios testified to the growing trendiness of the area. By night it yielded to the more menacing presence of junkies, prostitutes, pimps and drug dealers.

He entered the deli. As usual, a violent quarrel seemed to be in progress, held in Italian at top volume. From opposite sides of the store the owner and his wife were shouting simultaneously, encouraged from the floor by an old man seated on a wooden chair. Lloyd had learned by now that they were probably just discussing the time of the cheese delivery. He ordered a Parma ham sandwich, watching with enjoyment as the owner lovingly took down a side of ham, shaved wafer-thin slices on the machine, uttered a squeak of delight at their sheer perfection and laid them carefully inside a foot of fresh baguette. When Lloyd came outside, holding his beautifully wrapped package, he noticed a workman on a ladder across the street, pasting a new poster on to a billboard. A tropical sunset glowed in fiery reds and oranges; in the distance the trail of an airliner was barely visible. "A Passion for Travel," read the copyline. Lloyd grinned: he had written that himself. It seemed like a good omen. He started back toward the office at a leisurely amble, remembering.

It had all begun at a New York dinner party maybe seven years ago, when Lloyd had been seated opposite a wild-haired character called Tucker who had launched into a tirade against advertising executives. Assholes, he called them between slurps of Californian Cabernet Sauvignon, brain-dead airheads, the new mercenaries of the consumer army. More amused than insulted, Lloyd had announced that he was in the advertising business. It turned out that Tucker, age twenty-three, was marketing director for the media and rock music conglomerate, Passion. The Passion label had been one of the success stories of the previous decade. Every thirtysomething, Lloyd included, had grown up on their tapes and CDs, stamped with the distinctive heart logo, scarlet on black. That night he had traded rock trivia with Tucker until, credentials established, Tucker had explained his problem and invited Lloyd to pitch for the new business. It seemed that Passion now wanted to diversify into air travel. At the time this had seemed a wildly improbable leap. Air travel! It was like Bruce Willis saying he wanted to play Jesus Christ. Even Lloyd took a while to wrap his mind around the concept.

Tucker told him that the advertising agencies Passion had approached so far were all desperate to suggest ways of glossing over the features that did not square with traditional airline values—the company's newness, its maverick boss, its association with rock concerts and youth culture. Lloyd had turned the problem upside down. Instead of trying to pretend that Passion was American Airlines, he made the new airline fun, as hip and adventurous and youth-oriented as the music on the Passion label. When early rumors of the campaign leaked out into the advertising industry, how they had cackled and sneered! Nobody, they said, would want to fly with a company whose previous reputation had been for sex n' drugs n' rock n' roll. The truth was exactly the opposite. Lloyd had wooed the young people first, those who wanted to watch indie movies, listen to Passion bands on their headphones, and were delighted to eat simple packed lunches instead of microwaved cardboard.

Their success was almost frightening. Soon everyone wanted to travel with Passion, not just because it was cheap but because it was hip. The advertising budget tripled. Lloyd won his first—and only—Grand Prix, the Big Daddy of the advertising-industry prizes. Nobody realized that for its first year Passion owned only one airplane. Now Passion was poised to take over from Stateside as the dominant airline in the lucrative transatlantic trade. Next season, when they expanded the range of US destinations, would be the determinant. For Schneider Fox, Passion was their biggest single account and the chief reason for Lloyd's swift ascent up the company ladder.

What a genius I had in those days, Lloyd thought—what fire, what confidence! Where had the years gone? One minute he was a firebrand in his twenties, working most of the hours God gave him and fooling around the rest; the next, he had a fat corporate job, a live-in partner and thirty-four years on the clock. Correction: thirty-five.

Betsy had been very mysterious about the plans for tonight. Last year she had baked him a cake—chocolate fudge, he remembered, with candles. He had found the gesture curiously girlish, and the cake too rich, but he had been charmed all the same. It was nice to be adored. He wondered what surprise lay in store for him. An image of the black garter belt arose briefly and was banished. Control, please. Just as long as she hadn't bought him another of those ties that made him feel as if he should join the Republican party pronto.

After the dazzle of the street, the Schneider Fox reception area was dim and cool.

"I say, Lloyd, have you seen this? Your picture's in the paper." It was the receptionist, a young Indian woman with an accent as posh as the queen's.

"You're kidding." Lloyd strolled over to her. "How come?"

"It's in the new *Admag.* Gossip column, back page. Here, take it."

Lloyd read the article at his desk as he tore into the baguette, scattering crusty flakes. Two photographs accompanied it, a dopey one of himself taken at an awards dinner some years ago, kissing a trophy, and another that showed a man in shirtsleeves and suspenders, hair groovily cropped, posed cross-legged on a boardroom table. So this was Julian Jewel. For someone who had just dumped his employer he looked pretty impressed with himself.

Ah, My Jewel, Past Compare!

The canalside offices of Schneider Fox are awash with rumor after the shock departure of creative director Julian Jewel to Sturm Drang. It is understood that Jewel accepted a salary comfortably into six figures and a golden hello in the form of a brand-new red Ferrari. He joined his new firm on Monday after a celebratory weekend in Saint-Tropez.

"It's nothing personal," Jewel assures us. "Schneider Fox is a great company and it's been fun. But Hugo Drang and I have been mates ever since our Saatchi days. The chance to work with him again was irresistible." Not to mention seeing his name on the letterhead: word is the company is shortly to be rechristened Sturm Drang Jewel.

Ozzie supremo Harry Fox is rumored to be less than delighted by the manner of Jewel's resignation—a one-line e-mail message programmed to flash up on his screen at the end of play on Friday. But his response to our inquiries—"Julian who?"—suggests he is not reaching for his handkerchief just yet. Industry-watchers will recall Fox's tigerish assault five years ago on the prestigious but ailing Schneider agency in Manhattan, since which time the company's global turnover has increased fourfold.

Meanwhile, the big question is whether Jewel's key clients—including Wondersnax, Snifflies and Passion Airlines—will decamp to Sturm Drang. "Of course, I'd love to go on working with them, but I'm not counting my chickens," claims Jewel coyly. Very wise when there's a Fox about.

Ironically, Jewel was to have flown to New York last weekend to participate in the exchange program initiated by Fox to promote transatlantic goodwill and company loyalty. (Whoops!) Undaunted by Jewel's departure, Schneider Fox New York have sent their man anyway, whiz kid Lloyd Rockwell. Coincidentally, Rockwell masterminds the US account for . . . Passion Airlines. Fasten your seatbelts for a bumpy ride!

One clear winner in this everyday tale of adfolk is Susannah Wilding, flame-haired temptress of the art department at Schneider Fox London, who was whisked to the Big Apple in Jewel's place at twenty-four hours' notice. Grab a bagel for me, kid!

"You don't want to believe everything you read in the papers," rasped a voice.

Lloyd looked up to see Harry Fox filling the doorway, cigarette in hand. He rose awkwardly, brushing the crumbs off his suit.

"Ah, sit down, finish your lunch." Fox waved away Lloyd's politeness in a zigzag of smoke and settled himself casually in a chair.

Lloyd gestured at the magazine. "Are you concerned that we could lose any of Jewel's clients?" he asked.

Fox gave him a long look. He was a tall man, with an attractively angular face that could have been hewn from Ayer's Rock, and a rangy frame just beginning to betray middle age. Lloyd hadn't met many Australians, but he could tell that Fox was distinctly un-English. There was something in his unnervingly direct gaze and the swing of his shoulders that spoke of the lawless frontier, though when he smiled he looked like the charming fox of children's fables. He wasn't smiling now.

"Jewel's contract prevents him from approaching any of our clients for twelve months. He knows I'll be after him with a posse of lawyers if I catch him playing dirty." He flicked his ash into Lloyd's waste-bin. "And in the case of Passion, anyway, we have a secret weapon." He eyed Lloyd enigmatically.

"What's that?"

"You, of course. Aren't you supposed to be Passion's golden boy? It's time I put you to work. You don't think you're here for a holiday, do you?"

Lloyd laughed. "Not from what I've seen so far."

"I came to tell you that we're going to Lord's on Thursday," Fox said. "Client entertainment. I'll let you guess who the client is. You'll have the whole day to convince them how wonderful your new campaign is going to be. Think you're up to it?"

Was that the House of Lords, Lloyd wondered. *What kind of "entertainment" could possibly last an entire day?* He knew better than to ask. Harry Fox hated stupid questions. Aloud he said, "I'll give it my best shot."

"Good." Fox smacked his knees with the palms of his hands and stood up. "You still on for next weekend?"

"Of course. Betsy and I are looking forward to it."

"Did I warn you about the little monsters?"

"You did."

"And you're still coming?" Fox shook his head admiringly. "You Yanks must have nerves of bloody steel." And he was gone.

Lloyd subsided in his chair. Harry Fox was a challenge. Lloyd found him difficult to read. He was almost sure he liked him.

Chapter Eight

Betsy climbed crabwise up the narrow stairway, dragging two fistfuls of bulging supermarket bags. Her arms ached from the effort of holding them clear of the white pleated skirt she had put on to celebrate the arrival of summer. Pausing at the top of the stairs to catch her breath, she became aware of a sudden soft scampering from the hallway. Something furry and horribly alive squeezed through her legs, and a cat shot past her, heading for the open kitchen window. Betsy aimed a kick at it, missed the trick step down into the kitchen and crashed to her knees. There was an explosive chink of breaking glass and the drumroll of scattering tin cans. The cat yowled, scrabbled onto the windowsill and leaped free into the sycamore tree. Betsy saw her new potatoes, authentically dusted with organic soil, spill from one of the bags, chased by a foaming rivulet of champagne. A little lake of expensive mud formed on her newly washed floor.

"Shit!" she yelled. "Shit. Shit. Shit." Then, to nobody in particular, she added quietly, "Excuse me."

For a few moments Betsy breathed deeply through her nose, centering herself as her therapist had taught her. Then she rose from a squelch of lettuce, rubbed her knees tenderly and set about clearing up the mess. It wasn't too bad, she told herself. The avocado looked a little dented, but she could make it into guacamole. The Betty Crocker box was sodden, but thankfully the cake mix inside was sealed in plastic. Lloyd would get his favorite chocolate cake.

That damned cat! This was not the first time Betsy had caught it in the apartment. Not only was she allergic to cats, but this particular cat was the most loathsome specimen she had ever seen, a low-slung creature of leprous white with a piratical black patch across one eye that gave it a malevolent air. The thought of it roaming over the kitchen counters or spreading its hairy bulk across her pillow made her shudder. Something would have to be done.

Betsy wiped her groceries clean and put them away, wrapped the thick shards of champagne bottle in newspaper and cleaned the floor. Her first purchase in Britain had been a new sponge for the floor mop, to replace the stiff, emaciated corpse of its predecessor. She had spent the whole of last week giving the apartment a spring-cleaning. More than once, as she excavated yet another cache of fluff-encrusted ephemera from underneath cushions and down the sides of armchairs—paper clips, pistachio nut shells, wine corks, spent matches—the shadow of Ms. Susannah Wilding had darkened her thoughts. But now the bath gleamed, the windows sparkled, the tops of wardrobes and the underside of the bed were dust free. In the kitchen, spice jars marched in alphabetical order across scrubbed shelves. The oven no longer belched foul-smelling smoke when she turned it on. Betsy had even washed the curtains, braving the local laundromat that doubled as a refuge for mucus-smeared toddlers and old ladies with bandaged legs as thick as tree trunks. Betsy didn't understand London. While in America there were clearly designated rich neighborhoods and poor neighborhoods, here a peeling tenement packed with immigrant families could be right next door to a lawyer's astronomically priced home. It made her very uneasy.

When the kitchen was restored to order, Betsy opened the tall sash window wide to clear the champagne fumes. Honeyed air floated up from the backyard. It was almost pleasant. Betsy paused to lean on the windowsill, feeling the warmth on her arms, thinking how typical it was that the sun should have come out for Lloyd's birthday. He always seemed to get what he wanted.

The first time she had seen Lloyd he had been sitting in the sun. It was Labor Day weekend, and she was staying out on Long Island with an old school-friend. The highlight of the weekend was to be a tennis tournament that was held every year by some people who lived out toward Montauk Point. The rule was that anyone who wanted to stay for the evening barbecue had to play. Early on Saturday morning, armed with a sheaf of rackets, they had climbed into a station wagon and driven east, arriving at a sprawling clapboard house in a state of casual decrepitude that spoke of old money. Wicker furniture sagged on the deep porches. There were hammocks among the trees and a slope of yellowed lawn leading to the ocean. Their hosts were a hearty pair in late middle age, with wrinkled knees and unfashionably deep tans. Betsy saw at a glance that this was not her sort of crowd. She had been partnered with one of those terrier-like older men who like to stand at the net and shout "Mine!" It was not until the afternoon that she contrived to lose a match and escape into the house for a cooling shower. Afterward, she had strolled down to the water, drawn by a soft breeze that trailed plumes of cloud across a turquoise sky. The boisterous babble of the tournament faded and was replaced by the scurry of waves on sand and the rhythmic thunk of a boat knocking against wood. The trees cleared until there was nothing but blue sky and blue ocean. And there, alone, at the end of the boat dock, sat a lean man with dark, ruffled hair, reading a book. His air of calm self-containment had struck her as much as his looks. Betsy had wanted him at once.

With a self-possession she did not know she had, she had walked out to him and said, "Jay Gatsby, I presume," wanting him to know from the start that she was an educated woman, a thinker, a scholar.

Lloyd had just laughed, of course, but Betsy thought he had been quite struck when she told him that she had majored in English at college and was working on her doctorate at Columbia. He accompanied her to the barbecue, and over the spareribs and hot dogs Betsy was able to ascertain that Lloyd was college educated, solvent, heterosexual and apparently unattached. He seemed intelligent and honest, and he was certainly good-looking. She couldn't believe her luck.

It wasn't as easy as that, of course. When Lloyd didn't call her the following week, Betsy bought two theater tickets for the new

Arthur Miller play, due to open shortly. Somehow, she managed to make herself wait until the morning of the play, then called Lloyd to explain that she had been let down at the last minute and had a spare ticket. Would he like to come? He accepted.

Afterward they ate sushi and discussed the play, literature and life. At the door of the restaurant Betsy, well versed in dating rules for the thirtyish woman, hailed a cab and wished Lloyd goodnight before he could make up his mind whether to invite her home or make another date. Her strategy worked. He called her the next day to thank her for the theater and to suggest a date for the following weekend. That was the beginning. Over the next couple of months they went to movies, to galleries, to dinner; finally to bed.

That winter, during some of the worst blizzards New York had ever suffered, something went wrong with Betsy's central heating and Lloyd let her stay at his place for a couple of days. Then he got the flu, so badly that Betsy stayed another week to take care of him. She made him soup, read aloud to him and worked on her research notes while he slept. By the time he had recovered, she had also sewn all the missing buttons onto his shirts, taken his tape deck to be repaired and hung the curtains that had come back from the cleaners two months previously. It had been one of the happiest weeks of her life.

The evening before he was due back at work, Lloyd found her packing her bag in the bedroom. "But what about your heating?" he had asked.

"Fixed."

"What about all that reading you had to do?"

"Done."

And finally, as she had hoped and prayed, he had taken her in his arms and reproachfully murmured, "And what about me?" She had stayed.

That was almost two years ago. They had settled down into the social pattern of most couples—movies, friends, dinners, the occasional weekend in the country, low-key stuff. They rarely argued, largely because Betsy chose to give way. But she was becoming impatient. Practically every time Mother called, it was to announce the marriage of yet another of her friends' daughters, increasingly women younger than Betsy. "Any special news?" she would ask, with coy emphasis. It was Mother who had encouraged Betsy to accompany Lloyd to England—had, in fact, paid for the ticket. "Every man needs a little push now and then. Look at your father."

"Things are different nowadays," Betsy would reply, though sometimes she wondered whether the dynamics of courtship had changed all that much over the centuries.

She checked her watch guiltily. The morning was almost gone, and she had written nothing. Sighing a little, she fetched her glasses, seated herself at the computer in the living room and switched it on. She reached for the disk that contained the chapters she had written so far, and read the neatly inscribed label with a proprietary glow: *Prejudice and Persuasion: Themes of Slavery and Empowerment in the Novels of Jane Austen.*

Several people had warned her off so crowded an area of literary study. Betsy knew better. Previous critics had been so captivated by the superficial romanticism of the texts that they had completely missed the profundities. Betsy felt it was her mission to reinstate Jane Austen as a champion of women's rights and a serious commentator on social equality, particularly after Hollywood's crass attempt to claim her as the hot new scriptwriter of light romantic comedy. Personally, Betsy found nothing to laugh at in the novels. For three years she had labored to show that they dealt not with the trivialities of who married whom, but with the great iniquities of society: ageism (*Persuasion*), the exploitation of the Afro-Caribbean community (*Mansfield Park*), the gender bias of inheritance law (*Pride and Prejudice*), and anorexia nervosa (*Northanger Abbey*). This last analysis, drawing heavily on Freudian case studies, Betsy believed to be a genuine coup of original research.

Now she had reached *Emma* (fascism), and was in mid-exposé of the totalitarian state of Highbury. Betsy inserted her disk, reread the chapter so far, and started to type. Somehow, actually being in England had sharpened her distaste for its petty gradations of class, and she worked up quite a head of steam as she described the plight of exploited workers and unwaged widows. It was almost uncanny how each character exemplified an aspect of political theory or gender stereotyping. Betsy thanked God she was an American, living in freedom and equality. "Thus it is clear," she concluded, "that Austen is less concerned with her protagonist's choice of life partner than with the process of democratization that will enfranchise her claim to co-status with Knightley."

Betsy scrolled back through the pages, checking her spelling and honing her prose to perfection. Before she knew it, she had drifted into one of her favorite daydreams, the one where she finally allowed Lloyd to read her thesis and he returned afterward, awed and amazed, to pronounce her a genius. This developed seamlessly into her other favorite daydream, where he took her out to dinner and proposed formally, with a ring. She would accept, naturally, and then—then life would begin. Lloyd would be promoted to the board. They would buy a house with a yard. After a suitable interval Betsy would relinquish her academic career for motherhood. She would meet Lloyd off the commuter train, haloed by the setting sun at the wheel of their station wagon.

Sometimes she thought she would die if Lloyd didn't marry her. She took in his dry cleaning, ran his home, organized their vacations, let him choose what movies they saw, cooked dinner for his friends, almost always said yes when he wanted to make love. Right now, hidden at the bottom of the bedroom closet, were his birthday packages, already wrapped and beribboned: the new Wallace Stevens biography he wanted, a travel alarm clock and the handsome Brooks Brothers tie she had smuggled into England as a special surprise. There would be steaks for dinner and candles on his cake. What more could he want? What was he waiting for? Her eyes strayed to the pinboard behind the desk, where she had cleared a space for her postcard portrait of Jane Austen. She looked so neat, so knowing, so unknowable. *So what do you think, Jane?* Betsy challenged silently. It seemed to her that the portrait's mouth curled slyly. *It is a truth universally acknowledged that a man already in possession of everything a woman has to offer need be in no hurry to marry her.*

Betsy looked away and sank her head into her hands. What else could she offer him? With what key could she unlock that mysterious part of him that eluded her? She was sure that she could make him into the man she wanted—if he would let her. But there were aspects of his personality that she didn't understand, or even like: his friendship with Jay, for example, his silence about his family and the moods when he liked to lock himself away and listen to the saddest, sexiest music she had ever heard: Muddy Waters, Howlin' Wolf—even the names were weird. There were times when she didn't even know what he saw in her. If she knew, she could do it more—or better.

Out of the corner of her eye Betsy caught a stealthy movement in the doorway and spun around in terror. It was the cat again. It stood frozen in the doorway, giving her a long, blank look, then minced into the room, tail erect. Betsy sneezed helplessly, unstoppably, until her eyes and nose ran. What was happening to her? Why hadn't she brought her antihistamine pills to this dirty, godforsaken, cat-ridden land? She groped in her sweater for a handkerchief and held it over her nose until the sneezing fit subsided. A tide of rage and resentment ran hot through her body. She had told Lloyd about the cat, more than once. All he had done was murmur, "Oh, really?" in that absentminded-professor way he had.

Betsy rose from her chair and walked stealthily to the kitchen. First she shut the window. Then she got out a bowl and filled it with milk. "Here, kitty-kitty," she crooned, carrying the bowl back into the living room and setting it on the floor. Moving with exaggerated care, she picked up the waste-bin from under the desk, positioned herself at the edge of the couch next to the bowl and waited.

It took a long time. The cat stayed crouched in the shadow of the table, staring at her suspiciously. It washed itself from head to toe, with some unpleasant sound effects. Then it pretended to go to sleep. Eventually it strolled out into the room, assessing the contents of the bowl with the casual droop of an eyelid. It looked at Betsy. She smiled encouragingly, tightening her grip on the poised basket. At length the cat folded itself down and began to lap at the milk. Betsy made herself count to twenty, then launched herself from the sofa and slammed the basket upside down over the cat.

There was a squawk of panic. One sinewy leg remained free, clawing wildly at the carpet. The cat's tail flailed furiously as it struggled to back out of the trap. But Betsy was ruthless. She pressed one polished loafer, hard, on the cat's tail. With the other she stuffed the errant leg under the lip of the basket. The tail followed swiftly. Betsy sat down on top of the rocking basket, flushed and panting. With a coarseness that would have shocked Jane Austen right out of her little lace cap she shouted, "Got you, you bastard!"

Chapter Nine

Suze retrieved the copy from her computer memory, repositioned it on the screen grid and zapped the mouse. Her computer gave its usual frenzied cheep and flashed up the Matsuhana party invitation. She considered the effect. "It's design, Jim, but not as we know it," she muttered.

Still, it was what Sheri wanted, and Suze was in no doubt that what was good for Sheri was good for her. After one week at Schneider Fox New York her status as Sheri's protégée was established. Within hours of their bonding lunch, Sheri had squared Quincy, requisitioned a Mac, and installed both it and Suze in the office next to her own—Lloyd Rockwell's office, in fact, conveniently free. Instead of a hellhole down in the art department, Suze had a power desk, her own telephone and a view of the Hudson that made her heart sing. Dino said she was so lucky he wanted to do her chart for her.

There were penalties, of course. Last Friday Sheri had discovered that no one had designed the invitation for the grand opening of Matsuhana's first-ever retail store outside Japan. Matsuhana was the worldwide brand leader in sound and video systems, a byword for technological innovation and sleek design. Its store was to be at the cutting edge of retail design—part store, part amusement arcade, part showcase for electronic wizardry—situated on a prime piece of Fifth Avenue real estate. The party was less than three weeks away, and Schneider Fox had pledged to deliver an event of maximum glitz. It was clear that somebody had goofed.

Late on Friday, Sheri had called a rush meeting, explained that darling, head-in-the-clouds Lloyd must have forgotten this crucial detail, and had there and then hammered out a brief. The mood of the meeting was resentful. At this time of year, New Yorkers counted on slipping off early on Fridays. No one had volunteered to work over the weekend, and it therefore fell to Suze, as the new girl, to "prioritize" the invitation. Somebody very important was coming by this afternoon to give the artwork the OK, then it would be rushed to the printer and the invitation couriered. This was very New York. Suze had learned that any invitation that came by US mail wasn't even worth opening.

Suze hated jobs like this, where she was told exactly what to do, handed the dullest copy in the universe and asked to make it "fabulous." Her eyes ached from staring at the screen. She was longing for a cigarette. The sun had crept around the building to glare in at her office window, and she could feel it on her back, uncomfortably hot despite the air-conditioning. Irritably, she twisted her heavy hair into a rough knot on top of her head and secured it with one of Lloyd Rockwell's beautifully sharpened pencils. Then she double-checked that all Sheri's corrections had been made, put everything she needed onto a Zip disk and took it down to the art department to print out.

When she returned, she found Sheri ransacking papers on her desk. "Where have you been?" she demanded. "The party promoter's coming by any minute. I absolutely cannot keep him waiting."

"No need." Suze put a folder on the desk. "Exactly as you wanted it."

"What else have you got there?" Sheri asked suspiciously, noticing a second folder that Suze was holding.

"Just some extra color Xeroxes," Suze lied.

Sheri took out the invitation that Suze had mocked up and examined it keenly. The background was cool gray, washed over in a darker tone with a calligraphic device that looked vaguely oriental. The type was modest and beautifully spaced, the wording dignified, the famous black and orange logo placed discreetly in a corner. It looked elegant, expensive, supremely tasteful—and dull.

"I hope people will come," said Suze dubiously.

Sheri looked startled, then gave a forgiving smile. "I don't think you understand, Suzanne. Matsuhana has total command of the high ground in sound product—and I mean, like, globally. They are a multibillion-dollar corporation. Wall Street loves them. Their executives are profiled in *Fortune* magazine. They have major holdings in US telecommunications. They practically own Nevada—"

"Yeah, yeah," Suze interrupted. "Everyone knows the company is great. But, well, a Japanese party. Isn't that a contradiction in terms? All I can think of is raw fish and short men in suits bowing to each other. It's not exactly a turn-on."

"You think people might turn *down* this invitation?" Sheri was incredulous.

"Not businessmen." Suze tried not to sound scathing. "Or rich old people with nothing else to do. But I thought you wanted the party to be hot, young, hip. Perhaps things are different in New York, but in London we'd want to put out something more offbeat, maybe with a teaser or a gimmick to give the event a little twist."

"Gimmick?" Sheri's eyebrows rose another notch.

"For example, last year we launched this sexy lingerie business and enclosed a condom with every invitation."

"Condoms!" Sheri's eyes widened in shock. Before she could summon the words to comment further, there was a warm chuckle from the doorway, and a teasing voice said, "I always knew you career women liked to talk dirty. Sheri, how are you? You're looking gorgeous."

Framed in the doorway, sunglasses dangling from one tanned hand, was the most divine-looking man Suze had ever seen. Sunstreaked hair, laid-back smile, Glo-white T-shirt under a crisp black linen jacket: here was James Dean reincarnated.

Sheri accepted his kiss on her cheek with stunning sangfroid and introduced the man as Nick Bianco, party promoter. "And this is Suzanne, who is working with us on a temporary basis. She's from London," she added, as if to explain the condom lapse.

"Really? Wild place. I adore London." Nick's palm was smooth and warm against Suze's as they shook hands. Her stomach somersaulted. She wondered if he was married. She prayed to God he was heterosexual.

Nick picked up the invitation and started discussing it with Sheri. Suze's brain fogged over as she watched him sit down and cross his legs, placing one slim ankle on the opposite knee. Early thirties, she guessed. She couldn't see a ring. How did he get his jeans to look like that, at once so authentically faded and yet so miraculously clean? He must have just bought them at Calvin Klein. Unless they had been polished to this soft indigo bloom by the caresses of millions of adoring women.

". . . and thereby majoritize their market status," Sheri seemed to be saying.

Nick looked up from the design and gave Suze a dazzling blue stare. "Did you do this?"

"Yes, I . . . At least—not exactly." Of course he was heterosexual. No gay man ever gave women quite that kind of hungry, questing look.

"Because I like it, in fact it's fabulous, but I just wonder . . ." Nick turned back to Sheri. "The thing is, I'm planning to deliver a major scene here. That's why you hired me, right? Besides the usual suits, I've got guys flying in from the Hollywood sound studios, celeb DJs, rock stars, actors. I'm working on Bliss Bogardo to cut the ribbon. There's even a chance I could get The Truck."

"What truck?" asked Sheri.

"It's a band," Suze explained, hoping to redeem herself as a cool person.

"So what I'm asking myself is whether this"—Nick flapped the card—"is funky enough?"

"Now wait a minute, Nick." Sheri fixed him with her headlamp eyes. " 'Funky' is not a concept we discussed. We have six days to get this thing together, and I've already had to crawl to the printer. This is not the moment to go creative on me."

There was a difficult silence. Nick twitched one foot fretfully.

Gucci loafers, Suze saw, beautifully polished. "You're right." He sighed. "I wish you could have put a little more sizzle on the steak, but I guess I'll just have to be extra persuasive. Frankly, I think you've missed an opportunity."

Suze watched as he stood up, gave the invitation a final, withering look, and shut the folder. Any minute now he was going to walk out of her life, believing that she was responsible for this limp piece of design—and deaf and dumb to boot. Heartbeat accelerating, she reached for the other folder, the one she had slipped out of sight behind her computer. "Uh, Sheri," she gave a diffident cough, "why don't we show him the alternative?"

"Excuse me?"

"You know, the alternative version you asked me to rough out. Remember?" Suze pressed the folder into Sheri's hands and gave her a significant look.

"Oh. Sure. The alternative," Sheri said in a robot voice. She laid the folder on the desk and opened it.

This was the version that Suze had prepared in secret, partly out of frustration with the restrictions of her brief, partly out of experience. When a client was unhappy, it was always the designer who took the flak; she had learned to keep the odd ace up her sleeve.

There was total silence while Nick and Sheri took in what Suze had done. Instead of tasteful gray, the invitation card was brilliant orange, a Day-Glo version of Matsuhana's trademark color. Sheri's original copy was still there, but consigned to the foot of the card. What hit the eye first were the words "SOUNDS LIKE FUN," printed in huge, black, blocky type. The effect was startling. When the idea had come to her in the middle of last night, Suze had thought it inspired. Now, as the seconds passed, it began to look horribly vulgar.

"It was just an idea," she babbled. "Of course, it needs more work. I know it's not in line with the brief."

Nick lifted her mock-up from the desk. "It's perfect," he breathed reverently. "I love it. I *adore* it." His handsome face melted into a delighted smile. "How did you guys come up with such a great idea?"

"Well," Suze began importantly, but Sheri got there first.

"Sometimes, Nick, you just have to break the rules," she told him, with a pussycat smile. She put a proprietary hand on his elbow and steered him toward the door. "Let's go into my office and action this thing right away. You," she tossed over her shoulder at Suze, "can go home."

Suze watched, speechless, as Sheri led the way out into the corridor without a backward glance. Nick followed her obediently, but in the doorway he turned back and gave Suze a glorious wink. They exchanged a conspirators' smile that said as plain as words that while Sheri must be humored, there were only two people here who were hip, sexy as hell and the right side of forty.

Thoroughly overexcited, Suze had to go to the ladies' room to bathe her face in cold water. It was a humiliating feature of office life in America that you had to get a key every time you needed to go to the "bathroom," a cluster of primary-school-type lavatories that was kept locked against lurking rapists and toilet-paper thieves. Dee Dee was keeper of the key. Suze found her typing away in her cubbyhole, surrounded by plastic dry-cleaning bags.

"Going to a party?" Suze asked, trying to be friendly. She had the feeling that Dee Dee didn't approve of her, but couldn't think why.

Dee Dee gave her a sour look. "It's Sheri's stuff," she said shortly. "Please remember to bring the key back this time."

Suze retreated, feeling stung. It was true that last week she had found the key in her handbag when she had popped out to do a little shopping, but it was a perfectly understandable mistake. Anyway, who needed approval from someone who wore sleeveless blouses in beige Crimplene?

In the bathroom, Suze gave one glance in the mirror and let out an agonized yelp. What was that pencil doing sticking up out of the top of her head? Wayward tufts of hair sprouted from her scalp. Her zingy lemon-yellow dress (yellow was the "new white" this summer) had crumpled like a used tissue. She looked like a pineapple. Nick hadn't been smiling at her; he'd been laughing.

Suze tore the pencil out of her hair and threw it into the waste-bin. As she ran the cold water and soothed her flushed face, she brooded darkly on the kind of irresponsible man who could not only "forget" about the Matsuhana party, but also left pencils lying around to tempt people into hair abuse. Damn Lloyd Rockwell!

Chapter Ten

By the time Suze had struggled her way back to the apartment she was feeling hot and ill-used. Heat pulsed from the asphalt streets, yet there was hardly any sunshine, just a sullen, radioactive shimmer. Inside, the apartment felt airless and as cramped as a kennel. Suze went around checking the little metal boxes on the windows that she had initially thought might be loudspeakers—perhaps to blast out "America the Beautiful" on the Fourth of July: she had heard that Americans were terribly patriotic. Actually they were air-conditioners, and it seemed to be a rule of Manhattan life that their effectiveness was in inverse proportion to the outside temperature. No amount of fiddling or banging seemed to improve their performance. Instead, Suze took a long, cool shower, dressed herself in shorts and a singlet, lit a cigarette and tried to think of something interesting to do. "I am not lonely," she told herself. Once, she would have been straight on to Bridget for a girly gossip about Nick; nowadays she feared a lecture on diaper rash. There was nothing on television—quite a feat, really, considering the number of channels—and she was too embarrassed to go down to Video Heaven again. She decided that a serious snoop was in order.

The first cupboard stank of mothballs. Suze investigated the zipped hanging bags of women's clothes, just in case there was something fabulous she might have to borrow if anyone ever invited her out. But the floaty dresses and classic jackets did not speak to her. There was always something more appealing about men's clothes, and at the second cupboard Suze paused to breathe in the clean, male smell of laundered shirts and shoe leather. She had never seen such long, narrow shoes, all of the same classic, elegant cut. Maybe he wasn't such a fat businessman, after all. Out of idle curiosity she opened one of the shoe boxes on the floor and saw that it contained photographs—perhaps a secret porn stash! A quick riffle showed her that they were just boring old snapshots of boring people she didn't know. She replaced the lid.

Next she examined the books in the hall, detecting a his n' hers cataloging system. On the left were poems by Walt Whitman and Ogden Nash, biographies of Kennedy and Roosevelt, books on film and design, modern novels in hardback. On the right she found slim volumes by Joan Didion and Anaïs Nin, fat works of literary criticism, *The Joy of Cooking*, something called *Miss Manners' Guide to Etiquette* inscribed "To my darling daughter with love from Mother," and a lot of those books Suze had never got around to reading about how marvelous yet tragically oppressed women were. One title caught her eye: *Women Who Love Too Much.* That's me, Suze thought. Maybe it was just as well that she had blown her chances with Nick.

No brooding. She'd put on some music. In the living room, Suze craned her neck sideways to read the labels of the Rockwell sound collection. Bach, Chopin, Mozart, Scarlatti . . . She frowned. Classical music always made her feel as if it were Sunday afternoon and raining, and maybe she'd better just hang herself. Fortunately, there was a jazz section as well. Suze picked out a Sarah Vaughan CD, slid it into the stereo, then did what she had been longing to do ever since she arrived, which was to rearrange the living room furniture. Not only were the chairs oddly grouped—one here, another way over there, as if no one ever talked to each other—but if she moved the sofa she would be able to stand on it to see her reflection in the only large mirror in the house. She had just cleared the rugs out of the way and was discovering that the sofa was surprisingly heavy when the doorbell rang.

With a grunt of impatience, Suze stomped across the floor in her bare feet, undid the heavy metal lock and pulled the door open. *Hooray, a man.*

"Oh, good," she said, "you can help me move the sofa. It's in a completely daft place and I can't lift it." She led the way into the living room. "The thing is," she explained over her shoulder, "this isn't my apartment and I don't want to massacre the floor. Well, go on," she added, seeing the stranger still lurking in the doorway, "take the other end."

The man gave an amused shrug and did as she instructed. Within minutes all had been arranged to her satisfaction and the rugs replaced on the unscarred parquet.

"Thanks. That's brilliant." Suze pushed the hair from her eyes. "Who are you, by the way? I'm Suze."

"I know."

The man looked thirtysomething: medium height, stocky, with peroxide hair like David Hockney, dressed in white jeans and a striped seersucker jacket. Not bad, if you liked that kind of thing. He was smiling at her, a slow charming smile that seemed to suggest that he had seen it all but was still prepared to laugh.

"Jay Veritas," he said, shaking her hand. "I'm a friend of Lloyd's. He asked me to drop by and say hello. He didn't say anything about furniture-moving though." Jay put a hand to the small of his back and winced theatrically. "I think I might have pulled something."

"Rubbish." Suze laughed. "But you definitely deserve a drink. What shall we have?"

It seemed that Jay knew her kitchen better than she did. He got out a gleaming chrome liquidizer, assembled ice, orange juice and various bottles, and produced a frothy apricot-colored concoction that speared her throat like an icicle. "Totally divine," she pronounced, sinking back on the newly positioned sofa. "Where did you learn to do that?"

"Montana, New Mexico, Maine . . . I used to be a barman."

"Seriously?"

"Not very." Jay explained how he and Lloyd had worked their way from California to New York when they were nineteen, taking whatever jobs they could find. "We made a great team. We'd go into some bar in Nowheresville: first he'd show them what he could do on the piano, then, when they were hooked, he said he wouldn't work unless they gave me a job too."

"Lloyd?" Suze was surprised.

"He always got the better pay—and the girls. But let me warn you, never let him make you a cocktail."

"Not much danger of that." Suze got up and started poking around the room, looking for her cigarettes. When she found them, she held up the packet. "Do you mind?"

"Hallelujah!" Jay drew his own packet from the top pocket of his jacket. "I knew I was going to like you the moment I saw you. We can be social pariahs together."

They talked companionably, sipping their drinks and testing each other's brand of cigarette, while the light ebbed from the sky. Prompted by Jay, Suze burbled happily about her reactions to New York—its overwhelming physical beauty, its heady atmosphere of unlimited possibility and the liberation of being in a place where she could not be pigeonholed by her accent or her address or the school she had attended a decade and a half ago. "And I love being a tourist. Having scoffed at Americans taking photographs of London, I find myself doing the same thing here and I'm not even embarrassed."

Jay nodded. "Let's face it, it's tiring being cool all of the time—and we should know, right?"

Suze giggled. Jay wasn't camp at all, but there was a watchful quality about him that, added to his special brand of charm, made a connection in Suze's brain. *He's gay,* she realized.

"You're right about the furniture," Jay said, looking around. "It *is* better like this. In fact, now that I think of it, you've moved the couch back where it used to be, before Lloyd sold his piano."

"Why did he do that?"

"No room when Betsy moved in."

There was a small silence. Then Jay said, "Listen, are you hungry?"

"Starving."

"Let's go find some dinner. What do you feel like? American,

French, Italian, Chinese? Japanese, Caribbean, Cajun? Vietnamese, Greek?"

"Golly."

"Cal-Ital, Tex-Mex, Bengali-Slav, Chino-Latino, Kosher-Italian?"

"Stop!" Suze was laughing. "And I don't believe Bengali-Slav."

"Believe it. This is New York."

"Well, actually," Suze admitted, "what I secretly fancy is somewhere really New Yorky—tinkling piano, fabulous view, killer drinks with lots of ice and fancy straws. Humphrey Bogart, if you can manage it."

Jay made a horrified face. "You're just a crypto B-and-T."

"What's B-and-T?"

"Bridge and Tunnel people—the poor saps who have to commute from the 'burbs for some nightlife."

"We'd split the bill, of course." Suze gave him a coaxing look.

"In that case, I know just the place. You'll have to lose the shorts, though."

When Suze was ready they took a cab downtown. The rush of warm air through the open window made her feel as if she were on holiday. Her spirits rose and impulsively she turned to Jay. "It's lovely of you to ask me out. I've been dreaming of doing something like this ever since I arrived."

"Good. Although . . ." Jay hesitated, choosing his words. "This isn't exactly a date, you know."

"I know." Suze looked him in the eye, to show that she understood perfectly. "Don't worry, I've already found Mr. Heartthrob." She gave Jay a run-down of the afternoon's events, making him laugh at Sheri's lofty exit and a lurid description of her own appearance.

"I bet you looked adorable wearing a pencil," said Jay. "He's probably trying to track down your telephone number at this very moment."

"As if." But she couldn't help smiling.

When it seemed that any minute they would drive right off the edge of Manhattan into the East River, the cab climbed up on to a bridge. On the other side it turned sharply, swooped downward and deposited them in an uninspiring car-park. Jay led the way toward a low building and down a short flight of steps that seemed to rock under her feet. She was on a boat! In front of her was a bar, dim lights gleaming on bottles and cocktail shakers. Beyond that, across the river, rose the Manhattan skyline, sparkling with all the freshness and arrogance of a brand-new universe.

Jay scanned her face appreciatively. "Welcome to the River Café."

They sat at high stools at the bar and Jay ordered her something called a Perfect Manhattan, requesting that it be festooned with every paper umbrella and plastic swizzle stick in the place.

"How come somebody as fun as you is a friend of Lloyd's?" asked Suze. "I thought he was old and respectable."

"We're exactly the same age, thirty-five. It's just that Lloyd has a somewhat overdeveloped sense of responsibility. He dresses better than me too."

"What's his wife like?"

"They're not married."

"Girlfriend, partner, whatever."

"Very pretty. Dark hair, nice skin, the fragile type."

Automatically Suze sucked in her cheeks and tried to wilt a little. Various men in her past had claimed to find her pretty, sexy, even beautiful; no one had ever called her fragile.

"And is she nice? Do you like her?"

Jay looked thoughtful. "I don't think she cares too much for me. She thinks I distract Lloyd from Real Life. Last year, he helped me write the script for a movie I'm trying to make. Eventually Betsy called me up and told me 'in confidence' that it was affecting Lloyd's work. She was very nice about it—but she was telling me to back off."

"What did Lloyd say?"

"I never told him. Lloyd is different. He has interesting ideas. He makes me laugh. We talk about writing and movies and why the world is the way it is. Whenever Betsy's there we seem to be on some kind of schedule."

"Perhaps she'd like to tie him up in a nice neat parcel labeled 'husband'?" Suze suggested.

Jay did not rise to the bait. They moved to their table in the restaurant, and on principle Suze ordered dishes she'd never heard of—littleneck clams and seared yellowfin tuna with wild greens.

"And what about you?" Jay asked, refilling her wineglass. "Where's your boyfriend?"

"What boyfriend?"

"Women like you always have a man."

"Had," Suze corrected. Her mouth twisted. "Or so I thought." She picked up her fork and scored a line of crosses on the tablecloth, as if she could scratch out the memories. "Anyway, there are no women 'like me.'" She gave Jay a defiant look. "I am unique."

"Indubitably." Jay reached for his packet of cigarettes, shook out a couple and handed one to her. "Tell me."

And to her surprise, Suze did.

It was five years ago that she had gotten a job as a senior designer on the magazine section of one of the major Sunday newspapers. She was the new young talent, eager to make a mark; Lawrence Self was art director, a bachelor of forty-two with a shock of dark hair beginning to gray, snapping brown eyes under black brows and a reputation for being a difficult genius. He wore jeans to work, drove an Alfa Spider, smoked dope, mixed with actresses and artists and kept his money in a great wad of notes in his back pocket. Suze thought he was wonderful.

For the first time in her life she had worked as hard as she knew how, stayed late, cracked jokes, volunteered for every loony assignment—anything to keep her in the energy circle of this extraordinary man. She found that she loved the momentum of working on a weekly: first the casual, coffee-drinking dawdling, then the gathering panic as the deadline loomed and finally the adrenaline rush of putting the magazine to bed and tottering out to the pub to celebrate. Within three months they were lovers.

Lawrence—never, ever Larry—had grown up during the sixties and seventies. He had a laissez-faire attitude toward life that Suze found excitingly refreshing after the City clones, with their fixations on BMWs and bonuses. One day soon, he told her, he was going to give up this job bullshit, move somewhere warm and become a full-time artist. Marriage was one of the things he despised, along with mortgages, suburbs, Ford Escorts, overhead lighting and a typeface called Palatino, and Suze had quickly learned to despise them too.

"He taught me to see things, to look properly. At the weekend we used to go on what we called 'urban strolls,' looking at old churches, new office blocks, even the detailing on shop fronts or the design of iron railings. Lawrence was brilliant at pointing out where the architect had lost his nerve or had been overruled by the client. Or we'd go down to Bermondsey market, hunting for old wooden type, and experiment with new designs in Lawrence's studio." She sighed. "I did learn a lot. He made me take my work seriously, to stretch myself to produce the very best I could."

"Did you love him?" asked Jay bluntly.

"I adored him." Suze frowned. "Mostly."

Lawrence could be tetchy and moody. If he didn't like what she had done at work, he would take it out on her at home—though they had never actually lived together: Lawrence had explained how important solitude and privacy were to him. But they spent most nights and weekends together, unless Lawrence was feeling frayed.

"I took him up to meet my parents once, thinking they would get on because they're practically the same age, and they're all 'creative' in one way or another. Disaster!" Suze described how he had picked at her mother's cooking, lectured her father about the role of art in the life of the common man and made them all drive miles to look at some "marvelous" church, which turned out to be locked, then complained that the mud had ruined his shoes. Afterward he had apologized to Suze. "I'm like a fine wine, I'm afraid: I don't travel well."

Nevertheless, they might have gone on for years, had it not been for Araminta Smedley, known as "Minty," age twenty-four, possessor of an extremely rich father and a jobette in the newspaper's advertising department.

One day, driving back to his place from work, Lawrence had

confessed that he'd been "seeing" Araminta. Suze was furious, remembering all the recent times she had "respected his space," as he liked to put it, but in her heart she had been prepared to forgive him eventually. Then Lawrence had dropped his bombshell. Minty was pregnant. And she did not want to get rid of the baby.

What had hurt Suze most was that Lawrence had seemed barely regretful. He had looked at her winsomely, like a naughty child, as if to say, "With a sperm count like mine, what can one do?"

"Lawrence would never use condoms," she told Jay. "He said they didn't feel 'nice'—as if pills and coils and the anxiety of a late period were fun. I thought of all the contraceptive measures I'd taken, how careful I had been not to entrap him in any way. Then, bingo! In waltzes Minty and just grabs what she wants. It's so *banal*. Anyway, then I was in the ridiculous position of having to persuade him to take responsibility for the baby. But I still didn't get it. I thought he loved me, was in the same state of torment I was." Suze shook her head at her own stupidity, remembering how she had lost fifteen pounds in a week and spent her nights chain-smoking in a huddle on the sofa.

"The next thing I know, they're getting married. Isn't that sweet? And not just any old wedding. Oh, no, it's the full monty—church, bridesmaids, speeches. He even sent me an invitation—engraved, natch—and said I was childish when I wouldn't go.

"She isn't even that pretty," Suze told Jay indignantly, "just one of those drippy, flat-chested girls who's always photographed hugging a Labrador. So there you go." She gave a shaky laugh. "Not very original, I'm afraid."

"Poor Suze."

"The worst thing is feeling stupid. I really believed it all. I'd pontificated to all my friends about marriage being in the mind—a matter of trust, not of legal ties." Suze clasped her chest in a mock-heroic pose. "Afterward I just wanted to hide."

"And now?"

"Now *I*'m going to make the rules." She stabbed her chest with a forefinger. "I'm going to grab what I want when I want it, like everybody else."

"You don't mean that."

Suze let out her breath. "No," she agreed. "That's the trouble. I don't really want to screw around. I want to make love."

Jay nodded slowly. He began to tell her about the love of his life, an actor, whom he had lived with for three years—had hoped to live with forever.

"So what happened?" said Suze. A terrible thought occurred to her. "He didn't . . .? I mean—"

Jay gave an unexpected laugh. "You've been watching too many TV dramas. No, he did not die of AIDS. He's alive and well and living uptown with someone else. He just didn't love me, simple as that." Jay stubbed out his cigarette. "The problem is, I still love him—probably always will."

"Oh, Jay, I'm sorry." His simple words touched her. Had she ever loved Lawrence as much as that?

They stared sadly at one another.

Then Jay broke the mood. "Listen to us. Tragedy queens or what? Did I hear you say something about killer drinks, or were you just luring me on?"

They drank bourbon on the rocks and giggled at the piano player, who had exhausted his stock of Gershwin and was nearing rock bottom with "Send in the Clowns" and "My Way."

"Let's have a bad-lyrics competition," suggested Suze. "Hey, what did I say?"

For Jay was giving her a funny look. "Nothing. It's just that's one of Lloyd's favorite games."

I have a friend in New York, Suze thought happily, as she leaned against the wall of the elevator, feeling woozy. Jay had escorted her home, given her a hug and promised to invite her over to his place soon. There was a lurch as the elevator stopped at her floor, then the doors opened and Suze stumbled out, keys in hand. The first thing she saw when she entered the apartment door was the red light on the answering machine. She strode across the room and hit the button.

"Hi, this is Nick Bianco. We met this afternoon. A new club just opened downtown, and I wondered if you wanted to come with me on Thursday and check it out. If you're free, I'll pick you up around ten. *Ciao.*"

Screaming like a banshee, Suze dropped her handbag and ran dizzily around the room. Of course she was free! Oh, God, what was she going to wear?

Chapter Eleven

"When we beat them for the first time, you see, in eighteen-something, the Poms thought it was the death of English cricket. So when they next came out to us for a series, some of our sheilas decided to burn a stump and present the ashes to them in a funny little urn. Ever since then, this trophy's been awarded to whichever team won the series, though it never actually left Lord's . . . Are you with me so far?" Harry Fox swiveled round in the bench seat of the black taxi to raise an eyebrow at Lloyd.

"One little detail escapes me. What is a 'stump'?"

Fox laughed. "You'll see soon enough."

They were cruising slowly down a wide avenue. The sun shone down out of a cloudless sky. Ahead of them was a red double-decker packed with people standing ready to disembark; motorcycles and bicycles sped past. On both sides of the road a stream of humanity flowed in one direction: old men in Panama hats wearing blazers and red-and-orange ties, younger men in T-shirts carrying cool-boxes, women in summer dresses and hats, children tugging their adult escorts forward. All were converging toward a long brick wall that appeared on the right, over the top of which Lloyd could see the outline of a stadium. This was Lord's, ancestral home of the mysterious game called cricket. There was a buzz of good-natured expectation from the gathering crowd. Lloyd was surprised to feel a growing excitement himself.

Fox leaned forward and slid open a glass panel to speak to the driver. "We'll get out here."

Blinking in the sunlight, they joined the crush heading toward a gate in the wall. Fox produced a pair of tickets and they pushed through a creaking turnstile into an open space in front of the stadium, which was mostly grass. Some of it was fenced off with rope netting, and inside men dressed in white were hurling a red ball at other men who were trying to hit it with a club. "Those are the nets," murmured Fox vaguely, hurrying on toward the stadium itself, where they began to circle the perimeter in search of the right entrance. As they pushed through the crowd, passing stalls selling snacks and souvenirs, Lloyd caught snatches of conversation that baffled and delighted him: "He sent down seven maidens in a row." "It's never been the same since dicky bird." And, most perplexing of all, "We're praying for rain." A public-address system announced that blind cricketers would be giving a display in the luncheon interval.

They reached the hospitality boxes. A PR woman in a green blazer, carrying a mobile phone, led them up some steel steps and along an open walkway to a door marked "Schneider Fox." Inside the room was a large table covered with a cloth and laid for lunch. One wall of the room was virtually all window, through which Lloyd glimpsed the ground, beautifully mown into pale and dark green stripes, except for a worn-looking square at the center, where a man in a Panama hat crouched low, as if conducting a scientific experiment. The same scene appeared in miniature on a television screen mounted in one corner of the room, and Lloyd was bemused to note that the man appeared to be sticking a key into the turf. A waiter offered Lloyd a glass of champagne, which he declined. Then Fox beckoned him out onto the balcony, where a clutch of seats looked out over the pitch. It was an uninterrupted sea of green, except for some short poles sticking vertically out of the earth somewhere near the middle. "Those are the stumps," said Fox.

It was a spectacular setting. The stands around the ground were filling up, vibrating with color in the bright summer sunshine. To the left stood the "pavilion," an imposing colonial-style building of brick, trimmed with fancy woodwork; to the right a futuristic building resembling the *Starship Enterprise* seemed to hover over the stands, tethered only by a slender steel stem. Television cameras hung poised from gantries; scoreboards displayed an array of zeros. Overhead, an airship hung almost motionless in the bright blue sky.

A voice hailed them from behind. Lloyd looked around to see a pale-faced man in a suit, clutching a tightly furled umbrella.

"Roger, welcome!" Fox raised a hand. "I don't think you've met Lloyd Rockwell, our American hotshot. Lloyd, this is Roger Fotherington, our finance director." They shook hands. "Why don't you two get to know each other while I scout around for the rest of our party?"

He left the hospitality box and there was an awkward pause while Roger gave Lloyd a diffident smile, then stared thoughtfully at his polished brogues. "Don't suppose you see a lot of cricket in the States," he offered at length.

"Not a lot," Lloyd agreed, smiling.

"Pity. Good game. Client beano, you understand. Tax loss. Everybody happy."

Lloyd nodded. One day he was going to master this mysterious language known as English. "So, what are the rules?" he asked.

On the subject of cricket, Roger proved surprisingly fluent. The object of the game seemed to be to hit the ball and score as many "runs" as possible, though it turned out that the running was largely theoretical: if a hitter—or "batsman"—propelled the ball far enough, it was assumed that he *could* have run a certain distance, had he so wished. This struck Lloyd as very British. Much of the skill, according to Roger, lay in the way the ball was thrown—or "bowled": there were "googlies," "Yorkers," "chinamen" and a puzzling and somehow unsporting introduction called "the bodyline." The names for the field positions were sublimely ridiculous: "silly mid-off," "deep square leg," "short third man."

"And who are the stiffs over there?" Lloyd pointed at a row of middle-age to elderly men sitting in the front section of the pavilion, uniformly blazered and stern. "They look like some kind of jury."

Roger frowned. "Those are the MCC members," he corrected. "You see, Lord's is officially the Marylebone Cricket Club ground, though it's shared with Middlesex County Cricket Club—not that we're actually *in* Middlesex, you understand."

"Ah." Lloyd nodded. He noticed that there were no female members, but dared not ask Roger whether this was by choice or regulation. "So who's going to win?" he said instead.

"We are." Roger reached out and touched the wooden balustrade.

Lloyd was relieved when the rest of the party arrived, cutting short Roger's detailed history of the English team's appalling bad luck in recent matches against Australia. Harry made the introductions, and Lloyd found himself talking to Passion's marketing man, a lanky, handsome fellow called Piers. His manner was noncommittal. He seemed to know all about what Lloyd had done in the States and asked some searching questions about the forthcoming campaign to publicize the new routes. Lloyd realized that he was being grilled. He answered as honestly as he could, explaining which ideas were not yet fully developed and which were under review. After a while the atmosphere relaxed: Lloyd seemed to have passed the test.

Various announcements over the loudspeaker had gone unheard, but now applause made itself obvious. "OK, everybody, enough yakking," called Fox. "Let's watch the bloody cricket." From somewhere he had produced an ancient straw hat, which he pulled rakishly low over his eyes.

Lloyd followed him out on to the balcony. "Who's going to win?" he asked.

"We are."

For the next couple of hours Lloyd was deliriously happy. This was England as he had imagined it. The game was unbelievably slow; the crowd applauded politely; the mood in the box was one of gentle banter. Every now and then one of the players would utter a guttural exclamation and turn to stare inquiringly at an individual dressed in a white coat standing behind the "stumps," who sometimes put one finger in the air like a reproving nanny. As the players warmed up they handed him their sweaters, which he tied one on top of another around his waist. A succession of men made their way out from the pavilion to the middle and then back again a little while later. After what seemed like no time at all, play was interrupted as a cart was wheeled ceremonially onto the pitch.

"What happened? Is someone injured?" Lloyd asked anxiously.

"Good God, no. That's the drinks trolley."

Piers turned to his boss and pointed along the terrace. "Have you noticed that the opposition's here?" Lloyd looked to see where he was pointing. A few boxes away, an angry-looking red-faced man in his sixties was gesturing to somebody whose back was turned.

"That's Sir John Rex," Piers explained to Lloyd, "chairman of Stateside. He loathes us—thinks we're upstarts. He'll do anything he can to stop us encroaching on what he regards as his business. But here at Lord's we just ignore each other."

Play resumed its gentle, civilized course until lunchtime, when the cricketers walked off and the Schneider Fox party left the balcony for the greater comfort of the hospitality box. Lunch was cold chicken, lettuce and potato salad, washed down with white wine. While they ate, Piers talked more about Stateside. "They're determined to squeeze us out of the market. They've even been stopping our passengers at Heathrow and offering them upgrades if they'll switch airlines. We only found out about it when the car-hire company that takes our premium passengers to the airport tipped us off."

"Is that legal?" asked Lloyd. He noticed that Harry was listening to their conversation.

"Unfortunately, yes. But it's not a major problem. We're more worried about what they might try next."

"Any leads on that?" asked Fox.

"At the moment, no." Piers paused. "Though a rumor has reached us from the New York office that Schneider Fox is preparing a pitch for Stateside."

"But that's ridiculous," Lloyd cut in. "I can tell you beyond a shadow of a doubt that we would never contemplate such a thing. It would be a clear case of client conflict."

"Quite," Piers agreed. He looked at Fox and lifted his chin in the direction of the Stateside box. "To us they are the Enemy—are they your enemy too?"

Renewed applause signaled the resumption of play. They drifted back to the balcony; Lloyd was amused to see that, along the terrace, many of the neighboring balconies remained empty. He settled down to watch the cricket once more. Now that he had begun to understand the rules, he could sense the changing fortunes of the game. There was, he noticed, a certain bantering rivalry between Harry and the Englishmen in their party, reflecting the contest on the field of play. It seemed clear that both took pleasure in the other team's misfortune. This was not wholly unlike the feeling the English showed toward him as a representative American. Lloyd wondered how much being an Australian had influenced Harry's career in England.

Once more the players were leaving the field, to restrained applause. "Is that the end?" said Lloyd, looking at his watch. It was just after three thirty.

"Of course not," replied Roger. "This is only the tea interval."

Lloyd began to laugh. "The *tea* interval? The game stops for tea?"

"I don't see what's so funny about that," said Roger huffily.

Piers shot Lloyd an amused glance. "Why don't we stretch our legs?" he suggested. "I'll show you around the ground, if you like."

The two of them descended the steps from the hospitality boxes to ground level. There were plenty of other people circulating in both directions. Lloyd and Piers sauntered, the Englishman pointing out anything of interest as they passed. Suddenly a voice greeted them: "Oi, Piers, skiving again?"

Lloyd turned to see a man grinning at them from behind a pair of Ray-Bans. He leered at Lloyd as Piers introduced them. "Lloyd, this is Julian Jewel, of whom I expect you've heard."

"We've talked on the blower," said Jewel, sliding his sunglasses on to his forehead. His handshake was firm and friendly. "Hi, Lloyd. Glad to see my jumping ship didn't put a stop to your English jaunt."

Lloyd studied Jewel as he chatted to Piers. He was a short man, about Lloyd's own age, with a trendy haircut and a lime-green jacket. Everything he had heard about Jewel made Lloyd prepared to dislike him, but perversely, now that he stood there before him, Lloyd found himself warming to his energy and the mischievous gleam in his eye. When Piers suddenly remembered that he had to buy a souvenir for his godson, Lloyd was left alone with him.

"So, how are you getting on with the Passion people?" Jewel asked.

"Fine."

"And Harry? Clever bastard, isn't he? Though not too keen on me, of course."

"I like him."

"Well said." Jewel clapped him on the shoulder. "You're not worried about being away from the New York office for so long, then?"

Lloyd wondered if he was hinting at something. "Everything's under control," he answered blandly.

They chatted for a while about the latest lunacies in the industry; then Jewel looked at his watch. "I'd better get back to my lot." He rolled his eyes. "They're a load of bog-paper manufacturers from the Midlands. So dull they make even the cricket seem interesting. Give me Passion any day." He grinned cheekily. "They're a good client. Enjoy them while you can." And he disappeared into the crowd.

On his way back to the hospitality box, Lloyd realized he had taken the long way to circumnavigate the ground. He was debating with himself whether it might be quicker to turn back when he caught a glimpse of Harry Fox deep in conversation with someone in a doorway. As Lloyd approached, he recognized the other man: it was Sir John Rex. Lloyd was puzzled. What was Fox doing? He hesitated for a moment, then turned back the way he had come. He did not mention what he had seen when he returned to the box, nor did Fox say anything when he too returned a few minutes later. Lloyd felt vaguely disturbed by this, and wondered why. It was none of his business who Harry Fox talked to. Yet he was embarrassed about sharing in the deceit: it was like knowing that a friend was cheating on his wife. It made him uncomfortable.

He was still feeling unsettled by his chance discovery when he inserted the key into the lock of Susannah Wilding's apartment later that evening . . .

Chapter Twelve

As Lloyd mounted the stairs to the flat he could hear Betsy cursing. She appeared on the landing above him, uncharacteristically disheveled. There were cobwebs in her hair and a black greasemark on her nose. She was holding a hammer in that cute, limp-wristed way women did. Lloyd couldn't help smiling.

"It is not funny," Betsy enunciated grimly. "Something's happened to that tank thing." She pointed upward to the roof space. "Water's pouring out. I can't stop it. I've used every towel and newspaper in the place. My shoes are ruined. *Where were you?*"

"Meeting with clients," Lloyd answered, feeling that "watching cricket" might not go down well. Gently he pried the hammer from her grasp. "You should have called a repair man."

Betsy gave herself a pantomime smack on the forehead. "Now why didn't I think of that?" She glared at him. "Either they didn't answer the telephone, or they promised they'd come by first thing tomorrow." Betsy's face crumpled. "What kind of country is this? First there was that awful cat. Now a flood. It'll be a plague of toads next."

Lloyd put his hands soothingly on her shoulders. This was not the calm, competent Betsy he knew. "You go lie down, and take it easy. Here's my jacket. I'll see what the problem is. If I can't fix it, we'll go to a hotel." He rubbed her cheek with his knuckles. "Now scoot."

In the hallway a pull-down ladder was resting in a sea of wet newspaper. On the bottom rung was a small flashlight, part of Betsy's essential traveling equipment. Lloyd picked it up and ascended the ladder to the attic. There was the tank, with water spilling over the edge. Lloyd stepped carefully across the joists and shone his torch into the tank. Water was pouring in; the ball valve, which was supposed to close when the tank was full, had sunk below the surface. Lloyd rolled up his shirt-sleeve and reached in to pull it up again. Immediately the flow of water stopped. He fished around in his pockets and found a rubber band. Feeling pleased with himself, he secured the valve in place. He would have to get a new part tomorrow, but his makeshift repair would do for now.

Lloyd gathered up the filthy, sodden towels, descended the ladder and folded it back up into the attic hatchway. Poor Betsy. England seemed to make her tense. She had visited hardly any of the sights, saying that it was no fun to go alone. He assumed she spent the days working on her thesis, but so far he hadn't dared ask about her progress. The most animated he had seen her was when she told him about taking the intruder cat to the veterinarian to be destroyed. Lloyd had never set eyes on the animal. He had even wondered if it was a weird hallucination, expressive of Betsy's alienated state of mind.

Determined to find a way of making it up to her, Lloyd cleaned up the mess, stuffed the dirty towels into a rubbish bag and went to find Betsy. She was lying on the couch in the living room with a blanket over her legs, watching television.

Lloyd raised his arms in a he-man gesture. "I fixed it." He grinned.

"Thank goodness."

"Come on, let's go out and eat."

"Don't be ridiculous. I can't go out like this. Besides, my favorite program's coming up."

Lloyd tried again. "OK, I'll go to that Indian take-out place. We can eat in here, relax, watch TV together."

The curry was not a success. Lloyd over-ordered wildly and had to eat most of the food himself, while Betsy nibbled the poppadoms and exclaimed at the shocking level of sexual explicitness on British television. Eventually Lloyd wiped his lips and said, "I guess I'd better call Susannah Wilding to tell her about the leak."

"I doubt if she'd care, the way she keeps this place." Betsy yawned. "I'm ready for bed." She got off the couch, folded her blanket neatly and carried it to the door. "Why don't you ask her if the vacuum cleaner's working OK, just to see if she's even found it yet? And make sure she's watering the plants." Her face clouded. "I hope she hasn't filled the place with her men friends."

It felt odd to call his own number and to hear an unfamiliar voice say, "Hello."

"Is this Susannah Wilding?"

"Yes. Who's that?"

Lloyd explained.

"Oh, hi." She didn't sound very interested.

Lloyd had hardly begun to unfold the plumbing drama when she interrupted.

"Buggeration. That'll mean hundreds of pounds just to get someone to look at it. I hate plumbers, don't you?" He heard a sigh and almost blurted out that it wasn't his fault.

"Do you think you could very kindly get it repaired?" she went on, in her polite, English way. "I'll pay you back."

"No, no. It's already fixed. I just wanted to let you know. One of your rugs is kind of damp, but there's no serious damage. I fixed the leak."

"What, you personally?" She sounded surprised.

"It wasn't too difficult," Lloyd began modestly. "All I did—"

"Oh, God, you're going to start telling me about sprockets and bivalves. Honestly, I don't want to know. You're obviously a genius, and I'm getting ready to go out. Let's leave it at that, shall we?"

Lloyd felt snubbed. "Actually, a bivalve is a mollusk," he said with dignity.

"Probably what I'm going to eat tonight. Oysters, champagne . . . That reminds me: I know I'm a few days late, but happy birthday!"

"How did you know?"

"You got a postcard. I haven't got around to forwarding it yet. Sorry. Hang on and I'll read it to you." The receiver was banged down. Lloyd heard a rustling and an impatient exclamation as something clanged to the floor. "It's from Palm Beach, Florida—blue sea, palm trees, the usual—and it says 'Happy birthday from your loving father.'"

Lloyd felt his whole body stiffen. His "loving" father: that was a good one.

"Shall I send it on?" she asked.

"No."

"OK, I'll put it in your desk."

"No! I don't want it. Throw it away."

"But it's from your father." There was a baffled pause. "I keep all my dad's cards."

Didn't she know when to shut up? Lloyd forced a laugh. "I mean, it's only a postcard. Some mail came for you too," he hurried on, "an invitation, I think. It's got that square, important look to it."

"How exciting! Will you open it?"

Lloyd found the stiff cream envelope and slit it open. "It's a birth announcement," he told her, scanning the card. "Lawrence and Araminta Self have had a baby, Gioconda Lucia. Now there's a name to live up to . . . Are you there?"

"Yes, I am," she said, rather forcefully, Lloyd thought. "Does it by any chance give the weight? The size of a small elephant, for example? With tusks?"

Lloyd was beginning to feel out of his depth. "Ten pounds, seven ounces. Is that good?"

"Very satisfying, thank you. And you can bin that as well."

Lloyd decided to change the subject. "How's it going at work?"

"Very well. Although we had a terrible time with the Matsuhana invitation, thanks to you. I'm working on a special project with Sheri Crystal."

"Which project is that?" What did she mean, thanks to him?

"I'm not supposed to say. It's confidential."

"Not to me, for Godsakes." Lloyd laughed. "I am Sheri's boss, after all."

"Really?" she said, in a way Lloyd found maddeningly vague.

"Listen, I must go. Hot date and all that. Just tell me quickly how Mr. Kipling is."

Who the hell was Mr. Kipling? "Uh . . . I don't believe we've met him yet. Unless he's the old stager next door who's in love with his flowers."

There was a deep gurgle of laughter. "Don't be silly. Mr. Kipling's my cat—well, not really mine but we've sort of adopted each other and . . ."

Lloyd lowered the telephone receiver from his ear and held it to his chest, stifling her meandering burble. Oh, God, oh, Montreal. So *that* was Mr. Kipling! He felt a mounting, unreasonable rage at womankind. Why couldn't Betsy have asked someone before she had the damn cat put down? Why couldn't this Susannah Wilding person have indicated that Mr. Kipling had four legs and said meow?

". . . just a bit of milk, and odd leftovers," she was saying. Her voice was buoyant, her innocence of what had happened painful to listen to. He could not possibly tell her that the cat was no more.

Somehow Lloyd ended the conversation and hung up. His good humor had evaporated. He fixed himself a drink: Irish whiskey, with water, no ice and carried it back to the living room, trying to unwind. But the postcard from his father had upset him. He was concerned too, about work. What was Sheri playing at? What had Ms. Wilding meant about Matsuhana? Had Jewel been trying to hint at something? Why had Harry Fox been talking to Stateside? Eventually Lloyd decided he'd had enough for one day. He drank the last of his whiskey and walked through to the bedroom, in need of comfort. He wouldn't mention the cat business to Betsy just yet. Somehow he'd sort out the situation himself.

Betsy lay with her back to him, head on her hand, reading in bed. Soft hair fell away from her pale neck. Her arms were bare and smooth. Lloyd took off his clothes, not bothering with pajamas, and snuggled up to her warm back. Slowly he kissed his way up her arm to the strap of her nightgown and peeked over her shoulder.

"You reading?"

"Yes."

"Good book?"

"Very."

"Want to read me some?"

A deep sigh.

"Aw, please."

Betsy cleared her throat. " 'While it is part of the daily conversational commerce of women to touch base with each other about their desires and fears,' " she read, " 'men transfer their emotions onto the material world. Fearing that she may lose her job, a woman will express this anxiety to a co-female; a man in the same predicament will purchase a new car. While a woman may admit, 'I feel deeply upset,' a man will . . .'—want me to go on?"

Lloyd collapsed on to his back. "I think I'll go to sleep."

He turned away, drawing the covers around him. At least they had made love on his birthday. He mustn't be too demanding. In the dim light he had the impression that the walls were closing in on him. There was a faint silver gleam from the frame on the dresser. It was too dark to see the picture, but he could remember the laughing, generous mouth and that strange hair, the color of cinnamon. "A hot date," she had said, just like a teenager. Lloyd closed his eyes. He felt as old as a fossil.

Chapter Thirteen

Suze lay panting on the bedroom floor, naked apart from a liberal sprinkling of talcum powder. Why, oh, why, had she let Jay talk her into buying a rubber dress? It was like trying to get into a garden hose. A few moments ago the dress had got stuck around her shoulders, imprisoning her arms and threatening to smother her. Panicking, she had suffered a ghastly vision of herself found dead in the apartment, apparently the victim of some unspeakable autoerotic act, like those men found strangled with oranges in their mouths.

The dress itself was divine, a sleeveless low-cut sheath the exact color of an eggplant, with the same irresistibly tactile sheen, that reacted magically with her pale skin and bright hair. They had found it in a kinky shop down in the East Village during a rather long lunch break. She could still picture the look on Jay's face when she had pranced out of the dressing room, and the way he had said, "I don't know what you're trying to prove to this Nick character, but you look sensational." And she had snapped, "I'm not trying to prove anything. I *am* sensational."

Suze gave herself another shake of talcum powder for luck, squeezed the dress over her head and this time managed to unroll it slowly down her body, smoothing as she went. Phew! Too late now to wonder how she would ever get it off again. First she polished off the finger marks and talcum powder with a towel, then she completed her makeup and brushed her hair upside down so that when she tossed it back it fanned out like a tawny mane. Carrying her shoes, she padded along the hall to the living room and stood on the sofa to check out her reflection. Wow! Just as long as she didn't sit down or bend over. Or breathe. Earlier, Suze had put on some music to get herself in the party mood. Now she couldn't resist waving her arms about and trampolining gently on the couch springs, pouting at her reflection. She was happily warbling "Like a vir-ir-ir-ir-gin" when the entryphone buzzed.

It was Raymond, the doorman. "Your car is here, Ms. Wilding," he said, in a suspiciously restrained voice.

"What do you mean, my car? Isn't there anyone in it?"

"Just the chauffeur."

Crikey. Suze strapped on her shoes, gave herself one last shot of perfume and rode the elevator down to the lobby. As she started on the long line of carpet that led to the street, she saw what was waiting for her and her eyes widened. "Car" was not the word. It was a limousine as big as a shark, with smoked-glass windows and a uniformed man holding the door open with a gloved hand. Exchanging a glance of wild surmise with Raymond as she passed, Suze stepped in. The door closed with an expensive click.

Inside, it was like a playground for grown-ups. Two long banquettes of white fake leather faced each other across a small lawn of fluffy black carpet that reeked of air freshener. At the front, more smoked glass and a curtain with gold tassels hid the driver from view; on the back shelf was a telephone and fax machine. Almost the whole of one side of the car was a cocktail bar, complete with mirrored shelving, plastic champagne flutes and a fantail arrangement of pink paper napkins clipped to the bum of a wirework peacock. Multicolored cocktail sticks rose out of the peacock's head to imitate its crest. On the other side was an enormous television screen and what looked like a stereo system. Cautiously, Suze pressed one of the knobs and found herself watching a Spanish-language soap opera, which seemed to consist entirely of overdressed people wandering on and off the set, addressing each other in tones of controlled fury.

"Excuse me, ma'am," said a disembodied voice. Suze jumped guiltily and switched off the television. "Mr. Bianco sends his apologies for not meeting you in person. Something came up at the club. He'll meet you there. Meanwhile, please enjoy the vehicle facilities."

"Thank you," Suze said faintly to a little box she had located on the ceiling.

She opened the cocktail cabinet, which was lined with mirrors and luridly illuminated. Inside were miniatures and mixers of every description, teensy packages of smoked nuts and an ice bucket with an adorable little bottle of champagne resting inside. Was this a "vehicle facility"? Suze decided that it was. She eased off the cork and poured herself a frothy glassful. It tasted divine. This was the life. First she sat on one side, then on the other, then she lay down right across the back seat, lazily watching the buildings sail by. When the car stopped at a red light she could see the plebs straining to look in through the one-way windows, as though the stretch limo might contain Yoko Ono or Ivana Trump. Suze pulled faces back, knowing they could not see her. The telephone lay temptingly within reach. Neither her parents nor any of her London friends would thank her for waking them up in the middle of the night to boast, but just for fun she rang up the Speaking Clock and listened to the clipped voice telling her that it was three fifteen precisely.

The box in the ceiling crackled. "We're almost there, ma'am." Suze drained her glass, patted her lips with a napkin and peered out. She could see flashing lights and a swarm of people clamoring around a roped-off entrance, guarded by a man built like a fridge. Suze felt a clutch of anxiety. She remembered all the times she had agreed to meet Lawrence at a party, only to spend half an hour circling with a drink in her hand before discovering him holed up in a corner with a crony. How would she ever find Nick? As the limo whispered to a halt at the curb, the crowd swiveled to see which celebrity was arriving. They were all very young and very beautiful. Suze felt like dropping to the floor and asking the driver to take her around the block, but it was too late. The door opened. A blast of hip-hop hit her. Then a hand reached in to take hers and draw her gently out on to the pavement. There stood Nick, boyish in his cream suit, looking her over with frank delight.

"How could I have let you travel alone?" he asked in a slow, reproachful drawl, swinging her around to admire her from all angles. "I'm a boor, a cad, a total schmuck. Will you ever forgive me?"

Suze's usual banter deserted her. "I should think so." She smiled shyly.

Nick steered her through the crowd, which parted respectfully. The bouncer swung open the leather-padded door and Suze walked inside. A wall of sound hit her. The space was huge, with an industrial feel to it. Colored lights hung from high girders and raked across a mass of spinning, flailing bodies, turning them magenta and silver and aquamarine. Suze saw women wearing see-through dresses, PVC trousers, satin crop-tops and navel rings; men in leather, tight black T-shirts, denim waistcoats unbuttoned to show off their washboard stomachs. Up on the catwalk a transvestite was dancing in a repetitive, trancelike manner, teetering on six-inch platforms and occasionally tossing lollipops into the crowd. Suze tried not to goggle at his/her Perspex boobs inside which she was quite sure she could see live goldfish swimming. Around the dance floor giant screens projected strange, surrealistic images: wolves running through snow, tattooed musclemen doing circus tricks. Suze could feel the beat of the music pounding under her feet and rippling up her body.

"Let's go upstairs." Nick's breath was warm against her ear.

Looking up, Suze saw that a deep balcony ran all around the interior, reached by staircases balustraded with steel cabling. There was a bar at each of the shorter ends, tables and booths along the sides where people could drink and smooch and observe the snake pit below. Nick took her hand, wrapped it over his arm and shepherded her up the crowded stairs. Everyone seemed to know him, including a worrying number of extremely pretty girls. At the top, she felt a warning squeeze.

"Uh-oh. There's the model crowd, pigging out on their raw carrots and bitching about their agents. Quick, let's hide." He drew her deep inside a booth, handing her in on one side of the table and taking the seat opposite. "Sometimes I get tired of being polite." Suze slid across the tickly velvet. It was like being in a warm, secret cave. If they leaned close, they could just hear each other speak.

At once a man in spiked dreadlocks appeared beside them, wearing a necklace made of scarred metal fragments that might have fallen off a spaceship on reentry.

"Two vodkas and cranberry juice," Nick ordered, "and maybe one of those little bowls of caviar to keep us going." He cocked his head at Suze. "OK with you?"

"Lovely." Even in the club's weird voodoo gloom, he seemed to exude a golden glow. His eyes were frank and curious, his mouth made for smiling. He looked as if he had been raised on steak and corn and sunshine. She could practically feel his body heat. "Did you say this club just opened?" she asked, trying to sound composed. "It seems very successful."

"Last Saturday." Nick nodded. "We had a fashion show, a rap artist and a total queen of a DJ who insisted on his own special brand of mineral water. Pandefuckingmonium."

Suze leaned her elbows on the table. "What exactly does a party promoter do?"

"Makes sure the right crowd turns up. Creates a buzz. Checks that the ingredients are right—people, music, food, ambience."

"But how do you do that?"

Nick reached for a cracker and started to smooth caviar on to it.

"Basically, you schmooze. First you get to know the models, especially the young ones, new in town. Usually they're sleeping in bunk beds in some cramped godawful apartment and they're screaming to get out and meet people—magazine editors, movie producers, rich guys who can further their careers." He sprinkled the caviar with chopped onion and egg. "And, of course, the rich guys all want to meet the models. Then there are the fashion houses, who are always looking for an event to showcase their designs, or a music company that wants to premiere a new song. I just stir all the ingredients together, and bingo! Instant fun. Here, try this." He offered her his cracker and Suze took a bite, giggling as the crumbs fell into her cleavage. She tried to brush them off discreetly and caught Nick watching her.

"Wild dress, right?" She laughed nervously.

"It wasn't the dress I was looking at."

"So, um, going back to your job, does that mean you know lots of movie stars?"

"Sure. Let's say Jack's in town—or Dennis or Brad. These are cool guys, right, but they don't know the scene here. So they give me a call and I fix them up someplace, make sure the guy on the door knows they're coming, find them some female company, hustle them out the back way if the paparazzi sniff them out."

"And what if Demi comes to town—or Sharon or Winona?" Suze asked provocatively. "Do they get the same treatment?"

Nick gave a big, gorgeous laugh. He reached out and caressed her cheek with a warm hand that melted her entire body. "Don't tease." He filled up her glass. "Now tell me about you. I want every detail, from when you were born to the moment you got into that distracting dress."

Suze took a hunk of her hair and flipped it over to the other side of her parting, letting it slither down over one eye. "Well . . ." she began, "the first thing you should know is that my real name isn't Susannah, or Suzanne, or Suze, but S-I-O-U-X-I-E, pronounced Suzie. My parents met at a pop concert in the sixties. They were only twenty when they had me. Embarrassing, isn't it?"

But Nick seemed to find it fascinating. Bit by bit he drew out of her the whole romantic story of how her parents had met at nineteen, her mother a rebellious fugitive from her middle-class family in the gin-and-tonic belt, her father a coal miner's son dreaming of a different life. They had fallen in love at first sight, moved into a London bedsit together and eventually, weathering the voluble disapproval of both sets of parents, swapped curtain rings and got married. Suze was born nine months later. She had a drawer for a cradle and tea towels for sheets.

"And which one gave you your wonderful hair?" Nick took a thick swathe, letting it sift through his fingers. Suze's neck tingled.

"My father, though his is going gray now. My mother's was blond, way below her waist. They were very beautiful."

"I'll bet. What did you all live on?"

"My father had bought his first camera when he was fifteen. Of course, everyone in Derbyshire thought that was tremendously arty-farty—'That lad'll never swing a pickax, taking fancy snaps of flowers and such'—but he had a real talent. He got a job as a darkroom assistant and soon he was taking pictures of people like Twiggy and Marianne Faithfull. Actually, he was quite famous once." She swigged her drink, remembering the parties with candles and joss sticks, and the wonder of finding grown-ups lying peacefully on the floor. She had never felt neglected, just included in her parents' fun. They had taken her on their wanderings through North Africa and the Greek islands, magical places of heat and color where you could go barefoot and eat plump fruits warm from the tree. She told Nick about the time she had been washed in a courtyard fountain tiled with golden dolphins in a turquoise sea, about the bliss of lying in a sleeping bag on the sand, watching the flames of a campfire and listening to someone play the guitar.

A high-pitched beep interrupted them. Nick groaned, pulled a mobile phone from his pocket and pressed it to his ear. As he listened to the voice he raised his eyebrows apologetically at Suze, signaling his helplessness. "Mort, baby, how are you?" Rather than hang around waiting for him to finish, Suze took the opportunity to go to the ladies', a kind of concrete bunker which she found in the basement. Two giantesses with arms like spaghetti were gazing at themselves in the mirror, tweaking their identical blond hairstyles and waggling their bodies to the beat from the dance floor. Their eyes slid in Suze's direction and dismissed her instantly. As Suze locked herself in the cubicle she could hear them continue their conversation as if she didn't exist.

"So what was he saying?" gasped a baby voice.

"He asked if I wanted to come for a week on his boat in the South of France." The other voice was contemptuous. "I happen to know for a fact that he lost all his money on some Wall Street thing and doesn't even own a boat. As if I'm going to open my legs for a loser like that!"

"No way," came the shocked reply. "I wouldn't even *kiss* a guy worth less than five mil. I only came tonight because I heard Bliss Bogardo would be here. She promised to introduce me to a fabulous photographer, but she never even called."

"She does that to everyone. Bliss is a twenty-four-carat bitch. I heard she was in California, having her boobs done."

"What boobs?"

Suze could hear the pair of them snickering like chimpanzees. No wonder Nick preferred an intelligent woman like herself. Coming back upstairs, she found her way barred by a ridiculously handsome yuppie type who gave her a cock-of-the-walk look and said, "I wish you were my secretary."

"I wish you were mine," Suze shot back.

When she returned she found that Nick had finished his call. As she moved past him to return to her seat, he took her hand and pulled her onto the bench next to him.

"Finish your story," he said. "What happened to that sixties wild child?"

"Is this an interview?" No Englishman had ever been this interested or watched her so intently. "I'm afraid it gets ordinary after that—art school, computer design course, first job, et cetera."

"And your parents? What happened to them?"

"Nothing happened." Suze laughed. "They're still married, still in love, living on the edge of Wales. My dad teaches photography now but he still has his Harley-Davidson and drives us mad playing his old Jimi Hendrix records. My mother runs a plant nursery, specializing in herbs. She has a few cannabis plants at the back of the greenhouse so they can smoke the odd joint when they think I'm not looking. They're barmy, of course. But sometimes I think they're the happiest couple I know."

"'Barmy,'" Nick repeated, "I love that. So, Siouxie with an *X*, with such a great example, how come you weren't tempted to get married at nineteen yourself? What are you—twenty-five, twenty-six?"

"That sort of thing. But marriage—pfff." Suze tossed her head. "Things were different then, fun and free and romantic. Nowadays it's such hard work. Everyone is obsessed by ownership—owning houses, owning furniture, owning babies, owning each other. I don't want to be locked into one of those relationships where couples argue about who takes out the rubbish and say things like, 'We liked that film, didn't we, darling?,' as if they weren't two separate people. I'd rather be single than stick with anyone once the fireworks are over. Wouldn't you?"

She turned her face to his and their gazes locked. He was smiling into her eyes with a kind of surprised pleasure, as if he really did like her. Suze felt a jolt of excitement and tried to summon her defenses. It would be crazy to fall in love with someone just like that, on a first date.

Nick slid a hand down her bare arm. "Come on, let's dance."

Suze gave herself up to the music, letting the energy of the room flow through her, enjoying the steamy proximity of anonymous bodies. Lawrence had liked dancing, but his seventies-style head-shaking and stomping had always secretly embarrassed her. Nick rippled and spun, his body loose and sinuous. He had left his jacket upstairs and she could see the movement of his rib cage under his shirt. Though they hardly touched, his eyes held hers. Suze couldn't help smiling at him. She felt herself sinking helplessly, deliciously into a wash of sensation.

As the music throbbed from one track into another, her body grew hot and slick beneath the second skin of her dress. When they were both breathless Nick spun her off the floor, found a single empty chair in the shadows under the balcony and pulled her onto his knee. She could feel his heart pounding—or was it hers? He held her casually, his hand resting on the curve of her waist, while they watched the other dancers—or at least pretended to. Suze was aware of his eyes on her face, then of his finger tracing a line over the curve of her cheek and under her chin, turning her toward him. For a long, exquisite moment they stared into each other's eyes, while he rubbed his thumb gently across her lower lip. Then he smiled his lazy smile and said, "Another drink?"

They danced and drank, and drank and danced until the world began to spin, and Nick said that was enough heat and noise for one night. It was a relief to be out in the fresh air. The streets were deserted. The only sounds were the faint swish of car tires and a siren so far away it seemed as soothing and romantic as the hoot of an owl. Together they sauntered into the warm night, weaving a little from the multiple vodkas, her head in the hollow of his shoulder. Suze didn't know where they were, or where they were going, and she didn't care. Her brain had ceased to function. Her body felt light and liquid. She wanted to stay in New York for ever and ever.

They crossed a street and entered a square. The temperature cooled as shadowy trees closed about them.

"I hope there aren't any muggers," Suze said. Her voice sounded strange.

Nick laughed and squeezed her reassuringly. "I always walk through here. Once the pushers and tramps get to know you, they leave you alone. Besides, I have this."

Reaching into his back pocket, he drew out a piece of steel the size and shape of a comb and flicked his thumb across the top. A thin, dangerous-looking blade sprang out. Suze stared at it, fascinated and repelled. Before she could say anything, Nick bent down, sliced a red geranium from a flowerbed and presented it to her. "A flower for the flower child."

Further on they came to a fountain. Nick sat on the stone edge and drew her between his knees, hands at her waist, looking at her so intently she thought she might burst into flames. "*Never*," he said sternly, "cut your hair."

Suze rocked her hips lazily within his grasp. "And what about you, party promoter?" She gazed into his eyes. "Tell me where you were born, where you grew up."

"Oh . . ." He gave a dismissive shake. His gaze slid past her.

"Come on." She stroked his cheek. "It's only fair."

"There isn't much to tell. I'm from Oklahoma originally, what they used to call 'the dust bowl.' The life wasn't too great, and my parents split when I was a kid. Then, when I was fifteen, my mother killed herself."

"Oh, Nick." Suze dropped her forehead against his, closing her eyes, and laced her fingers protectively behind his neck. "Do you know why?"

"Worn out, I guess. She didn't leave a note. Anyway, I went looking for my dad, who was out in LA. He used to write me letters sometimes, and bragged about how he was working in Hollywood. When I finally tracked him down I discovered he was washing cars on one of the studio lots. That was my first job—assistant car-washer. Then I started running errands, fetching scripts, taking messages. Nobody notices a kid. But I watched them. Movie people are the most demanding in the universe. I got to know what made them tick. I learned how to make them like me."

Suze tightened her arms around him, wanting to banish that forlorn look. "How could anyone not like you?"

Nick gave a jerky laugh. "Why am I telling you this? Usually I say I'm from California and leave it at that. Nobody wants to hear the other stuff."

"I do." Tenderly Suze smoothed back his hair and began to kiss him very gently, first his eyelids, then the hollows under his cheekbones, then the velvet skin behind his ears. By the time she reached the irresistible curling corners of his mouth, they were both trembling. Her legs started to buckle. Nick gave a tearing groan and pulled her hard against him, holding her prisoner between his thighs. His lips closed on hers. Suze could feel his hands sliding down her back and curving over her hips, drawing him to her. Waves of heat rolled over her skin. She wanted to lie down.

Something was making a strange noise. Suze felt him reach into his pocket. There was a jerk, a splash, then silence. Nick had tossed his mobile phone into the fountain. She felt his lips move against hers, his hot breath enter her mouth as he whispered, "Let's go home."

Suze couldn't have told how far they walked, or how long, before they were stumbling up wooden stairs. At the top Nick leaned her carefully against the door while he got out his key. Drunk with desire, she watched dreamily as he bent his head to fiddle with the lock. "I love your neck," she heard herself say.

Then she was inside a high room of silver light and black shadows, and his lips were at her throat, traveling downward. "Not as much as I like yours," he murmured. "How do I get you out of this thing?"

She could feel him plucking at the straps of her dress, then sliding his hands up her thighs. Suze just arched her back and closed her eyes, letting his roaming hands turn her inside out.

"I think," said a husky voice in her ear, "I'm just going to peel you open like a gorgeous juicy fruit."

Suze heard a sharp click and felt something ice-cold on her naked flesh. Opening her eyes she saw the tip of Nick's knife resting in the hollow between her breasts. She shivered. As she watched, the blade snicked the *V* of her dress and slid soundlessly into the rubber like a knife through butter.

Chapter Fourteen

Oh, God. It was too early. Why had she drunk all that disgusting pink vodka? Whoever had invented work should be shot, along with the torturer who had put her head in a vise and forgotten to unscrew it. Suze squinted at the pallid dwarf in the elevator mirror and groaned. She had left her stomach somewhere around the third floor and her legs didn't work. Was it possible to get arthritis at thirty-two?

Moving like a sleepwalker, she located her office, took off the jacket she was wearing and hung it on the coatrack, wincing at the metallic clang. The jacket slid off, but bending down did not appear to be in Suze's current repertoire. She groped her way down the corridor to the coffee machine. The pot was empty.

"What happened?" asked a sardonic voice. "Did somebody die?"

Turning her whole body in case her neck snapped off, Suze saw Dee Dee watching her, arms folded. "Only my brain," Suze croaked. She aimed a hand at the coffeepot, fumbled the handle and sent the whole caboodle crashing to the floor, scattering coffee grounds. Very carefully she got down on her hands and knees and started scooping the mess into a plastic cup. Funny enough, she felt marginally better on all fours. Perhaps she could stay down here all day, like some novel kind of office pet. Or she could pretend she had just converted to Islam and needed to catch up on her praying. She practiced touching her head to the floor, just to see how it felt. Ouch. Then she felt hands at her shoulders, pulling her upright, and Dee Dee was marching her back to her office. Suze slumped gratefully in the high-backed chair.

"Thank you, Dee Dee. You're very kind." Suze gave an infinitesimal dowager's nod. It still hurt.

"You," Dee Dee accused, "have a hangover."

"Shh." Suze put an unsteady finger to her lips. "Don't tell Sheri. Important meeting this morning. Top priority. Got to *shine*."

"Hmm. Wait here."

Waiting she could do. By sheer willpower Suze held the usual office noises at bay. Time passed. She felt as perky as a slug.

"Aah!" She jumped. It was the telephone. Suze stuffed it in a drawer.

Dee Dee returned, carrying an ominous-looking glass. "Mr. Schneider was on this tomato juice and lemon diet a while back," she explained. "I knew there'd be some leftovers in his executive refrigerator. And don't worry about Sheri. She's in conference with Mr. Schneider and some bigwig."

Suze took the cup and peered inside. It looked like pig slop. "What else is in here?"

"Don't ask."

Suze closed her eyes, held her nose and drank the lot. "Eughgh!" She spat. A disgusting viscous liquid coated her mouth. Her stomach went into spasm. Her sinuses were on fire. Then a small time-bomb blew off the top of her head. Her eyes popped open. She felt . . . better. She practiced bending her head from side to side. The rolling lead ball that had been cunningly implanted in her brain overnight had disappeared. "Dee Dee, you're an angel! A genius!"

Dee Dee's round face blossomed into a smile. Really, she would be quite pretty if she lost a stone or two. "Let's go out and buy you something fabulous at lunchtime," Suze suggested impulsively. "Present from me."

"Maybe you should concentrate on your own outfit first. Aren't those trousers a little on the large side?"

Suze looked down, taking in the stone-colored chinos rolled up above last night's strappy shoes and belted tight, the man's white shirt hanging half in and half out, and the striped cotton waistcoat with its buttons done up wrong. A dim memory reached her of having woken up at the precise moment she was due at work, with nothing to wear except an object resembling a gutted garbage bag. Nick had done his best, grumbling and stumbling about, naked, and pulling things out of his closet for her. It was the Diane Keaton look, he told her. Suze thought Buster Keaton might be nearer the mark.

"Do I look totally ridiculous?" she asked Dee Dee.

"No, irritatingly enough. If you straightened your clothes and brushed your hair, you could probably pass it off as British street fashion."

Suze heard the caustic undertone. She was aware that her super-hip outfits had caused comment at Schneider Fox, not all of it favorable. New Yorkers were shockingly conservative dressers, at work anyway, and Suze had swiftly toned down the style of her wardrobe. "You mean, like the trendy crop-top I wore on my first day?"

Caught off guard, Dee Dee looked surprised. Her usual deadpan expression began to crumble. She caught Suze's eye, her smile broadened and the two of them burst out laughing.

"I loved those Eiffel Tower shoes, though." Dee Dee sighed wistfully. "London must be really wild if everyone goes around dressed like you."

After fifteen minutes in the ladies' room Suze was beginning to feel vaguely normal. What was a teensy hangover compared to last night? "Dynamite" was the word Nick had used. Her body fizzed at the memory. But this was no one-night stand. On Saturday he was taking her around the sights of New York; on Sunday evening he was coming to her apartment for dinner. Happiness swept through her. Here was the new Suze, no longer an object of curiosity at dinner parties or the pathetic prey of stupid men in suspenders. She was not a freak or a cast-off. The simple truth was that, until now, she hadn't found the right man.

At the appointed time Suze presented herself at Sheri's office. She had barely seen Sheri since the Matsuhana incident and was faintly apprehensive. But all Sheri said was "My, what an original outfit," before asking her to close the door.

"No calls, Dee Dee," she said into her speakerphone, so curtly that Suze felt a pang for her new friend. "Now, Suzanne." Sheri arched her neck and threw back her glossy hair. "First of all I want to tell you how impressively I thought you handled our presentation of the Matsuhana invitation."

"Really? You weren't—"

"You displayed not only the initiative to produce a wonderful design, but the tact to give no indication that there had been any conflict of view within Schneider Fox." She smiled warmly at Suze. "I'm sure you can understand that it would not have been appropriate to express my true feelings at that moment in time. I hope you will now accept my thanks and my congratulations."

"Of course." Suze tried to look nonchalant, but could not prevent a gratified smile tugging at her mouth.

"Because," Sheri went on, "we now have a most serious situation developing at Schneider Fox. I am going to need to rely absolutely on your help and your discretion." She looked solemn. "Nobody in this whole office knows what I am about to tell you except Bernie and me. Do you understand?"

Suze nodded. This was exciting.

Sheri folded her hands on the desk before her. "Rumors have reached us that one of our key accounts may be in jeopardy. I am speaking of Passion Airlines. It seems that they may be thinking of taking their business elsewhere."

"But why?" Suze couldn't help asking. "How could they? The ads have always been so brilliant, right from the beginning."

"I know," Sheri agreed. "It doesn't seem possible—and maybe it isn't. But Passion is our most valuable and prestigious account, and we have to devise strategies for dealing with what may be the biggest crisis in the history of this company. And I'm going to need *your* help."

"Right," said Suze decisively. "Er, why, exactly?"

Sheri explained the extreme delicacy of the situation. She couldn't ask Passion outright if they were leaving, nor did she dare to let the rest of the office know of the problem in case word leaked out. "Clients don't like uncertainty."

"So what can we do?" asked Suze.

"We convince them that we are too good to lose, that's what we do," said Sheri confidently. "After Christmas, Passion will be opening new routes, direct transatlantic flights to and from destinations all over the US. They need a new campaign that will reflect that. This has always been in the pipeline, but now Bernie wants me to action it urgently." Sheri looked important. "He's trying to schedule a meeting with the Passion marketing people within the next two weeks. Our job—yours and mine—will be to come up with a presentation that will impress the hell out of them. That way, if they were thinking of leaving, we'll change their mind. If they weren't, then we just look super-efficient."

"You want me to work on a major new campaign—to art direct it, do the layouts, presentation, everything?" Suze could hardly believe it.

"I want your input on every aspect, Suzanne. I wouldn't ask if I didn't think you could do it."

"Of course I'll do it." She couldn't wait to tell Nick. When he came to dinner, perhaps she could cook something really exotic to celebrate, like lobster. They could suck the meat out of the claws and then, when their lips and fingers were all buttery and warm—

"There's just one more point," Sheri was saying, in a tone of voice that Suze hadn't heard before, almost as if she were embarrassed.

"What is it?"

"God, this is so difficult." Sheri pressed her hands to her temples and took a deep breath. "The thing is, there's a chance—just a faint possibility—that our client doesn't have a problem with us as a company, but with a particular individual within this company." She paused significantly.

"I see." What on earth was she talking about?

"I mean the account executive."

"Ah-ha."

"I am speaking, of course, of Lloyd Rockwell." Sheri sounded edgy. "There have been one or two incidents recently when he has taken his eye off the ball. Well, you saw that yourself over that invitation. I know Lloyd is staying in your apartment in London and I have to be sure that you won't mention our work to him."

"Why would I?" Suze was amazed. "I've only spoken to him once in my entire life."

"I'm sure you wouldn't intend to say anything, but you know what men are like. They can be so territorial. Their poor little egos bruise at the slightest nudge. And Lloyd—well, I shouldn't really tell you this . . ." Sheri lowered her voice.

"Go on." Suze was agog.

"Well, one time after an awards dinner, Lloyd made a pass at me in the back of the cab. I handled it as tactfully as I could but he was terribly offended. He hardly spoke to me for days afterward."

"How creepy! Anyway, I thought he had a girlfriend."

"Since when has that bothered a man?"

Suze remembered Lawrence and Minty. "You're right."

"So let's you and I just do what women always wind up doing—pick up the pieces and get the job done. We can argue afterward about who deserves the glory." Sheri offered her hand. "Is it a deal?"

Suze shook it. "Absolutely."

"Good. Now the first thing—"

The telephone rang. Sheri stared at it disbelievingly, then snatched up the receiver. "I said no calls, Dee Dee." She listened for a few moments, then snapped, "Tell him I'm busy," and cut the line. She raised her eyes to Suze's. "Lloyd," she explained.

"Oh dear." Suze and Sheri exchanged a complicit half-smile, like naughty schoolgirls.

"There's nothing I can say to him right now," Sheri complained. "So why do I feel so guilty?"

"Don't," urged Suze. "After all, you're the one who's having to cover up for him."

"I suppose." Sheri sighed. "Now, where were we? Oh, yes." She patted a tall pile beside her. "Your first job is to master all the back history. And here's a draft of the profile for the new campaign, though it's pretty sketchy, I'm afraid. Our job would be so much easier if we could find Lloyd's meeting notes, but they're locked away in his computer.

Poor old Lloyd has always been very big on confidentiality. He goes crazy if you even ask him for a client's telephone number. We'll just have to wing it." She gave Suze a big, confident smile. "Two women have got to be smarter than one man, right?"

Suze walked out of Sheri's office feeling like Superwoman. For once, she had not been patted on the head or asked to realize someone else's grand plan, but personally selected for a special, secret mission. She swelled with the fantasy of herself promoted to agency art director, formidable in her power suit, taking command of a boardroom with the merest lift of her eyebrow, barking "No calls" into her speakerphone.

Dazzled by these visions of the future, Suze found that she was standing in the middle of her office. A shaft of sunlight slanted through the venetian blind, spotlighting Lloyd's computer with almost mystical significance. Suze stared. *If only we could find Lloyd's notes,* Sheri had said. Well, if anyone could hack into his files, it was she. A mere man, especially a bumbler like this Lloyd Rockwell, was no match for a clever woman.

Suze walked over and tentatively touched the keyboard. It wasn't really snooping. Besides, if she played her cards right, Sheri might find her a permanent job here in New York. Impressed by her brilliant career—and her cooking—Nick would suggest they move into a loft together. They would become one of those "hot couples" that were always being profiled in *Vanity Fair.*

Swiftly, Suze crossed the room and closed the office door. Drawing up a chair, she switched on the computer with a decisive snap.

Chapter Fifteen

Il Capriccio was a restaurant Betsy had picked out of her guidebook as "a real taste of Continental sophistication in the heart of London's theaterland." It turned out to be an old-fashioned Italian place of the rustic school. Fishing nets snarled with plastic crabs hung from rough-plastered walls. There were red candles in Chianti bottles, and tasseled menus the size of sandwich boards. When one of the waiters whipped Betsy's napkin from her wineglass, loosed the elaborate folds with an operatic flick and laid it across her lap, as reverently as if it were the Baby Jesus, Betsy caught Lloyd's eye and blushed. She was looking her best tonight, hair glossy, arms slim and tanned against her flowered silk dress.

Lloyd smiled back at her. That's all she needs, he thought: attention. Recently he had left her alone far too much. He knew that she was finding English life difficult and he wanted to compensate for her disappointment. Suddenly optimistic, he reached over and took her hand. "Let's make this a night to remember—a fresh start. I've always had a feeling something wonderful was going to happen to us in England, if we let it."

Betsy responded at once, squeezing his hand. "I hope so." Her glance lingered, eyes sparkling with anticipation.

Lloyd leaned closer. "Let's make love tonight," he whispered. "Properly—the way we used to."

Betsy nodded. She withdrew her hand. "I bought a microwave for the apartment today," she said. "You know, in compensation for that awful cat."

Lloyd laughed. "I don't get the feeling that Miss Susannah Wilding is exactly a microwave person."

"It wasn't cheap." Betsy straightened defensively. "Mother got hers for half the price at that discount store on Lexington." She shook her head. "I really don't know how the English can afford to live here."

Lloyd listened while she rattled off comparative prices of household items. She was just nervous, he concluded. It was so long since they had been alone like this.

"It was very thoughtful of you," he said soothingly. "I'm sure Susannah will appreciate all the improvements you've made. Now, let's order. Nothing microwaved here, I hope."

The food arrived on giant platters piled with potatoes and steaming with garlic.

"I have never seen so many carbohydrates in my life," Betsy gasped. "I'll have to live on lemons and hot water the rest of the week."

"Nonsense." Lloyd poured ruby-dark wine into her glass. "Live a little—a few calories won't hurt." He tore off a hunk of crusty bread with his teeth. "You've got a great body, Betsy. Give it a treat."

Betsy impaled a small lettuce leaf on her fork. "Did you see Mother's letter?" she asked.

"Uh . . ."

"You absent-minded old professor, you." Betsy sighed. "I left it out for you specially this evening. Anyway, the big news is that Mary Beth is getting married. Isn't that great?"

"Who's Mary Beth?" Lloyd mumbled, mid-prawn.

"For heaven's sake! Mary Beth, my oldest friend. We met when I was staying at her house." Betsy gave a mock pout. "Don't tell me you don't remember, or I'll cry."

But of course Lloyd remembered. It was a couple of months after the end of a disastrous love affair with a beautiful but flaky sculptress who lived in a warehouse in the meat district and created monstrous phalluses out of concrete. When she finally went into detox, Lloyd decided he'd had enough of women, and New York women in particular.

Then two close friends, a happily unmarried couple, invited him for a week's vacation on the Island. The three of them had swum, sailed, overdosed on seafood and played vicious poker into the small hours, but after a week of watching his friends trail to bed together, Lloyd had begun to feel lonely, shamefully lustful and freakishly single. It was in this frustrated frame of mind that he had accompanied his friends to a neighbor's party and found himself drawn to Betsy's slim, athletic legs and the polite way in which she dealt with her tyrannical tennis partner. A nice old-fashioned girl, he had thought approvingly. Later on they had met, quite by chance, and chatted over the barbecue. Lloyd remembered being impressed by Betsy's commitment to her academic work. He was a little hazy on what had happened next. He must have invited her to dinner—or was it the theater? Anyway, she had seemed wonderfully normal and undemanding after the sculptress. It was refreshing to talk with someone who didn't think Jack London was something you drank out of a bottle. Yes, on the whole he had chosen well. Lloyd felt a glow of self-congratulation. Betsy was just the sort of girl who *would* have a friend called Mary Beth. In fact, now he thought about it, he seemed to recall a large, gratingly cheerful young woman urging him to eat more coleslaw.

"Oh, *that* Mary Beth." Lloyd wiped a trickle of butter from his chin. "So who gets to be Mr. Mary Beth?"

"Don't." Betsy giggled. "She's not that bad. Apparently he's an older man, never married, some kind of corporation lawyer. Very respectable, Mother says. He has an apartment on the East Side, and he wants Mary Beth to give up work. They're going to have a huge white wedding at St. John's in September." Betsy's face sharpened with anxiety. "God, Lloyd, what are we going to give them for a present? They're both so rich they probably have everything."

"Sexy underwear," Lloyd replied promptly. "She's going to need it to rekindle his aging ardor."

"Be serious, darling. I thought a wonderful English teapot from Fortnum and Mason might be nice, or something from the Silver Vaults. Or maybe—"

"You decide," Lloyd interrupted. Then he saw from the way

Betsy folded her lips that he had somehow offended her. "I'm sorry," he said, "weddings aren't my strong point."

"No," she agreed.

Lloyd hastily crammed his mouth with more bread. In theory, he was in favor of marriage. In practice, it was hard not to think of all the blondes one would miss out on, and having to be home on time. Still, people did it every day. It couldn't be too difficult.

"I wonder what Fox's wife is like," he said aloud. Tomorrow morning they were driving down to Fox's house in the country in a hired car. It would be fun to drive on the wrong side of the road, legally.

"Whatever she's like, I'll be on my best behavior," Betsy promised, assuming a prim look. "I even bought a new dress."

Lloyd recalled the battered cricket hat. "Harry's not like that."

"Everyone is like that," Betsy corrected. "You're so naive, Lloyd. It's important to make a good impression. That's how other people get promoted."

"*I'm* the one you want to impress." Lloyd waggled his eyebrows insinuatingly. "Tell me about the dress. Is it preposterously short?"

Betsy clicked her tongue and gave an aggrieved sigh.

"Now what have I said?"

"That's not all there is to a relationship, you know. Of course the sexual element has its place, but there are other things."

"Of course there are other things, but—" Lloyd broke off in frustration. He frowned, trying to find the right words. "Sex is an expression of those other things. It's a—a sort of channel for everything we are, everything we mean to each other. It's a giving of our *selves*—not just our bodies—to each other. When we make love it should be . . ."

"'Should be,'" Betsy echoed. "Well, I'm sorry, Lloyd, but for me, life is a little more serious than that. When I think of all the laundry and cleaning and cooking I do for you, while you just prance off to work every day and pounce on me when you get home . . ."

"That's not what I meant." But he felt guilty all the same. "I know you're finding it lonely over here, but you were the one who wanted to come to England," he reminded her.

"Oh, I know. I'm not complaining, Lloyd. Truly. It's wonderful to be with you, to share your experiences. I just sometimes wish we could be a little . . . closer."

Wasn't this what he had just said? Lloyd speared a baby squid and chewed its rubbery legs.

"You were wrong about Passion having the cheapest flights, by the way," Betsy told him. "Mother got a call from another airline offering her a special deal for fifty dollars less."

"Really?" There was something odd about this, but Lloyd was too chilled by Betsy's reminder to pursue the thought. It had been decided—when, and by whom, Lloyd wasn't too sure—that the grand finale of their English trip would be a week touring the Lake District and Scotland with Betsy's mother. Lloyd had favored Paris but Betsy said it would be too difficult, what with people speaking French, and the plumbing system. The Lake District was famous for its rainfall. Lloyd dreaded incarceration *à trois* in some overheated car smelling of damp raincoat and fussy meals in moribund hotels. He knew that Betsy would turn coy and girlish in her mother's presence, while he became progressively more taciturn and lumpishly male. "When is she arriving?" he asked neutrally.

"In two weeks, as I've told you a million times. Don't worry." Betsy sneaked him a smile. "I've booked her into a hotel when she first gets to London. We're planning on doing major shopping. All you need to do is show up for dinner now and then."

Lloyd reached for her hand and kissed it. "You are a wonderful woman."

"I know."

Lloyd's spirits revived enough for him to order a lurid dessert floating in a bath of cream. Betsy chose chamomile tea, but having ascertained that there were absolutely no nuts in the dessert—the merest speck could cause a fatal reaction—she seemed happy enough to share it with him. He fed her slurpy spoonfuls while they talked of what they would do when they returned to New York. Betsy wanted to move, somewhere bigger, quieter, with a view of green. They debated whether to move downtown, or out of town, weighing price against space. Betsy's enthusiasm was infectious. She talked about a little house with a porch and a second bedroom for friends, of clean air, friendly neighbors, bicycles, nice stores, good schools—

"Wait a minute!" Lloyd interjected. "I don't care about schools."

Betsy gave a shy smile. "You may one day."

Lloyd found himself becoming quite excited at the thought of a study of his own, places to walk without fear of mugging or dog shit, maybe even room for a piano.

"Wouldn't it be wonderful?" Betsy breathed, leaning close.

Lloyd smiled back. He had never seen her looking so pretty and desirable.

Evidently the waiter felt the same, for he appeared at their table bearing two tiny glasses. "For the *bella signorina,*" he crooned. "On the 'ouse."

"*Signorina,*" Betsy repeated thoughtfully. "Is that Miss or Mrs.?" She sipped her drink and winced.

Lloyd didn't answer. He was still lost in a dream of perfect domesticity, with everything settled and orderly. It was all just there, in reach, the whole perfect package. All he had to do was reach out and pick it up.

There was a sudden blast of cool air from the door. A handsome woman with gipsyish looks entered the restaurant, carrying a basket heaped with red roses. Smiling boldly, she went from table to table: "Flowers for the beautiful lady?"

Later, Lloyd never quite knew what had got into him—pity for the flower-seller, a desire to recompense Betsy for her disappointing time in England, a craving to provoke an emotional high through one grand gesture. He produced a reckless handful of notes. "I'll take them all."

"Lloyd!" Betsy protested. "We can't afford—"

But quickly, before the generous gentleman could change his mind, the flower-seller deposited the flowers in Betsy's arms. They spilled everywhere, blood red against the white tablecloth. The other diners stared, entranced by the drama.

"Oh, Lloyd. How romantic!" Betsy gathered the roses to her face and inhaled deeply. "Does this mean what I think it means?"

Before Lloyd could answer, the unctuous waiter was at their table. "Luigi will wrap these for you," he announced, clicking his fingers to summon a minion. His soulful brown eyes rested for a moment on Betsy, then he kissed his own fingertips expressively. "You are a lucky man," he told Lloyd sternly, and retreated from their table humming the "Wedding March" in a jaunty baritone.

Lloyd watched him go, as through a mist. The waiter was bouncing his tray off his knee to the tune, and Lloyd found himself silently singing along. "Here *comes* the bride"—bounce—"all *fat* and wide"—bounce. His head felt as light as a bubble. A waterfall was pouring through his ears. Far away he could see Betsy's expectant face. She was smiling. Then her mouth moved.

"I love you, Lloyd."

In the flickering candlelight the cutlery seemed to rise from the table and explode into a million silver shards. Black spots danced in front of Lloyd's eyes. His spine stiffened, as if he had just received a freight truck in the small of the back. A voice was speaking—his own. "Betsy," he said formally, "will you marry me?"

Chapter Sixteen

"Isn't this the turn coming up?"

"I don't think so. It says Salisbury. We aren't going to Salisbury, are we?"

"No, but Harry's house is in that direction—they pronounce it 'Sawlsbree' here. You don't have to go all the way exactly to where a sign says, you know."

"I know that."

"Well, is this the right road or not?"

"I guess it might be."

"Could you take a look at that map?"

". . . Are we on a blue road or a red road?"

"We're on the motorway, kind of like the highway, and we've just passed a place called Basingstoke. You must be able to see that."

"I'm looking. It's just that the roads are so wiggly. Oh! What about this? I can see a black line with funny little marks across it."

"That's the railroad track. I'm turning off anyway."

Lloyd slowed the car, wondering what had been God's intention when He had decided to leave out the map-reading part of women's brains. It was a relief, anyway, to be out of the traffic. He had never seen people drive so fast. There was supposed to be a speed limit of seventy miles per hour, but clearly the English regarded this as a general principle, like socialism, not necessarily to be followed to the letter. As soon as he could, he stopped the car and leaned over Betsy's shoulder to show her the route. "Look," he pointed, "that's where he lives. Winterbourne Gummer, pronounced Winegum."

"It isn't!"

"You're right. It isn't."

She gave him a playful tap on the cheek, then pulled him close to nuzzle his ear. "Do you still love me?"

"Of course I do."

Gradually the roads became narrower and leafier, the air fresh and sweet with the smell of meadows and hedgerows. The countryside looked astonishingly green, considering that Britain was supposed to be in the grip of severe drought. On the way out of London they had heard a radio account of the heat wave that had now persisted for no fewer than five consecutive days. Couples were being urged to share their bath water, then collect it in buckets to pour on the garden. Old people were exhorted to postpone shopping trips until conditions were less severe, dog owners reminded not to leave their pets in cars. Scientists speculated on the imminence of desert conditions. Had he not been living here, Lloyd might have concluded that England had drifted out to sea and re-anchored itself somewhere around Tristan da Cunha. It was eighty-one degrees.

The road meandered up gentle hills, outlined green and yellow against a soft blue sky, then dipped into valleys cooled by small streams that sparkled in the sunlight. Along the way old-fashioned wooden signs, painted black on white, pointed the way to OVER WALLOP, MIDDLE WALLOP and NETHER WALLOP, to BROUGHTON and HOUGHTON, to WOODBURY RING and BARTON LACEY. They passed through villages so serenely beautiful it was hard to believe that real human beings lived there. Each had its own church and pub among a sprawl of thatched cottages with gardens ablaze. Lloyd felt a surge of elation. Was this happiness?

I, Lloyd Rockwell, am getting married. He tried to picture it: the ceremony itself, committing himself to Betsy for ever and ever, children, joint bank accounts, growing old, Betsy's mother . . . He frowned.

"What are you thinking about?" Betsy asked dreamily.

"I was just wondering how that airline knew your mother was flying to England. Which one did you say it was?"

"Stateside, I think. Who cares? Can't you forget about work for one day?"

At the end of a dusty lane that led down from a church they reached an impressive entrance flanked by old stone pillars.

Betsy tensed. "I wish you'd worn your nice jacket."

"I told you, Harry said it would be very casual." Immediately Lloyd felt guilty at his sharp tone. After all, he had stared into the closet this morning considering the exact same thing, before opting for chinos and a casual shirt. Was this a sign that he and Betsy were made for each other? He glanced over at her, immaculate in white linen, and smiled. "Besides, you look good enough for both of us."

They entered a driveway that looped between tall hedges and opened into a gravelled parking area surrounded by rich green lawn. In front of them was a large house of rosy brick, its windows shrouded with creepers. As they came to a halt, a girl and a boy, perhaps five and eight, erupted shrieking from the bushes. Apart from sneakers and random streaks of dirt, they were naked. Behind them cantered a golden retriever carrying a plastic duck in its mouth.

"What a darling dog!" Betsy exclaimed.

As Lloyd pulled the hand brake tight, he became aware of a presence. The little girl's eyes just reached over the window ledge. "Hello," she said expectantly. "Are you really a lord? Do you have any knights?"

"He's not a lord, you idiot." The boy shoved her out of the way. "Just an ordinary person called 'Lloyd.'"

Lloyd thought this was a pretty fair summary. "An ordinary person, however, who has brought largesse," he said mildly, reaching into the back seat for a plastic bag. "I'm sorry it's not wrapped."

Lloyd wasn't too sure what children liked. All he knew was that when he had seen the toy in a store display, it had made him laugh.

"It's a parrot!" squealed the girl in delight, pulling it from the bag.

"A very intelligent one too," Lloyd agreed. "Look, you have to turn it on here." He showed her a switch on the bird's perch.

"What can it do?" asked the boy skeptically.

Immediately, the parrot flapped its lurid wings and shrilly repeated, "What can it do? What can it do?"

The children were entranced, fighting to be the first to make it repeat silly things. There was a welcoming shout, and Harry Fox emerged from an archway at the side of the house, wearing khaki shorts and a disreputable sun-hat. Behind him came a slender, barefoot woman with the sort of pale coloring and light eyes that reminded Lloyd of folktales about women who turned into seals. Harry introduced her as his wife, Lorna.

"What a beautiful home!" Betsy exclaimed, handing her the lavishly wrapped hostess present over which she had agonized for days. Lloyd had kept himself aloof from the debate and now couldn't remember if she'd decided on the set of napkin rings or the embroidered hand towels.

"Say 'bottom,'" the boy was shouting.

Lloyd looked ruefully at Lorna. "I'm afraid that may not be every parent's favorite toy."

"Don't be silly." She smiled. "The only question is how soon we can get the children to bed so that we can play with it ourselves." Her voice was low and lilting, with a distinctive accent Lloyd could not place, her eyes frank and intelligent. He liked her at once.

In the cool hallway she paused. "I assume you'll want to be in the same room."

"If that's convenient." Lloyd cringed at his polite, hesitant tone. He became aware of thought-waves beaming from Betsy. Inexplicably, the words he knew she wanted him to say would not come.

"Aren't you going to tell them?" she prompted.

"Of course." He cleared his throat. "I—that is, we—in fact, yesterday—"

He felt Betsy link her arm through his. "We're engaged," she announced.

Lunch was a festive occasion, lubricated by champagne and eaten on the terrace in the shade of a rampant wisteria. Egged on by Betsy, Lorna told the story of how she had met Harry on a Scottish hillside near her childhood home. "He just sort of pounced," she said, in a droll, wondering way that made Lloyd laugh. "I don't even remember getting engaged. You certainly never gave me a ring, you old skinflint." She prodded her husband's leg with her foot. "To be honest I didn't even know his full name until we were in the church. If he'd told me his middle name was Hannibal I might have changed my mind."

"Love at first sight," Harry agreed. "Why not? If you see something, grab it. Isn't that right, Lloyd?"

Lloyd looked up sharply and met Harry's quizzical smile. Not for the first time, he felt that he was undergoing some secret test. Was Harry implying that he had missed an opportunity? Before he could think of a response, the boy spoke up. "But you had to get married. Otherwise"—his tone was aghast—"otherwise you wouldn't have been able to have *us*."

They lingered at the table, chatting over coffee, then lemonade, until the children bullied them into playing a family version of cricket, hampered by the presence of the dog, who believed the ball to be his and almost knocked Betsy over when she was trying to bowl. They were great kids, Lloyd thought. After the game, while Betsy went indoors to take a nap, he rolled up his trousers and chased them around the garden with the hose until they collapsed exhausted on the grass. Then he told them how his father had taken him camping in Canada when he was ten years old and they had seen a grizzly bear. Lorna promised him a job as a nanny if he ever tired of the advertising world.

When the light turned mellow and golden, they all drifted up the lane to look at the church. On the way Lorna told Lloyd the story of the sixteenth-century nobleman, son of the village squire, who had fallen in love with a local girl. The marriage was forbidden and when the girl found herself pregnant she had hanged herself from a yew tree. Her lover never married and when he came into his inheritance he had ordered the girl's body to be exhumed from the unconsecrated ground outside the church walls and placed in a lavish marble vault inside the church—big enough for two, so that when the time came he could lie beside her for eternity.

"What a sad story." Lloyd was moved.

"But romantic, don't you think? Imagine being that much in love with someone you can't see or touch."

Lloyd couldn't. Life seemed too urgent, too fast. Even the things right in front of one's eyes passed in such a blur that it was easy to make mistakes. Behind them he could hear Harry being nice to Betsy, drawing her out about her thesis and her future plans. Her replies made him smile. Evidently Lorna, too, had been listening, for at the lych-gate she paused and turned to speak to Betsy. "Did you know that Jane Austen's house is nearby? Why don't I drive you over there in the morning? You must be longing to see it. We can let the children run about in the garden."

"Oh." Betsy seemed hesitant. "That's very gracious of you, but we had planned that Lloyd would take me."

"Nonsense. Men are always bored by that kind of thing. Much better to let him go off fishing with Harry." She took Betsy's arm, woman to woman, and drew her up the path. "Now that you're to be married, it's vital to devise cunning ways of getting rid of your husband sometimes. You'll want to, I promise."

She turned with a mischievous smile to check that Harry was listening, and Lloyd, who was standing between them, intercepted a look so teasing and tender that it stabbed his heart with an emotion almost like envy.

"Your best bet at this time of year is a Greenwell's Glory, or a Kite's Imperial if it warms up and a hatch starts. That's the little white bugger." Harry pointed.

Lloyd took the small box of fishing flies, each ingeniously lodged in its own plastic compartment. He hadn't been fishing since he was a boy, using worms and a makeshift arrangement of string and sticks that he had dangled hopefully in the muddy creek at the back of his grandparents' house in Iowa. This was very different.

They were standing beside a little river. It was mid-morning. The stream ran clear and smooth over gravel, making gurgling and sucking sounds as it flowed, teasing long trails of green weed back and forth. The banks on either side had been mown smooth. On the way they had stopped off at an absurdly picturesque thatched fishing hut, where careful records were kept of the catches and a grubby map displayed on the wall. There was a terse account of piscatorial protocol, in which Lloyd saw no mention of worms. Trout-fishing in England was clearly a gentlemanly pursuit, where it mattered not who won or lost but how you played the game.

The setting was idyllic, the weather perfect, the air lively with birdsong and Sunday-morning church bells. But Lloyd was troubled. Last night he had woken up quite suddenly, as if a voice had spoken in his ear. He had gotten out of bed and stood at the window, staring out at the lawn silvered by moonlight, while he tried to trace the source of his anxiety. All week he had been tripping over little pieces of a puzzle that still made no pattern he could understand. But one thing his instinct told him: something funny was going on at Schneider Fox. This morning he had determined to find an opportunity to speak to Harry alone. There was no one else with whom he could discuss his unease. Sheri always seemed to be busy when he called, and Betsy was bored by shop talk. He opened his mouth to speak.

At that moment Harry put an urgent hand on his arm. "Look," he said quietly, "there's a trout just in front of that clump of weeds. Why don't you see if you can get him to rise to your fly? Remember, don't shadow the water or you'll spook the fish. This is hunting."

Lloyd clambered down the bank, awkward in the thigh-high rubber boots that Harry had lent him, brushing some green leaves as he went. Immediately his hand began to sting, and he shook it violently.

"Wimp." Harry laughed. "Don't you have nettles in America?"

Self-consciously Lloyd began to swish the rod back and forth in the air, as Harry had shown him. This morning they had practiced casting in the garden, and after half an hour Lloyd felt he was getting the knack of it. But that had been on an empty lawn, without a hook at the end of his line.

"Gently, man!" warned Harry. "Figure-of-eight. You're not trying to club them to death."

It was too late. The rod went slack and the line dropped in heavy coils in front of him. The nylon tip had formed an ingenious tangle. Meanwhile his quarry announced its departure with a majestic upstream bow-wave.

Lloyd sorted himself out and rejoined Harry, who gave him a sly grin. "Not as easy as it looks, eh?"

"No. Er, Harry . . . I've been wanting to talk to you about some things that are bothering me at work," he began in a rush.

Harry's genial expression vanished. "Listen to me, Lloyd." His eyes were cold. "I'm not much of a man for rules, but there's one that I never break. Family is family, and business is business. I never mix the two. Today you're my guest—mine and Lorna's. If you have something to say to me about Schneider Fox, tell me in the office. Have you got that?"

"Yes," answered Lloyd. Under the pressure of his fingers the fly box he was holding snapped shut with a sharp click.

"Good. I'm going upstream to have a bash," Harry continued, friendly once more. "Meet you back at the car in an hour."

Lloyd watched him go. He felt foolish but also irritated to have been so ruthlessly silenced. Just then an obliging trout rose within casting distance, in a run of fast water beneath a tree stump on the far bank. Crouching on one knee, Lloyd started to work out line. The fly dropped softly on the water, then began to drift downstream on the current. There was a "plop," and the fly disappeared.

Lloyd jerked the rod in surprise and felt an answering tug. Then the surface exploded as the trout leaped clear of the water, scattering droplets in the sunlight. It crashed down again and set off at a frightening speed, pulling the line screaming off the reel. But after a few wild dashes across the river, the fish began to tire, and soon Lloyd was able to draw it across his outstretched net. He lifted the fish out of the water and waded to the bank. He was trembling.

The fish lay panting in the net, one eye glaring defiantly at him. Lloyd was amazed by its beauty. Its sides were golden, speckled with dark brown spots. It looked full of life. To hold this wild thing trapped, at his mercy, was a powerful sensation. Lloyd hesitated. It would be satisfying to wipe that sly grin off Harry's face. He saw himself swaggering back to Betsy and Lorna, *homo hunter-gatherus*, jangling the buckles of his macho boots. But these seemed unworthy reasons to kill such a magnificent creature. Lloyd reached down and unhooked the fly. Then he lifted the trout with both hands and carried it to the water's edge, where he knelt down and gently placed it in the shallows. For a moment the fish lingered, as if unsure whether to trust this reprieve; then it shot forward into the deeper water and was gone.

Lloyd picked up his net and stood quietly by the water, breathing in an expansive lungful of clean summer air. He had done the right thing. As he turned to go, a much larger trout, a real monster, moved out from the bank below him. It had been there all along, the crafty fellow, waiting for him to get out of the way. Now the fish cruised into the fast current, carelessly conspicuous in the sunlit water, as if it knew that Lloyd presented no danger.

The sun was still high in the sky when Lloyd gave a final farewell toot of the car-horn to the children and turned out of the driveway. Summer days in England seemed to linger forever. It was hard to believe it was almost six o'clock. He rolled down his window to enjoy the country freshness while it lasted. His skin was pleasantly warmed from the sun. He felt well-fed, relaxed, content.

"Oof." Betsy let her head drop on to the headrest of the car seat. Her arms dangled at her sides, limp as noodles. "I'm exhausted. I can't believe how early those children got up."

"Was it early?" Lloyd swerved to avoid a pheasant in the road. Its feathers glowed green and bronze and crimson. "I didn't hear them."

"That's because of all that whiskey you drank. I thought we'd never get to bed."

"I was being polite. Lorna wanted to tell me about all the different Scottish malts." He grinned. "She was great, wasn't she? I love the way she lets family life wash over her."

"Ye-es." Betsy sounded uncertain.

"She seems to be able to make toast and laugh at the children's awful jokes and feed the dog and keep Harry in order all at the same time." He winked at Betsy. "You'll be like that one day."

"I don't think so."

"Sure you will."

"Not the dog part, anyway."

"You said it was darling."

"That was before it got dirty paw-marks all over my clothes. I'll have to take them over to Franco's when we get home. I don't think I could trust the British to get anything clean."

Lloyd kept silent. Some things women said were best left unchallenged. He tried another tack.

"I loved the way you teased poor Harry about becoming a housewife after you finished your thesis. I gather that Australian men aren't exactly famous for their feminist principles. He probably believed every word you said."

Betsy didn't answer for so long that Lloyd turned to check her expression. "Maybe I wasn't teasing," she said, with a strange little smile.

"What does that mean?"

"I didn't tell him I wanted to be a housewife, exactly. I just said I wasn't sure I wanted to be an academic."

"But—" Lloyd was thrown into confusion. "I mean, you've been studying English literature for years. What else are you going to do?"

"I'm going to be married to you, silly."

"Well . . . yes. But don't you want to pass on what you've learned? Or teach school or write books—or something? That's half the point of me working hard, earning the money to support us both until you're ready to do your own thing."

"It's not just your money. Don't forget my allowance."

"No. Of course." But Lloyd couldn't help thinking of all the expenses she didn't contribute to, like the rent, the bills, movies, dinners, vacations. Mostly her allowance went on clothes and things for the apartment, not necessarily ones he would have chosen himself. Then he felt ashamed of his meanness. "It's not the money that's important," he explained. "I thought you wanted an equal partnership, equal status—you know, what Virginia Woolf meant when she talked about 'a room of one's own.' I'd like you to have your own independent life, not just wait on me."

"I'll always want to keep my mind alive, naturally." Betsy closed her eyes. "Does your stomach feel funny? I'm not at all sure that salmon last night was cooked through. I couldn't believe how they served it with the head and everything. That awful white eye!" She shuddered. "By the way, did you call the Wilding woman about the cat?"

"Not yet." Lloyd had forgotten all about it. Now he quailed at the thought. What could he say?

"You can do it tonight, after dinner. Not that I could eat a thing." She yawned. "Will it bother you if I take a little nap?"

"Of course not." Lloyd felt oddly deflated. "I'm sorry you didn't enjoy yourself more."

"It's OK." She patted his thigh briefly. "That's what I'm here for—to support your career."

Lloyd drove on toward London with a reddening sky at his back, his mind floating free. Tomorrow he would talk to Fox and air his anxieties. Probably Harry would tell him he was worrying about nothing. After all, Lloyd had no evidence to support his vague suspicions. He hardly believed them himself. He wished he had got hold of Sheri on Friday. He would try again tomorrow. There was nothing he could do on a Sunday night, anyway.

Or was there? Lloyd drove on down the gray motorway, blind to the ugly fly-overs and dismal industrial complexes that cluttered the fringe of London. Imperceptibly, the pressure of his foot on the accelerator increased. A plan was forming in his mind.

Chapter Seventeen

Mozart or Phish? It was a tricky decision. On the one hand, she wanted to appear sophisticated and serious, not just a bimbo in a rubber dress; on the other, she wanted Nick to think her fun, not a stuck-up prig. Would jazz be a good compromise? She flicked through the CDs, her face in turn registering approval, bemusement and disdain.

It was a hot Sunday evening. Suze had just showered and was wandering about the apartment in her most alluring underwear, keeping cool until the last minute. Nick was due shortly for a perfect little supper *à deux*. Suze was rather looking forward to an evening in. She flitted from the kitchen to the living room and back again in a happy trance.

Yesterday had been the most romantic day of her life. They had met at noon under the clock in Grand Central Station, just like Lauren Bacall and Humphrey Bogart in an old film she had once seen. The cathedral-like ticket hall was high and cool, sliced with pillars of dusty sunlight. When Suze had spotted him in his dazzling white shirt and tight jeans, she could hardly believe this vision was waiting for her.

First they had descended to the Oyster Bar, where they had sat at the counter on high stools, drinking Bloody Marys and feeding each other slices of smoked fish. The bustling paneled room was the epitome of urbane New York, Suze thought. Nick's bare elbow brushed hers on the counter. Close up, and in daylight, he was handsomer than ever. He seemed delighted with her company: he admired her dress and teased her about her accent. Giddily, Suze teased him back: "Are you really pleased to see me? Or is that a mobile phone in your pocket?"

Afterward Nick suggested that they go to a private view of a hot new sculptor; one of his connections had slipped him some invitations.

"But I thought you were going to show me New York," Suze protested.

"You don't mean . . . tourist stuff?" Nick looked horrified.

Suze was firm. This was her first visit to New York, perhaps her last. He had promised. She didn't care how corny it was; she wanted to go sightseeing.

So that's what they did. First they lined up to ride the elevators to the top of the Empire State Building, giggling at the Japanese camera-freaks and taking turns reading to each other out of Suze's guidebook. Nick knew nothing about history or architecture, she discovered, and when they finally reached the 102nd floor, he had stared at the far, hazy view with such wonderment that she became suspicious. Eventually she had teased and tickled him into admitting that, in all his fifteen years in the city, he had never been up here.

Next they took a long, meandering walk through Central Park; it was much more fun than a London park. They watched the jugglers and clowns and kite-fanatics; they quacked at the ducks and rode on the old carousel; they kissed under the cool trees by the lake. But when Suze's eye alighted on one of the horse-drawn buggies, Nick drew the line. "What if someone saw me? Bliss Bogardo has an apartment around here. She could be at the window right now, checking me out with her binoculars."

"Who *is* Bliss—?" Suze had started to say, but at that moment Nick decided to kiss her, jamming her brain signals so that afterward she could do no more than stumble hip-to-hip with him across the yellowed grass, smiling dreamily.

When they were hot and exhausted they rode a cab down to the little dock on the Hudson, and took the Circle Line boat around Manhattan. As they slowly circumnavigated the whole magical island, sipping cold beer, Suze waved at the people on land—the poor saps who weren't in love—until Nick told her that two tourists had recently been shot dead from a bridge in the Bronx.

"I know what we can do afterward," Suze had said excitedly. She explained how her father had bought a bottle of champagne in some Manhattan club back in the sixties and asked for it to be put aside for his daughter until she came to claim it. "It was some kind of sales gimmick, I think. I couldn't have been more than a baby at the time." She put her hand on Nick's arm. "Oh, do let's go. Dad says it's one of his 'great spots,' and I can't think of anyone I'd rather share my champagne with."

"What's the club?" Nick asked, with professional interest.

"It's called '21.' Have you heard of it?"

Nick recoiled. "Jeez, Suze. I mean, businessmen go there. There are toy cars hanging from the bar, and stuffy old farts in armchairs. They've probably got Frank Sinatra on the sound system."

"Oh." Suze felt rebuffed. Hastily backtracking, she suggested a restaurant in SoHo she'd read about, which was so cool you had to reserve a table three months in advance, guessing that this was the kind of challenge Nick liked. She was right.

He flashed her a cocky smile, his good humor restored. "Leave it to me."

Suze listened with a guilty thrill while he called the restaurant and reminded them of all the celebs he'd brought them in the last year. "Bump a couple of nobodies off one of the corner tables," he drawled, winking at Suze, and she had leaned against him, burying her face in his delicious shirt-front, trying not to think of the people whose table they had pinched.

The place turned out to be rather ordinary, despite one or two faces she thought she almost recognized, and by the time Nick asked for the bill she was ready to let him take her home. After all the activity of the day, the flat seemed quiet and intimate. Suze left him in the living room while she made them Manhattan Killers on the rocks. He roamed the room curiously, scoffing at the furnishings and books and selection of music. "You can tell this apartment belongs to Mr. and

Mrs. Ordinary. No one's had chairs like that since the eighties. And look at this!" He waved a particularly gruesome CD at her over the kitchen doors.

Suze felt oddly defensive. There were some nice things about the apartment. She made herself promise never to reveal to Nick that she'd decorated her own flat herself. After a while, he came over to the kitchen and stepped inside. There was barely room for both of them. "Look at you," he teased, squeezing her waist, "the little homemaker. I don't think I've even seen my kitchen since around 1992."

"But where do you eat?"

"Restaurants, take-out places. Nobody cooks anymore."

"I do. Sort of."

"Aren't you sweet?" He was opening drawers and cabinets at random. "The people who live here must be pretty geeky. Imagine spending your money on pots and pans . . . What's this thing?"

"It's a pastry brush. You use it to—Ni-ick . . ." Suze giggled as he leaned over to sweep the soft bristles across the tops of her breasts.

Then he carried their drinks over to the sofa—the leather one, Nick insisted, with a provocative lift of his eyebrows—and lounged against the armrest, watching her with hungry, hooded eyes. Suze lit a cigarette, trying to appear cool; she didn't want Nick to think her a total pushover. But the leather proved too intoxicating. Suddenly Nick snatched the cigarette out of her hand and pulled her onto his lap, kissing her and tugging at her clothes. His hands slid into soft, secret places. Suze felt the briefest pang of conscience about doing this on someone else's sofa, before her mind dissolved into a mush of sensation. Nick's body was heavy and warm; she felt she was burning up. Crikey, she *was* burning up!—or, rather, the sofa was. Suze rolled away and stared aghast at her cigarette smoldering into the expensive leather. But Nick had just laughed, extinguished the thread of smoke in a splash of cocktail and pulled her back to him.

Now Suze was frowning at the unmissable black hole right in the middle of the sofa. What if the Rockwell people made her pay for a whole new one? She placed a cushion over the blemish and returned to the kitchen.

The only disappointing part of the day had been waking up early this morning to find Nick already gone. She had been looking forward to a long, lazy Sunday breakfast together. Nick had left her a note explaining that he had a deal going with some Australian soap-opera star who could only be contacted at weird hours, and that he would see her tonight—which he had spelled "tonite," with a little circle forming the dot of the "i." Oh, well, Suze thought, you couldn't have everything.

She glanced at her watch. *Help!* She'd better get organized. She had already discovered that producing the perfect little supper was not as easy as she had thought. All the shops seemed to be open on Sundays but half the ingredients had different names here. Rocket was called "arugula," spring onions were known as "scallions," and as for buying a perfectly straightforward carton of double cream—forget it. She had found it impossible to find anything that wasn't no-fat, lo-fat or pale sludge popping with chemicals. Never mind. Her menu was a model of sophisticated simplicity: rocket with shaved Parmesan ("parmajahno" in American), poached sea bass with baby vegetables and wild strawberries soaked in Cointreau. The pièce de résistance was to be homemade Hollandaise sauce, a recipe she had not previously attempted, but what could be so difficult about stirring a bunch of eggs and butter together?

She had just put the ingredients into the double boiler and was heading toward the bedroom to put on her dress when the telephone rang. If that was Nick ringing to cancel, she'd murder him.

It was Lloyd Rockwell. The man had a genius for ringing at inconvenient hours.

"Yes?" she demanded crisply.

"Hello." His voice was cautious. "I'm sorry to bother you again, but I'm afraid I have more bad news."

What now? Suze wondered. She hoped that little Hitler at the electricity board hadn't cut her off again just because she hadn't paid on the exact day. "Can you be quick? I'm in the middle of cooking."

"It's about your cat," he went on. "The thing is he's—well, the fact is, he's passed away."

"Passed away?"

"Dead, if you prefer."

"Mr. Kipling? Oh, no . . ." Suze pressed a hand to her mouth. She thought of all the times he had cheered her up, swaggering into the sitting room, boasting with the merest flick of his tail of unspeakably daring exploits on the rooftops of North London before collapsing into companionable sleep by her radiator. He had never been officially hers, but that was part of his attraction. He came when he wanted to; she fed him if she had anything at hand. He had been particularly fond of Marks & Spencer cheese flan, she recalled. A sob escaped her.

"Don't cry," he pleaded. "Please don't cry."

"What happened?" Suze sniffed. "Did he get run over?"

"Not exactly . . . You see, you must realize we didn't know he was your cat. When we found him coming in and out of the house, we thought he was a stray. So—I don't know how to tell you this, but we thought the best thing was to take him to the veterinarian. She said he was pretty near the end of his life anyway, and it would be difficult to find him a home so . . . so . . ."

"So you killed him," Suze finished savagely. "How could you?" she burst out. "A poor innocent cat just looking for a bit of company."

"I know. I'm sorry. Truly, I can't tell you how sorry. I see now it was a terrible thing to do. I know there's no way to make it up to you, though I would if I could."

He did sound sorry too. Suze snapped one garter against her thigh in agitation. She was upset and wanted to vent her anger on him, but felt he didn't deserve it.

"Betsy's bought you a present—a microwave oven. It's not supposed to be any kind of compensation, of course," he went on hurriedly, "just a small token of our apologies."

Suze scowled into the telephone. Microwaves were for dull people. As she stood, silent and mulish, she became aware of an odd smell.

"Oh, no!"

She dashed into the kitchen, trailing the long phone wire behind her. *Disaster!* In the Hollandaise-sauce pan was an evil-smelling brown custard. Suze went to snatch the pan off the stove, burned her hand, screamed and dropped the telephone receiver. Hopping with pain, she found an oven glove, put the pan on the draining board and ran cold water over her hand. She waved her other hand in front of her nose. The smell was disgusting. What would Nick think?

A disembodied voice was squawking at her from the floor. "Hello? Hello?"

She picked up the telephone receiver. "What is it now?"

"What happened?"

"I just burned my Hollandaise sauce, that's all. And he'll be here any minute. Everything's got to be perfect. I'm not even dressed." Rising panic made her voice squeaky.

"Maybe it can be rescued. What does it look like?"

Suze peeked into the saucepan. The suppressed memory of an afternoon spent with Bridget shortly after the birth of Timmy-wimmy rose from oblivion. "Baby poo."

"Uh-oh. That doesn't sound too great, I admit. Why don't you skip the sauce? Any man would be glad to have dinner cooked for him, sauce or no."

"You don't understand," Suze wailed. "This isn't 'any man.' It's got to be perfect. I mean, this is someone who throws away his dress shirts after one wearing."

"You're right, I don't understand. Hasn't the guy heard of laundries?"

"He says they can never get the collars right again," Suze mumbled. Even she thought this habit of Nick's a little extravagant.

"This man is not going to go for baby poo on his fish, is that what you're telling me?"

"Yes!" Suze snapped. "And he'll be here any minute, and I don't have any more shallots and—"

"Then we'll just have to make it another way."

Suze stopped waving her arms about. *"We?"*

"Sure. I'd like to help. It's the least I can do. What you want to do is look in the cabinet over the stove and find the white-wine vinegar. Second shelf, I think."

Suze hesitated, not sure whether to trust him. Most of the men she knew thought that food came in pretty little cellophane packets. She checked the cabinet anyway. Second shelf it was. This was impressive. "Got it," she said.

"OK. Now put three tablespoons of that and two of cold water in the pan and let it bubble. Meanwhile, get some more butter and egg yolks ready."

Suze found herself obeying. His voice was marvelously soothing. Maybe it would be all right after all. She found a flouncy little apron and put it on over her underwear, then started cracking more eggs, phone tucked into her chin. Suddenly she caught sight of the vinegar mixture. "Oh, no! That vinegar stuff is disappearing!"

"'Reducing' is the word. Calm down. You have to wait until there's only about a tablespoon left. Haven't you ever cooked anything before?"

"Of course," Suze replied loftily. She could do hard-boiled eggs, cheese on toast, baked beans . . . lots of different dishes. "My friend Bridget and I once gave a Suggestive Food dinner party," she offered. "The trouble was we got so sloshed on Sloe Screws that we incinerated the jumbo frankfurters and had to go down the road for a curry. We were eating breast-shaped strawberry mousses for weeks afterward."

He had a nice laugh. "What the hell is a Slow Screw?"

"Sloe gin and orange juice on the rocks. Divine, but lethal. Oops, there's only a spoonful left now."

"OK, pour it into the top of the double-boiler and stir in the egg yolks. Then start adding the butter, a glop at a time. And don't let the water underneath boil."

"A glop," Suze repeated thoughtfully. "That's the technical term, is it?"

"Tell me more about Mr. Perfect."

"Don't call him that. He's just really nice, and American, and good fun and . . ."

". . . and he likes you."

"And he *seems* to like me. Who can tell with men?"

"Ha!" His indignant voice was suddenly loud in her ear. "It's you women who are the inscrutable ones. The poor guy's probably standing outside the apartment door right now, with a bunch of flowers in his arms, wondering if you've remembered you invited him . . . Are you still stirring?"

"Yes. My recipe says it's supposed to 'coat the back of a spoon.' What on earth does that mean? I keep picturing a spoon with a little coat on it, like a dachshund."

He chuckled. "Tell me the rest of your menu."

Suze was just explaining precisely how she had marinated her strawberries when she broke off in astonishment. "Look!"

"Susannah, this is the telephone. Describe."

"It's gone all thick, and a sort of primrose color. It looks—you won't believe this, Lloyd, but it looks like Hollandaise sauce."

"Of course it does. Now add a few drops of lemon juice and some salt, and tell me how it tastes."

She did as he said and licked the spoon. "Totally divine. Why couldn't I do that?"

"You just did."

"Thanks to you." Suze stared into the pan with pride. "If you ever lost your job, you could always set up a cooking help-line. Wouldn't that be brilliant? My phone bill would be enormous."

"Listen . . . I wanted to ask if you could do me a work favor?"

"Of course! Anything."

"There's a file I need from the office. If I give you the name and the password, would you e-mail it to me from my computer?"

"Easy. Just let me write this down." Suze went into the living room and started rooting around the desk. "Is it you who's the manic pencil-sharpener?"

"Probably."

"You also have a terror of running out of tinned tomatoes, you have incredibly long feet and you're a hypochondriac. I've never seen such a medicine cabinet."

"That's Betsy. She likes to be prepared for any epidemics that may break out in Manhattan."

Suze tore off a piece of paper. "Right. Fire away."

Lloyd fired away and she scribbled down the details, promising that she would send the e-mail first thing on Monday morning. Lloyd sounded very polite and grateful.

Something was still troubling Suze. "Incidentally, how did you get Mr. Kipling to the vet? Usually he hates being touched."

There was a small pause. "In a plastic bag."

Suze spluttered. "Don't be daft. You can't put a cat in a plastic bag."

"You're right. I guess it was a basket. Actually, it was Betsy who maneuvered him into the, er, receptacle. She's very competent at that kind of thing."

Suze listened to his faltering tone, the tone of a man who hated lying and was doing precisely that. Suddenly she understood. "It wasn't you at all, was it? It was your girlfriend who got rid of him."

"No, no. Absolutely not."

She had never heard anyone sound so unconvincing. He must be taking the blame for his girlfriend. *Could anybody be that nice?* she wondered. He must have a flaw somewhere. She thought of a small test.

"One last question—do you really like Phil Collins?"

"Of course not! At least, not personally."

Just as she had thought: a girly present from a girly girlfriend. Suze smiled. "Thanks again for the cookery lesson. Bye."

She put down the phone and went to get dressed. Poor old Mr. Kipling . . . though he had been getting rather crotchety and smelly. She hoped he hadn't been too frightened at the vet's. In the bedroom, she found she was still clutching the piece of paper. She looked at it again and frowned, remembering what Sheri had said about discretion. Lloyd hadn't sounded particularly paranoid. On the other hand, it was important for Suze to stay in Sheri's good books.

Suze slipped on her dress, debating what would be the right thing to do. As she applied her lipstick carefully and batted her lashes to dry the mascara, she decided that she would tell Sheri about Lloyd's request before she sent him the file. It couldn't do any harm.

Chapter Eighteen

"Just a minute, Mr. Rockwell."

Lloyd paused in the Schneider Fox reception area. Approaching him was a sour-faced security man whom Lloyd had sometimes seen manning the reception when he worked late. Normally he barely looked up from his newspaper to grunt. Today he was bristling with self-importance.

"Yes?"

"Mr. Fox asked me to show you straight up to his office when you arrived."

"Fine. I'll just—"

"My instructions are 'at once.'"

"Uh . . . OK."

Together they walked up the stairs to the first floor and along the corridor to Harry's office. Lloyd was puzzled. Something important must have come up. Had he forgotten a meeting? This *was* Tuesday, right? Was he very late arriving this morning? He checked his watch. It was 9:15 A.M.

Lloyd shrugged. Every boss he'd known had been unpredictable and dictatorial in various measures, and it seemed that Harry was no exception. All yesterday Lloyd had been trying to talk to him privately without success; now here was Harry demanding to see him before he'd even gotten his coat off.

The security man knocked on the door of Harry's office, then gestured to Lloyd to go in and closed the door behind him.

Lloyd was surprised to see Piers standing with Harry at the

window. He smiled at Piers, but his smile froze when Harry turned to look at him. The normally enigmatic Australian looked angry. Lloyd felt a spurt of alarm. "What's happened?" he asked. The thought crossed his mind that Julian Jewel had, after all, lured Passion away from Schneider Fox. But it was impossible, unthinkable.

"I've asked Piers to join us because I think it's important that Passion knows exactly what's been going on," began Harry.

Lloyd stood looking at him, still carrying his briefcase in one hand with a raincoat folded over his arm.

"It's become clear to us in the last twenty-four hours that somebody has been leaking confidential client information," Harry continued. His tone was curiously formal. "Specifically, it appears that some passengers who booked Passion Premium transatlantic flights have been approached with a competitive offer from Stateside. They seem to have known exactly who the Passion customers were and what kind of deal they had been given."

"Yes," said Lloyd. "That makes sense."

Harry ignored him. "The information could have come from within Passion, of course," he went on, "but we think it came from Schneider Fox."

Lloyd shook his head. "Not a chance. As you know, we have been analyzing the response to our last promotion, but nobody outside my department had access to that data." He tried to guess where this was all leading.

Again Harry appeared to ignore what he had said. Piers was avoiding his eye.

"In the last twelve hours we've been running a security check to see if any Schneider Fox employee with access to that list has had any direct contact with anyone at Stateside. That's how we came across this message." Harry tossed a sheet of paper to Lloyd. It was a photocopied page from Dee Dee's message book. '*Tony says thanks for the list.*' "Recognize this?"

"Sort of." Lloyd nodded slowly. "Dee Dee—my secretary in New York—gave me this message last week. I was already in London when she took the call. But I've no idea who it's from or what it means."

"Are you also going to tell me you don't know a man called Tony Salvino, head of direct marketing at Stateside?"

"Well, no, I don't, though I've heard the name." Lloyd felt the first pricklings of danger. "Wait a minute, though. Are you suggesting that I've been leaking the list of Passion customers to Stateside?" The idea was so ludicrous that he almost laughed.

Almost.

"That's exactly what I'm suggesting." Harry's eyes were cold.

"But that's preposterous. I—I—I just couldn't do such a thing."

Lloyd looked appealingly at Piers, who shifted uncomfortably. "Harry, perhaps we should—"

"Open your briefcase." Harry jerked his head at Lloyd.

"What?"

"Put your goddamn briefcase on the table and open it."

Lloyd obeyed, tight-lipped.

On top was his newspaper. Harry tossed it aside, dislodging an apple, which rolled across the desk and smashed to the floor. A batch of memos and folders followed, then a clear plastic folder. Harry snatched it up, then passed it to Piers. "This good enough for you?"

Too late, Lloyd understood. "Wait—" he began.

"How much did they pay you, Lloyd?" Harry interrupted bitterly. "Lots of nice fat zeros, were there? I actually liked the bastard." He was talking to Piers now. "He and his fiancée came to stay with us only last weekend. I thought it strange the way he kept trying to pump me about Passion, but I didn't understand why until yesterday."

Lloyd's head was spinning. He knew he should interrupt, should explain why he had done what he had done, but he was bewildered. Nothing made sense. Why had Stateside thanked him? Did they, too, think that he was guilty?

"Bernie and I talked last night. We're terminating your employment with Schneider Fox as of this moment. Here is your letter of dismissal. I want you to leave the building right away." Harry Fox spoke as though his words disgusted him. "Schneider Fox employees will be instructed not to speak to you. You are to hand over all company property in your possession. We will clear your desk and return any personal items in due course. I warn you that you are still bound by the confidentiality agreements you entered into when you joined Schneider Fox, and if you attempt to use any further privileged information we shall take legal sanctions against you."

When Lloyd didn't move, Harry strode across to the door and flung it open himself. The security man was waiting outside. "Please escort Mr. Rockwell from the building."

"Harry—"

"Just get out. Now!"

Chapter Nineteen

There was a strident honk, a blur of red and a buffet of wind that rocked Lloyd back on his heels. An angry male voice shouted, "Are you effing blind?"

He was standing on the edge of the sidewalk a block or two away from Schneider Fox, facing into the traffic. His heart was hammering at frightening speed. He could hear himself panting, mouth open. How he had got here, he didn't know. Now he seemed unable to move. Trying to regain control, he forced himself to focus on something. On the ground were two black objects: tapering, rounded, maybe three or four inches across, with a smooth surface and a deep sheen—he made himself describe them, as if he were an expert witness at a murder trial. One of them moved. They were, he realized, the toe-caps of his own shoes. Abruptly he turned from the road, causing a young woman to pull her child sharply to her side and steer a cautious course around him. *Drugs*, said her frightened eyes, *or drink, or schizophrenia*. They were common enough around here.

The far side of the sidewalk was bounded by a stone wall, waist high, that formed the parapet of a bridge over the canal. Lloyd leaned his forearms on it, trying to slow his breathing. His head drooped. He stared down, down, down. The water below was a deep, dark, inviting green.

He had been fired. He had been thrown out of his office and told never to return. He had no job, no purpose, no place to go each day, no salary, no future. His colleagues thought him a cheat and a liar—worse, a criminal.

There was a ringing in his ears, which swelled until it seemed that he could hear again the echoing slam of metal doors and the scream of electric bells. A stench of cheap food and sweat and disinfectant rose in his nostrils. He saw the once-confident figure unbearably diminished in rough uniform blue, and the eyes that haunted him—pleading spaniel eyes. Overcome with revulsion and guilt, Lloyd pressed his face tight into his shoulder until the world went dark.

Try to think. What could have happened? Only two days ago he had been Harry's guest, laughing with his wife, playing with his children. Could Harry have been playing some double game all along? Lloyd lifted his head and looked down along the canal. Someone was fishing. Lloyd thought of how he had tried to raise his worries about Passion with Harry on the riverbank, and wished he had been more persistent. Why did he always have to be so goddamn polite? He ran his finger around the tight collar of his shirt, then impulsively ripped off his tie, his badge of office servitude, and flung it into the water. Only when he saw it floating limply did he remember that it was one Betsy had given him.

Betsy . . . Lloyd felt a faint stirring of warmth. There had been a time, early in their relationship, when Betsy had taken a whole week off from the library to take care of him when he was sick. They were hardly even going out at the time. It had been a truly selfless gesture. The memory of Betsy's calm presence filled his thoughts. She had known exactly what to do. Drink your soup. Lie down. Put on another blanket. Time for some medicine. She had been so soothing and competent. He could remember the gloriously comfortable feeling of resigning himself to another's control.

Betsy was intelligent. She had a trained mind, clear and direct from years of academic study. She would be able to figure everything out for him, and tell him what to do next.

Before he realized it, he was walking the familiar route home, up Caledonian Road with its laundromats and hardware stores, along his favorite street, where each house was guarded by a pair of domestic-sized sphinxes, and on through the quiet squares with hidden gardens, leading to the sanctuary he already thought of as home. He ran up the stairs of the apartment, shouting her name. What if she was out? But Betsy appeared on the landing, a startled expression on her face.

"What are you doing here?" She came down the hallway to meet him. "Where's your tie?"

He put his arms around her and for a long moment he held her close, breathing in her fresh, familiar smell, feeling her body warm and reassuringly alive against his.

"What is it?" she asked again, freeing herself.

"I lost my job."

"What?" Betsy looked horrified. "Why? What did you do?"

"I—" Lloyd shook his head. "I don't know." He explained what had happened—the suddenness of it, the shock.

Betsy put a comforting hand on his shoulder. "There must have been some kind of misunderstanding, Lloyd. These English people probably don't understand the business. Why don't you call Bernie and explain what's happened?"

"If Harry didn't believe me, Bernie certainly won't."

"Is there anyone else who might know what's going on? How about Sheri?"

Sheri! Yes, she might be able to make sense of this. After all, she knew more than anyone else about what they were planning for Passion. "You're right," he said. "I'll call her."

"You can't call her yet. She'll be asleep. Why don't I make you some coffee and run you a bath? You look terrible. Try to relax for a while."

Lloyd couldn't wait longer than twelve o'clock English time; seven in the morning in New York. Sheri would be awake but still at home. He was feeling a little calmer now. He took the phone into the bedroom and dialed her home number, listening to the familiar American purr, so different from the English ring.

"Hello?"

"Sheri, it's Lloyd—I need to speak to you."

There was an intake of breath and then a click as the receiver was replaced. Lloyd felt a shock of realization. *She already knew that he'd been fired!* He sat stunned for a moment, then went to find Betsy.

She was sitting at the computer, looking studious. It almost made him smile to see how quickly she snatched off the reading glasses that she so hated to be seen wearing. She jumped up and came across the room to him. "What's the story?"

"She wouldn't talk to me." He flopped into an armchair.

Betsy looked at him thoughtfully. "Lloyd, you know you could find that this is a blessing in disguise. You could take a job somewhere else. I never thought Schneider Fox appreciated you as they should. Lots of men are on the board by the time they're your age."

"Betsy," Lloyd said patiently, "*think!* Who in the entire advertising industry is going to employ someone who's passed on a client's secrets to its biggest rival?"

"But you didn't." There was a long pause. "Did you? Because if you did, you know I'd forgive you, darling." She thought some more. "Maybe the rival would hire you."

"Of course I didn't do it!" Lloyd banged the arm of the chair with his fist, hard enough to make her spring back. "For fuck's sake," he shouted, "I don't even know exactly what they think I did."

"OK," she said at last, in a small, wounded voice. "There's no need to use language."

Lloyd scoured his hand back and forth through his hair. "There must be some crucial misunderstanding. If I could only think straight, I might be able to figure out what it is."

His gaze veered wildly around the room, as if for inspiration. But all he saw were the tall books on art and design sloping this way and that on the bookshelves, the metal lamp with the loose connection that made it flicker, Fred Astaire tap dancing—all the strange, funny landmarks of someone else's life that had now become partly his own. He stood up. "Let's go home. I'll look for another job. We could move to another city—Chicago, Seattle." He strode toward the telephone. "We could be on a plane tonight."

"But we can't go now!"

"Why not?" Lloyd snatched up the receiver, desperate to take positive action.

Betsy was staring in amazement, almost laughing at him as if he were deranged. "Have you forgotten Mother?" she asked, in a gentle, reproving voice. "You know she's arriving next week. She's been looking forward to this trip so much. We can't disappoint her."

Betsy was standing next to him now, holding out her hand for the receiver. He gave it to her without comment. But somewhere deep within him a fire began to kindle and take hold. He paced around the room, straightening books, fiddling with objects on the mantelpiece, feeling caged and frustrated, wanting to lash out.

"Written any great prose today?" He peered at her computer screen. "Let's see, what have we here?"

"Don't look," Betsy said sharply. "It's private."

"'Silver (sterling), crown pattern, eight settings,'" Lloyd read aloud. "'Spode china, Greek key pattern, eight settings. Double sheets . . . Oxford edged pillowcases . . . electric waffle-maker' . . ." He felt the flames leap and roar. "Don't tell me you've found Jane Austen's long-lost shopping list?"

Betsy reached around him and tapped a few keys. The screen went blank. "I just thought we should get our wedding list in at Bloomingdale's. They get so busy at this time of year."

Lloyd thought his head might explode. He grabbed Betsy's shoulders. "Betsy, I have lost my job. No job means no money." He gave her a shake. "Don't you understand? The way things are going right now, there isn't going to *be* a wedding!"

Chapter Twenty

Suze frowned dubiously at the scratched and peeling door, then stepped back to peer up at the square, red-brick building. It looked like an abandoned factory. Could anyone really live here? She double-checked the address on her piece of paper, gave a shrug and pressed the bell.

Almost at once, the entryphone crackled. "That you, Suze?" It was Jay's voice, all right. "Come on up! Fifth floor."

Suze pushed open the door and crossed a bare, concrete hallway to the elevator. It was the industrial type, with heavy mesh gates you had to close yourself. *I hope he doesn't ask me about Lloyd*, she thought, as she clanked slowly upward.

It had been a terrible day at work. The shocked atmosphere had hit her as soon as she'd entered the office that morning, and when she saw the memo from Bernie waiting on her desk she understood its cause.

> *Lloyd Rockwell's employment with the company has been terminated following the disclosure of a conflict of professional interest. On lawyers' advice, employees are instructed not to communicate with Rockwell, or to answer questions from the press. I know I can rely on your cooperation.*

Poor Dee Dee had been in tears. Suze was jolly upset herself, at the thought that her job-exchange might be cut short. No way was she leaving New York. For the moment, she could only assume that

Lloyd was staying on in London: thank goodness, otherwise she'd be kipping on somebody's floor by now. Or sleeping in Nick's bed . . .

When she pushed back the elevator doors she found Jay waiting for her in an open doorway, wearing disgraceful jeans, snow-white sneakers and a T-shirt with the words "WHY ME?" printed in giant black letters. The very sight of him cheered her up.

"Hi," he said, giving her a casual kiss. "You look like you need a drink." He stepped back to let her in and Suze entered one of the most extraordinary rooms she had ever seen. In fact, it wasn't a room, but a double-height space about twenty times the size of her London flat, with a row of big, square windows that offered glorious snapshot views of Manhattan. The really wild thing, however, was that every surface was covered with plates, posters, statues, ashtrays, lamps, bric-a-brac of every description—all showing the image of one man.

"Crikey!"

"Welcome," said Jay, "to the world's largest collection of JFK memorabilia." He paused for dramatic effect. "Possibly the world's *only* collection."

"I knew there must be a reason why I liked you, Jay. You are seriously bonkers."

Jay shrugged. "Let's just say I'm the obsessive type. I was born the day Kennedy got shot. Take a look around, if you want, while I get us something to drink. How about some ice-cold Chardonnay?"

"Heaven."

Suze dropped her handbag on a chair, slipped out of her uncomfortable work shoes and started snooping around. Off the tennis-court-sized central space were various antechambers—a small kitchen, a large bathroom, an enormous bedroom, and various walk-in closets. At the far end, a door led into another vast space that was clearly Jay's studio, crammed with cameras, cans of film, reflectors and expensive-looking editing equipment. There were desks and telephones and at least two dark rooms. On the walls were classic film posters and framed awards. Suze was impressed. It looked like a serious operation.

"Wine coming up!" Jay shouted to her.

She crossed back over the smooth parquet and sank into a white sofa by the window. Jay handed her a large glass. She took a sip and uttered a groan of pleasure.

Jay sat down in a chair opposite her and stretched out his legs. "So tell me," he asked, "how was the big date?"

"Sensational. Jay, I can't begin to tell you."

"Try."

So Suze tried, and Jay listened as she told him how handsome Nick was, how stylish, how witty, how considerate—

"Did the rubber dress go down well?"

"Oh, it went down all right." Suze smirked.

"This guy Nick sounds perfect. I wish I was going out with him."

"Hands off!" They laughed. "Jay . . . do you think it's possible to fall in love with someone you don't really know?"

"It's possible."

"I really think I might be in love with him. He's so . . . well, he's just so everything."

"I can see he's got a lot going for him."

"I honestly think he might be The One . . ." Suze burbled on happily while they sipped their drinks, watching the sun set fire to the buildings one by one. Gradually her disgruntled, nervy feeling slipped away, to be replaced by one of supercharged bonhomie. She sank back into the cushions, wriggling her toes.

"Do you live here alone?"

"Usually. Sometimes a boyfriend stays for a while." Jay grimaced at the word. "Have you noticed how the word 'boyfriend' has acquired a new meaning these days? It used to be that young girls had boyfriends, whom they married one day, at which point the boyfriends became husbands. Then everyone stopped marrying, gays started coming out, and it got to be embarrassing to call the forty-year-old man you'd been living with for ten years your 'boyfriend,' and we made up all these new words, 'partner,' 'lover,' 'significant other.' Nowadays 'boyfriend' means a bit of fun, nothing serious, someone for a night or a week or the occasional bedfest—for men and women both. A boyfriend is by definition someone whom you will absolutely not marry." He shot her a sudden, probing look. "So what about Nick? Is he a boyfriend?"

His question threw her into confusion. Suze drank some more wine. "I'm not really into marriage."

"Good answer!" Jay chuckled at the evasion, reading her thoughts. He stood up. "Let's go eat, before I turn into a sociology professor."

"Hooray!"

"Are you feeling brave?"

"Completely reckless."

"OK, leave it to me."

Jay took her around the corner to a small Japanese restaurant, where he mysteriously ordered "a boat for two." When it arrived, Suze gasped. Nestled inside a huge wicker tray, which was indeed boat-shaped, were exquisitely arranged rolls of raw fish, vegetables cut into stars and flowers, seaweed parcels and transparent, pale pink slices of ginger. She seized her chopsticks with a moan of greed.

"So, how are things at Schneider Fox?" asked Jay.

Suze squirmed. She didn't feel like telling him about Lloyd just yet.

"Well, you know I'm working on a special project with Sheri."

"Oh, yeah, the famous Sheri."

"Yes." Suze folded her lips. "Jay, I don't expect you to understand this, but she's a wonderful person to work with. She's so strong and assertive and focused. And she really relies on me. It's very . . . empowering." Only this morning Sheri had confided to her how they needed to pull out all the stops to convince Passion to stay, now that Lloyd had gone. They were making a presentation to Passion in only ten days. *"I cannot do this without you,"* Sheri had said.

"And the best thing about her," Suze went on, "is that she doesn't take any shit from the men at the top."

"Really? How about Bernie? What does she take from him?"

Suze flushed. "You don't understand her at all," she told him coldly.

There was an awkward silence while they picked at the fish.

"Suze," Jay began gently, "isn't it about time you told me about Lloyd?"

Suze was shocked. She dabbed her mouth with her napkin, playing for time. "You mean, you know—about his being sacked?"

"Of course I know. He's my best friend. He called me this morning to tell me about it."

Suze poked at a heap of ginger, feeling irritable. If he'd known all along, why hadn't he said anything? "So what did he tell you?"

"That he's been accused of passing confidential client information to a rival company."

Suze sniffed. "And I suppose he denies it?"

"Of course he does."

"Well, I happen to know that he did it." She shook back her hair, avoiding his eye. Sheri had told her that morning about the Tony Salvino call.

Jay began to look angry. "How do you know?"

Suze was getting really irritated now. "I just do. I'm not supposed to be talking to you about this. Anyway," she went on, "what I say is, if Lloyd can't keep his hands to himself when it comes to women, why should he when it comes to work?"

Jay slapped his chopsticks on the table. "What the fuck do you know about Lloyd and women?"

"Don't shout at me." Suze was almost in tears. "Sheri told me herself that Lloyd had pounced on her in a taxi."

"Oh, well," said Jay sarcastically, "if *Sheri* says so . . ."

Suze was quiet for a moment. She knew she was right, but she could see that her words hurt Jay. "Why would Sheri make it up?" she asked, in a reasonable voice. "Look, I've never even met Lloyd. As far as I'm concerned he can shag anyone he likes. I just know that the evidence proves that he is guilty."

"Suze, Lloyd is the last person in the world who would do something like this, because . . . Oh, what's the use?"

Suze was desperate not to let the evening end on a bad note. "Because of what? Tell me."

"Why should I? You don't care about him." He rose to his feet. "Come on, let's go."

As they were leaving the restaurant, Jay said, "Lloyd doesn't have a crooked bone in his body. His problem, if he has a problem, is that he's too straight."

Later that night Suze lay in bed thinking about what Jay had said. Whatever Lloyd might or might not have done, he had a true friend in Jay—someone who would fight for him when he was down. Suze could see why anyone would like Jay, but she didn't know what Jay saw in Lloyd. Men were such a mystery. Abruptly her thoughts switched to Nick. After the Hollandaise sauce rigmarole, he had phoned—late—to say he wasn't coming. A rock star had turned up unexpectedly and needed entertaining for the evening: Suze would understand, when he told her who it was. Actually, Suze had not been particularly understanding, but Nick's charm had worn down her resistance, and she had let him coax her into agreeing to a weekend together—*this* weekend.

She hugged herself with excited anticipation, imagining how it would be. They were going to a little seaside place Nick knew. She would have him all to herself, away from the distractions of the city: two simple people enjoying simple pleasures. They would swim and sail and eat lobster, then climb the stairs of some rickety old inn to make love in the breezy muslin tent of a four-poster bed. She couldn't wait.

Chapter Twenty-one

"So how did you do yours?"

"I guess you'd call it plantation style. *Gone With the Wind* meets *Out of Africa*. Lots of wicker. I can give you my decorator's name if you want."

"Thanks, but I couldn't desert Helga. She's so creative. I was thinking of a *Citizen Kane*–type office thing, but she feels ancient Rome is more me."

"My wife would like that. She adores ruins."

"Kitty? Is she here?"

"Hell, no. I married Carla Gland last fall. Kitty's living up in Malibu with her spiritual adviser. This alimony thing really hurts, huh?"

"Tell me about it."

Suze gave a small, desperate cough. She was standing on the crowded porch where Nick had left her, sandwiched between two men with silver hair and glowing suntans, combined age about 150, she reckoned, but in a frightening state of artificial youthfulness.

"Are you redecorating your houses?" she asked brightly.

Their faded eyes, sculpted boyishly open, assessed her without interest. "Our jets."

"Oh dear," said Suze. "I think I must be at the wrong party."

Retreating, she squeezed her way through the linen jackets and little black dresses, past bare, tanned backs and defiantly patterned shirts, until she reached the steps, where she balanced her drink on the wooden balustrade and looked out. Cocktail time in East Hampton: quite a sight.

Before her stretched a lawn decorated with knots of beautiful, chattering people and shadowed by the cupolas and pediments of the vast white mansion at her back. Beyond the grass was a strip of sand swept to pale perfection by waves that had rolled three thousand miles from the coast of Portugal. Everything in view boasted money—the rich green of the grass, the clipped hedges that screened an Olympic-size swimming pool, the silent servants proffering toothpicked delicacies. Even the sea itself, lit by a low evening sun, looked like molten gold.

Nick had picked her up from Schneider Fox shortly after lunch. Sheri had been surprisingly relaxed about letting Suze go early—encouraging, even. "It will be an experience," she had said, with a knowing lift of her eyebrows that Suze found faintly disconcerting. Nick drove a red two-seater convertible with the air-conditioning on and the top firmly closed against Manhattan's sticky, debilitating heat. The traffic, he warned, would be unspeakable; certainly it seemed to make him uncommunicative and edgy. But for Suze, joining the mass weekend exodus made her feel like a real New Yorker. As they crossed the East River, she had looked back at the city, scorched brown under a smothering sky, and felt excitement rise.

Slowly they had sloughed off the clutter of suburbs and industrial complexes. The roads narrowed. Color leached into the landscape. Manhattan's murky waters brightened to a true ocean blue. Suze began to see place-names that sounded vaguely Indian—Patchogue, Napeague, Montauk. For the last few miles Nick had put the top down and they sailed through hedged lanes, past antique shops and roadside fruit stalls, tooting at bicyclists. There were smartly railed horse farms and cutely restored windmills to lend a rural gloss, but Suze did not take long to realize that Long Island was not exactly "the country," more a vast holiday resort. Her fantasy of a quiet seaside village faded and was eclipsed altogether when they turned at last off the lane and entered what was evidently a grand private estate. She could hear the whisper of banknotes in the hush of cooling trees, the hiss of tires on the smooth driveway and the crunch of gravel as they parked outside a row of small clapboard houses, painted Shaker blue.

On the drive out, Nick had explained that they would be staying the weekend as guests of a man called Shrine Wackfest.

"Who?" Suze giggled.

"Shrine Wackfest is one of the wealthiest men in the United States," Nick continued, with a hint of disapproval at her irreverent laughter, "and a fabulously generous patron of the arts. Without him, Herb Damon would be nobody."

Suze said she didn't care who he was as long as they could go swimming the second they arrived. She didn't dare admit that she'd never heard of Herb Damon.

Dumping their bags in the "cottage"—actually a luxurious bedsit with bathroom, kitchenette and small, private patio—they had pulled on their bathing suits and chased each other into the sea. It was cold enough to make Suze squeal, and soon they had retreated to the beach to exchange salty kisses and let the sun melt their bones into delicious laziness. Sandy and glowing, they returned to the cottage to test the bed. It was absolutely fine.

Eerily, their clothes had transported themselves into drawers and onto hangers, though Suze had seen no one. She blushed when Nick pulled something from the wardrobe and turned to her, swinging the hanger from one fingertip. "What," he asked, with a lascivious grin, "is this?"

It was a sexy little black basque that Suze had bought at the last moment, anxious in case Nick got bored with her. Neatly folded on its hanger, criss-cross laces dangling, it looked absurd. She hated the thought that some servant had sniggered over it. "It was supposed to be a surprise," she mumbled, "for later."

"Well, well," he said, "I look forward to later."

While they showered and changed, Nick outlined the program for the weekend. "Cocktail party tonight, dinner at the new Italian seafood place, then a pool party. Tomorrow, after everyone gets back from the gym—"

"The gym? There's a party at the gym?"

"Of course not. But people have to keep in shape, you know."

"Can't they go for a walk? I thought this was 'the country.'"

Nick rolled his eyes. "After we get back from the gym—"

"Not me."

"OK, after everyone else gets back from the gym, there'll be a barbecue, then we'll ride motorcycles on to another cocktail party—"

"But we haven't got a motorcycle."

"You hire them, dummy." Nick's tone made her feel naive. "Then dinner, a firework party farther up the point, maybe a nightclub."

"Won't we be too drunk to ride the bikes home?"

"The help comes and picks them up in a truck."

"Oh." Of course.

"Then on Sunday we'll sail over to another house for brunch, maybe play some tennis, then head back to the city. Think you can stand it?"

"It sounds like a very complicated way of having fun."

Nick laughed. "Suze, believe me, this is going to be the most fun you ever had."

Suze smiled to herself as she watched Nick's little rituals of shaving and perfect cuff adjustment. He was in rock-star mode tonight, dressed all in black with a fancy gold watch to match his hair.

They heard a car pull up and Nick walked swiftly to the window. "Look who's here!" He waved Suze over.

A man of about fifty, with slicked-back dark hair and wraparound sunglasses, was walking up the path to the next-door cottage.

"That," Nick said, with a note of triumph, "is Manfred Zarg, the Hollywood producer. Shrine's got him on the hook to make a movie. He wants to close the deal this weekend."

Now, standing on the porch, Suze self-consciously smoothed the skirt of the dress Nick had sent her in compensation for the rubber ruin. It was a halter-necked black thing by Donna Karan. Suze wasn't sure it was quite *her*, but Nick had expressly asked her to bring it, saying it would be "right." She would have worn a tea towel to please him.

Suddenly she caught sight of him at the heart of a small group, telling a story, making them laugh. Even from here she could see his eager smile. He looked across toward Suze and signaled to her to come over. Delighted, she descended the steps of the balcony. When she joined the group Nick introduced her to a woman of about her own age, wearing granny glasses and what looked like pink silk pajamas.

"You two have got to meet." Nick sounded thoroughly over-revved. "Laura's into advertising too. She's totally brilliant."

Suze gave her a friendly look. "Are you a designer as well?"

The woman twitched her glasses. "I prefer to call myself an artist."

"Don't we all?" Suze laughed. "But one has to live. What sort of clients do you work with?"

"Actually, I'm not into that commercial scene. My work is subversive, more like a parody of the genre."

"Ah."

"I like to take images from the conventional advertising spectrum and construct my own iconography."

Suze was trying to understand. "And—what?—people buy your work and hang it on their walls, is that it?"

There was a small pause. "Right now, I'm refining my style. I don't want to peak too soon. Excuse me, I've just seen my dealer."

"What does she live on?" Suze asked Nick when the woman had moved on.

"She doesn't need to work. She's a Peabody."

"Pea*brain*, more like."

Nick chuckled. "I love English girls," he told her, putting an arm around her and squeezing her tight.

Together they cruised the party. Nick pointed out literary agents, entertainment lawyers, fashion editors, clothes designers, architects and several men with names like Raleigh and Todd who mysteriously "ran their own funds."

These were, he told her, *la crème de la crème*.

"That's Chester Delaware, the writer." Nick waved a hand. "He's still not married—you should see the women fighting over him. Shrine's bought movie rights to one of his pieces for *Esquire*. And look, there's Shrine himself."

Shrine Wackfest turned out to be a plump man of about forty who could have been an accountant, except for his tremendous air of self-importance, evident even at a distance.

"Shouldn't we go and say hello?" Suze asked. "I'd like to thank him, at the very least."

Nick looked at her as if she had said something quaint. "Shrine just likes to have the right people here. He doesn't need to meet them."

Suze wanted to laugh, but at that moment she was distracted by a horrifying sight. "Look!" She tugged at Nick's jacket. "That plane's about to crash."

"That's the seaplane, you dope. Probably some celeb. Let's go see."

He took her glass and placed it with his own on a passing tray. Hand in hand, they walked to the terrace overlooking the shore and watched as the tiny plane splashed into the sea and glided right up to the end of the dock. The door opened and a girlish leg appeared, followed by the remainder of a woman in her sixties. She wore a tiny black dress with spaghetti straps and had strange orange hair cropped close.

"Hey, it's Lois!" Nick stood up to wave energetically and was eventually rewarded by a kiss blown from scarlet fingertips. "You must know Lois Trout, the fashion queen. She had a brain tumor, but they operated just in time. Now everyone's copying her hairstyle." He looked at his watch. "Will you be OK for a few minutes? I'll be right back."

"Not more calls?" Suze pouted.

Nick took her by the arm. "Come over and meet Melissa and the gang. They'll take care of you."

He led her back toward the house, introducing her as "my friend from London" to a group of knockout blondes, who made Suze feel like an overweight dwarf.

"I love Nick, don't you?" sighed Melissa, watching him go. "He's so cute. When I first came to the city he was *soooo* nice to me."

The others joined the chorus—a little too enthusiastically, Suze thought. "But none of you actually went out with him," she suggested, looking around the circle of faces.

"You mean, like his girlfriend?" Melissa gave a hoot of laughter. "How can you date a guy who's always partying? Besides, he's married to his mobile phone."

Their talk turned to the new crocheted tops from Galliano and Suze drifted away, unnoticed. Suddenly tired of all the chitter-chatter, she scooped up another cocktail and passed through an opening in the hedge. The pool was quiet and empty, a tempting blue. Suze thought how much fun it would be to stay behind with Nick when the others went to dinner. But she knew he would think that impossible. She began to understand the tension she had sensed in him from the moment he picked her up outside Schneider Fox. *He's on duty,* she thought.

In the stillness she became aware of a repetitive tapping noise which she traced to the Italian-style loggia at one end of the pool. She could hear somebody counting: "Thirty-five, thirty-six, thirty-seven . . ."

Inside, bouncing a ping-pong ball on a bat, was a girl of perhaps fifteen, wearing a simple white dress. She smiled at Suze, but went on counting until she missed. "Fifty-one!" she said breathlessly. "That's my best so far. I was trying to see if I could get to a hundred."

"Don't you like the party?"

"Sure." The girl shrugged. "It's just I don't know anybody."

"Join the club." Suze smiled.

The girl was astoundingly pretty, long-legged and athletic-looking with shiny dark hair to her shoulders and turquoise eyes fringed with black. She didn't look like a New Yorker, and her accent sounded Southern.

"Are you here with your parents?" Suze asked.

"No." The girl's disparaging tone gave the word about six separate syllables. She accompanied it by a screwball grin that made Suze laugh out loud. "I'm with some other girls—you know, models? My booker said I had to come, but I don't know what I'm supposed to do." She waggled her bat. "You want to play ping-pong?"

They played three games. Suze learned that she was in fact seventeen, that she had five brothers and sisters and a dog called Chummy, and that it was her dream to own a house with an upstairs. Until two months ago she had been working in a tobacco factory somewhere in North Carolina. Now she was signed to a big New York agency, who had decreed she should be called Pierre. Her real name was Jodie. It was clear that she was desperately homesick.

"My boyfriend's got a mobile phone," Suze offered. "I'm sure he'd let you ring your family if you wanted to."

"They all go bowling Friday night. But thanks."

Now it was almost dark. Suze became aware of a stir of social panic, as people began discussing where to eat. She saw them jabbing their phone buttons, frantic for a reservation. Over the whine of mosquitoes came the sound of cars beginning to rev. "Shall we go back to the party? I think we're all supposed to be going out to dinner."

"Finally," cried Jodie. "I could eat a horse."

The restaurant was outrageously overcrowded. At the entrance was a huge aquarium where you could look your dinner in the eye before dispatching it for slaughter. Nick took command of their group, cajoling the waitresses, arranging for tables to be put together, organizing the seating. Suze found herself at the other end of the table from him, next to a tubby man who seemed somewhat overdressed in a three-piece suit. Suze recognized him as Chester Delaware, "the writer."

"Sowah," he drawled, turning to her, "what do you make of this event?"

"It seems very impressive."

"Impressive . . ." He considered the word carefully. "Yes. I think it's meant to impress, don't you?"

"Well, I'm impressed."

"Good. Tell me, what line of work are you in? Or are you just famous for being famous?"

"I'm a designer."

"Clothes, magazines, software?"

"I'm in advertising. Schneider Fox, if that means anything to you."

"Aha. So you're one of those people who try to persuade us to buy things we don't really want or need, is that it?"

"Something like that." Suze wasn't sure if she was enjoying this conversation, but it was less vacuous than some of the snippets she had picked up from around the table.

"Fiber is the secret of my life, totally."

"She's a Virgo, so what can you expect?"

"I've become so spiritual since my surgery."

"Now don't take this the wrong way," said Delaware, waving a crab claw to illustrate the point, "but don't you think that advertising is almost always a form of lying? And if so, what does that say about the people who work in the business?"

Suze gave him a straight look. "It certainly can be a form of lying," she said, "just like journalism, or politics, or movies, or investment banking or practically anything else. I know that there are some corrupt people working in advertising, as there are everywhere. It's up to the individual to maintain his or her integrity, isn't it?"

The writer gave a supercilious smile. "How adorably naive." Then he turned to talk to his neighbor on the other side. Suze finished her meal in silence, stealing looks at Nick.

At last dinner was over. They shared a car with a group of others. Back at the house, a band was playing on the balcony; the pool was lit up. An immaculately dressed black man explained that, if they preferred, guests could watch a screening of Manfred's latest film in Shrine's private movie theater in the basement.

Suze danced with Nick, trying to recapture the magic of their first date, but his eyes were elsewhere, seeing who was with whom, checking out the scene. At around two in the morning he disappeared once again to phone Australia. Suze found a lounge chair near the pool and sat at the edge of a group, wondering if anyone would talk to her. Eventually one of the men turned around. He stared at her, then leaned over confidingly. "The last time I was here, Bliss Bogardo was sitting right where you are now. My God, she was beautiful." He gave a deep sigh of regret, and stood up. "Time for a refill."

Suze decided to see if the film was on, and was just approaching the house when she noticed a figure walking purposefully toward the parking area. She started to run, wobbling in her party shoes, calling out, "Nick? Wait for me."

He turned and gave her a tight smile. "I won't be long. I said I'd go get some stuff for Shrine." He jangled a key-ring.

"You're going in the car?" An image rose in Suze's mind of the two of them racing through the night with the top down, like Cary Grant and Grace Kelly, wind in their hair and moonlight on the ocean. "Great!" She put her arm through his. "I'll come with you."

Nick shook his head. "You don't want to come. Stay and enjoy the party."

"Honestly, I'd like to come. I've hardly seen you." She leaned into him coaxingly. "It's no fun partying without you."

Gently he disengaged himself. "Really, I have to go alone."

Suze searched his face. He looked guilty. She couldn't help glancing over at the car, wondering if he had another woman stashed in there. It was empty. "Where are you going?" she persisted. "Why can't I come?"

Nick looked away impatiently. "I told you. I have to get something. It's . . . private."

In the silence between them, sounds of the party came floating up from the shore—bursts of laughter, a girlish scream, a splash. Suze's perceptions sharpened. She could feel the gravel through the thin soles of her shoes. Watching Nick's troubled, handsome profile, she suddenly understood. "Oh, I get it."

Nick stared at the ground, saying nothing.

"Nick, why you?" Suze caught his hand, trying to make him look at her. "What if the police stopped you?"

"I just said I would." He stood stiff and unresponsive. "As a favor."

"Oh, really?" It seemed he was willing to do favors for anybody and everybody, except herself. She dropped his hand and folded her arms. "So you're a drug dealer now, is that it?"

"Don't be stupid." His head jerked up and they stared at each other for a tense moment. Then, almost as if he were pleading with her, he added, "It's not a crime to want to make people happy."

He stepped close and cupped her face in his hands. All the fight went out of her. Automatically she twisted her head to caress his fingers with her cheek.

"Listen," he said persuasively, "why don't you go back to the cottage and put on that black lacy thing and wait for me?"

She watched him drive off, waiting until the taillights had disappeared around the curving driveway and the roar of the engine had faded to nothing. A movement caught her eye and she saw that two of the maids were chatting with a man from the kitchens, sharing a smoke under the trees by the edge of the parking area. They were all still in uniform. The maids were Filipinos; the man looked Mexican. For the first time it occurred to Suze that every single one of the people she had met today was white.

Reluctant to go straight back to the cottage, Suze decided on one last walk along the beach. At the poolside, the party was getting frisky. Some of the women had discarded their swimsuits. She could hear rustlings and suppressed laughter in the hedges. Suze took off her shoes and wandered down the sand until she was alone with the stars and the moonlight and her own liquid shadow. The ocean whispered at her feet and Suze paused for a long while, letting it lap her toes. Then she turned back. The house was lit up like a historic monument. Architecturally, she now realized, it was a dog's breakfast. How Lawrence would have howled with pain at its jumble of Doric columns, *faux* Palladian pediments and Dutch window gabling. The thought made her smile sadly. "Did you love him?" Jay had asked. Suze sighed. Whatever she had felt, she knew now it wasn't the sort of love she wanted.

Back in the cottage again, Suze showered, perfumed and laced herself into her corset contraption. It looked great, but somehow she felt more sordid than naughty. She pulled on one of the guest dressing gowns and went out on the patio for a cigarette. Nick didn't like her smoking.

A few minutes later she heard laughter and peered out of the darkness to see a couple weaving their way down the lighted path. She recognized Manfred Zarg. To Suze's surprise, the girl with him was Jodie. She almost called a greeting, but thought better of it. None of these people were what they seemed. The man opened the door of the cottage next to Suze's and the two of them entered.

When Nick came back she was sitting in a low armchair, with *Vanity Fair* positioned discreetly across her lap and the table lamp on the dimmest setting. She felt the pose a little contrived, but it seemed to have the desired effect. Nick gave her a long, hard stare and growled, "Come here."

More out of nervousness than anything else, Suze shook her hair over one eye and answered, "Come and get me."

"Aah, so that's how you want it!" Within seconds Nick was out of his shoes and jacket. He pulled her out of the chair, spun her around and rammed her against the high wooden end of the bed.

"Hang on," she began, half laughing. "You could at least take off your clothes."

He yanked up her legs and tipped her back onto the bed. She felt the fastener between her legs pop open. "You'll like this," he said, plucking at his fly.

But she didn't. Not one bit. Her legs were in the air, her neck and chest squashed tight. "Nick, wait! I'm not—"

He wasn't listening. He thrust forward, pressing her thighs painfully wide. Suze bit her lip with the brutality of it. "Please . . ." she begged. She reached out for him, thinking that it would not be so bad if they were somehow in this together.

Nick plunged in deeper. His hands closed over her wrists, clamping them to the bed. "You little wildcat, you."

Suze began to get frightened. Her neck was so cramped that she could barely breathe. She thrashed back and forth, trying to get a purchase on the bed. Tears of pain and humiliation gathered in her eyes. Nick swayed above her, his face fierce with concentration on something she could not share. His eyes stared into hers, but they were blank, elsewhere. He might have been a stranger.

There was a sudden, piercing scream from next door. Suze heard a deep bellow of anger, then a horrible pulpy thud. Nick's hold relaxed for a second, and Suze managed to raise herself on one elbow. "What was that?" she croaked.

"They're having fun." He pushed her back down. "Like us."

There was more yelling, a crash of glass, then a much worse sound—a desperate, repetitive mewing. Suze couldn't bear it. She drew back her legs and pushed and kicked until finally Nick staggered back, trousers open, T-shirt rucked halfway up his chest. He had the dazed look of a bull in the ring.

In an instant Suze had rolled off the bed, snatched up the dressing gown and run to the door. Pain stabbed her body at each step.

"Where are you going?" Nick slurred.

Suze didn't even look around. Tying the belt tightly, she raced in bare feet across the prickly grass and rapped on the door of the cottage.

"Jodie, are you in there? Are you OK?"

Silence. Suze banged again, louder, pressing her ear to the door. She heard movement, a rustle. The door opened. There was the big Hollywood producer, eyebrows politely inquiring, formidable even in his paisley silk dressing gown, which he held clutched about him. The belt, she noticed, was missing. Across the back of one hand was a smear of scarlet lipstick. "Hi," he said blandly.

"Hello," Suze faltered. She became aware of her disordered appearance. The cottage was completely silent; the door at the end of the hallway was shut. Could she have made a mistake? She swallowed. "Is Jodie here?"

"It's four in the morning. Goodnight." He began to close the door.

Suze stepped forward. "I know she's here." She pressed her hands against the door, looking him in the eye. "I'll come and get her if I have to."

His small, scary eyes crawled over her face. Then he gave a big, phony smile and called over his shoulder, "You want to go home, girly?"

There was a stealthy sound from the end of the hall. Suze saw the handle turn, the door open, and Jodie appear, naked, holding a pathetic bundle of clothes over her crotch. Lipstick was smeared into a crude, baby-doll shape around her mouth and, as she crept nearer, Suze saw that someone had also drawn lipstick circles around her nipples. "Hello, Jodie," Suze said, trying to sound normal. "Do you want to come next door with me?"

Jodie stood silent, afraid. The man swung the front door wide. "Well go on, if you're going," he said genially. But as Jodie scuttled past, he thrust his face into hers and whispered viciously, "Why didn't you say you preferred girls?"

Suze put her arm around Jodie and hustled her next door. Nick had disappeared. Jodie sat on the edge of the bed, eyes wide, teeth chattering. She didn't seem hurt. Suze pried the bundle of clothes from her clenched fingers and drew in her breath. Around Jodie's wrists was a belt of paisley silk, tied so tight that Suze could not work it loose. Looking around the room, her eyes fell on Nick's jacket. Sure enough, in one pocket was his knife. She cut Jodie free, then got a warm, wet towel from the bathroom to bathe her wrists and wipe her face. "He put some white stuff, like sherbet, on his wrist and told me to sniff it," Jodie said, in a shivery whisper. "I knew it must be some drug, but I felt great—for a while. Then I was in his room and—"

Suze stroked her hair. "Shh. Don't think about it. You're safe now." She helped to dress Jodie in a pair of her own jeans and one of Nick's shirts, and then got dressed herself, feeling a stab of disgust as she took off the black thing and left it on the floor. She was checking her wallet, wondering if she had enough money to get Jodie a taxi home, when the front door of the cottage opened.

It was Nick, immaculately dressed and in control.

"All taken care of," he said to Jodie, with a smooth smile. He didn't even look at Suze. "There's a car outside, ready to take you back to the city now. I'll make sure your clothes get sent over." He came over and knelt down beside her, gently taking one of her hands. "OK, sweetheart? Mr. Zarg understands you just heard some bad family news and he'd like you to have this to cover your air ticket home." Turning Jodie's hand palm-upward, he closed her fingers over a wad of folded bills. Then he shepherded her outside, while Suze watched from the doorway. She saw how carefully he helped her into the car, and how he waited like a gentleman until it had driven away, and felt the beginnings of forgiveness. How would she have managed without him? As he came back up the path, she called out eagerly, "Oh, Nick, thank God—"

Nick put the palm of his hand on her breastbone and slammed her backward into the cottage, closing the door behind them with a flick of his foot. His face was hard. "Don't you *ever* do that to me again!"

Suze reeled against the wall. "Do what?"

Nick's eyes blazed. "You know who that is?" He jabbed his finger in the direction of the next-door cottage. "That's the producer who Shrine wants to make his movie. I told you that." He advanced on her accusingly, forcing her backward down the hall. "I even put you next to the goddamn writer at dinner. Shrine paid a million bucks for his story. The whole point of this weekend was to get the producer on board. Imagine how thrilled Shrine's going to be to hear what happened tonight."

Suze couldn't believe what she was hearing. "But that poor girl," she reminded him. "We couldn't just ignore her. He was *hurting* her." Unconsciously, Suze folded her arms around her own body.

"She was OK." Nick looked at her stonily. "What did she expect, going to a man's bedroom in the middle of the night?"

"She bloody well was not all right," Suze protested. "What's the matter with you? Anyone could see she was scared to death. He gave her coke. She didn't even know what it was!"

They glared at each other. Suze didn't say anything, but her thoughts must have showed in her face. "Don't you look at me like that." Nick's face snaked close to hers. "I didn't give her the drugs."

"You could have," she said hotly. "You were happy enough to leave me alone and go off to get them for your precious Shrine. Can't you see, Nick?" Her voice rose. She ached with pity and disappointment.

"He's not your friend. None of them are your friends. They treat you like—like some sort of pet poodle."

The second the words were out of her mouth, Suze regretted them. But it was too late. Nick grabbed her by the arm and yanked her close, breathing hard into her face. "And what's so great about you, huh? How come you get to look down that snooty nose of yours and tell me how to behave?"

"I'm sorry," Suze began. "I didn't mean—"

"You're not rich. You're not famous. You're not even that great-looking. Jesus, I spend my life surrounded by beautiful models. Who needs you?" He flung her away. "Stupid English bitch, I only took you out in the first place because Sheri asked me to."

The room went still. "What?" she asked wonderingly.

"You don't think I'd pick you of my own free will, do you?" His voice was scathing. "Sheri said you were lonely, that you needed distracting. It was a favor, for old times' sake."

Old times? Suze felt her whole body cramp. She twisted away, wrapping her hands around her stomach.

"Yeah, that's right." Nick stood at her shoulder, vibrating with anger. "Sheri and I have been around the block a couple of times. And I'll tell you one thing." He jabbed his finger into the flesh of her arm. "Sheri knows who's boss in the bedroom."

Suze pressed her hands to her ears. "Stop it," she sobbed. "Please."

But he couldn't stop. "Little Miss Sixties Wild Child, Siouxie with an *X*. You know what you are? You're a fraud. 'Ni-ick, look at me in my sexy underwear. Look at me playing peek-a-boo through my hair.'" His mimicry was unbearable. He pulled her around to face him. "I'm the somebody." Nick thumped his chest. "I'm the one inviting you to great parties and introducing you to important people. What have you got to give me that's so great?"

His face was ugly with dislike. Suze couldn't believe that he was capable of looking at her like this. "I don't give a stuff about the parties and the people," she burst out. "I thought we liked each other. I thought we were equals. I didn't know it was a contest."

"Answer my question. What have you got to give me?" he repeated.

Suze bent her head, sobbing. "I gave you—"

"You gave me nothing," he shouted, beside himself. "New York is full of girls ready to lay down their bodies at the lift of my finger. Girls prepared to just do it. There's none of this crap about equality. I don't need some little feminist bitch from London telling me how to behave."

"Feminist?" Suddenly Suze was furious. Her head snapped back. "It's not feminist to dislike old men tying up young girls. It's not feminist to object to being practically raped. It's not feminist to think men and women can treat each other like human beings." She was spitting, gasping, smearing tears across her face. "You disgust me," she shouted. "I disgust myself." Her blurred vision focused on something small and shiny lying on a low table: Nick's knife. She snatched it up and flicked it open. "Let's just complete the image, shall we?" she shouted. She grabbed a hunk of her hair and slashed at it with the knife.

"Suze . . . don't!"

It was horribly easy. The hair came away in her hand, soundlessly, like the stalk from a rotten apple. "Is this how you really see me?" She hurled the hair at his shocked face. It drifted harmlessly to the floor. "Is this *feminist* enough for you?"

One more slash; then the delirium left her. Suddenly she felt close to collapse. "I gave you—" Suze could barely speak now. She took a shuddering breath. "I gave you myself."

Then she flung the knife on to the floor at his feet, snatched up her wallet and ran out of the cottage.

It was already light outside. Along the horizon a line of violent orange was seeping into pale gray sky. Suze ran blindly. She could hear herself panting. Suddenly she was in the car-park. A chauffeur was leaning against the bumper of his car, arms comfortably folded, waiting. When he saw Suze stumbling toward him he straightened in alarm.

"Are you going back to New York?" Suze shouted in desperation. "Could you give me a lift?"

"Excuse me," called a petulant voice behind her. "This is my car."

Suze turned to see a tall, skinny girl in sunglasses approaching across the dewy lawn. She wore skin-tight white leggings, cut off at the calf; her wet, newly washed hair was tied back with red polka-dot ribbon. Behind her trailed a Mexican houseboy, eyes lowered, carrying a gigantic suitcase in one hand and a set of brightly colored workout weights in the other.

"Could I come with you?" Suze tried to sound normal. "I have to get home. It's an emergency."

"Impossible. I'm doing a fashion shoot on the top of the Empire State in two hours' time. I require absolute privacy."

"Please," Suze begged. Damn it, she was starting to cry again.

The girl walked straight past her. Suze watched as she folded one long leg like a chicken, ducked her head and climbed into the car. She settled herself on the springy seat, big enough for four, shifting her tiny bum this way and that so that the ridiculous hair-bow bobbed up and down. It was the last straw.

Suze stepped after her and thrust her head into the car. "Who do you think you are anyway?" she yelled. "Minnie Mouse?"

There was a hiss of shock. Very slowly the girl lowered her sunglasses to examine every inch of Suze's ravaged face. "I'm Bliss Bogardo, of course. Get in, honey."

Chapter Twenty-two

My life is over, thought Lloyd, as he wheeled his trolley along the supermarket aisles. Now that he was unemployed he'd joined the underclass of sad failures condemned to drudgery. There were a surprising number of men doing the same thing: Lloyd felt sure they were all rejects like him. How long before he too was wearing tracksuit bottoms and zipped nylon jackets with ditzy logos on them, forced to live on processed food?

It was Sunday afternoon. Betsy had sent him out to do the shopping. "Since you're not contributing financially," she had said briskly, "you might as well help me with the chores." She was right, of course. No law laid down that shopping was women's work. In the pre-Betsy days he'd enjoyed nothing more than dropping by Balducci's and emerging with more cheeses and salamis and weird-looking fungi than any sane person could eat. Nevertheless, he now felt demeaned. Hypnotized by Muzak, dizzied by the bright assault of thousands of products, he shuffled along at a depressive's pace. *Coffee*. Check. *Cereal*. Check. *Butter*. Check. *Flour*—hmmm. Plain? Wholemeal? Self-raising? Lloyd clutched Betsy's neatly written list at eye level as he studied the packages on the shelf. In the end he decided to take one of each.

All week he had floated in limbo, confused and defeated. For the first time since he'd been a teenager he had watched television indiscriminately, one program after another, until news bulletins and car ads and hospital dramas and the mating habits of marmosets created a cacophony in his head, loud enough to silence the anxieties that came in the night. He had taken to walking at random through London, sometimes for five or six hours, exhausting his body.

He still couldn't grasp what had happened. He'd heard nothing from anyone at Schneider Fox, not since a motorcycle messenger had dropped off a box containing his few personal possessions from the London office on Wednesday afternoon. After Harry's threat of legal action, he dared not initiate contact himself. Sheri's reaction to his one telephone call had been mortifying. She thought he was a traitor. They all did. What hurt was how easily everyone seemed to accept his guilt. Dee Dee had not called. No one was interested in his side of the story. No one seemed to believe he might have a different story to tell.

The life he had thought was his had been sliced clean through. A strange thought occurred to Lloyd. Could his father have felt this way?

Betsy was doing her best to be supportive. She had begun to suggest job opportunities elsewhere. "I'm sure Daddy could get you a position at Champs to tide us over," she offered one day at breakfast. Betsy's father was a taciturn workaholic who had more or less cornered the market in a new kind of dog food that came in odorless pellets. "A little while back they were looking for someone just like you in their New Jersey office." The walk that Lloyd had taken after that remark held the record.

Jay was the one person whose faith in him was absolute: "Get yourself a lawyer, man. Fight back! Beat the bastards!"

But Lloyd couldn't. He didn't have the will. He didn't know any English lawyers. What could he prove anyway? He had not even dared to call Susannah Wilding about the apartments. She was sure to be wondering if he and Betsy were returning early; it was bad manners not to put her mind at rest. But he kept putting it off, almost as if he were embarrassed. Why, for heaven's sake? This was a woman he hadn't even met. He knew nothing about her except that she was messy, wore black garter belts, couldn't cook, liked Bessie Smith, went out with men a lot and was one cat short. Betsy had made him promise to call her this afternoon. He was not looking forward to it.

After an hour and a half Lloyd had been up or down every aisle at least three times, backtracking for missing items. Curiously, he still couldn't find any English muffins. Instead, he bought a bag of something labeled American doughnuts—clearly a luxury item from its classy packaging and stupendous price. Waiting in the long checkout line, he opened the bag and drew out the smallest doughnut he had ever seen. He took a bite. Tasteless, dry, larded with fat, drenched in powdery sugar: yup, they were American, all right. How delightfully unpredictable the English were.

At the store exit there was a large area lined with magazine racks. As Lloyd carried out his bags, he noticed the latest issue of *Admag* and steeled himself to take a look at the job ads. You never knew, they might need copywriters in Outer Mongolia. He thumbed through the back pages, recoiling from the usual inflated vocabulary of "key postholders," "aggressive initiatives" and "strategic targets." There was nothing suitable. It chilled him to see that practically every post stipulated an applicant under thirty-five.

As he let the remaining pages flip past, preparing to return the magazine to the rack, Lloyd was horrified to catch sight of his own photograph. The caption underneath read: "*Rockwell . . . Did he jump or was he pushed?*" Lloyd clutched the magazine closely, as guilty as a murderer confronted with his own "WANTED" poster, and scanned the article with mounting trepidation.

> Mystery surrounds the abrupt departure from Schneider Fox of blue-eyed boy Lloyd Rockwell, halfway through his four-week stint in the UK. MD Harry Fox is keeping schtumm, but one internal communication seen by *Admag* referred to an "unacceptable breach of client confidentiality." Rockwell, currently in London as part of SF's transatlantic exchange program, has been unavailable for comment. It is not known whether he will be seeking another post in the industry.
>
> Rockwell had been tipped as a possible successor to SF's aging New York boss, the legendary Bernie Schneider. Rockwell's US colleagues confess themselves "shocked" by his unspecified

transgression. Rockwell was recognized as one of the top copywriters in the business and had been responsible for many of the agency's most innovative campaigns, in particular those for Passion Airlines. His unexpected departure follows hard upon that of Passion's UK minder, Julian Jewel, who quit to join Sturm Drang only three weeks ago. Speculation now inevitably surrounds the future of the Passion account. If Passion dumps SF, Sturm Drang would seem an obvious alternative.

Meanwhile, a persistent rumor links SF with Passion's chief rival, Stateside Airlines. Yesterday Harry Fox dismissed such speculation as "Total balls. We would never contemplate taking on two such directly competing accounts."

Perhaps not . . . but if Passion were to quit the agency, the way would be clear for SF to pitch for Stateside. Expect more musical chairs as rivalry for the lucrative transatlantic trade hots up . . .

Lloyd found he was trembling. He slapped the magazine shut. *I didn't do it!* he wanted to shout—perhaps had shouted. Certainly the uniformed assistant was eyeing him suspiciously from behind her cash register. He took the magazine over and paid for it. When she gave him his change he fumbled the handover. Coins spilled from his hand and went spinning and bouncing in all directions. Lloyd retrieved them from the floor, crouching like a beggar. His humiliation was now complete.

When he got home he found Betsy engrossed in tourist leaflets: the Wordsworth Experience, Tartan Heritage Trail, *Braveheart* Country. He showed her the *Admag* article.

"Oh, no . . ." She paled. "How could they do this? I told them we didn't want any publicity."

"Told them?" Lloyd was stunned. "You mean, they called up? Here? Why didn't you tell me?"

"I thought you'd be upset. I was trying to be tactful."

Lloyd was too angry to speak. He did not need protecting: he was not a child. He stomped into the kitchen and put away the groceries, banging cupboard doors. In a fever of self-pity he wiped down the kitchen counters, emptied the garbage, replaced the plastic liner and cleaned the stove. If he was to be a domestic drudge, he might as well act like one. Finally, when he'd run out of excuses for further procrastination, he picked up the telephone and dialed.

"Hello?" said a muffled voice.

She sounded as if she were still in bed. Lloyd checked his watch, wondering if he'd got the times mixed up, but no—it was eleven in the morning in New York. She couldn't be asleep. Of course, there were other things people could do in bed.

"Susannah? I'm sorry to disturb you. Am I calling at a bad time?"

"Oh, it's you." Her voice was flat, unwelcoming. So she too believed he was a crook.

"Look, I'm sure this conversation is as awkward for you as it is for me. I guess you heard I lost my job . . ."

"Yeah." She sounded barely interested. Maybe she had the flu.

". . . and I thought we should discuss the apartments."

"OK."

"OK what?"

"OK, let's discuss them. You want to come back tomorrow? Fine. You want to stay another ten years? Fine." Her voice faltered. "I really couldn't care less."

Lloyd was taken aback. Had he upset her? While he searched for the right response, he heard an unmistakable sound. She was crying.

"Susannah . . . are you all right?"

"Yes. No. I don't know." She sounded desperately sad.

"Is it anything you want to talk about?"

There was a loud sniff. "I just split up with my boyfriend, that's all."

"Do you want me to hang up?"

"No, it's just normal. My life's always in a mess."

"I'm sorry. It wasn't—" He hesitated. "Not . . . Mr. Hollandaise Sauce?"

"Don't!" He heard a ragged sob, followed by more sniffing.

"Are you in bed?" he asked.

"Yes. Why?"

"Bedside table. Second drawer. Kleenex."

He heard a fumble. "Thanks." Then she said, more robustly, "It wasn't my cooking, at any rate. He didn't even turn up for dinner, the rat."

Lloyd smiled at this flash of bravado. "There you go. Rats aren't worth crying over."

"I'm crying for myself. I'm so stupid." There was a wavery sigh. "I think I'll give up men." She blew her nose somewhat fiercely, then added, "Sorry about this. It doesn't matter."

"Susannah, of course it matters. I wish I could make you feel better."

"There is one thing you could do to cheer me up," she said at last.

"What's that?"

"Start calling me Suze. The last person to call me Susannah was my headmistress."

"OK. Listen . . . Suze, if you want to come back right away, I'm sure we can find somewhere else to go." Lloyd couldn't believe what he was saying. Betsy had instructed him not to let her come back until next weekend at the earliest.

"I'm not running away," she answered, with surprising force. "I came here to have fun and I'm bloody well going to."

"Good for you." To his surprise, Lloyd found that he was almost enjoying this conversation. For the first time since Tuesday his gloom lifted. "I know what, why don't I tell you one of my jokes?"

"No, thanks."

"Let's see . . . Two guys meet in the hardware store. One says, 'I gave my mother-in-law a new chair for Christmas.' 'Really?' says the other. 'How does she like it?' 'I don't know,' comes the reply. 'She hasn't plugged it in yet.'" Lloyd heard a watery snort. "See, you laughed."

"That was sheer pity. It's a terrible joke."

"You try, then."

"I can't . . . There's only one joke I can ever remember."

"That's the one I want to hear."

A big sigh. "If you must. Here goes: Where does Caesar keep his armies?"

"You know, I've always wondered that. Where *does* Caesar keep his armies?"

"Up his sleevies!"

Lloyd's splutter of laughter turned into an unstoppable, childish giggle that brought Betsy into the living room, eyebrows raised in mild inquiry. Seeing that he was still on the telephone, she waggled her fist, miming the gesture of tipping a watering can. Lloyd sobered up. "Betsy's just come in. She wants to know how her plants are."

There was a long, guilty silence.

"Excellent!" Lloyd exclaimed, nodding reassuringly at Betsy. "I'll tell her. Keep up the good work."

Simultaneously he heard Suze mutter, "It's not as bad as killing people's cats." Touché.

Betsy was hovering, as if she might ask Lloyd to interrogate Suze further on household matters. "I guess I'd better go now," he said.

"OK." She sounded surprised. Had he been too brusque?

"And take a tip from me. If you're feeling down, don't watch TV and drink, especially at the same time. You'll want to cut your throat."

"What do you suggest instead? Rearranging my knickers drawer?"

What a great word "knickers" was, so much more evocative than "underpants" or—Lloyd addressed himself to her question. "Well . . . you like Fred Astaire, don't you?"

"How do you know that?"

"The picture on your wall—which I love, by the way. Nobody can listen to Astaire and cry at the same time. I've got a terrific tape. You'll find it—"

"Don't tell me. Popular music, subcategory vocalists, sub-sub category male, under A. It's taken me three weeks, but I've cracked your system."

"Oh." She was teasing him. He sort of liked it. "It's better than piling everything up into a great Leaning Tower of Pisa and waiting for it to fall over," he retorted.

"The Leaning Tower, may I point out, is still standing. And explain this: why have you got Fats Waller under P?"

"Ah. That's P for piano."

She laughed—a real, warm-blooded, spontaneous laugh. Lloyd felt strangely gratified. He could picture exactly where she was, her view of his Stella print above the chest of drawers, how the sun would be beating at the windows in a yellow glare. He caught a distant brash blast of traffic from the street. So far he hadn't missed New York one iota; now he felt a prickle of nostalgia.

"Sorry I blubbed," she said.

" 'Blubbed'?"

"That's posh girlspeak for sobbing your heart out. It's what you do at boarding school when the lacrosse captain snubs you."

"If you say so."

"And thanks for the pep talk."

"Any time. Why don't you get up now and put on some music, and—?" He stopped. What did women like to do to make themselves feel better? He had an inspiration. "And wash your hair," he concluded, feeling very clever.

"Ohhhhh . . ." It was a rising howl of anguish.

"What did I say?"

"*Nothing*. God, I hate men!"

And that was it. She had hung up. Suddenly Lloyd was back in the red living room, alone, with rain rustling out of a gray sky and a dead phone in his hand.

Suze replaced the receiver and collapsed back into her pile of pillows, staring at the white ceiling. She knew it well. She had lain here in the stifling heat like a beached starfish, ever since Bliss Bogardo's car had dropped her back at the apartment early yesterday morning. Lloyd was right. Now it was time to get up and confront the world. She would begin with herself.

Her legs felt wobbly as she stumbled across the carpet into the bathroom and prepared to stand on tiptoe, as usual, to see into the mirror. Even though she had steeled herself for this moment, Suze was shocked by what she saw. Her eyes were squinty and pink, her skin blotched from hours of crying. But the stomach-churning tragedy was her hair. Instead of tumbling waywardly to her shoulders, it flopped jaggedly to ear level in the worst kind of pudding-basin shape, as if cut by a blind maniac. Her neck was laid pathetically bare, and in the unforgiving light she saw faint lines etched across it. With nothing to distract the eye, her nose looked as big as the Flatiron building. Suze gazed in misery. This was the real her: dull and plain and old.

Abruptly she turned away and sat on the edge of the bath, rocking back and forth, her face in her hands. Nick's words still screeched through her brain: "bitch," "fraud," "Little Miss Siouxie with an *X*." Suze ached with humiliation. She had an image of herself tossing her hair like a spoiled child, telling Nick about the Harley-Davidson and Twiggy and smoking joints, and how the things other thirty-year-olds wanted were too boring for her. No wonder he had thought she would go along with all that stuff at the Hamptons. Fresh tears seeped through her fingers. No one had wrecked her life for her. No one had needed to. She had done it herself.

For some reason Lloyd's voice saying, "Not Mr. Hollandaise Sauce . . .?" in his funny, hesitant way floated into her thoughts, and almost made her smile. She wiped her tears. He had been very nice to her. Mind you, he couldn't see how ghastly she looked. She wondered what he looked like. Her image of him was confused. There was the boring businessman she had first pictured; but how could Jay have a friend like that? It was obvious he was hopeless at his job, and worse; he had got himself fired, after all. But today he had sounded . . . nice, kind, sympathetic. Suze made a horrible grimace at these saccharine words. Since when had she cared whether a man was "nice"? Next thing she knew she'd be on the flower rota at the village church.

Would Fred Astaire really cheer her up? She could at least give it a try. A little while later she was standing on *Webster's Dictionary* in front of the bathroom mirror, a pair of scissors in her hand, while old Fred lilted on about dancing and romancing, which rhymed in American but made you feel silly if you were English and tried to sing along.

Though not as silly as her haircut. Each time she thought she had evened up one bit, she had only to move her head for new strands to appear from nowhere and ruin the effect. At this rate she was going to end up looking like a principal boy. She would have to go out early tomorrow and get it cut properly, before work, pretending it was some divinely divine new style that only she was hip enough to have cottoned on to. As Suze twisted her head to reach one last dangling lock at the back, she lost her balance and fell off the dictionary. Why was that wretched mirror so inconveniently high? Then it occurred to her that this was where Lloyd shaved. He must be very tall.

Suze remembered the box of photographs she had once found at the bottom of one of the cupboards. She had nothing else to do today, and she was curious. It would do no harm to take a peek.

Sitting cross-legged on the bed she removed the lid of the shoebox with a guilty thrill, promising herself that she would replace it at once if the contents were too personal. Trying not to disturb the order, she started at the bottom, fingering through the photographs, pausing at the ones that looked interesting. The first picture she picked out showed a cool dude in shades, sitting on the outsize hood of a huge American car: not Lloyd, obviously. But the next, a boy of about fifteen, wearing shorts and a singlet with a number on the front, could have been him. He was tall and long-legged, with dark hair curling about his ears and a frank, blue-eyed stare that made him look very American. He was holding a cup and grinning, as if he had just won a race. There were several more of the same boy—some younger, some a little older, one clearly with his parents. The father looked just like the boy, but with a stylish, adult charm. Another showed two much older girls as well—sisters, perhaps. They were an attractive family, all tall, with a glow of American prosperity, photographed on boats, on beaches, at barbecues, often posed in front of the same colonial-style red-brick house. She found one picture of an older Lloyd, looking daft in an academic gown and mortarboard, tassel dangling. Every detail of his pose showed the struggle between pride and self-conscious mortification. Suze smiled, remembering how she had felt when she went to secondary school and her parents insisted on photographing her in her new school uniform.

Suddenly Suze came across a face she recognized. Here was Jay—looking very street-cred in ripped jeans and the sort of skin-tight T-shirts people wore in the early eighties. Behind him was a huge, flat-topped rock rising out of sand and scrub that made her think of Texas or Utah. This must have been taken on the famous trip across the States that Jay had told her about. Jay was thinner and younger and less blond, but the quizzical smile was the same. She felt a surge of affection. There were several more photos of Jay, some with another man who Suze gradually realized must be Lloyd. Suze's interest perked up. Grown-up, with nicely muscled legs and hair funkily long, Lloyd was distinctly tasty. He was, in fact, Mr. Mean and Moody himself from the car photo she had first picked out.

The car featured prominently in a series of pictures that plotted Lloyd's and Jay's course west to east across America, some showing Jay in barman's kit with bow tie and Lloyd in the kind of white uniform they wore in hamburger joints. So that's when he had learned to cook. Other shots showed Lloyd playing the piano in dark bars. One had a swirly inscription on the back that read, "Hi, lover boy! Dontcha forget the Blue Coyote and your everlovin' Darlene," with a smiley face drawn underneath the signature. Well, well.

More girls appeared in pictures probably taken at college—haunted-looking Sylvia Plath wannabes in black, thoroughbred blondes, good-sport types in NYU sweatshirts. Then there were a couple of black-and-white shots taken at professional functions—Lloyd wearing a black bow tie in a party of strangers, giving a speech, shaking hands with a nameless dignitary. Right at the top of the box Suze found an envelope of typical holiday snapshots. Many of them featured a slim, serious-looking woman in white linen and a straw peek-a-boo hat, her arm laced through Lloyd's.

Suze sighed. Of course: the happy ending. Coupledom, domesticity, swagged curtains, dinner parties. How depressingly predictable. Scowling, she packed the photos back into the box and replaced it in the wardrobe. Then she got dressed and went out for a long walk, trudging around Central Park with her hands in her pockets, eyes averted from human contact. She could not stop herself thinking of Nick and the time they had come here together. Then she had felt desirable, pretty, happy, fun. And Nick—had he been pretending all along?

On the way back she stopped at a take-away place and ordered a pizza the size of a dustbin lid. She ate the whole thing straight out of the carton, sitting at the dining room table as the light faded, watching the couple opposite go through their usual routine: fetching dishes, eating, talking, watching television. After the pizza she felt fat, garlicky, unlovely and unlovable. She would change her life, she decided, flicking the ragged ends of her hair with a fingernail. Fresh fruit, exercise, eight pints of mineral water per day, as recommended by women's magazines: monastic discipline would rule. She could almost feel how it would be, her skin glowing, her body smoothly muscled. A new energy would radiate from every pore. She would be self-reliant and mysterious. "Heavens, Suze, you look marvelous!" people would tell her. "Been on holiday?" The wonder would no longer be why she was not married, but where in the world to find a man good enough for her.

The fantasy sustained her for the time it took to drop her clothes on the Rockwell carpeting, brush her teeth, rub in her night cream and climb into the rumpled bed. She lay on her side in the dark, listening to her heartbeat echoing in her ear—boom-boom, boom-boom—and wondered if she was going to be alone for the rest of her life.

Chapter Twenty-three

"Glad you could make it, Ms. Wilding."

From the far end of the conference room, Bernie Schneider stared coldly at Suze. There were perhaps fifteen people already seated around the table, their paraphernalia of notepads, pens, artwork and paper cups ranged neatly before them. The clock on the wall read nine thirteen.

Fuck a duck. How was she to know that this morning's meeting would be brought forward to nine? Suze considered herself bloody brilliant to have found a hairdresser prepared to squeeze her in at such an early hour; evidently it hadn't been early enough. She had not planned quite such a triumphal entrance for her new shorn look.

The only empty seat was next to Sheri. Suze slunk into it, feeling a faint distaste at her proximity to the woman Nick had said was so great in the bedroom. Sheri acknowledged her presence by the faintest stretch of her lips. Suze could sense that she was excited, like an actress waiting in the wings. Her shining blue eyes were fixed on Bernie, waiting for him to continue.

"OK, people," he resumed, "end of spiel. Our mission, I repeat, is to convince Passion that Schneider Fox is still the right agency for them. I'm going to hand over to Sheri now to outline the concepts we're working up for Friday. She's in the driving seat on this one, and I want you to know that she has my full confidence."

"Thank you, Bernie." In her suit of ice blue, golden hair pulled back into an immaculate French pleat, Sheri looked like the Queen of the Valkyries. She glanced around the table, establishing eye contact.

Then she began to speak, in a low, fervent voice. "This is an inspirational moment for us all. We have the opportunity to transition into a whole new phase of our creative partnering with Passion. Many of us are experiencing sadness and shock about Lloyd Rockwell, but remember the famous quotation: 'No man is an island.' This business isn't about individuals. It's not about egos. It's about sharing, about teamwork, about giving 100 percent. On Friday I want to walk into that presentation knowing that each and every one of you is with me in spirit, saying, 'Go, Sheri! Go, Schneider Fox!'" She raised her fist in a power salute and there was a spontaneous outbreak of applause from around the table. Suze twisted her hands in her lap, embarrassed. "Now," Sheri continued briskly, "to work."

For the next two hours they bandied statistics and research data, examined reels and debated visuals, choosing and refining the concepts for the final presentation. Dee Dee kept her head down throughout, silently taking notes. Schneider watched Sheri with a proprietorial half-smile, occasionally lowering his head to record great thoughts into his tiny Dictaphone—probably ordering his lunch, Suze thought, eyeing his triple chin. At the end he roused himself to make the usual corporate pep talk about how important it was for the company that this presentation should succeed. He expected total commitment, even if that meant working around the clock. Suze flushed a little when she heard this. Tonight, she decided, she would work late. After all, she had nothing else to do.

As the meeting broke up, Sheri indicated to Suze that she should follow. She walked purposefully back to her office with Suze in her wake, pausing only to dump a load of papers on Dee Dee's desk. Once they were both inside her office she shut the door and leaned back against it, closing her eyes and exhaling deeply.

"Are you all right?" asked Suze.

Sheri opened her eyes again and beamed a smile. "Absolutely fine. Goodness, what an original hairstyle! You English are so unconventional." Her eyes narrowed assessingly. "You know, I think you should be at the presentation on Friday. Ross Bannerman himself is coming. You fit the Passion image. You can wear one of your strange outfits." She frowned. "No bare flesh, of course. Now, I need your help . . ."

Suze left Sheri's office feeling cheered. It seemed that she was to have a key role in the upcoming presentation. Hah! She wasn't a nobody, whatever Nick had said. Men always liked to make you feel small; it was women who were supportive in a crisis. So what if Nick and Sheri had once slept together? It was a free world, and the incident was way in the past. And even if Sheri had suggested that Nick take her out, wasn't that just the kind of consideration one woman showed to another? She had been wrong to feel humiliated. It was a sisterly thing.

Suze decided to reward herself with a tripette to the street-level coffee shop. There had been no time for breakfast this morning, and her nicotine level was dangerously low. As she walked down the corridor she could see poor old Dee Dee, slaving away at the photocopier. Something about her stance, still and secretive, troubled Suze, and as she came closer she understood why. Dee Dee was crying. Suze put an arm around her shoulder. "Hey, what's up?" she asked gently.

Dee Dee shook her head, unable to speak. She was clutching a sheet of paper—a letter, perhaps. Suze looked more closely, wondering if it might be a love letter, but it was just office stuff. She rubbed Dee Dee's arm encouragingly. "Tell me."

"His handwriting . . ." Dee Dee wailed. "It brings it all back. And I feel so guilty. I haven't even spoken to him." She began to sob.

Suze could make no sense of this, but it was clear that Dee Dee needed comforting. "Come on, let's get out of here." She turned her toward the elevators. "What you need is some serious caffeine."

Once downstairs, Suze settled Dee Dee at an outdoor table, found her some paper napkins to mop up her tears and bought them a coffee and croissant each.

"I'm on a diet," Dee Dee sniffed.

"Bollocks."

Dee Dee gave a weak, hiccuping laugh. "What does 'bollocks' mean?"

"Tell you later. First of all, you're going to tell me what's upsetting you."

Dee Dee was still holding the piece of paper in her lap. She laid it on the table.

"Lloyd wrote this. It was in the pile Sheri wanted me to Xerox." She raised round, guileless eyes, shimmering with tears. "He was so special. I'll never find another boss like him. He made me feel like I was someone important, one of the team, not just some dumbo secretary."

"Lloyd was your boss?" Suze was surprised. "I thought Sheri was."

Dee Dee glowered. "She is now. You missed the part of the meeting where Bernie announced that he'd made her acting creative director. 'Acting' is right. If I wasn't a nice girl I'd call her a nasty word beginning with B."

" 'Banana'? 'Blancmange'? 'Bandicoot'?" Suze was rewarded by a glimmering smile. "Come on, Dee Dee. Sheri may be a bit bossy but you have to admit she's frightfully impressive. It's great to see a woman in charge, for once."

"You wouldn't understand," Dee Dee said bitterly. "You're one of her favorites."

"Well . . ." Suze hesitated. This wasn't the right moment to blow her own trumpet, though surely it was obvious that Sheri had singled her out because of her talent?

"She even gave you Lloyd's office, right next door to hers."

"Is that why you weren't very friendly to me at first?"

Dee Dee looked embarrassed. "It's just the way you took right over, looking so perky and fiddling with his stuff. It's like you knew he was never coming back."

"Don't be ridiculous." Suze bridled at Dee Dee's accusing tone. "I knew nothing about Lloyd when I came here. I still don't. But I've heard the rumors. Sheri's been really worried about the Passion account—quite rightly, as it turns out. Lloyd was letting things slide badly."

"I don't believe that for one minute." Two bright spots appeared on Dee Dee's plump cheeks. "Lloyd's work for Passion has been the talk of the industry. He's won awards. He's been asked to give seminars at business schools." She glared at Suze defiantly.

Suze sipped her coffee. Dee Dee's fervor was convincing. "So you thought Lloyd was good at his job?"

Dee Dee looked at her as if she were mad. "He's brilliant! Everyone knows that. Why do you think they made him creative director?" She leaned eagerly toward Suze. "The thing about Lloyd is that he can take even the crummiest company and find at least one good thing about it. That's what he focuses on. That way, he says, you've not only got the trust of the customer but you make the company feel so good about itself that it starts raising its standards. Once your campaigns are positive, you can make them fun. Lloyd is good at that."

Suze nodded slowly. This was the way she liked to work too. "And he didn't ever strike you as disorganized?"

"Lloyd?" Dee Dee burst out laughing. "Lloyd's lists are famous. I used to kid him about having to write a list every night of the clothes he was going to wear the next day."

"He forgot about the Matsuhana invitation," Suze reminded her.

Dee Dee pursed her lips. "Lloyd gave Sheri a five-page briefing memo on that a week before you even arrived. I typed it myself."

Suze chased the last flakes of croissant round her plate with her finger, feeling uneasy. She began to replay the tape of the last three weeks in her mind, editing out everything Sheri had told her about Lloyd. She remembered Lloyd's neatly sharpened pencils, his fiendishly precise music-cataloging system, the way he had lied so poorly about who had dispatched Mr. Kipling.

"Dee Dee, you said you felt guilty about Lloyd. Why?"

"I was the one who took the message that incriminated him. I even wrote it down, for everyone to see." Dee Dee sank her head in her hand.

"That wasn't your fault. He did get the call, after all."

"Yes, but when I gave Lloyd the message, he didn't know who it was from," Dee Dee argued. "He kept going over and over it. I know he wasn't lying." She sighed. "Anyway, the really bad thing was that the London office found a confidential list in Lloyd's briefcase. I wormed the story out of Bernie's assistant. No one knows how he got it, but that was pretty much the nail in his coffin."

Suze felt her face flame. "List?" she asked casually. Surely it couldn't be the list she had e-mailed to Lloyd?

"Confidential client information. I don't know what exactly, but whatever it was . . ." Dee Dee drew her finger across her throat. "The thing is, I can't believe Lloyd would ever do anything underhanded. He's not that kind of person."

"But—" Suze began. Then she shut her mouth. This needed thinking about. For the first time it occurred to her that Lloyd might be wholly innocent, as Dee Dee claimed. If it wasn't for her, he might still have a job. She felt rather sick.

The streets were beginning to fill up now, with office workers on their lunch break. They looked busy and focused, rushing to fit in their errands or hurrying back to their desks carrying food in brown paper bags. Suze found herself imagining what it would be like not to have a job, to stare out of the window day after day after day, watching other people with appointments to make and trains to catch, while the phone stayed silent and there was no reason even to get out of bed. "Dee Dee," she said briskly, "I want you to show me that message book you mentioned. I want to see that Matsuhana memo. And I'd like to borrow this, if I may." She picked up the piece of paper with Lloyd's handwriting.

"Sure." A spark of hope kindled in Dee Dee's eyes. "What are you going to do?"

"We'll see." Suze hadn't the faintest clue. But she thought she knew where to start. "Tell me honestly, why do *you* think Sheri's been so nice to me, treating me like a . . ."

"Teacher's pet?"

Ouch. "I was going to say protégée."

"You're an outsider. You're out of the political loop. You'd believe anything she said. Also—" Dee Dee stopped short.

"Yes?"

"Well, look at you." Dee Dee waved a hand. "Sheri probably assumed you'd be thinking about clothes and boyfriends all the time and you wouldn't notice too much what was going on in the office."

Suze felt her skin prickle. Was this really how other people saw her? An empty-headed bimbo, too self-obsessed to care what went on outside her own tiny world? It was as if someone had handed her a mirror into which she had smiled confidently, only to see an ugly stranger. *I'm not like that!* she wanted to protest. But Dee Dee's candor was devastating. Perhaps she *was* like that. One way or another she had hurt people—Dee Dee, Lloyd, even Nick.

"I see," she said faintly.

Dee Dee was gazing critically at her. "Why did you cut your hair?"

"What?" For a moment Suze didn't know what she was talking about. She put up a hand and fingered the crisply cut ends, remembering the hot, darkened room in the Hamptons—the tangle of white sheets, Nick's savage face, his knife spinning to the carpet. She thought of those self-pitying hours spent staring into the mirror at her ruined looks and felt ashamed. It didn't seem important any more.

She summoned a self-deprecating, sideways grin. "A success—not?"

"I liked it better long," Dee Dee confessed. "You looked more human."

By that evening Suze's new role as a dedicated workaholic was beginning to pall. Everyone else had gone home hours ago. Daylight had faded, to be replaced by a nighttime ration of strip lighting that functioned only in the public areas, leaving the rest dark. The untenanted offices seemed spookily alive, as if possessed by poltergeists flashing e-mail messages onto computer screens and setting the fax machines whirring. After so many hours at her computer Suze felt radioactive. She was starting to experience odd spells of dizziness when her body seemed to swoop and sway toward the screen. There was a throbbing spot right between her eyebrows that felt almost as bad as a hangover. Suddenly she remembered Dee Dee's miracle cure: lemons and tomato juice, as she recalled, purloined from Bernie Schneider's private fridge. There might be ice as well.

Leaving her shoes under the desk, where she had long since kicked them off, Suze padded out to the elevator and rode one stop up to the twenty-second floor. When the doors opened, she peered out cautiously. There was no one in sight. All was silent. Suze stepped boldly into the corridor. She could see at once where Bernie's office must be by a rash of exotic potted plants and a stretch of superior carpeting that led to a suite of rooms tucked into a corner of the building. The first room she came to was a tiny kitchen. Suze smiled. This was easy.

There was no tomato juice in the fridge, just several tubs of yogurt, some tonic water and a dozen Snickers bars, but in the ice compartment Suze spotted a bottle of vodka. She was trying to wrestle off the cap when she heard a faint noise. Anxiously, she poked her head out into the corridor. Nothing. Then a small movement caught her eye. It was the elevator indicator. Someone was coming up.

Suze watched the numbers flashing up on the illuminated panel. Nine, ten, eleven . . . There were forty-five floors in the building, she told herself. The chance of the elevator stopping precisely here was tiny. Nevertheless, while she poured out her drink she stood in the doorway of the kitchen, keeping track. Nineteen . . . twenty. The pace seemed to be slowing. Christ! Only a glass wall separated her from the brightly lit corridor; she couldn't stay here. She shoved everything into the nearest cupboard—glass, bottle, ice-tray—and looked for somewhere to hide. Instinctively she turned in the opposite direction to the elevator. There were three more doors, then a blank wall. Suze tried the handle of the door opposite: locked. The next door opened into a small private lavatory, but there was nowhere to hide and she daren't lock it. Now she heard the faint bounce of the elevator as it came to a halt. There was one door remaining. Oh, God, the handle wouldn't turn! The elevator doors hummed open. She could hear voices. *Quick!*

Suze wrenched the handle the other way and practically fell into a huge room, lit from outside by the pinprick lights of a thousand skyscraper windows. She looked around wildly. Under the far window was a huge sofa, but it was pushed tight against the wall. She thought of crouching behind some sculpture thing on a plinth, but it was too small. The voices were getting closer. *Nightmare!* Then she saw the desk, a massive modernist statement with smooth panels almost to the floor on three sides. Gibbering silently, Suze sank to her knees on the soft carpeting. She scuttled under the desk and drew in her feet a millisecond before the door opened.

"Wait. I'll get the light," said a voice.

"Oh, no. Leave it a minute. This is such a fabulous view."

Suze closed her eyes in anguish. Bernie and Sheri.

She heard the swish of stockings, then a voluptuous sigh. "Oh, Bernie, when you sit in this big office and look down at all the little people out there, you must feel so proud."

There was a smug chuckle. "I guess I haven't done too badly."

"Badly? You're only the most successful advertising man in the whole of Manhattan. I've had one ambition since I started in this industry, and that was to work with Bernie Schneider. There's so much one can learn from an experienced man."

"That's certainly nice to hear. Listen . . . why don't I get us a drink?"

Suze froze. Oh, no! He would find the ice tray missing. What if he discovered all that stuff she had thrown in the cupboard?

"Thanks, Bernie, but I couldn't—not on top of all that wine we had." Sheri gave a low, teasing laugh. "You're not trying to get me drunk, are you?"

"Well . . . I mean . . . of course not."

"Maybe afterward, hmmm? I want to show you these layouts first. I've hardly dared to let them out of my sight. I'd feel so much better if you could keep them in your safe, once we've finished."

"Sure thing."

There was a thump as something was placed on the desk above Suze's head. She heard the click-click of a briefcase opening and the rustle of papers. A lamp went on with a soft snap. "I'll spread everything out here, so you can get the picture. Oops, was that your pen? I think something fell off your desk."

"Forget it. The cleaners can pick it up."

Two pairs of shoes appeared side by side under the panelled front of the desk, inches from Suze's nose—men's loafers with tacky gold buckles, and patent leather high heels that narrowed sharply to Cruella De Vil toes.

"This is one of the ideas we've ostensibly been working up for Friday," Sheri was saying. "Naturally, I never intended for us to actually present it. But if Plan B comes into operation, all we have to do is this"—another rustle—"and bingo! What do you think?"

Bernie was breathing rather heavily. "Let me take off my jacket. It's kind of stuffy in here." The black loafers retreated.

"Of course I hope we can keep Passion," Sheri went on, "but this way we're covered, however Ross Bannerman jumps."

Bernie's shoes reappeared somewhat closer to Sheri's than they had been. "How did you get Quincy's department to do this? There's no way it could ever be a Passion ad."

"Stop worrying, Bernie." Sheri's voice was as smooth as honey. "Quincy's never even seen it. I used that designer woman from London. She's just a babe in the wood. She knows nothing. That's why I chose her."

Under the desk, Suze stiffened indignantly and almost cracked her head on the underside of a drawer. As she crouched back down into a new position, she caught sight of a small chrome object gleaming faintly on the carpet. That must be what had fallen off the desk. But it wasn't a pen. It was Bernie's Dictaphone.

"That was smart. You know, I really think this is going to work. In a way, Rockwell has done us a favor . . ."

Rockwell! Suze didn't know what the two of them were talking about, but whatever it was sounded distinctly fishy. Stealthily she reached out and picked up the Dictaphone. Through a small Perspex window she could see the reel running; the fall had switched it on. Suze slid the volume dial to "MAX," and gently replaced the machine on the carpet.

"One good thing," Bernie was saying, "if this thing with Stateside comes off, maybe I can get that asshole Fox off my back."

"A couple of months from now, he could be begging you to buy him out."

"You're quite a girl, Sheri, smart as well as beautiful. You know, when I retire, it would be comforting to know the agency was in good hands."

"Retire?" Sheri managed to sound as amazed as if he'd just announced his intention to form a rock band. "I don't believe it! What are you—fifty-two, fifty-three?"

"I'll be sixty-one this winter."

"Bullshit." Sheri stretched the word out into a long, low siren call of seduction.

Bernie rose to the bait like a greedy trout. "I'm still firing on all cylinders," he growled, "and I mean *all*."

For several moments after that no words were spoken, but the slithery sounds and panting breaths told their own story. Suze listened in dawning horror. Bernie's shoes were now toe-to-toe with Sheri's. An acrid tang of male sweat seeped into the air, overlying Sheri's perfume. Right in front of Suze's eyes, an ice-blue jacket suddenly plopped to the floor.

"Oh, baby," groaned Bernie, "I've been wanting you so much."

"Me too . . ." There was a sudden gasp. "Oh, Bernie," whispered Sheri. "Just look at it. I don't know if I can fit the whole of that huge, gorgeous thing inside me . . . Now, just a minute, Bernie. Wait for—uhhh!"

Sheri's shoes were suddenly whisked from sight. Suze felt a tremendous thud above her head, and the desk began to rock and judder, its joints squeaking. It was like being trapped inside her own personal Mount Etna. She watched Bernie's trousers concertina slowly to his ankles and turned her head away. On the other side, locks of golden hair dangled from the edge of the desk. Poor old Sheri. There now followed a series of slurping noises, interspersed with sharp gasps of breath, as if Bernie and Sheri were having a race to see who could eat the most Kentucky Fried Chicken. Pained grunts from Sheri suggested that she was getting indigestion early in the game.

"Wouldn't this—ow!—be more—ahh!—comfortable on the couch? . . . Bernie? Sweetie? . . . I could show you some of my special tricks."

Suze watched them stagger across the room like two drunks. Bernie clutched his trousers at knee height, his elephantine rump sagging from blue boxer shorts patterned with gold crowns. Sheri was half naked, her skirt rucked up around her waist. "Come on, big boy." She toppled Bernie on to the sofa. "This time I'll be on top." And flinging out one long leg, she straddled his bulk as if mounting an exceptionally fat pony. They were off.

It was time to leave. Suze switched off the Dictaphone, removed the tape and tucked it inside her bra. She replaced the machine on the carpet, leaving the flap open. With a bit of luck, Schneider would think the tape had fallen out and been swallowed by a vacuum cleaner. Then she began to squirm her way commando-style out of her hidey-hole, past the legs of Bernie's executive chair and around to the side of the desk. Here she was screened from the couch. The half-open door was before her, but to reach it she would have to cross perhaps eight feet of carpet in full view of the sofa and illuminated by the slanting light from the hallway. Did she dare?

The sounds from the couch were settling into an insistent rhythm. Suze had the feeling that Sheri would not prolong the pleasure beyond what was strictly necessary. It was now or never. She rose carefully on to all fours. There was a loud crack from her knee-joint.

"What was that?" asked Sheri sharply.

"Don't stop," Bernie yelled, "or you're fired!"

The noises resumed. Slowly, silently, Suze crawled across the carpet to the doorway. All they had to do was turn their heads and they would see her. Any second she expected a shout of outrage.

None came. She had escaped. Rising to her feet, Suze ran down the corridor, calculating swiftly. She would have to risk the noise of the elevator, she decided: the doors to the stairs would be locked. But her timing must be perfect. Finger poised over the "DOWN" button, Suze listened with total concentration to the muffled noises from Bernie's office. It sounded a little as if a large woodpigeon were locked up with a yappy Pekinese.

Then suddenly Sheri was shouting, "You're the best! . . . The biggest! . . . The baddest! . . . The Berniest!"

Her words seemed to do the trick. "I'm coming," bellowed Bernie. "This is it! Oh, God . . . Oh, God . . ."

Suze pushed the button. While the lovers panted for the final frontier, the elevator rose silently. They came together.

Chapter Twenty-four

Betsy sat on the edge of the bath in her nightgown, turning the little pink and white package around and around in her hands. Balanced on the rickety chair beside her was a tall glass of water, in case she still hadn't drunk enough. Next to it lay her wristwatch, to check the timing. She had locked the bathroom door—not that it mattered, since Lloyd had still not come home. Everything was ready. What was she waiting for?

Taking a deep breath, she opened the package and set out the little pieces of plastic equipment. They looked way too flimsy and cheap for their momentous function. She unfolded the leaflet of instructions and started to read. The process was frighteningly simple. In less than five minutes' time she would know the answer. Pink or white. Yes or no. Good or bad. Suddenly cold, Betsy wrapped her arms around her ribcage and rocked nervously back and forth. The truth was that she no longer knew what she wanted.

Until last Tuesday, it seemed that everything was turning out as she had hoped. Lloyd had proposed. Mother had been silenced at last—if silence was the word. After the initial babble of delirious rejoicing, in which Betsy had detected an unnerving echo of Mrs. Bennett praising Lizzie for capturing the disagreeable but delightfully monied Mr. Darcy, her mother had not so much withdrawn her maternal attention as shifted its focus. When was the wedding to be? She needed to know in good time so that all her friends could be there to witness Betsy's triumph. What about the color scheme? She wanted to order her outfit. Where would Betsy and Lloyd live? How soon was she to become a grandmother?

Into this bubbling broth of happy speculation Betsy had not dared to drop the cold, hard stone of Lloyd's dismissal from Schneider Fox. There was no point in worrying Mother before she flew over. Besides, it was embarrassing to confess that the man she was about to marry was currently out of work. If Lloyd would only hurry up and get another job it might not be necessary to tell Mother at all. They could simply announce his new post as a triumphant promotion.

But Lloyd was not hurrying. He was not telephoning his contacts. Lloyd was doing nothing except hanging around the apartment like a saggy old birthday balloon, or disappearing for hours on end. Lots of people lost their jobs. Betsy had read about them in newspapers. Why did Lloyd have to make such a big drama out of it? Even before the Schneider Fox trouble Betsy had sensed him changing, as if some virus in the English air had infected his character, weakening the elements she loved and strengthening those she feared. How could he have enjoyed those Fox children, for example? On the way back from Chawton they had totally destroyed her sense of communion with the spirit of Jane Austen by singing "Waltzing Matilda" at top volume from the back seat. And this awful apartment: Lloyd had amazed her the other day by saying it had "character." She had even caught him listening to some Jimi Hendrix tapes he found here. Since he had lost his job, the only time she had heard him laugh was on the telephone to the Wilding woman. Telling jokes! He had said more to her in one phone conversation than he had to Betsy in days.

Then there was his unreasonable fixation about *her* getting a job. This had never been part of the scenario. Honing her intellect in an environment of cultured tranquillity was one thing. The thought of actually working in academia—the rigors of research, the scramble for tenure, term papers, classes, the squalid banality of real, live students—was enough to bring on one of her migraines. It wasn't wrong to expect a man to provide a home, security and lovely furnishings. That's what marriage meant.

Betsy felt a spasm of panic. She stood up and paced the floor in small, tight circles until she caught sight of herself in the mirror. She looked sad-eyed and strained. Next birthday she would be thirty-five. Closing her eyes, Betsy smoothed her fingers across her forehead and temples in a gentle, repetitive motion until her thoughts settled. She had invested two years of her life in this relationship. Lloyd had proposed and she had accepted. It could be her last chance. Suddenly decisive, Betsy took her sample and filled the plastic tube to the black line. Lloyd might try to persuade her that he was a poor marriage prospect, but he would never run away from his own child.

Betsy had completed the next stage of the process and was waiting for the required three minutes to pass when she heard the phone ringing. Suddenly fretful that something might have happened to Lloyd, she abandoned her vials, struggled with the door lock and hurried to pick up the receiver. "Yes?"

"Hello. Could I speak to Lloyd, please? Sorry to ring so late, but it's frightfully important."

She might have known. It was that Susannah person, she was sure—not that the English woman had the courtesy to give her name, or to address Betsy as if she were a real human being and not some answering service.

"Lloyd's not home right now," she said repressively.

"Blast!" came the exasperated reply. "Where is he? Will he be in soon?"

"May I know what your call concerns?" Betsy was not going to admit that she had no idea of Lloyd's whereabouts. "Perhaps he can reach you when . . . when his business is concluded. If, that is, you wish to leave your name and telephone number."

There was a ripple of laughter. "Heavens, how rude of me! This is Suze Wilding, and of course you know the number as I'm in your flat. You must be Beth."

"Betsy."

"Of course. Betsy. Well . . . hello at last."

"Hello."

There was an uncomfortable pause.

"I'm actually ringing about Schneider Fox," persisted the voice.

Just hearing the name fired Betsy with anger. "Lloyd doesn't want to hear from Schneider Fox again. He doesn't need Schneider Fox. There are lots of other jobs, you know."

"Ye-es," came the doubtful reply. "But that's not really the point, is it?"

"It seems pretty much of a point from where we're sitting."

"But surely the important thing is to clear his name. Jay thinks so too."

Betsy marveled at her casual confidence. It sounded as if she had been living with them all for years. She assumed her frostiest tone, the one Mother used with repairmen. "You have been discussing Lloyd with Jay Veritas?"

"Yes. We've become quite good friends. He's lovely, isn't he?"

Lovely? That sardonic, cigarette-smoking homosexual with unnatural hair color? Betsy felt as if she were losing her grip on her own private universe. Here was a woman she had never even met, a total stranger, using *her* telephone, probably lounging on *her* bed, acting as if Jay was her best friend, telling Betsy what was best for her own fiancé—and all in that patronizing, polite, English voice that seemed to dismiss her as of no account. It was time to take control. "Please give me your message. I'll make sure Lloyd gets it."

"I can't do that. It's a bit complicated."

"I'm sure I could understand if you spoke very slowly."

"I didn't mean it that way. It's just that I have to talk to him personally. I . . . well, I owe it to him."

The suggestion that this woman and Lloyd had some secret business that Betsy could not share flooded her veins with venom. "Speaking of owing, I hope you're going to appreciate the microwave I bought for you. They're such a boon for you single women."

"Oh, great!" the voice flashed back. "If there's some stray cat I fancy getting rid of, I won't have to bother with the vet. I can just cremate it myself."

Betsy gasped. Lloyd promised that he had taken the blame for the cat incident. How could he have lied to her? She opened her mouth to deliver a crushing retort, but the English woman got there first. "I'm sorry," she said crisply. "That was very rude. Look, this conversation is going nowhere. If you want to help Lloyd, I suggest you ask him to ring me. OK?" And she hung up.

Betsy was trembling. She glared vindictively around the living room, hating its gaudy clutter. Who did these uppity career women think they were? Suddenly she remembered what she had been doing and ran to the bathroom with an anguished cry. The test well was colored neither pink nor white, but a muddy gray-green. Betsy snatched up the instructions and read what she already knew. She had waited too long and the test was negated. The kit could not be reused. She would have to buy another.

In a rage of frustration she swept up all the containers and stuffed them violently into the box, ready to throw away the whole stupid mess. But of course she couldn't. This was England. The English didn't believe in wastebaskets in the bathroom—like they didn't believe in table napkins or iced water. Betsy started kicking the bath panel and went on kicking until she burst into tears. Sobbing pitifully, she limped into the living room. She located the wastebasket through a blur of tears and dropped her trash into it, then collapsed onto horrible Susannah Wilding's horrible couch. Never had she felt so alone and abandoned. Where was Lloyd?

The minutes passed. Betsy's tears dried. At length she reached for the telephone and began to dial. Mother would know what to do.

Three miles away, in the heart of Covent Garden, Lloyd was standing at the bar of the Lamb and Flag. My kind of pub, he thought woozily, surveying the low dark beams, yellowed plaster and the polished brass of the beer-pump handles. The yeasty air and genial roar of conversation were pleasantly narcotic. He sipped his drink and stared about him absently, moving occasionally to peer at old prints and odd memorabilia. "I should be getting home to Betsy," he said to himself, but the words made no impact.

He had gone out right after breakfast so that Betsy could get on with her thesis. It must be aggravating for her to have him cluttering up the apartment. Today his aimless wanderings had taken him southward toward the river, into a tangle of twisting streets and high-walled alleyways that must once have formed the heart of Dickens's London. Garlick Hill, Oystergate, Cinnamon Street, Tobacco Dock: the names conjured up a teeming, bustling world of entrepreneurial vigor, alive with color and exotic scents. Now the British Empire was long gone, the businesses were extinct, the buildings deserted. One narrow passageway brought Lloyd to a steep stone stairway, slimed with green, that led down into the pewter water. He stood for a while looking westward, with the sour smell of the Thames in his nostrils, watching cloud-shapes form and dissolve over the turrets of the Tower, where a succession of tyrants had rid themselves of dangerous rivals and unwanted wives. Gloom, decline, decay, the oppressive weight of history: the area suited Lloyd's mood to perfection.

Afterward, he had followed the river's sinuous loops as far as Chelsea and almost back again until, exhausted, he had stumbled into a movie theater and fallen asleep even before the advertisements had finished. When he came out he was hungry. A plate of "shepherd's pie" had filled the cracks; several whiskies had taken away the taste. Now the day was almost over. Once again, he had managed to complete it without feeling a thing.

As he stepped back from his perusal of a framed eighteenth-century cartoon, Lloyd nudged the elbow of another drinker and made him slop beer onto the floor. The man grinned at him sheepishly. "Sorry," he said.

Lloyd shook his head with a slow smile. He was charmed by the ingrained politeness that made the English apologize for their physical presence, as if having a foot stepped on or an eye almost gouged out by an umbrella spoke were social faux pas that deserved censure. "My fault," he countered. "Let me buy you another."

"I shouldn't really."

"Me neither, but I'm going to."

"Right. Cheers. Half a bitter, then."

Lloyd relayed this mysterious request to the barman and bought himself another malt whiskey. The appeal of English beer—a tepid, dark infusion of the leavings at the bottom of your average garbage pail—eluded him.

They sat down together and began talking. The man was in his late forties, smartly but not expensively dressed, a salesman, perhaps, or a middle manager.

"You're an American, aren't you?" he said. "I can always spot them."

"It must be the hair between the eyes."

The man looked blank for a moment, then gave an uncertain laugh.

"And how about you?" Lloyd went on politely. "Do you live in this neighborhood?"

"Me? No. Too noisy. We're out Wimbledon way. Nice for the children—grown-up now, of course."

"So what brings you into town?"

The man gave him a peculiar smile. "I'm at a conference, aren't I? The wife's not expecting me back until the small hours."

"But . . . where's the conference?" Lloyd was bewildered. "Why aren't you there?"

"Because they don't want me anymore. They don't need people with twenty years' experience. They have computers now, and young lads out of college with 'qualifications.' " He enunciated the word with scorn.

"You lost your job," said Lloyd, recognition dawning.

"Three weeks ago last Friday."

"And you haven't told your wife?"

"I can't." The man put his hand on Lloyd's sleeve. He brought his needy eyes close. "You see that, don't you? I've been the provider all our married life. She couldn't cope with it any other way."

Lloyd shrank away. He couldn't help it. "But what do you do all day? Where do you go? You can't just sit in a pub."

"Couldn't afford it anyway, could I? No, I'm still turning up at the office. They've given me a project—sorting out the filing. I know all the history, you see. Of course, they can't pay me any longer. I wouldn't expect that. But it keeps me off the streets."

Lloyd was appalled. "But that's—" he began. Then he saw the pain of humiliation in the man's eyes. How could anyone bear the weight of such an impossible deception? "Of course," he said. "I understand."

Five minutes later Lloyd was striding toward the Underground, fleeing from his pathetic companion and a sense of rising panic. *I am not like that!* he told himself. *I am not a sad failure. People do not pity me.* A fine rain was falling. Light gleamed on the slick sidewalks from restaurants and bars. Inside, Lloyd saw groups of laughing friends and couples leaning close, and felt so sharp a severance from the rest of the world that he was frightened. He jerked his head away. He mustn't look. He mustn't think. It seemed to him that dark, dangerous thoughts lurked in his subconscious like misshapen sea-creatures from the lightless depths. If they came to the surface, who could say what he might have to confront?

Outside the Underground station, a handwritten notice warned passengers of long delays owing to "*a body on the line.*" Lloyd shivered at the sinister phrase and pulled the collar of his raincoat tightly about his bare neck. He couldn't afford a taxi. The bus system was unfathomable. He would have to walk.

The lights were out in the apartment when he got back. On the floor outside the bedroom he found a note. *Your little friend Ms. Wilding wants you to call "urgently." I have a migraine. Don't wake me when you come to bed.* Lloyd screwed up the piece of paper, then unscrewed it and peered once more at the neat script. Was Betsy mad at him again? Scowling, he stuffed the note into his pocket and lumbered down to the kitchen. He wasn't ready to go to bed yet anyway. He needed another whiskey.

Carrying a generous tumblerful to the living room, Lloyd lay down on Ms. Wilding's crazy couch and settled his head on a mound of cushions. His body felt agreeably weary, his mind fuzzy. There on the wall was old Fred, tap dancing his socks off. Idly Lloyd hummed a few bars of "A Foggy Day in London Town": great stuff. He wondered whether Suze was getting over the rat boyfriend. Maybe he should find out. According to Jay, Suze didn't have much luck with men. She'd been strung along for years by some older man who had treated her badly. With a grunt of effort he manhandled the telephone onto his stomach, nearly falling onto the floor in the process. It could be that he was a little drunk.

"Hi," he said familiarly, as soon as she had answered.

"Is that you, Lloyd? Hooray! Where have you been?"

Lloyd was in mid-yawn. "In a pub," he said indistinctly.

"Well, get your brain into gear. I have hot news."

Lloyd listened while she babbled on about getting trapped in Bernie's office and witnessing some kind of lovefest between Bernie and Sheri from under Bernie's desk. Extraordinarily, she had tape-recorded their conversation. She sounded high-spirited and purposeful. He smiled and closed his eyes. It was nice listening to her voice.

"You see what this means?" she prompted.

"Sure. Bernie and Sheri are having an affair. Let them, is what I say." Lloyd waved his arm in the air, spilling some whiskey on her couch. "It's a free country."

"For God's sake, pay attention. You can't be that drunk. What it means is that something is going on. Something to do with the Passion account—and with you."

Lloyd took a swig of his drink. "So what? I don't work for Schneider Fox anymore. Hey—maybe they should rename it Schneider Fux." He chuckled for some time at his witticism.

"Don't you care about Passion?" persisted the voice.

"Nope."

"Or about losing your job?"

"Nope."

"Or about everyone thinking you're some kind of crook?"

Lloyd opened his mouth to reply, but no words came. Suddenly he was seventeen again, reading the newspaper headlines his mother had tried to hide from him. His body sagged. He felt utterly defeated. "You sure know how to make a guy feel good," he said at last.

"I want to do more than that," came the crisp reply. "I want to help you get your job back."

Lloyd sat up. "Huh?"

"Don't you want it back?"

"Oh . . ." Lloyd squirmed. "It's too late now. Harry and Bernie will never change their minds. Everyone in advertising thinks I'm a criminal. No one believes me."

"I do."

Her calm, simple statement took his breath away. She believed him! He felt like a floundering swimmer who had found a foothold on solid rock. "Why?" he asked.

"All sorts of things. Dee Dee and Jay, for starters. Both of them are certain you would never do anything dirty. Then there's the conversation I heard tonight—weren't you listening? And don't forget I've been living in your apartment and working in your office for three weeks, and talking to you on the phone. I know I've been frightfully dim, but it suddenly dawned on me that the Lloyd Rockwell I was getting to know was totally unlike the person Sheri kept telling me about. Honestly, Lloyd, she's been systematically running you down ever since I got here."

Lloyd frowned. "I'm sure you're wrong there. Sheri's ambitious, but I can't believe that she would deliberately set out to sabotage another person's career."

Suze's cynical hoot echoed down the line. "That's because you're too nice. You need a nasty, devious mind like mine to appreciate how other people work. Don't you understand? Sheri wants to be top dog. First she gets rid of you. Then she grabs the agency's star client. Meanwhile, she's bonking poor old Bernie's brains out so that he'll believe anything she tells him."

Could this be true? For the first time in days Lloyd allowed his brain to function. He remembered how unconcerned Bernie had been about the collapse of his trip to England; it was Sheri who had seemed upset. And when a new exchange had been miraculously sorted out a few hours later, who had telephoned the good news? Sheri. Then there were all those unreturned calls. He tried to slot more pieces of the puzzle into place, but they didn't fit. "What about the list of Passion customers I got you to send me? Sheri couldn't have known about that."

There was a low moan. "Yes, she did. I told her. That's when she still had me believing you were some bumbling idiot who was an embarrassment to the agency. And while I'm in confessional mode, I might as well tell you I've also accessed all your confidential computer files and given your notes on Passion to Sheri." Her words came out in a defiant rush. "I'm really sorry, Lloyd."

Lloyd said nothing. He felt hurt and angry. "A bumbling idiot": the words stung. He hated the thought of people trawling through his private files. "How could you do that?"

"I don't know," she answered miserably.

But over the next few minutes, as she explained her side of the picture—how she had understood that Passion might leave because Lloyd had mishandled the account, how flattered she had been to escape creepy Quincy and accept the temporary role as Sheri's personal art director—Lloyd began to understand. "Even before you got the chop, Sheri was obsessed with Passion," Suze went on. "Now it's become her personal mission: save Passion or die. She's had us all working overtime for a mega-presentation on Friday."

"*This* Friday?" Lloyd felt a sharp stab of exclusion.

"Yes. Ross Bannerman's coming in person. But tonight, in Bernie's office, I distinctly heard Sheri say, 'We're covered whichever way Ross Bannerman jumps.' What do you suppose that means?"

"No idea."

"We'll figure it out. The point is, I'm on your side now. I'm going to help you fight back. All we have to do is prove you didn't leak that list, and demonstrate to Passion that you're the man they want in charge of their advertising."

Was that all? Lloyd sighed. "The trouble is, everyone thinks—"

"Never mind what they think," interrupted Suze. "Look, Lloyd, we're in the advertising business. We can make people think ten impossible things before breakfast. Driving cars is sexy. It really, really matters which washing powder you use. Stuffing your kids with scrambled cow-entrails and chips is fun." She clicked her tongue impatiently. "This isn't about what people think, it's about the truth. You *are* innocent. You *are* good at what you do."

A glorious feeling of sanity rolled over Lloyd. If she believed in him, maybe he could start believing in himself again. "All right," he said. "Let's do it. Though frankly I can't see how."

"You will," she said breezily. "Dee Dee says you always come up with something brilliant at the last minute."

"That's different. Put me into that boardroom on Friday—" He broke off. "Except that I'm three thousand miles away, and Schneider Fox wouldn't even let me into the building and I don't have access to the information I need. Or an art director."

There was a weighty pause. "Ahem," said Suze.

Of course. She was a designer—a good one, too, he'd heard. Lloyd felt a trickle of excitement. "You don't mean that *you* . . .?"

"Why not? Come on, Lloyd, we have to do it." Her enthusiasm was exhilarating. "I'm going out now to get this tape copied and couriered over to you," she went on busily. "Tomorrow I'll fax you all the stuff I can lay my hands on for the presentation. See what you make of it."

"Thanks, Suze, I—"

"I'll ring you the second I get back from work. It will be quite late your time, I'm afraid."

"That's OK. Listen—"

"The thing is, I don't dare ring you from work in case Sheri catches me." She stopped politely. "Sorry, did you want to say something?"

Lloyd smiled. "Yes, I did. I wanted to say thank you for helping me like this. Even if it all comes to nothing, I appreciate what you're doing. You've given me back my faith in myself. If it wasn't for you—"

"Pff. Think nothing of it. You helped me with my cooking. You cheered me up. I'm just returning the favor. Actually I want to get back at Sheri for making such a fool of me. Also—" For the first time her fluency faltered. "Well, it's the right thing to do, isn't it?" Then she groaned. "Yuk. Do I sound horribly pious? I hope I'm not about to turn into a nun."

Lloyd gave a shout of laughter. "I think you sound wonderful," he said.

In the surprised silence that followed he could practically hear the barricades of British reserve going up. "Oh. Well. Jolly good." Her voice was clipped. "Speak to you tomorrow. Bye."

After she had gone Lloyd sat quietly for a while, a lingering smile on his face. Then he leaped to his feet. "Come, Watson, the game's afoot!" he said aloud. Going over to the desk, he moved aside Betsy's papers and rooted about, looking for some paper and a pen that worked. It must be very late, but his brain was zinging. At length he wrote down:

1. Customer list—check
2. Presentation—Friday
3. Harry?
4. Stateside???

His mind sped ahead. Full of optimism, he allowed himself to imagine what it would be like to have his reputation reinstated, to be himself again. Yet one cloud lingered at the edge of this rosy horizon. What was it? Lloyd looked up from the desk and propped his chin on his hand, chasing the source of his disquiet. The revelation, when it came, was shocking. He did not want to marry Betsy.

At once a flood of guilt and anxiety rose to drown the thought. Betsy was loving, vulnerable, dependent. She was good to him—spoiled him, even. He had chosen her, out of all the women in the world. He couldn't let her down.

But the thought bobbed up again. This time Lloyd examined it squarely. He admitted to himself that Betsy had not given him the support he needed over the Schneider Fox crisis. She shrank from confrontation, just as he did. Together they would make a timid, dull couple, soured by resentments. Reaching into his pocket, Lloyd took out her note and smoothed it open. *Don't wake me when you come to bed.* Was this what their life would be like? He remembered Jay's reaction to the news of his engagement, a flat "Congratulations," delivered with all the joyousness of a death-knell. A chill settled about him. He was about to marry the wrong woman.

Lloyd stuffed Betsy's note into the wastebasket. As he did so, a crumpled carton caught his eye. Automatically his brain shifted into gear, professionally assessing the message of its pale colors and self-effacing lettering. What was the product? Body lotion, perhaps, or one of those hair-removing creams women used that stank to high heaven.

Lloyd bent down and turned the carton around so that he could see the label. "Home Pregnancy Test," he read. The sudden noise inside his head was like the squealing of car tires, just before a crash.

Chapter Twenty-five

That night Suze slept the deep, unbreakable sleep of the virtuous and on waking discovered two surprises. One was the collection of clothes she'd abandoned in the Hamptons, mysteriously delivered overnight in a brand new Louis Vuitton bag. How very Nick. Unzipping it, she found a message: *Siouxie sweetheart, please call me—N.* There followed four different telephone numbers. Suze put the note aside. Had she mentioned to anyone recently that she hated men? Her second surprise was a long fax from Lloyd, which Suze read with gathering excitement. This was going to be fun.

Fired with energy, she swept into the Schneider Fox building as if she owned it, made a detour past Dino's workstation and sweet-talked him into "borrowing" some art department equipment, and was already at her desk, head down, by the time Sheri arrived. Suze observed her royal progress down the corridor with grudging admiration. Not by one misplaced hair or the faintest flush to her cheek did Sheri betray her after-hours romp with Bernie. Suze waited a decent interval, then appeared diffidently at Sheri's open door. "Awfully sorry, Sheri, but I've got a doctor's appointment this afternoon. I'm afraid it may take rather a long time. I'll work at home tonight to make up." Encountering Sheri's outraged stare, Suze lowered her eyes and tried to look bashful. "Gynecological thingy," she muttered.

"Oh . . . All right. But I want those spreads finished and ready to put on slide tomorrow."

"No problem," sang Suze, retreating briskly. Brilliant. She had just bought herself several hours of extra time. She was going to need them.

Next she found Dee Dee and lured her to the ladies' for a secret pow-wow. When Dee Dee emerged, there was a determined angle to her chin and the light of battle in her eye.

By lunchtime Suze was seated under a grapevine in the courtyard of a divine little Greek restaurant in the Village. Placing her forearms on the table, she leaned across to Jay, eyes sparkling. "Guess what?" she confided. "Lloyd is innocent!"

"You don't say?" Jay's quizzical half-smile made her want to swat him.

"I do say."

"It must be true, then."

"Oh, fiddle-dee-dee." Suze tossed her hair—or tried to. Unfortunately, eight inches or so were missing. "If you can't be serious, I won't tell you *all.*"

Jay raised his eyebrows at her. "Seriously, could I stop you?"

Over the retsina she regaled him with the Sheri/Bernie minidrama, and explained how she was going to redeem herself with Lloyd. "Schneider Fox is crazy to have let him go. I'm sure he's been set up. Now we're going to prove it."

"We?"

"Lloyd and me, of course. He's already started to work out the most fantastic plan. We'll both have to be incredibly brave and brilliant, and I expect it will all end in disaster but—"

"But what?"

"I don't know—but it's such fun, I suppose. There's nothing like working really hard on a project with someone who's absolutely on your wavelength, and you keep egging each other on to more and more wonderful ideas." She laughed and settled back in her chair. "It's so funny, the way I imagined him when I started this exchange—a fat American businessman, aged about 112, and dull, dull, dull." She clutched Jay's arm in mock panic. "He's not dull, is he? Swear to me he's not dull."

"How could any friend of mine be dull?" Jay looked shocked at the very idea. "I tried to tell you before that you were wrong about Lloyd, but you were so wrapped up in your new boyfriend you wouldn't listen. How is Mr. White, by the way? Good weekend?"

Suze drew back. One hand strayed unconsciously to her new short hair. Somewhat to her surprise, she found she didn't want to wallow in recollected misery. She summoned a rueful smile. "I made a mistake. Or perhaps he did. Frankly, I don't think East Hampton is my scene." To divert him she started to tell Jay about the ghastlier guests.

"Ah, the B list." Jay nodded sympathetically. "Bulimics, babes, bratsos, big shots and blondes. Was it total hell?"

"Worse. What's the A list, then?"

Jay took a sip of his wine. "Alcoholics, actresses, aristos and assholes," he pronounced.

"You're making it up." Suze giggled. "Anyway, whatever the list, I wasn't on it. Perhaps I'm not as sophisticated as I thought."

Jay gave her an assessing look. "Perhaps you're growing up?" he suggested.

Suze eyed him warily. She had always hated it when people said that. Lawrence used to tease her about becoming a "grown-up" one day, prompting images of herself preparing advance meals for the freezer, or having her hair sculpted into waves under a drying helmet. Now it struck her that there were other ways of growing up, not all of them bad.

"Tell me more about Lloyd," she said, changing the subject. "I still can't understand why he didn't make a fuss when he got fired. You have to admit, the way he just accepted everything made him look very guilty."

Jay fiddled with the menu, searching for words. "People are complicated," he said at last. "They find reasons not to do the obvious thing."

"Like what?" Suze demanded. "Sorry, am I being nosy? It's just that he sounds . . . quite nice, actually. I'd like to understand him better."

Jay smiled at her. "Let's order," he said.

They decided to share a selection of starters, which arrived in small bowls temptingly scattered with fresh herbs and paprika. Sunlight filtered into their green cave.

Jay picked up a marinated green pepper and nibbled at it thoughtfully. "OK," he began, "I'll tell you about Lloyd, because I think I trust you. But this isn't tittle-tattle, you understand." He pointed the pepper at her warningly. "It's not something you bring out as a tasty piece of gossip at one of your tony English dinner parties."

"I'd never do that!" Suze responded hotly, though even as she spoke the words she felt an uncomfortable shock of recognition. The old Suze had done such things. Lowering her eyes, she dipped a piece of pita bread into the smoky eggplant paste. "Go on."

"First," he said, "you have to understand the American suburbs, particularly those green little towns outside New York with cute red-brick shopping malls and nice white churches, where everyone's so rich and privileged the whole place is awash with problem teenagers. All the dads commute to the city, and all the moms divide their time between shopping and the country club. That's the kind of place where Lloyd and I grew up. My dad was a big shot lawyer, Lloyd's was a stockbroker—very successful, very charming. I'm an only child, and by the time Lloyd was born his sister was already ten, so we were both loners in a way. We liked books and ideas and language, and had the same sense of humor."

"Weird, you mean." Suze grinned.

Jay bowed his head in acknowledgment. "As we grew up we became rebels, naturally. When all the kids at school were into bubblegum rock or heavy metal, we were listening to the Sex Pistols. We dressed in black and read Thomas Pynchon and brooded about the meaninglessness of life over our chocolate milkshakes. We despised television, except for English imports like *Monty Python* and *Fawlty Towers*. I think there may even have been a stage when our regular greeting to each other was '*Salut, mon vieux*.' I tell you, we were cool, man.

"At around fifteen, we got sent away to our different preppy schools up in New England, two spoiled brats being groomed to inherit the earth. When we remembered, we wrote each other long letters full of profound observations and rapier-like wit. In the vacations we'd come into the city and hang out at Tower Records, or I'd drag him into the art movie-houses to watch Bergman and Renoir. Lloyd knew I was gay, of course. He was the first straight person I ever told. It never seemed to matter.

"The summer of my junior year, a boy at school—a real jerk called Murray Rose, only we called him Runny Nose—came up and asked me in a sneery way what I thought of my friend Rockwell now. He showed me a newspaper headline from our local paper. It read, 'Swindler Rockwell Arrested.'"

"Swindler!" Suze repeated. "What had he done?"

"It turned out that there had been some irregularities in Mr. Rockwell senior's dealings with his clients' investments. He made the classic mistake of temporarily borrowing from one fund to make up a shortfall in another while he waited for the big dividend that would get him out of trouble."

"But it never came?"

"It was messier than that. Lloyd's dad had been having an affair for years with his secretary. It was one of those situations where he kept promising to divorce Lloyd's mother, but of course he never did. One day the secretary got tired of waiting, so she huffed and she puffed and she blew down the whole house of cards."

"How horrible!"

"Worse than you can imagine. As financial scandals go, this one was pretty small potatoes, but the trouble was that Lloyd's dad had been Mr. Popular—pillar of the golf club, school governor, life and soul of every party. He radiated energy and confidence, with the result that half the town had invested their savings in him. When it all collapsed, they were vindictive as hell. Nobody hates to lose money more than rich people, have you noticed that?"

"What did they do?"

"Oh . . . petty, mean-minded things. Rocks through the windows, garbage in the swimming pool, nasty telephone calls. The first morning after Lloyd came home from school, he opened the back door and found the family dog lying dead on the porch. It had been shot in the head."

Suze jerked away from the table with a cry of disgust.

"Nice neighbors, huh?" Jay grimaced. "That's when Lloyd's grandparents came and took him away—his mom's parents, of course. They were 'protecting' him. His father was already in jail. No one would raise the bail to keep him out until the trial. I don't know if Lloyd even got to see him."

"Poor Lloyd. He must have felt completely abandoned. And I suppose you couldn't help if you were away at school."

"I could have done something." Jay's face darkened. "But I didn't. Not a thing. I didn't write, I didn't call, I just hoarded the knowledge like a terrible secret disease. I guess I didn't know what to do—I was only seventeen. Adults did what they did, and kids just watched. But I hate myself for it now. By the time I got home for vacation, Lloyd's dad was on trial, and Lloyd and his mother had moved to California. I went on living my normal, selfish teenager's life. I missed him, though."

"How did you make contact again?"

Jay lit a cigarette and leaned back in his chair. They had both forgotten about their food.

"On my eighteenth birthday I decided to break it to my parents that I was gay, that I wanted to be a filmmaker and no way was I ever going to law school. I was pretty full of myself in those days. Probably I didn't mince words in making it clear to my dad just what I thought about becoming a workaholic fat cat like him. Anyway, there was a big bust-up and I lit out for San Francisco, where I'd heard the sun always shone and people were happy and practically every other person was gay." Jay gave a wry smile. "I hated it. Everyone was so goddamn easygoing I thought I might fall asleep and never wake up again. No one had mentioned the word 'fog' either. The good thing was that I hooked up with Lloyd again. He was pretty freaked out. Dad in prison, Mom poor and alone and spitting poison, a high school where the other kids hated him for being an East-coast preppy."

Suze sat with her chin propped on her hands, trying to imagine what it must have been like. Nothing as bad had ever happened to her. She felt a sudden welling of warmth for her own family and friends. How lucky she was!

"I thought it was time we both got out," Jay continued. "Lloyd had this old car. We decided to go traveling and take any job we could find while we figured out what to do next. It took us about nine months to work our way to New York. By then, Lloyd had himself pretty well under control. I went to film school, Lloyd went to college and life returned more or less to normal."

"And what about Lloyd's father?"

"It could have been worse. He was transferred to one of those middle-class places where you can take a degree and practice your golf swing, and he got parole after five or six years. Still, prison is prison. When he came out he didn't have a cent, Lloyd's mother had divorced him and none of his children wanted to know him—Lloyd included."

Suze nodded slowly. "He sent Lloyd a card for his birthday. Lloyd told me to throw it away."

"There you go." Jay frowned. "Personally I think he was more of a fantasist than a criminal, but Lloyd seems to want to blank out the whole episode. He gets uptight about doing the right thing. This trouble at Schneider Fox—I get the feeling he's been waiting half his life for something awful to happen to him, just like it did to his father."

They sat together in silence, smoking their cigarettes. Suze thought it must be lonely to carry such a secret from one's past. "He's lucky to have you for a friend," she told Jay.

"I'm the lucky one," Jay countered fiercely. "I'd hate to lose him again."

Suze stared at him in surprise. "Why would you?"

Jay started to answer, then a guarded expression came over his face. "Circumstances alter," he said cryptically.

Before Suze could press him further, he leaned over and gave her cheek an affectionate rub with his knuckles. "I'm glad you're helping him. No one could call you uptight. You probably bring out the best in him."

Suze blushed. "I don't know about that," she mumbled. As he withdrew his hand she caught his wrist and turned it over so she could read his watch. "Christ! I must get on. That's really why I asked you to meet me. I need your creative brain—and your film equipment." She gave him a coaxing smile. "Can we go back to your studio now? I'll explain the problem."

They paid the bill and walked up the stairs that led from the restaurant's secret courtyard to the pavement. At the top, Suze turned to Jay. "Thank you for explaining about Lloyd. I won't tell anyone else."

"I know you won't." He ruffled her hair. "I kind of like the new Suze. You look like a wayward angel."

Suze was still thinking about Lloyd. "If you think it would be fairer, I wouldn't mind if Lloyd knew something personal about me." She paused. "I mean, you could tell him about Lawrence, if you like."

Jay dropped his cigarette to the ground and extinguished the tiny spark with his shoe. "I already have."

After an hour in Jay's studio, Suze headed back for the apartment, her head full of plans and new thoughts. It was a beautiful afternoon, clear and hot, with a cooling breeze from the river. Suze stepped out along the now-familiar streets, at one with the busy throng of passersby. In front of her, Manhattan's great buildings rose into the sky like a sheaf of arrows targeted on the sun. She was happy.

Back in the apartment, she changed into cut-off jeans and an old T-shirt, studied Lloyd's fax once again and set to work. For the next two hours she made phone calls one after another, trying to track down things she needed. Then she turned on the computer and switched her mind into creative gear. Lloyd's ideas were good; she thought she could see ways of making them even better. She was sitting at the desk, surrounded by a sea of paper and colored card and open magazines and phone directories, when there was a ring at the door. Surprised, Suze padded across in her bare feet and opened it cautiously. Confronting her was a handsome woman in her sixties, swathed in flowered silk and clutching a formidable handbag.

"Why, hello," the woman gushed. "I'm Mrs. Rennslayer." Her expectant smile tightened fractionally under Suze's blank stare. "Betsy's mother," she explained.

"Oh." Stifling her annoyance at the interruption, Suze swung the door wide. "Come in," she said politely.

Mrs. Rennslayer's heels rapped across the parquet. "I'm here to pick up some clothes for Betsy. She's having trouble with your British weather. I did try to telephone, but all I got was the busy signal." She swung around and eyed Suze reproachfully.

Suze gestured at her papers. "I've got a lot of work on."

"So I see." Mrs. Rennslayer skirted the spreads laid out on the floor and forged her way into the living area, eyes darting about appraisingly. "Oh! You've moved the couch!" She bustled over to it and started plumping up the cushions. Next, she straightened the shade of the table lamp.

"I think you'll find the clothes in the bedroom," Suze suggested. "Why don't I make you a cup of tea while you sort things out?"

"How gracious of you to offer. Don't worry, I won't disturb you one teensy bit. I'll just creep into the bedroom and get what I need. I'd like to use the bathroom, too, if I may."

"Of course."

Suze put on the kettle and returned to the computer, but her concentration was broken. She could hear Betsy's mother opening and closing drawers, and clanging hangers—probably having a good old snoop. Instead of focusing on the job in front of her, Suze's mind filled with a painful inventory of her unmade bed, the pile of underwear draped over a chair and the muddle of skin creams and half-read paperbacks on her bedside table. She heard the lavatory flush and the water rumble. Eventually Mrs. Rennslayer reappeared, freshly combed and lipsticked, carrying a small airline bag. She wore a puzzled expression.

"Isn't the vacuum cleaner working?" she asked.

"I expect so." Suze was taken aback. "Why?"

"I thought I saw a dust ball under the bed. Betsy has to be so careful about dust. Her system is very sensitive."

Suze bit her lip. "The kettle's boiled."

Mrs. Rennslayer followed her inquisitively to the kitchen. In the doorway she stopped with a gasp. "My goodness!"

"Sorry about the mess."

There was a sorrowful sigh. "I guess you working girls don't have time to clean up. Oh, no, dear, not those awful mugs. Let's have the nice china tea set. I always think tea tastes so much better when it's properly served."

After Suze had put sugar in the sugar bowl, milk in the flouncy little jug, tea in the teapot, silver spoons on the saucers and carried the whole lot out to the dining table, she and Betsy's mother sat down opposite each other. Suze tucked her dusty feet out of sight. She felt somewhat underdressed for a formal tea party.

"So." Mrs. Rennslayer cocked her head to one side. With her beady eyes and frosted hair fluffed into a crest of soft curls, she looked like a sly parakeet. "I understand you work for Lloyd."

"Well, we work for the same company. I'm on the design side."

"It's wonderful how successful Lloyd has become. Betsy is so proud of him."

"Yes," Suze agreed cautiously. Had no one told the woman that Lloyd had lost his job? How odd.

"I imagine you two know each other very well, professionally speaking?"

"Actually, I've never met him."

Mrs. Rennslayer's eyebrows rose. "But he writes to you. Didn't I see a letter lying on the table?"

Suze looked up sharply. What was she getting at? "A fax," she agreed. "We're liaising over a *confidential* project."

"My, my, 'liaising.' It must be nice for Lloyd to know he has a little helper back home while he takes charge of the London office."

Suze fought against mounting resentment. She could not think of a riposte that would not betray Lloyd. "More tea?"

"Thank you." Mrs. Rennslayer took a handkerchief from her

sleeve and dabbed at the corners of her mouth. "What a wonderful opportunity this must be for you, to come to the United States and see how we live here."

"I've enjoyed it very much," Suze answered coolly. "Do I gather you're about to visit England for a taste of our culture?"

Mrs. Rennslayer eyed her suspiciously. "I'm going to see my daughter," she corrected. "But of course I love England. It's so quaint."

"Quaint?" Suze was tired of this game. "You obviously haven't been there since you were young, Mrs. Rennslayer. You'll find that the wattle-and-daub houses have all but disappeared now. We've been civilized by Coca-Cola and *The Oprah Winfrey Show*."

Mrs. Rennslayer clanked her silver spoon in her saucer, lips pressed tight. After a moment, she raised her head and fixed Suze with an insincere smile. "I imagine you have a boyfriend back in England?"

"Not at the moment."

"Don't worry, dear." Mrs. Rennslayer placed a liver-spotted hand on her arm. "You'll find someone."

"I'm not worried." Suze practically shook her off. "I'm not looking for anyone."

"That's good. Men never like to be chased." Mrs. Rennslayer's gimlet eyes bored into Suze's. "Fortunately, my Betsy's never had trouble in that direction. But not everyone is as talented and attractive as she is." Her whiplash glance skimmed across Suze's tatty T-shirt. "Lloyd just worships her, you know."

"That must be nice." Suze stared back stonily.

A silence fell.

"Oh, my Lord! Look at the time." Mrs. Rennslayer rose grandly from the table. "It's been lovely visiting with you, but I can't waste my time chitter-chattering."

"Please don't let me keep you." Suze jumped to her feet and almost ran to the door. She waited with her hand on the lock while Mrs. Rennslayer gathered her belongings and checked her appearance in the mirror. Suze studied her cold, complacent profile. She bet there were absolutely no dust balls under the marital twin beds back at Château Rennslayer.

Betsy's mother patted her hair. "Yes," she went on, "this is such a busy time for me, with my trip coming up—and the wedding preparations, of course." She paused expectantly.

"Oh?" Suze made one last attempt at civility. "Is someone getting married?"

Mrs. Rennslayer spun round, opening her eyes wide. "Surely Lloyd has told you?"

"No." Suddenly Suze felt small and foolish. "Told me what?"

"Why, that he and Betsy are getting married."

"Married?" Suze's hand slid from the doorknob. "Are you sure?"

"Of course I'm sure." Mrs. Rennslayer gave a rich laugh, though her eyes were steely.

"He never mentioned it to me."

"It's hardly a business matter." Mrs. Rennslayer extracted a pair of white gloves from her handbag. She fastened the clasp with a snap. "They've been engaged for almost two weeks." Her voice was triumphant.

"You mean they got engaged in London?"

"Isn't it romantic?" Mrs. Rennslayer loomed beside her, waiting for the door to be opened. "Thank you for your hospitality." She offered her fingertips for Suze to shake. "I don't imagine we'll be meeting again." She sailed out to the elevator without a backward glance.

Suze shut the door and leaned against it in a daze. Thank goodness that was over, she told herself. Now she could get on with some work. But oddly enough, when her entryphone buzzed some ten minutes later she found that she had lit a cigarette instead and was staring blankly out of the window.

"Delivery for you, Ms. Wilding." It was Raymond's chirpy voice.

Suze remembered all the things she had ordered by phone. Americans were so efficient. Perhaps one of them had already arrived. "Thanks. I'll come down."

As soon as he saw her, Raymond darted into his office. "It's your lucky day," he said, beaming as he emerged with an enormous bouquet.

Astonished, Suze accepted an armful of crackly cellophane. Her first thought was that Lloyd might have sent her flowers as a thank-you. That would be one in the eye for Mrs. Know-it-all Rennslayer. There and then she ripped off the envelope and tore it open. Written on the card inside, in the childish hand of an anonymous florist's assistant, were the words, "From Nick Bianco."

Suze crushed the card in her hand and strode back toward the elevator, letting the flowers swing head-down at her side like an old tennis racket. She didn't want them. The minute she got upstairs she would squash them straight into the garbage can.

"I love your hair," Raymond called after her.

Something in his voice—his directness, his simple eagerness to please—shamed Suze. How spoiled and selfish she must seem. Her footsteps slowed. She turned. There was Raymond, ears akimbo, smiling his innocent, optimist's smile. Suze walked back to him. "Raymond, do you have a girlfriend?"

His smile broadened. "I have a wife, Rosita. We got married three months ago."

"Jesus, Raymond, you look about twelve. Listen . . . I don't really need these." She held out the flowers. "Why don't you give them to Rosita? Tell her you love her."

"She knows that already."

"Women can never be told often enough. Go on. Take them."

Suze watched a procession of emotions cross Raymond's guileless face. In the end professionalism won: the tenant was always right, however unhinged. "Thanks. They're beautiful." He took the bouquet reverently. "Have a nice day now."

Riding up in the elevator, Suze hunched herself into a corner, her empty arms folded tight. Her reflection glared back at her from the dusky mirror, scruffy and mulish. I'm thirty-two years old, she thought, and I know nothing—nothing!—about people. Why hadn't Lloyd told her he was getting married? Hadn't she earned the right to his trust? Of course, it was no business of hers who he married, but he had put her in a false position. She had been made to look ridiculous and it was his fault. No wonder she was annoyed.

Back in the apartment, she cleared the tea things and dumped them into soapy water, grimacing at Mrs. Rennslayer's cup with its red lipstick rim. Why would Lloyd want to saddle himself with such a ghastly mother-in-law? For that matter, why would he want to marry an ice-maiden like Betsy? Then she remembered the photographs: men were always suckers for a pretty face. "Fragile," Jay had said. And Betsy had been to a proper university, not just art college. She understood about microwaves and how to keep houseplants alive. No doubt a tidy housewife type would suit Lloyd, with his tidy mind.

Suze dried her hands on the back of her shorts and thumped open the swinging doors to the living room. Well, thank God I'm not a little domestic wonder, she reflected, pacing about the apartment. She must have felt quite strongly about it, for she repeated the thought to herself several times. Eventually her restless circling brought her back to the low table where the telephone was. For a while she stood staring at it, shuffling her thoughts, then picked up the receiver and dialed. When a voice answered, she hesitated only for a moment.

"Hi, Nick," she said brightly. "It's Suze."

Chapter Twenty-six

"Mrs. York? This is Lloyd Rockwell from Customer Services at Passion Airlines, calling to check that you're happy with your arrangements to fly to London next month."

Lloyd rubbed a hand wearily over his stubble, as he repeated the same old words. It was two o'clock in the morning. His face was stiff with insincere smiling. Over the past couple of hours he must have made fifty calls.

Mrs. York said she didn't know anything about their travel arrangements; she left that kind of thing to her husband. Next was Mr. Young; he wasn't home. Mrs. Yussef told him she had a sick baby and hung up on him. Ms. Zabar told him to mind his own business. But with Mrs. Zimmerman he struck gold. "We're not flying with Passion now." She sounded embarrassed. "We switched our ticket."

"I'm sorry to hear that." Lloyd reached for his pencil. "May I ask why? We always like to know if customers are unhappy with any aspect of our service."

"Oh, no," she told him kindly. "We've always traveled with Passion before. Our son's married an English girl. We like to visit with them every summer. The only reason we're going with Stateside this year is that it's cheaper."

"I see. I'm just surprised because we like to keep our prices as low as we can. You must be quite a bargain-hunter."

"Not really. Someone called up—a nice young man like you. He said that if we switched to Stateside we'd save fifty dollars each. That's a lot of money to us."

"Of course it is! I understand. How do you suppose he knew you were planning to fly to London?"

"Well . . . Aren't these things all on computers nowadays?"

"That must be it. Thank you for your time, Mrs. Zimmerman. And I'll tell you what I'll do. I'm going to send you a one-hundred-dollar voucher against any future Passion flight to London. Maybe we can persuade you to switch back to us."

"Why, thank you!"

"Just one more thing. Can you remember when this other gentleman called you?"

"I may be seventy-two, but I've still got my marbles. It was the week before last, right after I got back from my pottery class. I go every Monday."

"Mrs. Zimmerman, I'm impressed. Thank you. Have a wonderful trip."

Lloyd replaced the receiver and made a note next to Mrs. Zimmerman's name on the list in front of him. Then he slumped back on Suze's sofa, tapping his teeth with a pencil. Out of the people he had called so far, chosen at random from his list, he had reached thirty-five. Eight of them had told him, in one way or another, to bug off; of the remaining twenty-seven, twenty had been directly offered a cheaper flight by Stateside.

Twenty people; that was two thousand dollars' worth of vouchers he had promised. If he was wrong—if Passion didn't honor the deal—he would have to find the money himself. Plus a huge telephone bill he would owe Suze. It was a price worth paying to redeem his reputation.

Beside him was a large pad of lined paper on which he had written several questions. He poured himself yet another cup of coffee from the pot on the low table in front of him, and looked again at the computer-generated list, now covered with his notes. The answer was there somewhere; it had to be.

The list was printed on continuous paper, listing alphabetically all those who held current reservations for Passion's economy-class transatlantic flights. Schneider Fox had online access to Passion's bookings so that each list was up-to-date at the time it was printed;

this one in front of him had been secretly printed out yesterday by Suze and couriered to him. Each entry showed the name, address and telephone number of the person making the booking, the dates of the booking and of the flight, and various codes indicating the number of people traveling, the fare paid and any special promotions that might be applicable. These were not very complicated: Passion had a policy of trying to offer one standard fare for each class, part of the no-frills philosophy that underpinned everything the airline did.

Lloyd began systematically to check the entries for the seven people who had not been approached by Stateside against those who had, comparing details. A sense of purpose sharpened his brain, clearing the fog. He felt liberated to be doing something—anything—at last. It was a laborious process, but by the time he reached the last one he knew he was on to something. His hopes rose another notch, and spontaneously another idea popped into his head, a long shot, but worth a try. He reached for the phone and called one more number, this time without referring to the list. A child's voice answered. "Hello?"

"Billions of blistering barnacles, is that Billy?"

"Uncle Lloyd!" The welcome in the child's voice made Lloyd grin with pleasure. They chatted for a minute or two, before the boy's mother came on the line.

"Lloyd, is that you? I thought you were still in London."

"I am."

"For goodness' sakes, what time is it over there?"

"I've been working late. Nancy, I'm sorry to bother you about this, but has anyone called recently offering you a cheap flight to England?"

"Sure. A guy from Stateside called about two weeks back. He seemed to think I'd already booked a flight with Passion, so I played along. I sent you a note about it, just like you asked. I guess no one in the New York office thought to pass it on."

"I guess not."

"Is everything OK?"

"You did just what I wanted."

"I'm glad to help if I can. Tell me quickly, before I burn dinner—how are you enjoying it over there?"

What could he say? "It's great."

"And how is Betsy?"

"She's great, too. Of course, she's asleep right now."

His sister laughed. "Same old Lloyd. Chatty as a clam. Are you ever going to come visit us? Billy will be going to college before you know it. How about Thanksgiving? Betsy would be welcome too, of course."

"Maybe," Lloyd parried automatically. He heard a faint sigh and realized how unenthusiastic he must sound—how cautious and non-committal. This was his family, after all. "I'll try," he said.

"Really?" Her eagerness shamed him.

"I'd like to. Uh . . . who else is coming?"

"If you mean have I invited Dad, yes, I have. Now, don't go silent on me, Lloyd. I know he messed things up for you, but it was such a long time ago. He gets lonely. He'd like to see you."

Lloyd plucked at the phone wire. "I'll let you know," he said curtly and cut the line.

At once, he picked up his pad of paper and returned to his problem. It was fiendishly difficult: he had to prove that he was *not* guilty, which when you thought about it was a lot harder than proving that someone *was* guilty. What he had just discovered from his sister was not conclusive proof that he was innocent, but it was . . . Lloyd's mind drifted off. He found himself counting the months to Thanksgiving. Only five—not enough. He pressed his hands to his temples, trying to force his brain to concentrate. Obstinately, it darted down murky byways of memory, flushing out long-buried emotions. Lloyd got up and went over to stand at the window. Outside, dawn was breaking over London. The sky was pearly with promise.

On such a morning, eighteen years ago, he had sneaked out of his grandparents' house and hitched a ride to the State penitentiary. Visiting hours weren't until after lunch, they said, so he had sat down with his back to the high wall, watching delivery trucks come and go and listening to the sounds of a prison waking up—the shouts and bangs, the tramp of feet and bursts of casual masculine laughter, punctuated by sudden bells. He knew that there had been a mistake and that it was up to him to rectify it. He was the only son. All his life he had waited for an opportunity to prove himself worthy of his father's attention. Now here it was.

When the sun was high, other visitors started to show up, lawyers in tight suits glancing impatiently at their watches, mothers yelling at their children to behave. For them this was routine. When the gates clanked open, Lloyd followed them inside. The visitors' room was just as he had imagined it: large and gray, with double desks facing each other, divided by glass. "I'm here, Dad. Just tell me what to do": Lloyd had prepared his confident opening words. But as soon as he saw his father's face they had shriveled to a dry nothingness. His father looked ashamed. His hesitant half-smile was like a monstrous disfigurement. *He was guilty!* For Lloyd the shock was intensely physical. He had risen from his chair, recoiling in fear and revulsion. Then he had fled. Behind him he had heard the crack of his plastic chair tumbling to the floor.

Lloyd turned from the window, banishing the memory. For years he had told anyone who asked that his father was dead—even Betsy. He was used to the lie. Nancy didn't understand. It wasn't hatred that he felt for his father, or shame or disapproval: it was guilt. Lloyd wasn't sure there was a way out of this, unless it would be to offer up his own experience of disgrace and shame and cowardice. But not at Thanksgiving. Not with Betsy.

It was time to go to bed. Lloyd yawned and stumbled across the room to straighten his papers. He was weary, but he had made progress tonight. He had two leads to follow, faint leads but they might take him somewhere. So what was nagging at him? There had been something peculiar about his conversation with Nancy. Then he remembered: he hadn't told her he was getting married.

Chapter Twenty-seven

"Do we need to have such a mess everywhere? We've got to be out of this apartment by Saturday. How am I ever going to clean up?"

It was six o'clock the following evening. Lloyd had been working all day again, and the living room was littered with coffee cups, bottles of mineral water, printouts and sketches and notepads covering every surface and much of the floor. He sat on a little island of carpet, surrounded by paper. He was feeling pretty spaced out, but he could not allow himself to be distracted. "I'm sorry, Betsy, but I must finish this. It's important." He picked up one of Suze's faxes. There had been four today alone, full of good ideas, wild suggestions and a forest of question marks. He wondered how she was getting on.

"More important than me?" Betsy posed coquettishly in the doorway.

"Yes," he answered brutally. "At this exact moment, more important than you. I'm trying to figure something out. It could be good for both of us." Lloyd didn't want to say any more than that. There was no point in giving her false hopes.

Betsy picked up one of his papers at random, gave it an exasperated glance and let it drift back to the floor. "Let it go, Lloyd. You lost your job. Period. Passion is someone else's problem now." She came over to him. Lloyd could smell perfume. Her voice softened as she touched his hair and asked, "Why can't you think about me for once?"

Lloyd sat back on his heels and studied her. "What exactly is it you want me to do?" he asked.

"Come shopping with me tomorrow."

"Shopping!"

"I thought we could buy my ring. A girl doesn't feel truly engaged until the ring's on her finger. I know Mother's going to want to see it."

Lloyd's temper rose. Did Betsy really think that he looked like a man ready to go shopping for some ridiculous ring that would probably cost a month's salary that he didn't even have? Before his thoughts could explode into words the telephone rang.

"That'll be the theater agency," she said, with maddening certainty, "confirming our tickets for *Les Miserables.*"

But it wasn't. Betsy's expression changed as she held the receiver to her ear. Then she held out the phone to Lloyd in much the same disdainful way that she had dangled the black garter belt. "It's your girlfriend. Again."

Lloyd took it with a sense of relief. "You mean Suze?"

Betsy stalked from the room. "No doubt you'll be busy chitter-chattering together for the next several hours." She slammed the door.

Lloyd blew out a gust of breath and flopped into a chair. He put the receiver to his ear. "Hey, I was just thinking about you." He grinned. "I've made some interesting progress on those—"

"I'm ringing you about the material you said you'd have ready," she interrupted him coldly.

"What?" Lloyd was puzzled. "Suze, is that you?"

"I want to remind you that it's vital I receive it by Friday."

Lloyd frowned. She was being very snippy. What had he done? "Jesus, what's with you? You know I'm working on that stuff as hard as I can. We both are."

"So you say. I don't think you've grasped the importance of this presentation. Both Mr. Schneider and Mr. Fox will be there."

How snooty she sounded, enunciating each word as if he were a cretin. Lloyd's jaw tightened. "Of course I realize—"

"Is that or is that not Veritas Studios?" she asked icily.

"Quit fooling around. You know perfectly well—" Then Lloyd

understood. She was speaking in code. Veritas Studios—that was a reference to Jay. Of course! He leaned forward eagerly. "I get it. Someone's come into your office and you don't want them to know what you're saying. Is that right?"

"Yesss!"

"OK, OK, I'm a moron. Is it . . . our horizontal friend?"

"Exactly." He caught a wobble of amusement in her voice.

"And you want to tell me . . ." Lloyd's mind clicked back over their conversation. She had put a special emphasis on one particular phrase. He had it! Both Mr. Schneider *and Mr. Fox* . . . "You want to tell me that Harry's going to be there on Friday. Hmm." Lloyd wasn't sure if this was good news or not. "Thanks for letting me know."

"So you'll be taking appropriate action at once, will you?"

"Um . . .?" What did she want him to do? A dreadful suspicion entered his mind. He and Suze had already discussed the difficulty of getting Bernie to give them a fair hearing while Sheri had him by the balls. But Harry was a different matter. He might be angry with Lloyd, but his brain still worked. "You're not saying you want me to see Harry first, and somehow convince him that we have a case?"

"That would certainly be helpful."

Lloyd glowered. The memory of his last meeting with Harry was still painful. She had no idea what she was asking. "He'd never listen to me."

"You can do better than that."

God, she was tough. "You don't understand," Lloyd protested. "There's no way I can get in touch with him. The office has instructions not to take my calls. I can hardly accost him in the street. I can't call him at home because—" He broke off. It was hard to explain how he could still feel warmth for Harry's family, or how he could respect the rigid line of demarcation between home and work drawn by the man who had fired him. "He had us down to his house in the country. He was so disappointed in me," Lloyd finished lamely.

"Look." Suze's tone was uncompromising. "My boss is standing over me and she's not looking happy. My job is on the line here. If you don't pull your finger out, neither of us will be getting further work from Schneider Fox."

Lloyd was silent. She was dead right.

"Let me know what progress you've made," she went on, sounding like herself for the first time. "I'll be waiting for your call." The line was disconnected.

Lloyd dropped the receiver into its cradle. Huh. He scratched the back of his head. Huh, again. It was all right for her: anyone who could sit under an office desk while her bosses had sex on top of it clearly hadn't a nerve in her body. She knew Harry Fox better than he did; why didn't *she* make the approach? Lloyd's gaze roamed about the room. Her personality was present in everything he looked at—the bold color of the walls, the dashing line of the cleverly faked curtains tacked up with drawing pins, the exuberantly piled books and scatter of zany postcards. He couldn't escape her. Suze had linked her fortunes to his; now they were inextricably entwined. He had lost his job; now she was risking hers to help him get it back. Lloyd straightened his backbone and got to his feet. He couldn't let her think he was a wimp.

First he tried the Schneider Fox office number, but the line had already been switched to the recorded message. Without giving himself time to change his mind, Lloyd looked up Harry's home number and dialed it. After several rings, a woman's breathless voice answered. In the background Lloyd could hear children whooping. It was probably bath time.

"Lorna? It's Lloyd Rockwell."

There was an intake of breath. "Oh, dear. I wish you hadn't phoned." Her voice was reproachful.

"I know. I'm sorry. I wouldn't be doing it if I didn't have something important to tell Harry. Is he there?"

"You've upset him dreadfully. He's been shouting at all of us for days."

"Harry's wrong about me," Lloyd told her. "I'm sorry if that sounds rude, after all your hospitality, but it's the truth."

Lorna paused. "He's not here anyway."

"What time will he be back?"

"Not for several days now. He's off to New York on business."

Lloyd squeezed his eyes shut. He was too late.

As he wondered what to do next, he heard a giggle. "I know where Daddy is," said a piping voice he recognized—Harry's daughter.

"Get off the phone, you cheeky monster!" said Lorna. "Bedtime! Harry's at some function tonight," she continued, sounding more friendly. "He's flying tomorrow. But I don't think much of your chances."

Lloyd was silent. Neither did he. But he had to try. "Can you remember which function—or where?" he asked. "It's important."

"I'm afraid not. Selective deafness tends to afflict married people, as you'll no doubt discover."

"He's gone to the rewards dinner," continued the little voice importantly. "Daddy says you have to eat a chicken made out of rubber. Then you get a reward."

"Off!" shouted Lorna. Lloyd heard a crash as the phone extension was replaced. "I'll have to go, Lloyd. I'll tell Harry you rang."

But Lloyd was hardly listening. A surge of hope fizzed through his veins. He knew exactly where he could find Harry. "Lorna, what would your daughter like best in the whole world?"

"*What?*"

"Forget it. I'll think of something. You're a wonderful woman. Good-bye."

Lloyd burst into the bedroom, where Betsy was lying on the bed with the curtains drawn. She looked on aghast as he flung open the closet and started unbuttoning his shirt.

"Have you seen my dark suit?" he demanded. "What do you think 'black tie' means? Is that a tuxedo? God! Why do I *never* have any clean white shirts?"

Betsy struggled on to one elbow. "There's one at the back." She pointed. "I ironed it this morning. What's happening, Lloyd?"

"I have to go out for a few hours."

"Where? Can't I come?"

Lloyd dressed swiftly, too preoccupied to answer. He hadn't worn a suit in over a week. Tying his tie, buttoning his starched cuffs, he felt in command again. He brushed his hair smooth and stooped to look at himself in the mirror that was always too low. His reflection stared coolly back. He looked OK. Betsy watched him mutely from the bed. She was very pale, he noticed. A question surfaced in his mind, but she had said nothing and he hadn't dared to ask. Suddenly tender, he bent to kiss her forehead. It was the formal, distracted kiss of a soldier going to war. She clutched his sleeve. "But where are you going?" she repeated.

Lloyd straightened to his full six feet two inches. "I'm going to get my job back."

Chapter Twenty-eight

The hotel was an ugly, grandiose building on Park Lane, the sort of place where Edwardian dowagers might once have chaperoned young girls to chilly balls. Lloyd approached it at a brisk pace, nervous yet determined. Taxis were drawing up outside, disgorging funky-looking women and fastidiously dressed young men. Rowdy groups jostled toward the hotel on foot, trading gleeful insults. This was the advertising crowd: Lloyd recognized them by their confident laughs. The *Admag* Awards was the annual jamboree of the industry, an event of major boozing and bitchiness. Everyone who was anyone in the business would be here. How would they react to someone who was no one?

Lloyd lifted his gaze to the high trees of Hyde Park, gathering his courage. The evening that lay ahead could be humiliating and unpleasant; he owed it to himself—and to Suze—to rise above pride and fear. He smoothed down his tie, wishing he weren't the only man without a tuxedo, then squared his shoulders and stepped through the entrance.

At the rear of the hotel lobby, a table covered in a cloth barred the way to the function room. A thin-faced woman sat behind it, checking the names of arrivals against a list she was holding. As Lloyd approached, she beamed a phony smile of professional welcome in his direction. "Good evening, sir. May I see your invitation please?"

"Of course." He reached into his jacket pocket and drew it out, savoring the irony that this had been one of the items returned to him by the motorcycle courier from his office at Schneider Fox.

The woman ran a finger down the list in front of her, turning over several pages. Then she frowned and began the process again. A line began to form behind Lloyd. "Buck up, angel," called a cocky voice, "or the champagne will run out like it did last year!"

"I'm sorry, sir." The woman looked up at Lloyd, her face now expressionless. "Your name does not appear to be on the list."

"There must be a mistake."

"I'm afraid I have strict instructions not to admit anyone who isn't on this list. Perhaps if you could speak to one of your colleagues . . .?"

"But surely my invitation speaks for itself?"

"Those are my instructions." She glanced toward a uniformed security man standing by the door, who moved forward ominously.

Lloyd's fragile confidence wilted. He had fallen at the first hurdle. He retreated into the lobby, uncomfortably aware of the speculative glances that followed him. Over the years he had attended dozens of events like this, but always in a group of colleagues, sometimes even in the starring role of an award-winner. Like everyone else he had complained of the banality of the menu, the crassness of the judges and the viciousness of the inevitable morning-after hangover; all the same it had been a familiar world, *his* world. Now, as he positioned himself inconspicuously by a marble pillar, self-conscious in his business suit, he felt like an outsider.

"Well, well, you're a brave man," said a voice in his ear.

Lloyd looked round to see Julian Jewel, smiling impudently at him. "Something tells me you're not with the Schneider Fox party. Am I right?"

"Very perceptive of you." Lloyd was not in the mood for badinage.

"So who are you with?" Jewel persisted.

"I'm not with anybody."

"Then what the hell are you doing here?"

Lloyd sighed. "It's a long story, Jewel."

"I love long stories. Let's go through and you can tell me over a glass of fizz."

Lloyd flapped his useless invitation, feeling foolish. "They won't let me in."

"Oh, crap. Leave it to me."

At the desk, Jewel told the thin-faced woman that Lloyd was with the Sturm Drang party. His bumptious charm did the trick. Confidence, thought Lloyd. It's all about confidence. "Thanks," he told Jewel.

They took the escalator to an upper floor, where the party was in full cry. A young woman wearing startlingly few clothes and wound about with chains approached, bearing a tray of champagne flutes; Jewel took two and handed one to Lloyd. "I gather that you've been a naughty boy," he said.

"No. That's why I'm here."

"It did sound a bit out of character. So why the bust-up? Have you been rogering one of Harry's koalas?"

Lloyd was craning his neck, looking around the room over Jewel's head. "It's Harry I've come to talk to. Will you let me know if you see him?"

Jewel's eyes sparkled with anticipation. "Can I be referee?"

Suddenly Lloyd saw a woman he recognized. Smiling, he raised a hand. She caught his eye, then turned away. Inwardly, he flinched.

"Listen, don't let me spoil your evening," he said to Jewel. "You got me in here, and I'm very grateful, but you must want to be with your friends. I'll be fine by myself."

"Rubbish. You must join our table. Hang on, and I'll have a word with Hugo. I'm sure he won't mind. He loathes Harry." Jewel slid into the crowd like a sleek seal.

Lloyd stood alone in the babble of noise and blaze of high chandeliers. *Where was Harry?* He should be here by now.

Lloyd found that his glass was being refilled, this time by a young man in a leather thong and gold body paint. He recalled reading that the theme of this year's Awards was "Submission."

"Hi. Don't I know you from somewhere?" A woman was standing in his path, blond, attractive, flirtatious.

"I don't think so."

"I know!" Her eyes opened wide. "I saw your photo in *Admag*. What was the article about? I've a hopeless memory."

"He's wanted by the police," said Jewel, reappearing at their side. "If you're interested, there's a large reward."

Jewel was accompanied by an older man with unruly gray hair and a clever, dissipated face, who struck Lloyd as somewhat the worse for drink. "Great you can join us—anything to annoy the opposition." Hugo Drang pumped Lloyd's hand vigorously. "Bloody Fox pinched one of my best accounts. Tell me," he poked Lloyd in the ribs, "what's the definition of a well-balanced Australian?"

Lloyd looked blank.

"A man who's got a chip on *both* shoulders." Drang laughed heartily.

Together they walked through to the banqueting hall, a cavernous, high-ceilinged room of tawdry opulence. Round tables laid for dinner crammed the space; on the far side of the room was a raised stage with a podium, backed by a large film screen. The noise was terrific.

"It's a bit like a brothel, I always think," said Jewel. "In that sense absolutely appropriate to this evening."

Chaos reigned for several minutes as people milled around the room in search of their tables. The Sturm Drang party had been placed near the back, and while Lloyd waited for the surge to subside so that he could sit down, he once again scanned the crowd. There was a ramrod back topped with crinkly hair he thought he recognized: yes, it was Roger, the cricket freak from Schneider Fox. Straining his eyes in the atmospheric gloom, Lloyd followed his progress and saw him raise his hand in a greeting. An answering hand rose from a table near the stage. Lloyd's nerves knotted. It was Harry.

Now what? Creating a scene at the Schneider Fox table was not going to get him anywhere.

Jewel introduced Lloyd to his colleagues, as if it were perfectly normal for him to be there. An extra place was set for him, between Jewel and a female designer—Cleopatra haircut, scarlet lipstick, tiny stretchy dress: dazzling in a scary sort of way. Lloyd hoped Suze didn't look like that. Food began to appear on the table. He pushed it distractedly around his plate.

"Apparently this place used to be a skating rink," Jewel offered. "A chap told me earlier. In the War it was a favorite hang-out of your compatriots, Rockwell, including Eisenhower and Patton. You should feel at home here."

Lloyd smiled. "I'm being made to feel very welcome."

"Well said! Now, Lloyd, since I'm being so nice to you, tip me the wink. Do you think we've got a chance with Passion?"

"Surely I'm the last person you should ask."

"On the contrary, you're the only person who hasn't got an ax to grind."

"Well . . ." Lloyd hesitated. Jewel was a friend of Piers, and Piers had not looked happy when Lloyd had last seen him in Harry's office. It was all too possible that Passion would move agencies. Then he remembered Suze's fighting words: *You are innocent. You are good at what you do*. He must be positive. He would not admit the possibility of failure. "In my opinion you haven't got a chance with Passion. I'm sorry."

"Interesting." Jewel nodded thoughtfully. Then he gave a sly grin. "I think we might have a go anyway."

The beginning of the ceremony was signaled at last by a blast of portentous music. A minor celebrity appeared on the stage and tripped his way to a podium to the sound of thunderous applause. The bright spotlights showed Lloyd that Harry was still in place. Should he go over there now?

A giant screen began to flash up a succession of ads for jeans, deodorants, drinks, cars, toys, cereal and "social" issues like homelessness or cruelty to animals. Some of the work—and many of the acceptance speeches—made Lloyd wonder why he was so eager to get back into the industry. One image provoked an outbreak of raucous cheers and cutlery-banging at the Sturm Drang table. Lloyd had seen the poster, for women's underwear, all over London, and it had made him smile every time. "Whose idea was it?" he asked.

"Mine," said three different voices.

"And now it gives me great pleasure to present the award for the best voiceover in a television commercial, which is sponsored today by Vision Computer Services. The nominations are as follows . . ." Lloyd ran a finger around his collar. He couldn't eat and he didn't dare drink. The room was simmering with heat and noise. As the latest winner descended the steps from the stage, he scanned the Schneider Fox table yet again and found one person missing. Harry had disappeared.

Lloyd looked wildly around the room. A movement at the back caught his eye. He saw a beam of pale light as a door opened, then the outline of a tall figure. This was the chance Lloyd had been waiting for. He got to his feet and moved through the tables toward the door through which he had seen Harry go out. Hardly anyone looked up as he passed; they were all watching the presentations. Lloyd found himself in a lobby; a sign indicated where Harry must be. Now that the moment had come, Lloyd felt sick with apprehension. It was still not too late to find an exit and escape into the night.

Steeling himself for the ordeal ahead, Lloyd pushed his way through the door.

Harry was standing at a basin, washing his hands. Their eyes met in the mirror. Harry's face turned ugly.

"You've got a hell of a nerve showing up here tonight." He flicked the water from his fingers with a violent gesture.

"I came to see you."

"Well, you're wasting your time. Whatever you have to say, I'm not interested." He turned from the basin and moved toward the door.

Lloyd stepped into his path. "Don't you want to keep the Passion account?"

"Don't push your luck, Rockwell." He was very close now. Lloyd thought Harry might hit him.

"I can prove to you that I didn't leak that data to Stateside." Lloyd held his gaze. "The person who did is still working for you."

Harry looked at him hard. "Why should I believe you?"

"Why shouldn't you, Harry? If I had really been the robber, do you think I would have left my fingerprints all over the place? Do you thank that Tony Salvino would have been naive enough to leave a message with my secretary if we were in cahoots? Anyway, why would I have done it? I loved my job. Did you think that I was going to work for someone else?"

"Yes."

"Come on, nobody would give a serious job to a person who had leaked such important client information, would they?"

"So what are you saying?"

"I'm saying that someone else leaked that data and pinned it on me. If you'd just give me a chance to explain, I can prove to you that I didn't do it."

"OK, prove it."

Lloyd slid the small cassette recorder out of his pocket and placed it on the marble top beside the washbasin.

Harry's face tightened with distaste. "I don't like spies." He took an angry step toward the door.

Lloyd's heartbeat was racing. *Quick!* He pushed the ON button.

"Of course I hope we can keep Passion, but this way we're covered, however Ross Bannerman jumps . . ." Sheri's voice sounded tinny in the high, tiled room.

Harry stopped. He shot Lloyd a sharp glance as Bernie's reply rumbled out of the machine, then listened to the rest of the conversation staring impassively at his shoes.

"If this thing with Stateside comes off, maybe I can get that asshole Fox off my back." Lloyd switched off the tape.

Harry raised his eyes to Lloyd's. "Is there more?"

"Nothing you'd want to hear."

"Who did the recording?"

"That's not relevant."

"You can fake these things," Harry suggested.

"You can. But I didn't."

"Even if you didn't, it doesn't prove anything."

"Not by itself, no. But there's more."

Lloyd could see that Harry was of two minds. "Hear me out," he pleaded. "If I don't convince you, then you won't hear from me again. That's a promise."

The silence that followed was broken by the squeak of the door and a sudden roar from the banqueting hall as a middle-age man entered the room. His eyes swiveled curiously to Lloyd and Harry, then he went into a cubicle and clicked the lock shut.

Lloyd waited. There was no more to say. He had done his best.

"Breakfast tomorrow." Harry's voice was matter-of-fact. "The Ritz, seven thirty. I'm flying to New York at midday. I'll give you half an hour."

Chapter Twenty-nine

After the simmer of the streets, with their frenzy of after-work traffic, the hotel lobby was cool and civilized. Sheri led the way across the Aubusson carpet, her head held high. A handsome young bellhop stepped smartly out of her path and extended a gloved hand to open a door marked Hades Bar. Suze followed Sheri inside and found herself plunged into near-darkness. As her eyes adjusted, she made out a small zinc-topped bar illuminated by atmospheric blue bulbs, behind which a faceless barman loomed white. Tables hugged the walls, each surrounded by deep, plush chairs. Most were empty. There were no windows. It was the sort of place, Suze thought, where a rich woman might meet her secret lover—or her drug dealer.

It was the evening before the presentation. Suze had been working late again when Sheri had breezed into her office, high on an adrenaline rush, and insisted they go out for a drink together. "Isn't tomorrow your last day with us? Come on, let's celebrate."

This was the Sheri who had dazzled Suze on her first day in the New York office—persuasive, impressive, irresistible. Caught on the hop, Suze had been unable to think of a reason not to go.

They sat down opposite each other at a table furnished with a tiny domed lamp and a bowl of superior salted nuts. Sheri settled herself with a contented sigh. "I love this place. Hardly anyone in New York knows it's here."

"It's great," Suze agreed, enjoying the feeling that she was one of a select few.

"So, what do you say?" Sheri asked, when the Bloody Marys had arrived. "Are we ready for tomorrow?"

Suze raised the chilled glass to her lips, feeling faintly treacherous. "Everyone's worked very hard," she parried.

"*You* certainly have." Sheri bobbed her head approvingly. "I congratulate you, Suzanne. I had the impression that English people took a lot of tea breaks and went home early."

"Actually, we have the longest working hours in Europe. It's a matter of style," Suze explained. "We like to pretend that our achievements are effortless."

"How peculiar! You English are a mystery to me. I wonder what else you're hiding?"

Suze fidgeted with the nut bowl. Was Sheri hinting at something? But Sheri smiled serenely, and changed the subject. "Tell me, when are you flying home?"

"Saturday morning." Suze felt a flutter of anticipation.

"You'll be back," Sheri assured her. "There's no place in the world like New York. I could help you find a job here, if you wanted."

"I'd love that." Suze leaned forward eagerly. Then she remembered why this would be impossible. "At least, one day, perhaps."

Sheri wagged a finger at her. "'One day' is a phrase I do not allow in my vocabulary. Opportunities don't come around twice. You have to grab what you want off the candy tray." She threw out one arm imperiously. "Waiter! Two more Bloody Marys over here."

Suze saw with surprise that Sheri's glass was already empty. It seemed that tonight, for once, Sheri was declaring herself off duty, off the leash.

"So many women flunk out of their careers," Sheri continued. "They get pregnant, or they can't take the responsibility, or they watch with big doe-eyes while some man grabs the big job." Her voice sizzled with scorn. "Look at me. I have a great job, a good address, money in the bank. You could have the same. The secret is knowing what you want, and not letting anything—or anyone—stand in your way."

Suze tried to picture herself in a sleek penthouse in New York or London with an important job, a large income and a huge designer wardrobe. Was that what she wanted?

"Don't get me wrong, I'm not one of those 'feminists,'" Sheri said scornfully. "I just know what I want out of life."

"What about men?"

"Sure, they can be a help—especially the older, married ones who don't get laid often enough." Sheri winked.

"No, I mean 'relationships.'" Suze grimaced apologetically at the word. "I mean love."

"I don't love, Suzanne, I fuck. That's what men want, and I do it well." Her face twisted. "I've had lots of practice."

"And you've never wanted to get married?"

"Why buy when you can rent? With marriage all that happens is that you stop doing what you want and start doing what your husband wants you to do—going to the supermarket, entertaining his friends, fixing up his home, moving to a strange city for the sake of his job. That's all on top of your own job, of course. Then when you're all worn out he tells you you're not as much fun as you used to be and moves on to wife number two. Who needs it?"

Suze nodded. She had often expressed similar views herself. "I dread being married to a man with his jacket hanging up in his car," she confessed.

"There are worse things." Sheri's voice hardened. "Like men who beat up their wives, then leave them in some trailer park with a bunch of kids and no money."

"Still, I suppose marriage doesn't have to be like that." Suze was thinking of her own parents. "Two grown-up people can simply like being together."

"Sure they can. It's called sex."

"No. I mean—" Suze stopped, confused by her own thoughts. She had a private image of herself, curled up in an armchair reading a book, with unwashed hair and wearing an old pair of jeans, and having a man look across at her and say, "I love you," and mean it. This was too corny for words. Instead she asked, "Haven't you ever wanted children?"

Sheri waved a dismissive hand. "My apartment's so small. Where would I keep them? Take my advice, Suzanne. If you want to be successful in this world, like me, you can't afford to waste time on relationships."

Suze thought of the years wasted with Lawrence—wasted not because he had married someone else but because he had kept her bound within his own limitations for so long. She'd never seen it quite that way before. And after Lawrence had come Nick. Where she had expected romance, she had found hurt and humiliation.

The darkness made her bold. "Do you mind if I ask you something?"

"Go ahead."

"Is it true that you asked Nick Bianco to take me out?"

"Didn't you like him?" Sheri looked surprised. "I can tell you, in some circles he's regarded as one of the most desirable men in town."

"He's very charming," Suze admitted. "Unfortunately, it didn't work out."

Sheri gave a full-blooded laugh. "I wasn't expecting you to *marry* the guy. Every girl deserves a fling now and then."

"Nick implied that asking me out was a kind of favor to you."

"Men are such blabbermouths."

"So it's true?"

A gleam of private amusement lit Sheri's face. "Sort of. You have to remember I didn't know you so well then. Maybe I didn't want you asking too many questions about your work."

"Why would you worry about that?"

Sheri paused to consider. Then she leaned across the table toward Suze. The lamplight sharpened the shadows under her strong cheekbones and the thrust of her chin. "I'll let you in on a secret. I've been developing a little insurance policy in case Passion decides not to stay with us."

Suze opened her eyes wide. "I don't understand."

"The fact is, I happen to have some good contacts at Stateside."

"So?" Suze tried to sound casual.

"And I'm sure I could swing that account on board if Passion doesn't come to the party," Sheri finished smugly.

"So you win either way. How clever. I don't think I'd be brave enough to try anything like that. Weren't you worried about client conflict?"

Sheri's nostrils flared with disdain. "Rules are for little people. You have to see the big picture."

Despite everything Suze couldn't suppress a flicker of admiration for Sheri—a lone woman, manipulating these large companies for her own ends. There was an ingenious symmetry about her plans. Suze felt a lurch of guilt about what she was plotting with Lloyd. It was still not too late to ally herself with Sheri and a glittering future in New York.

Sheri pressed home her point. "Suzanne, if you want something, you have to reach out and grab it. Why not? You have talent and you have guts. You don't want to be Miss Ordinary, do you?"

"No," Suze replied uncertainly. She looked away. More shadowy figures had gathered in the small bar. She watched them murmuring to each other in the gloom, like priests and sinners at the confessional. Sly shafts of light flashed on a signet ring embedded in a man's hairy hand and lingered on the curve of a glossy, stockinged calf. Suze blinked and stretched her eyes, feeling half blind.

"You have to go for what you want, Suzanne." Sheri's eyes glittered with zeal. "And remember, we girls have an advantage."

"What's that?"

"We can make men do what we want." Sheri smiled lasciviously. "I remember when I was a little kid, maybe nine years old, and a fair came to town. I didn't have any money to go, but I found a place where you could squeeze through the fence. And there it was! All these lights and glamour and bright costumes. What I absolutely craved was a beautiful doll that was the first prize in the shooting gallery. She had real hair and a big stiff skirt with sequins and lace.

She was so perfect, so clean. I'd never had a brand new toy in my life. I used to go every night and stare at her. On the last night of the fair, the man running the booth told me I could keep her if I gave him a kiss. Well, he was kind of dirty-looking, and it turned out to be a little more than a kiss, but it wasn't so bad. And he gave me that doll! I couldn't believe how easy it was."

Suze stared, too shocked to comment. She had been to fairgrounds too, and had coveted the fluffy vulgar prizes, but she had always gone with her hand held tight, or high on her father's shoulders. "Where's your family now?" she asked.

"Who knows?" Sheri knocked back the last of her drink. "The point I'm making is that deciding what you want is the key to success. While other people are hesitating about the right thing to do, you can snatch the prize from under their noses."

"Like Lloyd Rockwell, for example?" Suze asked daringly.

"Lloyd?" Sheri screwed up her eyes as if she could barely remember him. "He wasn't so bad, in a WASPy kind of a way. Those polite, preppy types are always the biggest pushovers. I even maneuvered him into making a pass at me once." She chuckled. "It lasted all of sixty seconds, but after that I pretty much had him by the balls."

A wave of revulsion broke over Suze. And when she surfaced, it was as if all her illusions had been swept away. For the first time she saw Sheri clearly: how she fed off the power and talent of others. The image of Sheri astride Bernie on the black sofa arose in her mind, filling her with disgust. Sheri was a parasite, with no ideas or creativity of her own; at the center of her being was a void.

Suddenly Suze wanted to get out. She made a show of looking at her watch. "Gosh, I must go."

Sheri didn't seem to hear. "Winners and losers," she murmured, "that's what it's all about." She gripped Suze's arm. "You can be a winner—like me."

Suze held herself still. She could feel Sheri's moist palm, warm on her bare arm. She saw the manicured perfection of her pink, polished nails, the expensive elegance of the watch that trapped her slim wrist in a chain of gold. Sheri was lonely, Suze realized, with a twinge of pity.

She stood up abruptly. "Thank you for the drinks. I still have work to finish," she explained.

"Attagirl." There was the faintest slur in Sheri's voice. "That's what I like about you, Suzanne. We're two of a kind."

Chapter Thirty

"Market indices show that forty-two percent of married couples plan to visit Europe at some stage in the near future . . ." Sheri tapped the bar-chart on the screen with a stick. This morning she was dressed in fire-engine red. She looked marvelous.

Suze gripped the edge of her chair, her heart racing. She had lain awake most of last night, worrying. Since six o'clock this morning she and Dee Dee had been in the office, making the preparations. What if it didn't work? What if they were wrong? What if—? Suze forced herself to concentrate on the man at the center of the boardroom table. Ross Bannerman, the founder of Passion, had a face more familiar than the president's: you could barely open a newspaper or magazine without seeing his cheesy grin somewhere. It was an odd sensation to see him here now, in the flesh, with Tucker, the marketing director, and another Passion colleague, whose name Suze didn't catch. She wondered what they were making of Sheri's presentation.

From the start Sheri had been in overdrive. She had insisted on conducting a rehearsal beforehand, and now that Suze saw her in action for the second time she realized that every word Sheri mouthed was scripted. Suze almost felt sorry for her: Sheri was trying so hard, but Suze could tell that her whole approach was wrong for Passion. Even her swanky suit jarred with the casual wear of Bannerman's tieless team.

Harry was looking cool, as he always did. He had nodded a greeting to Suze as he entered the room, but had said nothing.

Bernie had opened the meeting by referring to the "Rockwell Incident." It was regrettable, Bernie had said, but Lloyd had been fired; the incident was closed. Today's meeting was to plan the future, not to dwell on the past. Schneider Fox had devised an entirely new campaign, which would fuel Passion's drive to replace Stateside as the market leader in the transatlantic airline business. Spearheading that campaign would be Rockwell's replacement, Sheri Crystal.

After a good half hour of guff, Sheri presented a sixty-second film showing a businessman shaking hands with a colleague outside an office building; relaxing in the care of an attractive (but not too attractive) flight attendant; and then being welcomed by his wife and children in an airport arrivals lounge. A woman's voiceover boasted breathily, "We look after you better"; the same copyline accompanied stills from the film in a series of print and billboard mock-ups.

It was well produced—Suze had done much of the work herself—but the content was uninspiring. When the tape ended, there was dead silence.

"It's good, isn't it?" Bernie said, with grating bonhomie.

Sheri had resumed her place at the table and was staring down, twiddling a pen in both hands.

Bannerman and Tucker exchanged a look. Suze held her breath. Then Bannerman spoke. "I have to say that it's not what we've come to expect from Schneider Fox. In the past, you've always created something that traded on Passion's distinctiveness. We'll have to think about it."

"It's bland." Tucker was blunt. "It might as well be an advertisement for Stateside."

Sheri opened her mouth to say something, then shut it again. Bernie put on his most ingratiating smile. "Well, we certainly appreciate your frankness," he said. "I guess we'll need to do some more work."

"I think we'll need to explore our options," said Tucker brutally. He began to gather up his papers.

Suze swallowed. She must speak now, before it was too late. "In that case I'm sure you'll be interested to see our alternative presentation," she said, hoping that she sounded more confident than she felt. Out of the corner of her eye she saw Bernie look inquiringly at Sheri, and Sheri shake her head. She prayed that Dee Dee was ready. "It won't take very long," she continued. "I want to show you a rough video mock-up, just to give you an idea." Before anyone could tell her not to, she slotted another tape into the machine.

The tape she had spent hours preparing took one minute to play. After twenty seconds Bannerman was smiling; after fifty he was laughing. "That's more like it!" He slapped the table. "It's much more *us* than the first presentation, much more like what you did for us way back." As he was saying this, his eyes turned from Suze to where Harry was sitting. There was a pause.

Dee Dee, where are you? Suze screamed silently.

"I'm glad you picked up on that, Mr. Bannerman," Sheri cut in smoothly. "That's exactly what we wanted. We thought we'd try the other presentation first, to see if you might want a change of direction, but this is the option we think is best."

"I see," said Bannerman, a little dubiously. "Well, you had me fooled. Anyway, let's go with the second option."

"It will be our number-one priority." Sheri gave him a dazzling smile.

She's going to get away with it, thought Suze, in rising panic. All that work Lloyd and I have put into this just to benefit Sheri. She glanced around the table. Bannerman and his team were getting ready to leave. Sheri had recovered her poise. Bernie was grinning. Only Harry sat absolutely still.

"One thing, Ms. Crystal," said Tucker. "That great music in the background. It was familiar, but I couldn't place it. What is it?"

"It's . . . um . . . ah . . . Oh, it's so silly but it's slipped my mind." Sheri looked inquiringly at Suze. Suze met her gaze, saying nothing.

"Suzanne?" Sheri prompted. There was an edge of panic in her voice. For several seconds they stared at each other in silence. Suze was aware of Bernie shifting uncomfortably.

"It's Miles Davis, from his album *Kind of Blue,*" said Lloyd's voice. Suze nearly wept with relief. There was a crackle of static from the video screen, and a man's features appeared. "With John Coltrane on sax and Bill Evans on piano," he added.

The stunned silence erupted into uproar. "What the fuck is he doing here?" demanded Bernie. *He's not here*, thought Suze, swallowing a hysterical giggle. Sheri's face looked frozen with panic. The Passion team whispered to each other.

"He's here—at least, he's linked to us by videophone, at my invitation," said Harry Fox abruptly. "Rockwell outlined this presentation to me in London yesterday morning. And he's convinced me that he wasn't responsible for leaking the Passion bookings to Stateside."

Bernie shot a sharp glance at him. He looked worried.

"Go on," said Bannerman.

"I think Rockwell should tell you himself," replied Harry. "Go ahead, Lloyd."

"Thank you, Harry," said Lloyd. "When I was accused of leaking data to Stateside, I couldn't understand what had happened. For the first week after I was fired I confess I didn't know what to do. Then a good friend," he paused for a moment, "encouraged me to try to clear my name, and I decided to try to find out what was going on."

Suze was standing stock still in the middle of the room, staring at the screen. There was Lloyd, the man in the photographs, the voice on the telephone, put together at last. He was wearing a dark suit and a plain light shirt, as she had instructed him, to look good on screen. And he did look good; in fact, he looked great. His face was calm and confident. His eyes were blue.

"I began by calling up Passion customers," Lloyd continued, "and I found that many of them had been approached by Stateside. Somehow they had accessed the list, as you rightly concluded, Harry. I knew it wasn't me who'd leaked it to them, and I also knew that somebody had tried to pin it on me by planting a phone message where it was likely to be discovered. That suggested it was somebody close to me trying to cover up his—or her—traces."

"That's just what I said!" Sheri gave Bernie an accusing look. He ignored her.

"On the other hand," Lloyd continued, "it wasn't somebody familiar with the procedures for using such lists—anyone who was would know that we had inserted dummy names in the list to prevent this kind of abuse. I called one of those dummies on Tuesday night—my sister. Sure enough, she had been approached by Stateside."

Bannerman and his colleagues were staring at the screen, intent on Lloyd's words. Suze saw Tucker make a note.

"My next step was to try and find out *when* this list was leaked. As some of you will know, Schneider Fox has online access to data on Passion bookings. Earlier this week I got hold of an up-to-date list. By calling a large number of Passion customers and comparing the booking dates of those who had been approached by Stateside with those who hadn't, I was able to establish to within a few days when the leak occurred."

"How does that help us?" asked Bannerman.

"Well, for one thing," Lloyd replied, "the leak occurred after I had left New York, when I no longer had direct access to the Passion data. That helps me—though, of course, I *might* have been able to leak the list of customers from London with the help of a confederate."

Suze noticed that Harry was smiling.

"But there is another aspect which is much more significant," Lloyd continued. "To access this data requires the use of a password. Only a few people are authorized to access the data and each has his—or her—own password. For security reasons these passwords are kept confidential. I know my password, but I don't know that of any of my colleagues. But the computer knows them and the computer will be able to tell us who accessed the data during the period it was leaked to Stateside. I guess whoever leaked the list of passengers didn't know that his or her password would have been logged at the time."

Sheri choked and then rose to her feet. "I hope none of you are taking this seriously," she said. "It's clearly a setup, engineered by Rockwell and his accomplice, Suzanne Wilding." She pointed to Suze.

"Rockwell has already shown himself to be disloyal. Now Wilding has gone behind my back too. I would not be surprised to find that *she* was the one who supplied confidential client information to Rockwell after he was fired by Schneider Fox."

She paused for dramatic effect, and for a moment Suze thought Sheri might yet win them over. Then Bernie spoke. "Ms. Crystal, as of this moment I am placing you on indefinite leave. Please leave the building immediately."

Sheri's face froze. She looked at Bernie. Finding no response, she turned first to Harry and then to Bannerman. They looked away. Anger blazed in her face. The features Suze had once so much admired turned ugly: her eyes were wide; her lips drew away from her pearly teeth: she looked like a Barbie doll on speed. She snatched up her case and strode to the door. "You'll be hearing from my lawyers." Then she left, slamming the door behind her.

Bernie was the first to speak. "Rockwell, I owe you an apology. Please consider yourself reinstated with honor."

Harry coughed. "Actually, Bernie, I've already offered him a job with the London office."

Suze could see that Lloyd was trying to stay cool, but delight and relief animated his whole face. She kept smiling encouragingly at him, as if he could see her.

"Jesus, guys, what kind of a company is this?" asked Bannerman. "Listen, Lloyd, while these two are fighting over you, why don't you jump ship and come to work for me? If you can meet me here in New York on Monday, we'll talk about it."

"Thanks, everyone." Lloyd was grinning openly now. "I'm flattered by your confidence." If he was being ironic, his face showed no sign of it. "This morning I had no prospect of a job, and now I've got three terrific offers. I hope you'll understand if I take a few days to decide my next move."

Schneider, Fox and Bannerman all made noises of agreement. "I'd just like to say one more thing," Lloyd went on, "and that's to pay tribute to Susannah Wilding. She had faith in me when nobody else seemed to. She encouraged me to try and clear my name. And this Passion campaign is as much her work as mine. Thanks, Suze, for everything."

Lloyd smiled down out of the screen. Then there was a crackle and his image disappeared.

Chapter Thirty-one

"Isn't this lovely?"

Betsy's mother surveyed the imposing dining room with an approving smile and allowed Lloyd to pull out a chair for her. "So much better than that poky table by the kitchen they wanted to give us. You can't let these people get away with tricks like that." She settled herself in the seat with the best view of the small garden, while Betsy and Lloyd ranged themselves on either side.

Betsy let out a tiny sigh of relief. She had spent days of investigation before picking this hotel. It was within walking distance of Harrods and it had character—Mother was big on character—but it also had modern bathrooms and unstained mattresses: Betsy had checked. The only hiccup so far had occurred over the forty-watt lightbulb in the bedside lamp, but Room Service had promised a more powerful replacement as soon as it could spare someone to go to the drugstore. She allowed her gaze to wander around the lofty room, with its framed foxhunting scenes, gilt bracket lamps and ornate plasterwork. The effect was a little chilly, perhaps, but undeniably English. Most tables were still empty. She recognized the few other diners as fellow Americans, accustomed to eating earlier than the British: it was still only six thirty.

Betsy perused the menu, glad to see that the food wasn't too fancy. She was hungry, having eaten nothing all day except a flabby so-called croissant at Heathrow Airport. This morning she had traveled out on the subway to meet her mother, alone, since Lloyd had pronounced himself too busy to accompany her. Fortunately, Mother had accepted her explanation that he could not leave the office on a normal working day. Subjecting her mother to a return journey on the subway was, of course, out of the question, though it was irritating that the taxi had cost almost a hundred dollars and taken forever to reach the hotel through the commuter traffic. Perhaps it was just as well that Lloyd hadn't come. It was so important that this evening was a success.

So far, so good. Lloyd was politely inquiring about her mother's flight. Betsy was already familiar with the saga of delays, long lines and the dearth of baggage carts due to striking Stateside staff.

"You see, you should have traveled Passion after all," Lloyd teased. "They take care of their employees as well as their passengers, so no one needs to strike."

"I think this English welfare system is to blame. People here don't seem to want to work. There weren't any problems at Kennedy."

"Now, Mother, let's not get into that," Betsy interceded. Experience had taught her that politics was not an ideal topic of conversation between her mother and Lloyd.

"Drinks, sir?" A waiter stood at their table, pencil poised, head cocked ingratiatingly.

"Do you serve iced tea?" Betsy's mother inquired.

"Oh, I think we can do better than that." Lloyd had been lounging back in his chair, looking relaxed and unusually handsome, Betsy thought, if a little unkempt. When they got home, she would tell him he needed a haircut. Now he leaned forward and grinned at them both. "Let's have some champagne."

Betsy saw her mother give a doubtful frown. "Is there something to celebrate?"

"Lots," replied Lloyd exuberantly. "Including your arrival in London, Mrs. Rennslayer."

"Why, thank you, Lloyd dear. You know, now that you're going to be one of the family, I really think it's time you started calling me 'Happy.' Unless you'd prefer 'Mother.'"

"Whatever makes you happy, Happy." Lloyd winked at Betsy. She gave him her be-on-your-best-behavior glare.

He had been in this impish mood ever since she had returned home to change, leaving her mother at the hotel. They had spent the afternoon shopping. Even as she had approached the front door, tired and laden with large crackly bags, she had heard loud music pounding out of the stereo. She found Lloyd lying on the living room floor, in jeans and bare feet, with all the windows wide open, surrounded by CDs. As soon as he saw her, he jumped to his feet, picked her up, bags and all, and carried her triumphantly about the room until she had yelled to be put down. She had almost wondered whether he had been drinking, though it wasn't even six o'clock.

Eventually she had persuaded him to turn off the music and explain what had happened. She had not been able to follow every twist of the plot, with its printouts and computer passwords and videolinks, but two points emerged. First and most wonderful was that Lloyd had been offered his job back. To Betsy this seemed like a miracle, an eleventh-hour reprieve from breaking the news of his unemployed state to Mother. Not quite so thrilling was the realization that a key role in Lloyd's rehabilitation had been played by Susannah Wilding. Lloyd had been irksomely effusive on this point. For some time Betsy had been wondering what this Wilding woman was like. Mother's report had not been wholly encouraging: messy-looking and insolent, but the sort of woman, Mother supposed, that certain men might find attractive. Still, now that everything was working out at last, Betsy could afford to be magnanimous.

The champagne was ceremonially transported to their table in a silver bucket, swaddled in white napery like a royal baby. When it had been poured out, Lloyd fingered the fragile stem of his glass and cleared his throat.

"Oh no," Betsy's mother objected, before Lloyd could speak. "You can't toast yourselves. Let me." She raised her glass. "To Betsy and Lloyd. Eternal happiness." She took a tiny sip and smiled bravely. Mother didn't care for alcohol. "Darling, have you decided where you're moving yet? It would be so wonderful if you could be near us. You know Daddy and I would be happy to help financially."

"Who said we were moving?" Lloyd shot Betsy an accusing glance.

"We've only discussed it," she put in hurriedly. "Why don't we order our food?"

When the menu had been thoroughly interpreted and debated, and the accompanying wine chosen, Lloyd raised his champagne glass again. "We have something else to drink to tonight. I want to celebrate the fact that today I have received no fewer than three job offers."

Mother was impressed. "That's wonderful, Lloyd! Are you a vice president at last?"

"Who cares about the title? The important thing is to enjoy your work, to feel stretched. And guess what, Betsy?" He looked across at her excitedly. "I forgot to tell you that Jay called today. He's finally sold his movie to a Hollywood distributor. Isn't that fantastic?"

"Who's Jay, dear?" asked Mother.

"A friend of Lloyd's." Betsy did not expand on this. So far she had managed to conceal from Mother that Lloyd's best friend was a, well, homosexual.

"Maybe Betsy told you that I helped Jay write the script?" Lloyd continued. He speared a prawn and chewed it with relish. "In fact, I wrote most of it. Jay says the studio may want to commission more work from me." He laughed happily. "Watch out! Next thing you know, I'll be lying by the pool at the Beverly Hills Hotel, talking telephone-number deals."

Mother stiffened. "Hollywood would not suit Betsy. It's such a corrupting atmosphere."

"Think of all that sunshine, though—and the ocean! I could handle that kind of corruption for a year or two. If I hit some troughs, I could always play piano bars to keep us going. By the way, Betsy, I've decided to buy another piano when we get home. We can make room, if we throw out some of the furniture."

Betsy sawed at her *magret de canard* with grim concentration. She did not care for Lloyd in this mood. She knew perfectly well that he had no intention of going to Hollywood: he was being deliberately provocative. "Tell Mother about the real jobs," she said, hoping to steer him back on course.

"Well, one is with Passion, but that's not a firm offer, just a possibility. I'm meeting the big boss in New York next week. Oh, yes," he continued, "I'm afraid that means I won't be able to accompany you on the trip."

"What?"

"Lloyd, you can't let us down!" Betsy dropped her knife and fork with a clatter. She felt like bursting into tears. "Who's going to drive the car?"

Lloyd looked surprised. "You both have licenses, don't you? You just point the car and drive." He raised his glass and took a careless swig. "I've already booked a flight going out tomorrow night. By the time you get back, Betsy, I'll have the apartment in shape and my job fixed up."

There was an uncomfortable silence. Mother was dabbing her mouth with her napkin, eyes downcast. "Let's just pray we don't get a flat tire," she sighed, "or wind up murdered in some strange hotel room."

Lloyd laughed. "Of course you won't."

Betsy couldn't believe how heartless he sounded. She touched her mother's hand. "We'll be all right."

"I know we will, Betsy." Her mother returned her grip comfortingly. "It's the lack of consideration that bothers me. I'm afraid that's something you're going to have to learn about men."

"More wine, anyone?" From the other side of the table, Lloyd raised a bottle and smiled at them with almost insulting good humor. There were times, these days, when he seemed like a stranger. Betsy was beginning to doubt if she would ever be able to keep him in order.

"I think we have all had enough," Mother said firmly. "And my steak was tough. I always say you can't beat American beef."

Betsy could see Lloyd preparing to issue a retort. "What about the third job?" she prompted, heading him off.

"Schneider Fox London have a vacancy. It's a very successful outfit, Mrs. Rennslayer, and it's on the up. I have to say I'm tempted."

"But that's impossible! It's been bad enough for poor Betsy to be away from home all these weeks. I don't know how many times she's been on the telephone to me, sobbing her heart out."

Lloyd was looking betrayed. Betsy attempted a dismissive laugh. "Mother, you're exaggerating. It did seem awfully rainy at the beginning, but we've had lots of interesting experiences."

"I admit that I have had to go to work some of the time," Lloyd said pointedly, "but that's given Betsy a chance to write her thesis and soak up some English atmosphere. We've been out to dinner and the theater. We've gone sightseeing. We even had a sunny weekend in the country."

Betsy felt her mother's sympathetic gaze. "Is that where you met the awful woman who couldn't discipline her children?"

"She wasn't awful," Lloyd protested. "She was delightful. How could you say such a thing, Betsy?"

Betsy was beginning to feel like a circus performer, trying to balance on two galloping horses with minds of their own. "Why don't we discuss this another time?" she suggested.

Her mother took no notice. "But, Lloyd, you can't possibly be thinking of *living* in England?"

"Not forever," he agreed. "I don't want to do anything forever. It's good to move around, try new things, not get trapped. But I need to talk everything over with Betsy and we haven't had a chance yet. We'll let you know when we've made our decision."

Mother bridled. "That is not a satisfactory answer."

Anxious to prevent further argument, Betsy opened her mouth to speak.

Her mother flung up a commanding palm. "No, Betsy, I will not be silenced! Someone has to speak up for you. I think it would be very selfish of Lloyd to take you away from your home and your family—especially at this particular time."

"And what particular time is that, Mrs. Rennslayer?" asked Lloyd. His tone was even, but his upper lip had a pinched look to it that Betsy recognized. He was getting angry.

"Moth*errr*," she warned.

"I don't pretend to approve of what has happened, but a mother cannot harden her heart against her little girl—however she has behaved."

"Mother, please—"

"Betsy is not a little girl. She is thirty-four years old."

"You know what I'm talking about, Lloyd."

"No, I don't. Do you, Betsy?" Lloyd was looking very stern.

Betsy began to panic. There was something she had not yet brought herself to explain to her mother. She could see disaster hurtling toward them all. She began to stumble out excuses, but Mother simply turned up the volume. "I am referring, of course, to the baby."

"But I never said—"

"What baby?"

"It is an American baby. It *belongs* in America."

"Betsy, what's she talking about?"

"Mother, please let me explain—"

"No grandchild of mine is going to be born under socialist medicine!"

"Mother, *shut up*!"

There was a ghastly silence. Betsy's hand crept to her mouth. What had she said?

She became aware that a large object had appeared next to her. Glancing sideways, she saw a glistening chocolate cake exuding jam, a bowl of blood-red berries, something yellow submerged in cream. She wondered if she was going to throw up.

"Something from the sweet trolley, madam?" intoned a sepulchral voice.

"Give us five minutes," said Lloyd, with aplomb.

"I am going to my room." Mother rose majestically from the table. "I have no wish to interfere in matters that apparently do not concern a mother." Her wounded eyes swiveled to Betsy. "I will talk to you later, Elizabeth." She walked from the room, handbag clasped to her heart. As she reached the exit she tottered and gripped the door jamb for support.

Betsy half rose from her seat. Then she felt a hand on hers.

"Good for you," said Lloyd warmly.

His touch released a gush of tears. "I shouldn't have said that." Betsy groped for her handkerchief.

"Yes, you should. It doesn't mean you don't love her. She has to understand that you're grown-up enough to run your own life."

"Am I?" Betsy hung her head. At this moment she didn't feel capable of running anything. Her mother's reproachful eyes scorched holes in her conscience.

"You're also grown-up enough to tell me that you're having a baby."

Betsy's head jerked up. Lloyd was watching her steadily. He looked calm, but remote. She felt almost frightened of him.

"It's not that I didn't want to talk to you," she tried to explain. "I never seemed to find the right moment. You've been so . . . strange these last couple of weeks."

"Strange?" He laughed abruptly. "Can you blame me?"

"And then when I found out for sure, there didn't seem any point in making a big drama about what might have been."

"'Might have been'?" Lloyd pounced on her words. "You mean you're *not* pregnant?"

"It must have been a stomach bug. I did a test, but I didn't do it right. So then I had to buy another kit and wait until you'd gone out of the house to try again. Except you were always telephoning or fiddling with your papers." Betsy hoped he was beginning to understand how difficult he'd been to live with. "I finally got a chance the night before last, when you went off to that big party. The result was negative."

"You're not going to have a baby," he repeated wonderingly. Betsy was hurt to see how relieved he looked.

The dessert man was trundling toward them again. "Not tonight, thanks," Lloyd said, forestalling his patter. "We'll have the check." He turned to Betsy. "How come your mother seemed so convinced you were pregnant?"

Betsy hesitated, framing her answer. "She happened to call the first time I did the test. You were out and I was lonely so I told her what I was doing. She was so excited. She went off into this big fantasy about grandchildren and birthday parties and having us live nearby so that she could babysit."

Lloyd grunted. "And what about the father?" he asked. "Were you planning to inform him at some stage?"

"Of course I was, Lloyd. But you were always so busy. Then I discovered that there was nothing to tell."

"And you haven't told your mother you're *not* pregnant because you didn't want to disappoint her, is that it?" Lloyd sounded bemused, but he seemed to swallow it.

"I wanted to tell her in my own time." Betsy twisted her napkin in her lap. She did not pass on Mother's view that there was nothing like a pregnant fiancée to keep a man on his toes in the run-up to a wedding, a dangerous period during which relentless discussion of flowers, bridesmaids and engraved invitations had been known to make many a prospective bridegroom turn tail.

She looked guiltily at Lloyd. He looked warily back. The silence between them lengthened.

"You don't have to marry me, you know, Betsy," he said gently.

"But I want to!" she protested. *Was this true?* Panic gripped her. She wanted to go back to the way things were.

"Do you?"

Betsy could only nod. The right words had deserted her.

Lloyd reached across to her. "Come on. Let's take a little walk."

Outside it was still light but the traffic had quieted. They left the hotel and walked toward the park. Lloyd put his arm around her. It felt comfortable, and familiar. Betsy could hardly stand the thought that he might ever become a stranger.

By the time they returned the sky was dusky, noisy with nesting pigeons. Lloyd paused on the steps of the hotel and disengaged himself. He smiled into her eyes with such a sad, affectionate look that Betsy's whole body flushed with sudden heat. Never had he seemed more attractive. If he had asked her, she would have gone upstairs with him right there and then.

"It's been a tough evening," he said. "I think we both need time alone to think. Why don't I see if I can find you a room here tonight?"

Chapter Thirty-two

As the plane leveled out from its climb, Suze pressed her cheek against the cold window and squinted down through a milky dawn sky. A frill of white showed where the silver sea met flat, mottled land, and she wondered if she was looking at Long Island—if, a few hours from now, the smart crowd would emerge from mansions and cottages below, groomed for another weekend of whoop-de-doo. Then the plane tilted and she felt a burst of joy as she caught a final glimpse of Manhattan, angled against the horizon, looking as peaceful and as static as a monochrome postcard. "I'll be back," she whispered.

The view disappeared in a rush of cloud that spattered the window with moisture. Suze closed her eyes. Her ears were fuzzy with the thrum of the engines, her limbs sluggish in the pressurized atmosphere. Images formed and dissolved in her mind: Lloyd's disarming grin when Harry, Bernie and Bannerman all offered him jobs; Sheri's office, stripped of its pictures and flower vases; Dee Dee's face when Suze presented her with a pair of the Eiffel Tower sandals she had so coveted, ordered by phone and couriered from London at reckless expense; a yellow flash in the dark street as Raymond opened the cab door to let her climb into its musty interior. It had been four in the morning when she said good-bye to the apartment. As the driver gunned his car through empty streets, Suze had rolled down the window to breathe in the city's warm exhalations for the last time, watching through half-closed eyes as the gaudily necklaced buildings flashed past.

The past twenty-four hours had been exhilarating but exhausting. Once Harry and Bernie had carried off the Passion team to a celebratory lunch, the rest of Schneider Fox had decided it was playtime. As news of Sheri's dismissal spread, Suze found half the company crowding into her office, avid for a blow-by-blow account. Their blood-lust was disconcerting: she had been unaware of how much Sheri was disliked—or how much Lloyd was missed. A sentimental, valedictory mood prevailed. People Suze scarcely recognized squeezed her hands and said how wonderful it had been knowing her. She had been presented with a farewell card and a squashy parcel that turned out to be a six-foot inflatable Chrysler Building, complete with battery-operated light. Suze promised that it should take pride of place in her London bedroom. Halfway through the afternoon Harry had poked his head around the door, grinned at the melee and given her a thumbs-up sign: "See you in London." Bernie never reappeared. The word was that he had gone straight on to his primal-screaming session.

By five o'clock the office was empty; everyone had taken off for the weekend. Suze swept her few personal possessions into a plastic bag and took a last look around. She would miss the wide blue view from the window. Her eye alighted on one of Lloyd's sharpened pencils; she popped it into her bag for good luck and closed the door.

The sight of the apartment, strewn with papers and coffee mugs and half-filled suitcases, made her want to weep. Instead, she called up Raymond and after a stiff bout of bargaining wrote him an enormous check to cover cleaning, restocking the fridge and a fresh supply of boring old houseplants. Then she showered off the contaminations of the day, washed her hair until it squeaked and prepared herself for one last evening in New York.

The restaurant was predictably chic, with minimalist styling and subdued lighting. It was eight o'clock when she arrived—early by Manhattan standards—and the tables were empty. She had not promised that she would come, only agreed under pressure that she might. But there he was at the bar, as he had said he would be, the golden boy with his all-American smile.

"Hello, Nick." She kept her voice casual.

He jumped off the bar stool and came forward to kiss her on both cheeks. "Great to see you! Let's sit down." He led her to a corner table—"his" table, she was sure—and ordered her a drink. He was very self-possessed. It was hard to believe that this was the man who had turned so vicious only a week before.

"Thanks for coming." His blue eyes were sincere. "I want to apologize. I couldn't let you leave town thinking badly of me."

Suze said nothing. His phrasing gave him away: Nick wasn't really interested in her, but in himself.

"I hated that argument we had in the country," he protested. "It was my fault. I was a little uptight that weekend."

Uptight? What a useful weasel-word that was, excusing a multitude of sins. Suze twisted her glass around and around, trying to block out the images of his savage anger. "What happened to the movie deal?" she asked.

Nick flashed her a sunny smile. "*Perfecto.* All fixed up. Zarg's forgotten all about that little problem we had."

And what about Jodie? Suze wondered. *Had she forgotten?*

"Good." She gave him a smile. "There's something I want to know. Tell me honestly, did Sheri really tell you to ask me out?"

Nick look embarrassed. "I said a lot of things that night I didn't mean. I was mad at you. All Sheri did was to tell me that you were new in town and might be lonely—but only because I was pumping her about this great-looking English girl she had working for her." He leaned across to her. "I liked you. You know that. I loved that day we had, doing goofy things in Central Park. It was nice. It was . . ." He frowned, searching for the right word. When he found it, he sounded faintly surprised. ". . . normal," he pronounced.

Suze studied his face. She thought she believed him. "I'm beginning to think I am rather normal," she said, with a sigh.

"You're gorgeous," Nick replied automatically. "Maybe when I've finished having fun I'll be normal too." He didn't look enthusiastic about it. "You don't want to go believing people like Sheri Crystal," he continued. "The first time I did some work with Sheri, she made a play for me. Then I found out she was balling another guy—Tony somebody. All she wanted was to get my ideas for free." He looked disgusted.

"Tony who? Do you remember?"

Nick shrugged. "Some Italian name . . . But who cares about Sheri?" He held out a hand to Suze and gave her his irresistible bad-boy smile. "Friends?" he asked.

Suze's eyes wandered over the smooth, tanned planes of his face, noting the curl of his smile and the tousled forelock, just asking to be smoothed back. He was a gorgeous hunk of manhood. She didn't fancy him one bit. "Friends," she agreed, putting her hand in his. They shared a long smile. She felt the balance of their relationship swing between remembered highs and lows, and settle somewhere comfortable in between. She had been silly, but she hadn't been used.

A purring noise interrupted the amicable silence: Nick's mobile phone. Politely, he let it ring, in case she had anything more to say. Suze watched anxiety cloud his face. She burst out laughing. "Go on, answer it. You know you're dying to."

"Well, if you're sure . . ." He slid it out of his pocket.

Suze stood up. "I must go anyway. I'm meeting somebody."

Nick blew her a distracted kiss, already on to the next excitement. In the doorway she paused to look back at him, lounging in his chair, talking enthusiastically into his little black telephone. "Hey, Larry, great to hear from you!" She felt a spurt of tenderness. Then she had turned her back on him and walked free.

A hand touched her shoulder. It was the stewardess, wondering if she wanted lunch. Suze sat up in alarm. Crikey! If it was already lunchtime by the English clock, that meant dinnertime was only eight hours away. Her stomach began to flutter—though not with hunger. Tonight, at long last, she was going to meet Lloyd Rockwell.

They had arranged to have dinner in her favorite Notting Hill restaurant, during the narrow slice of time between the arrival of her plane and the departure of his. Lloyd had sounded excited about meeting her; probably he was just being polite, because of the help she had given him. No doubt actually seeing her would prove a disappointment. Nevertheless, Suze felt a ripple of pleasurable anxiety. Could he possibly be as nice as he sounded on the phone? She had rather liked the look of him on the videolink, but then she had only seen his face, and a fuzzy version at that. He might have a beer paunch or bad breath. Jay said he was very intellectual: would her conversation bore him?

Last night, after leaving Nick, she had picked up Jay in her cab and taken him to the 21 Club, where they had finally drunk the bottle of champagne that had been awaiting Suze for thirty-odd years. One by one they had raised their glasses to Jay's movie, Lloyd's rehabilitation, Suze's boardroom triumph, Suze's dad, eternal friendship, true love and tobacco. It was a wonderful evening. In between the bouts of sentiment, Suze had fished for clues about Lloyd.

"Will he like me, do you think?"

"I don't know. He's pretty picky."

"Well, will I like him?"

"His taste in ties is terrible."

Half giggling, half exasperated, she had gone on pestering him for details until he brought her up short. "You haven't forgotten Betsy, have you?"

She had, temporarily. Somehow, Suze had never quite believed in Betsy.

To Jay she had said, "Don't be silly. Betsy Whatsername isn't even going to be there. This is a business meeting—combined post-mortem plus key exchange plus sorry-I-broke-your-wineglass sort of thing. It's not exactly romantic."

The stewardess reappeared, offering drinks. Suze considered ordering an enormous vodka; then she remembered reading that drinking alcohol in airplanes was disastrous for the skin. Feeling very adult and responsible, she asked in dignified tones for a bottle of mineral water, a pillow and a blanket.

She drank her water, then slipped off her shoes and replaced them with the slippers provided. Perhaps she ought to get some rest. She didn't want Lloyd to think her an old hag—not that it mattered. She slapped on some face cream. Then she pulled down the window blind and covered her eyes with the shade. She groped for the airline pillow and snuggled under the blanket. In five minutes she was asleep.

"Ohhhh, yeah . . . oh, yeah. Everything's gonna be all right this morning . . . WHOO!"

Lloyd turned up the stereo to full blast and boogied back to his breakfast. The window was thrown wide. Midday sunshine warmed his back. He was wearing shorts, sunglasses and nothing else. He felt good.

"I'm a man," he growled alongside Muddy Waters, shaking his cereal packet in time with the pounding bass drum. *"I spells M . . ."*—he poured a slurp of milk from the bottle—*". . . A"*—he dug his spoon deep—*". . . N"*—he tossed the toasted flakes into his mouth and dispatched them with a virile crunch. Under the table his bare foot thumped out the insistant blues beat on the floorboards.

The flat was a wreck. Lloyd stared around vaguely at the piles of paper, books and acquired oddments he had halfheartedly begun to collect. Yesterday afternoon, in celebration of his triumph, he'd bought over three hundred dollars' worth of blues CDs at some beaten-up store near King's Cross: yet more stuff to pack. The bedroom was worse. He had spread out his clothes on the unmade bed, but had got no further. Who was going to fold his shirts? Betsy usually did the packing, but . . . Lloyd stopped tapping his foot and looked solemn. This morning she had called from the hotel; at the end of their long conversation she had told him that it would be better if they didn't meet today, she would collect her things some time when he was out. She had sounded subdued. He hoped her mother wasn't bullying her. Last night she had been so sweet. Lloyd gave a mournful sigh.

Still, he mustn't allow himself to feel too down. He had a job—a choice of three, in fact. Betsy was not pregnant after all. *And he was not going on vacation with Betsy's mother!* Lloyd waved his spoon euphorically in the air, spattering the furnishings with soggy cereal. *Whoops.*

More calmly, he poured himself another cup of coffee. Outside the sky was a pure, cloudless blue. Trees shimmered olive and silver in the sunlight. His last day in London stretched before him, full of possibilities. He might go into town and see an exhibition. He could check out the second-hand bookstores in Cecil Court. Then there were presents he needed to buy: for Dee Dee, for Jay, for Lorna's irrepressible little daughter and, of course, for Suze. Especially for Suze: he owed everything to her. He would give her the present tonight.

Oh—and packing. Lloyd shrugged. Probably he could clear the whole shebang in ten minutes, once he put his mind to it. He clattered his dishes together, ready to take them into the kitchen, and turned up the music another notch. It had been a long time since he had felt free to play it as loud as he liked.

I love the way you walk as you cross the street. How did Suze walk? He'd never even met her.

But he would tonight. Lloyd did his syncopated chicken walk down the hallway and clashed his cup and cereal bowl together. *Baby, I wants to be loved.*

They were going to meet for dinner. She'd suggested the place; it was sure to be as wild and upfront as she was. What should he wear? Suze would probably think most of his clothes dull. Hmmm . . . A daring thought struck him. Why not buy something new, just for tonight? Splash out! He would head down to Covent Garden after breakfast and show his credit card some major action.

Lloyd piled his dirty dishes in the kitchen sink, alongside the whiskey glass from last night. Then he wandered into the bedroom. He picked up the photograph from the chest of drawers. She looked pretty: he grinned. Too pretty: he scowled.

He put the picture back. What was he thinking of? All they were going to do was exchange keys and catch up on some work details. Nevertheless, as Lloyd shrugged himself into his shirt, with Muddy Waters still rampaging through the flat, he couldn't help snarling under his breath. "*I'm a hoochie-coochie man. I never miss. When I makes love to a woman, she can't resist.*"

Chapter Thirty-three

Suze negotiated the bizarre entranceway, with its miniature Japanese-style water-garden, and climbed the wooden staircase on teetery heels. Behind her a muscled doorman-cum-bouncer carried her bags. As she mounted the stairs the buzz of sophisticated chatter grew louder. She could hear the clatter in the kitchen, where the carrot-haired chef regularly threw tantrums and caught a gust of coriander as one of the waitresses carried out a tray to the dining room. At the top, the tired-looking blonde, who always reminded Suze of a 1930s hatcheck girl, gave her a hard look, then smiled. "Hi. Wilding, isn't it?"

"That's right." Suze smoothed her dress. "Is it OK if I leave my cases here? I've come straight from the airport."

"No problem." She swung open the hatchway, then consulted her reservations book. "Your table's in the far corner, by the window."

"Right." Suze swallowed. "And, um, has by any chance—?"

"He's already there."

Suze nodded. Her mouth was suddenly dry. The blonde was watching her with a look of faint amusement. Suze rubbed her lips together, lifted her chin and walked into the restaurant.

She saw him at once—a lean figure in a pale jacket and indigo-blue shirt, half turned to the open sash window so that he could look down onto Portobello Road. One long arm was crooked on the back of his chair. His profile looked thoughtful. For some reason, Suze smiled.

As if she had called his name aloud, he turned his head and

stared straight into her eyes. He rose from his seat and stepped forward to meet her. "Suze? Is it you?" He looked delighted.

"Hello." Heavens, he was tall. She stopped awkwardly, uncertain what to do. She knew him so well that shaking hands seemed absurdly formal, yet she could hardly kiss someone she'd never even met. For a moment Lloyd seemed similarly stumped. Then he put a warm hand on her back and steered her with casual authority to the table. He pulled out her chair, in that old-fashioned way Americans had, and seated himself opposite, smiling at her with amazed curiosity as if she were a surprise present he'd found in his Christmas stocking. Suze felt herself flushing under his scrutiny. In the flesh, with his rangy shoulders and penetrating blue eyes, he was disconcerting.

"You cut your hair," was the first thing he said.

"Oh, God. Don't look." Suze placed both hands on top of her head. "Is it a total disaster?"

"Absolutely not. I like it. You remind me of that movie star—you know . . ."

"Yul Brynner?"

Lloyd burst out laughing. She had heard him laugh many times, but the physical details of his expressive eyes and straight white teeth were new. "I don't see you starring in *The Magnificent Seven* just yet." He chuckled. "*The Magnificent One*, maybe." He leaned forward, eyes alight. "Because that's what you've been, Suze. You know that. Without your help I'd be nowhere. Up the creek. In the gutter. Down the tubes."

"Pfff," said Suze. "Anyway, it was fun."

"Fun?" Lloyd shook his head in wonder. "You put your job on the line for me. I call that heroic." He reached out and lifted a bottle from the ice bucket. "Have a glass of champagne. I'm pretty much living on the stuff these days." He filled her glass and raised his own. "To us." They clinked glasses. His eyes lingered on her.

Suze took a sip and gave a contented sigh. Beside her the window was open. The air was rich with heady metropolitan smells—diesel fumes and summer leaves and delicious cooking. Above the rooftops the sky was glowing ultramarine, spattered with peachy clouds. She felt cool and sleek in the sleeveless silvery dress that she had packed in a cocoon of tissue paper at the top of her case. At Heathrow, she had spent almost an hour dolling herself up for this meeting, wanting to look good. Lloyd's expression told her that she had succeeded.

A waitress appeared at their table and handed them a couple of menus. The restaurant specialized in girls of offbeat beauty, decked out in long white aprons wrapped over black micro-skirts, with hair and lipstick in wanton colors. They were part of what Suze liked about the place, along with the handsome proportions of the room, its glorious big windows framed by long crimson curtains and its eccentric decorations. Roman-looking busts, garlanded with gold-foil laurels, stared blindly from high shelves; by the entrance was a topiary swan in a stone pot; a stuffed parrot perched on the bar.

"I'm paying for dinner," Lloyd said masterfully. "If you want to make me happy, you'll order all the most expensive dishes on the menu."

"Great! I already know what I want."

"Then let's order."

"But you haven't even looked at the menu yet."

"Oh. Yes. OK." While Lloyd studied the menu, Suze stole a concentrated look at him. He had a strong face, with dark eyebrows that slanted up to his temples and a decisive-looking nose. He was thin, but substantial, with none of that English skimpiness. In swimming trunks, for example, he'd probably look—

"Everything looks delicious. I can't decide what to have. What are sweetbreads?"

"Animal innards—the pancreas, I think."

Lloyd checked to see if she was joking. "Maybe I'll pass on that."

The waitress reappeared and took their order. Not having eaten on the plane, Suze found she was ravenous. She propped her elbows on the table and smiled at Lloyd. "What time does your plane leave?"

"Midnight. But I've got to check in at ten."

"Piffle. Those airport people don't feel happy unless they've herded everyone together hours in advance. If you leave it late, they have to let you jump the queues and you breeze through. That's what I always do."

"Really?" Lloyd looked unconvinced. "Maybe I could get there a little late. I already checked my bags at the airline office. How long will a cab take from here?"

"At this time of night, only half an hour."

Lloyd raised one eyebrow.

"All right, forty minutes. Max."

Eventually a cab was ordered for ten. Suze could see that Lloyd thought this tremendously daring.

"By the way," he said, "don't let's forget. We must give each other the keys." He reached down to a small canvas hold-all by his chair, unzipped one of the compartments, extracted her keys and handed them over. "You'll find the other set in your apartment."

Suze was still hunting through her handbag, trying to screen its bulging cornucopia from his sight. Coins, tweezers, pen tops, lighter, breath freshener, safety pin, miracle lip-restorer—*Christ, where were they?*

"Do you always travel this light?"

"Ha, ha."

"Hey, isn't that one of my pencils?"

Suze looked embarrassed.

"Keep it." He gestured magnanimously.

Eventually Suze found the keys sandwiched between the folds of her checkbook and passed them to Lloyd.

He hefted them in the palm of his hand. "I guess I really am going back." He sighed. Then his fingers closed around the keys and he dropped them into his jacket pocket.

"So Betsy's not going back with you?" Suze fished.

"No. She's staying in England, to take a trip with her mother."

"I expect you're sad not to be going too?"

Lloyd fiddled with the pepper grinder. "Well . . ."

"One salmon blini with lime chutney, and one *risotto nero.*" The waitress placed the dishes in front of them both. "Enjoy your meal."

Suze waited for Lloyd to say more about Betsy.

"Tell me more about the presentation," he said.

In between forkfuls, Suze gave him the full picture: Dee Dee masterminding the videolink from an outer office, calming her nerves with a jumbo-pack of cinnamon doughnuts; Harry half smiling like a sphinx; Bannerman and Tucker almost comatose from Sheri's barrage of statistics. "And you should have seen them when you came on!"

Lloyd shrugged modestly.

"That stuff about the passwords was brilliant. How did you figure it all out?"

Lloyd sipped his champagne. "I made it up."

"Lloyd!"

"It worked, didn't it?"

Suze looked at his face—confident, amused, in control—and let out a gust of laughter. "I wish you could have been there. By the end, Bernie looked as if he'd swallowed a whole pig."

"And some humble pie?"

"Absolutely."

"How was Sheri's presentation?"

"Bor-ing . . . Almost like a parody."

"Poor Sheri. So much ambition, so little talent."

"Ye-es. I see that now."

"And Passion really liked our ad?"

"They loved it. It didn't look at all bad, actually, considering I had to use videotape and cobble odd bits and pieces together."

"Hooray for you."

"They were your ideas."

"Hooray for us, then." They toasted each other once again.

"Jay was a star," she said. "He's so nice. I really like him."

"Well, I can reveal something. He likes you too. He was telling me just yesterday—at some length. He said I had to meet you."

"How funny. He told me the same thing about you."

Soon Suze was floating on a delightful little bubble of alcohol and flattery. She listened while Lloyd talked about his work on the Passion account, laying down his knife and fork and gesticulating in the air. He had expressive hands, with elegant wrists and long fingers. She wondered what it would be like to—

"Kiss," he said suddenly.

"Wh-what?" Suze felt herself blush.

"Kiss—Keep It Simple, Stupid. Don't you have that expression over here?" He looked up inquiringly. Her embarrassment must have shown, for his whole face sharpened with intensity, as if he knew exactly what she was thinking. A spark of excitement arced between them.

"Yes. Of course we do." She seized her water glass and took an inordinately long drink, staring at the tablecloth.

As the waitress laid out their main course, Suze reflected on what it would be like to go out with someone nice, who wouldn't abandon her at parties to get drugs for other people; someone intelligent, who wouldn't patronize her, or regard her as a pleasant diversion for an empty weekend.

"Tell me," she asked, "what do the words 'Prince of Denmark' suggest to you?"

"Hamlet, I guess. Why?"

"Nothing," Suze answered airily. Then her face became stern, as she remembered Betsy.

"Mr. Kipling must have been special." Lloyd was looking solemn. "'The cat that walked by himself.'"

"Huh?" said Suze, through a mouthful of *frites*.

"The Kipling story," he explained. "Rudyard Kipling. I assumed you named your cat after him."

Suppressing a bubble of laughter, Suze nodded in agreement. Lloyd was looking splendidly serious; she didn't want to dash his illusions about her literary erudition. Actually she had named the cat after a brand of prepacked baked goodies called Mr. Kipling's Exceedingly Good Cakes, because he was so greedy. She had been working on the account at the time.

She swallowed her mouthful. "I have a confession to make as

well. Your leather sofa: I'm afraid it's acquired a rather large black hole, courtesy of a burning cigarette."

"Oh." Lloyd frowned. Then his mouth curved. His eyes glinted. "You know what? I hate that couch. I always hated it. It was some crazy idea of—well, of a friend of mine, to recreate the atmosphere of an English gentleman's club. Now that I've been in England, I realize that such things can't be bought. They have to be distressed over the centuries by aristocratic rear ends and port glasses. Frankly, I think a cigarette burn has added several hundred dollars to its value. How's your fish, by the way?"

Suze glanced at her plate in surprise. Some food had definitely disappeared. She was quite unaware of having eaten it. "Very good."

"That's all?" His eyebrows shot up. "Not 'divine'—or even 'divinely divine'?" He was teasing her, with a look that gave her goosebumps. She shivered and ran her hands up her bare arms.

"Are you cold?" Lloyd's face sharpened with concern. "I'll shut the window."

"No, don't. I love London in the summer—when it's warm even at night, and you can smell the trees, and hear people enjoying themselves."

"Then take this."

Before she could protest he had stood up, peeled off his jacket in one fluid motion and was bending over her to drape it around her shoulders. She slid her arms inside the silky lining, warm from his body, and pushed up the overlong sleeves, breathing in its masculine smell. She couldn't help hugging it to her.

"There are still some things I don't understand," she said, trying to steer the conversation away from dangerous territory. "For example, did Harry know what was going on?"

"Only that Stateside might come on board if Passion dropped us. He didn't know what Sheri was up to, of course—or not until I told him."

"I see. What will happen to Sheri, do you think?"

"My guess is that she'll get a job with Stateside. I think she must have worked her magic on Tony Salvino. By the sound of that tape you sent me, she had certainly cast a spell on Bernie."

It was Suze's turn to raise her eyebrows.

"What's that look supposed to mean?"

"From what I heard, Bernie wasn't the only one to be enchanted by Sheri's lovely legs."

Lloyd confusion was a joy to behold. "But that—I never—She just—"

"You copywriters have such a great way with words."

Lloyd bowed his head, conceding victory.

At that moment a voice said, "The taxi has arrived, sir."

"What? Already?" Lloyd looked amazed and checked his watch. "Ask him to wait for a while, will you?" When the waitress had gone, he leaned forward. "Suze, can I ask you something?"

"I should think so." *What was he going to ask?*

"Why did you decide to help me?"

"I'm not sure. At first I believed what Sheri told me. I began to change my mind because the people I really liked—Jay and Dee Dee—always believed in you. And then when I realized that you'd been set up, it seemed so unfair. Also—" She paused, staring at her plate.

"Yes?"

She looked up into his eyes. "I began to like you myself."

"What about that time when you called me, and then Sheri came into your office? You sounded so stern! For a while there I thought you really were mad at me."

Mrs. Rennslayer's ghastly smile surfaced in Suze's mind. "Of course I wasn't."

The daylight had ebbed away now; the room inside darkened. Suze and Lloyd seemed drawn together into their own private pool of candlelight. Suze let her eyes wander over his thick, dark hair and along the faint line of muscle in his shoulders, and rest on the triangle of flesh at the base of his throat. He caught her peeking.

"I like your shirt." She blushed again.

"I'm glad. I bought it today." His eyes added, *Especially for you.*

Suze tore her gaze away. He was engaged to someone else. "I hate to say this, but you really should be going."

"Oh, yes," he said, without enthusiasm. "I'll get the check."

He waved over one of the waitresses, then put a hand on her arm to draw her close so that he could whisper in her ear. A smile puckered her burgundied lips. Suze felt unaccountably jealous.

"Now that I'm such a big shot, I get to have things delivered," Lloyd offered grandly, in answer to Suze's questioning gaze. "Why don't you look out the window for a while?"

"Why?" Suze was mystified, but obeyed.

"I like to admire your profile. You have such a superior nose."

Suze rolled her eyes. "I hate my—" But at that precise instant a bare arm intruded into her vision. The arm belonged to the tired blonde—not looking tired at all but holding a small wicker basket, which she placed on the tablecloth in front of Suze. She exchanged a saucy look with Lloyd and departed.

Suze unhooked the lid of the basket and looked inside. "Ohhh . . ." she breathed.

The kitten was the size of a grapefruit, smoky gray with four white feet and a white throat. Its eyes were the color of a stormy sea, and quite unafraid.

"It's a he," Lloyd explained.

Suze lifted the kitten gently out of the basket. "He's gorgeous," she murmured, holding him close. "Much more handsome than Mr. Kipling, I have to say."

"Younger, too," Lloyd pointed out. "Just what you need to take care of you in your apartment."

Suze bent her head and breathed in the smell of warm kitten. Other men might have given her more expensive presents; none had ever given her one that indicated so much thought, or presented it in such a stylish way.

"Oh, Lloyd, thank you! He's absolutely—Ow!" Laughing, Suze put her hand to her mouth to lick the small scratch. "What a tiger!" She glanced at Lloyd through her eyelashes. A smile curved his mouth and his eyes were soft, as if he was looking at the most wonderful creature in the world. Suze's lips parted to say something. Then one of the waitresses paused to stroke the kitten and the moment was lost.

Their table had now become the focus of attention. There was a rippling chorus of coos from the women; the men were looking perplexed, as if they'd missed a trick. Suze had a vision of a mass raid on the pet shops tomorrow. She put the kitten back into the basket, calming him with a stroke of her finger across his head. His newly sprouted whiskers gave him a supercilious expression that reminded Suze of her dinner partner in the Hamptons. "I think I'll call him Chester," she said. She closed the basket and as she did so caught sight of her watch. "God, Lloyd, your plane!"

Lloyd looked at his watch. "Jesus! How did that happen?" He got to his feet, picked up his small case and gave Suze a wild stare. "What about you? How will you get home?"

"Never mind about me. Go!"

He just stood there. "I don't want to go."

Suze gazed helplessly back. Then she rose from the table. "I'll come to the stairs with you." She didn't want to say good-bye to him here, with half the restaurant staring.

Out on the landing she leaned against the cold stone wall. Lloyd swayed close to her. He looked dazed.

"Well, good-bye," she said weakly.

Slatted shadows fell across his face from the iron balustrading above. She saw the shallow dip in the line of his upper lip. Her throat tightened.

Suddenly he grabbed her hand. "Come down with me. Please. You can wave me good-bye."

He pulled her down the stairs, making no allowances for her high heels or tight skirt. He wouldn't look at her. Outside, it was dark, with the faintest rustle of wind. Lloyd opened the cab door. Then he stopped. "I have to go." His eyes were still averted, but his fingers laced and unlaced themselves through hers, launching rockets of sensation throughout her body. "I have to go," he repeated.

The taxi engine coughed into life. At last Lloyd turned his head and looked at her. His eyes were narrowed into fierce bright slits.

For a moment she thought he was going to kiss her. Then he wrenched his hand free and climbed into the cab, slamming the door behind him. He folded down one of the jump seats and sat so he could face her through the open window.

The driver revved the engine. He was really going. Suze couldn't bear it. "Lloyd?"

"Yes?" He leaned forward eagerly.

They stared at each other for five full seconds. A stray breeze ruffled his hair. He looked very serious. Suze licked her lips. "Don't forget to tell the driver it's Terminal Four."

"OK," he said, with an effort.

Suze stepped back on the pavement, out of reach, and clasped her arms tightly behind her back. The cab began to move. "Good-bye."

"I'll call you," he said.

The cab sped away, square and black as a hearse. As it braked at the corner, Suze saw one of Lloyd's long arms unwind from the window to give a last wave. The cab turned the corner. He was gone.

Suze took a deep breath of taxi fumes, and blew them out again in one big, decisive gust. Well, that was that. She scrabbled for a cigarette in her bag, and managed to light it after three goes. What was the matter with her? She felt energetic enough to walk ten miles, yet so languid she could have lain down right then and there on the pavement. Hugging her elbows, she walked to the end of the block in short, jerky steps. At the corner she turned back, puffing furiously. In no time she had reached the next side street. She paced back again. A faint moan escaped her. It was no good denying it: he was gorgeous—funny, nice, clever, generous, divine-looking, with wonderful hair and eyes and the sexiest hands she had ever seen. She could almost feel those long fingers smoothing back her hair, or unbuttoning her—Suze spun on the sole of her shoe, turning away from such siren images.

He had gone. That was all there was to it. She might as well go home. She tossed her unfinished cigarette into the street. It was time she gave up smoking. No one liked it. She was ready for a change.

Somehow she managed the palaver of ordering a taxi and getting her bags and the cat basket stowed inside. She slid into the far corner of the leathery old seat and leaned on the armrest, blinking as the street lamps passed.

Lloyd had liked her too: she was sure of it. She remembered the expression on his face when he had said, "I don't want to go." But he was getting married to Betsy. He had gone. His final words were, *I'll call you.* Yeah, sure.

The cabdriver was dodging through the back streets of North Kensington, as if he had a record to beat. Suddenly he braked hard, nearly catapulting Suze onto the floor. "Bloody typical!" he snarled. Suze looked up to see a pair of lights coming straight toward them down the narrow passageway between the parked cars. Muttering to himself, the driver pulled over to allow the other vehicle through. The road looked familiar, Suze thought: this was where Bridget and Toby lived. She slid across her seat to look out of the window, and there, sure enough, was the tall gray house with its brass dolphin door knocker and lavish curtaining. The shutters on the ground floor were still open, the window raised high to admit a cooling breeze. A lamp shone inside. Suze could see Bridget and Toby, sitting opposite each other at their bleached beechwood table. Bridget was resting her chin in her hand, smiling at what Toby had to say. They looked companionable, affectionate, content. There wasn't a baby in sight.

Then the taxi moved off and the snapshot picture disappeared. But its mood lingered in her mind. Maybe coupledom wasn't so bad. It didn't necessarily mean you had to spend your entire time thinking about soft furnishings. It might be nice to have someone to watch out for you, and to care how you behaved. Suze wondered if she hadn't sometimes been a little dismissive of other people's lives.

After the experiences of the last few weeks, her old London life seemed unappealing. She wasn't sure how easy it would be to sink back into the old routine of work, TV, episodic fitness programs and casual dinners with friends, punctuated by the odd late-night supermarket raid.

Within minutes, it seemed, they were in Islington, and the cab-driver was asking directions. Suze peered out of the window as he turned into her street, with its familiar landmarks—the Greek corner shop, the house that always had a pile of old mattresses outside it, the tree she liked, with orange berries in autumn. And here, by the third lamppost, was her house, looking friendly and faded, and smaller than she remembered.

Suze paid off the cab, unlocked the front door and staggered with her belongings into the narrow communal hallway. "This is your new home," she told Chester. "You'll like it." There was an answering rustle from the basket.

Leaving the heavier bags for later, she opened her own inner door and climbed the stairs, carrying the basket. As she approached the first landing she became aware of three things. She could hear breathing. The light was on in her bedroom. And a mad-looking woman whom she had never seen before was standing on the step above her, one arm poised to strike. In the split second before Suze screamed, she noticed that in the woman's raised hand was an object that—but for its state of sparkling cleanliness—might have been her very own frying pan.

Chapter Thirty-four

Gorgeous: that was the only word for her. No, not the only word—also exciting, funny, adorable, sparkling and sexy. As the taxi careered around a roundabout, Lloyd's brain spun dizzily, remembering how she had looked at him with those wonderful hazel eyes.

Hazel? He frowned. Was that the best he could do? Her eyes were like glowing drops of amber. No: like twin topazes, or the burnt gold of angels' halos in stained-glass windows, or maybe . . . He sighed. Her eyes were full of fun and had looked at him tenderly. It was enough.

How did she manage simultaneously to appear incredibly stylish and as if she had just fallen out of bed? Lloyd's imagination summoned up her smooth, white skin, which flushed apricot when she was embarrassed, and her tobacco-leaf hair, spangled with copper. He thought of the seductive curve of her arms and how her mouth curled up at the corners, even when she was serious. He liked the hearty way she ate her food: she was a real woman with real appetites. He wondered . . .

Lloyd coughed and adjusted his position on the taxi seat. He hoped Suze hadn't noticed how he kept having to look out of the window, or pretending to concentrate on his food, to stop himself overheating.

The miracle was that she had seemed to like him too—or was she just being friendly? It was a long time since Lloyd had considered himself single. He wasn't sure how men and women behaved on dates these days. Of course, it hadn't exactly been a date.

She was clever too. And she was brave and bold.

So why was he leaving her behind? Why hadn't he told her how he felt? Why hadn't he pulled her into his arms and kissed her, as he had wanted to? Why hadn't he told her he was free?

Because he was cautious and cowardly, that's why. There had been a moment when he might have told her about Betsy—how they had agreed, with varying measures of pain and relief, to part—but he hadn't been able to think of a way of saying this without it sounding like a crass come-on.

Or was he just afraid of rejection? Years of living with someone had made him soft; he had suppressed the aggressive instinct of a male on the prowl. He was a wimp.

Lloyd stared broodingly at the floor of the taxi. Damn, damn, damn. He lost himself in a wash of self-pity. Damn Betsy. Damn the universe. Damn even Suze. Why did she have to be so damn pretty?

Lloyd blinked his eyes and focused on the chunky office blocks and fine 1930s factories flashing past. It looked as though he had already reached the outer fringes of London.

I'll call you. Of all the stupid things he might have chosen to say, this was the worst, the classic exit-line of a casual Romeo. How could he?

Of course, she must already have a man in her life. Coward that he was, he had not found a way of asking outright, but she was sure to be taken. Girls as attractive as Suze were never available for more than a nanosecond between the breakup of one relationship and the start of another. For all he knew, she was already back together with Mr. Hollandaise Sauce. If not, doubtless there was someone in London waiting to pounce—a handsome viscount with a Ferrari, who would whisk her to Paris for weekends, or an arty type who would write her poems. Lloyd wanted to bite the upholstery.

He closed his eyes despairingly. Perhaps he even moaned aloud, for the cabdriver slid open the window behind his head and shouted, "Can't hear you, mate, can I?"

Lloyd tensed. This was his moment. It was perfectly simple. People did it all the time in movies: *Hey, buddy, turn the cab around.*

Fast. I'm heading back to town. Lloyd opened his mouth and spoke. "Did I tell you it was Terminal Four?"

The taxi thundered on into the night, leaving her further behind with every moment. Lloyd raked his fingers through his hair. He had to leave: what else could he do? It was only yesterday that he and Betsy had split up. To pick up with another woman the very next day seemed, well, ungentlemanly. Suze would think him volatile. She'd already had a couple of bad experiences with men—what blind, brainless bastards they must have been! Lloyd unclenched his fists, forcing himself to think logically. It wasn't fair to make advances to a woman and then jump on a plane to New York. He and Suze lived thousands of miles apart. He had met her just once. The whole thing was impossible. He would put her right out of his head.

They were approaching the airport. Lloyd stared out gloomily as an obese airplane hauled itself into the sky. The cab pulled up outside the terminal building. Lloyd paid the driver and jumped out before he could change his mind.

The terminal was busy. A gridlock of baggage carts blocked the check-in desks. Lloyd glanced at the clock: it was already eleven thirty. It occurred to him that living with someone like Suze could be a nerve-racking business. At that moment, over the general babble of squealing children and holiday-happy whoops and the rumble of the luggage conveyor belt, he heard his name being called on the loudspeaker: someone was paging him. He felt alarmed, then elated. Could it be Suze?

When he fought his way to the right desk and announced his name, the uniformed man looked reproving. "Check-in was an hour and a half ago, Mr. Rockwell. Your flight is already boarding. May I see your ticket?"

It was strange not to have Betsy standing over him while he searched through all the zipped pockets of his bag. When he located the relevant documents he was told sternly to make straight for the gate. He took his place in the snaking line for Passport Control, shambling forward listlessly, dazed by the noise and glare.

Get a grip Rockwell. OK: it had been wonderful meeting her. What she had done for him at Schneider Fox had been wonderful. She was wonderful. They'd had a wonderful evening. Now it was time to go home.

Suddenly, it was his turn at the passport counter. The official looked at his photograph—the usual wild-eyed portrait of a mass murderer—then peered forward to scrutinize Lloyd's face. His expression was impassive. *I don't have to go,* Lloyd told himself. He looked around for a telephone. He could call Suze's flat. He smiled as he imagined how she would answer, in her eager, impatient way, and how he would say . . . What would he say? A loud thud interrupted his thoughts, as the official brought down his stamp hard. "Thank you, Mr. Rockwell." He handed Lloyd his passport.

Lloyd took it automatically. The line at his back surged forward, forcing him into the no-man's-land of the duty-free shopping mall. Officially, he had left England. He felt dead inside. Lloyd began following signs to the gate. It was too late to turn back now.

Chapter Thirty-five

"Don't!" yelled Suze, cowering on the shadowy stairway.

The strange woman tightened her grip on the frying pan. "Get out of my apartment or I'll call the police!" she shrieked.

"What do you mean, your apartment?" Suze straightened boldly. "It's *my* apartment." Her eyes strayed to the frying pan. It seemed a curious object to steal.

The truth dawned on them both at once.

"You're Betsy Rennslayer."

"You're Susannah Wilding."

"I thought you'd moved out."

"I thought you were coming back tomorrow."

"Who said so?"

"Who told you that?"

"Lloyd," they chorused. The two of them exchanged a long, speculative look.

Suze waited for her pulse to slow to normal, then picked up her bags. "Is it all right if I come up, then?"

"Well, of course!" Betsy moved aside. "What a terrible welcome this must be for you. I apologize."

"Not at all." Suze led the way into her sitting room. How nice it looked! She had missed her little flat. She put down her belongings and turned to Betsy. "There's obviously been a muddle. I'm sorry if I frightened you."

Betsy was giving her an intent, not wholly friendly stare. Suze tucked her hair behind her ears, suddenly self-conscious. Her mind was full of Lloyd. Her feelings must be plastered across her face.

"Lloyd didn't tell me you were coming tonight," Betsy repeated obstinately.

Suze drew an impatient breath. Then she thought she understood. Betsy had been expecting to sleep here tonight. Probably she had been on the verge of putting on her nightie and getting into bed—Suze's bed. Suze recoiled from the image. The idea of spending the night with the woman whom Lloyd was going to marry was unbearable.

She steeled herself to be polite. "Do you mean you haven't anywhere to sleep tonight? You can stay here, if you like. I'll go on the sofa."

"That's nice of you." Betsy looked surprised. "But it's OK. I'm staying at the hotel with Mother. I came over to pick up my clothes and make sure Lloyd had cleaned up, the way he said he would." It was clear from the set of Betsy's jaw that Lloyd had not fulfilled this function to her satisfaction. She put her hands indignantly on her tiny hips. "I sometimes think men just don't *see* dirt the way we do. At least, some of us do," she added.

Suze wasn't listening. So this was the woman Lloyd wanted to marry. Betsy was pretty, she had to admit—small and irritatingly slender, with a high, pale forehead that set off her dark hair and eyes, and a dainty little doll's nose about half the size of Suze's own. There was a helpless air about her, which men probably loved. Jealousy rose in her throat. She grabbed the frying pan from Betsy's hand. "I'll put this away," she said brusquely. "Then I'll call you a taxi."

Betsy's startled face told her how rude she sounded. "I'm sorry," Suze said ruefully. "I'm a bit tired from the traveling. Can I get you a drink?"

Betsy hesitated, as if this were a crucial decision. "Oh, why not? I'm worn out. Nothing too strong, though." She flicked her skirt under her bottom and sat herself neatly on one of Suze's straight-backed chairs.

On her way to the kitchen, Suze peeked into the other rooms.

They all looked the same as ever, but somehow better, fresher . . . cleaner. The bedroom curtains were truly scarlet again; there was a new mat in the bathroom; the kitchen looked friendly and welcoming, its open window-sill crowded with luxuriantly blooming geraniums. She frowned dubiously at the frying pan in her hand: presumably it was hers; she seemed to remember a blackened, mottled affair. She stored it in the usual cupboard. Here, too, mighty Ajax had been at work. Homemaking must be Betsy's big talent: not necessarily a bad one, Suze conceded. An object she had never seen before gleamed on the kitchen counter: her brand-new microwave oven, boon to the single woman. Suze opened the door curiously, then closed it again. Once she'd stopped despising the thing, it might turn out to be rather useful.

Back in the sitting room she handed Betsy a weak spritzer and sat down on the sofa, cupping her glass of wine. Lloyd must be halfway to the airport now. Misery seeped into her veins.

"So why did you come home early?" asked Betsy.

Suze opened her mouth. Absolutely nothing came out. Didn't Betsy know about her dinner with Lloyd? If not, where had Lloyd told her he was going tonight? Suze felt a hot blush spread across her face, as the seconds ticked by. God, this was embarrassing! Suddenly she thought of an inspired way out.

"It was the keys—yes, that's right, the keys. You see, yesterday when Lloyd and I were, um, having a business discussion on the phone, we suddenly realized we wouldn't be able to get into our own flats. Ha ha ha." She gave a manic laugh. "So we thought, why not meet for a drink? And a little something to eat. And swap keys. You know, before his plane left." Suze tried to look casual. "Didn't he mention it?"

"No."

"You should have joined us." Suze's cheeks ached from jaunty smiling.

"Should I?"

"Except it would have been boring for you. Work stuff, you know. Boring, boring, boring." Suze threw out one arm in an extravagant gesture and knocked her wineglass off the table. It flew halfway across the room and fell to the floor with a forlorn tinkle.

Suze gave a sob of dismay and went over to kneel uncomfortably on the hard floor, picking up pieces and dropping them into the wastebasket. Suddenly she felt utterly despairing. *I love him.* She bent her head, trying not to cry. Her chest ached with the effort.

Behind her back she heard Betsy say, in a low, wondering voice, "He didn't tell you, did he?"

Suze turned. She could feel the tears, wet on her eyelashes. She didn't care who saw them. "Tell me what?" She sniffed.

"Isn't that typical?" Betsy murmured to herself, shaking her head and smiling. Then, more softly, "Isn't that nice?"

Suze stood up. "What?" she asked painfully. "What didn't he tell me?"

Betsy's eyes traveled slowly to her face. She examined Suze as if coming to a decision. "Lloyd and I broke up."

"Broke up?" Suze faltered. It seemed her heart had stopped beating.

"We're not getting married."

"Not . . .?" Suze repeated.

"I guess we finally realized we wanted different things." Betsy was silent for a while, looking sad. "And lately," she continued, "I've had the feeling he was thinking about someone else." Her eyes darted inquiringly to Suze's.

Suze blinked with shock. Her heart was beating after all. "No," she said firmly. "Honestly, Betsy, no."

"I knew right from the beginning there was something about you," Betsy sighed. "Suze this, Suze that. I could hear it in his voice when he talked with you on the phone. He even told you that awful hardware-store joke he thinks is so funny."

Suze didn't know what to say. She began pacing up and down the room, squirming under Betsy's scrutiny.

"Then you helped him with his work. I don't understand how exactly, but I could see he thought you were wonderful."

Suze tried to hide the huge, foolish smile stretching her face. "It was no big deal. I just didn't like the way the New York office was treating him."

Betsy continued as if Suze had not spoken. "I have to admit, I got pretty jealous."

"But I didn't even meet him until tonight!"

"Oh, I'm not saying we broke up because of you. It would have happened some time—better now than after we'd gotten married. But what about tonight? Why didn't Lloyd tell me he was meeting you, unless he felt there was something between you two?"

"But there isn't! Lloyd is very nice, of course. I like him. But there's nothing—I mean, we didn't—" Suze faced Betsy. "It was a purely platonic business meeting."

"Really?" Betsy folded her arms and gave Suze an appraising stare. "Then how come you're wearing his jacket?"

There was a moment of absolute stillness. Suze looked down. Then she put her hands to her chest. Betsy was right. She was wearing Lloyd's jacket.

"I was cold," she explained. Betsy's eyebrows soared.

The two women looked at one another. Betsy's eyes were wistful, but not hostile.

Suze started patting the pockets. "What about his money? And his ticket?"

"Lloyd hates carrying things in his jacket. It's one of his funny little ways."

At that moment, Suze felt something in a side pocket. She drew it out and held it up. It was the set of keys she had handed Lloyd at dinner—the keys to his New York apartment.

"Uh-oh," said Betsy. "The doorman gets very grouchy if anyone wakes him up in the middle of the night."

The same thought occurred to them simultaneously. Both consulted their watches with identical, synchronized flicks of the wrist, as if they had been practicing for weeks.

"Isn't there a cab rank around the corner?" Betsy mused.

"You don't mind?"

"He's worth it."

Suze felt herself inflating like a hot-air balloon, expanding with joy, high with impossible hope.

"Meow," said Chester.

Suze jumped. She had forgotten all about him. Now what? She couldn't possibly leave an adorable baby kitten alone in a strange flat.

Suze looked at Betsy. Betsy looked at Suze: it was clear that she understood the situation perfectly. A resigned expression settled on her face. "I'll take care of the cat," she enunciated in flat, martyred tones.

"Will you really?" Suze beamed.

Betsy sneezed. "Just go." She closed her eyes.

"But how will—? What if—? Aren't you off on holiday tomorrow with your mum?"

Betsy looked coy. "There's been a change of plan. 'Mum' "—Betsy mouthed the word experimentally—"has decided to spend the week at a health farm. I'm going to Italy." Her face was transformed by a shy, glowing smile. "There's this Italian count I met at the hotel. He's—" Betsy broke off. "Get going," she ordered. "It's a chance in a million, but you might just catch him."

Chapter Thirty-six

Gate 26. Only two more to go. Lloyd checked his watch: eleven fifty-five. He should be hurrying. The passage stretched before him like a tunnel, as far as he could see. A succession of advertisement panels lit the route into the gray, flickering distance. The people mover bore him slowly, inexorably forward along its black path. He didn't even have to exert himself to walk.

Gate 27. Now the passage was almost deserted; anonymous murmurings eddied back and forth. Outside, he could hear the roar of aircraft engines.

Gate 28. This was it. Lloyd stepped off the people mover. He could see that the waiting room was empty. He turned toward it at a leaden, sleepwalker's pace; he couldn't bring himself to run. As he approached, a familiar copyline caught his eye: "Passion—it's the only way." Lloyd gave a mocking, inward sneer. The photograph showed a young couple in a hammock on a tropical beach. The image was seductive, the mood upbeat, the message optimistic. How crass, he thought, how falsely persuasive. Airplanes weren't fun; travel was not romantic. There was no happily ever after. He thought of all the fantasies he had purveyed for other people. Buy this, do that and your life will be wonderful. But real life didn't come pretty and slickly packaged. Real life was cruel. Real life showed you the most desirable woman in the world, then snatched her away.

A uniformed woman awaited him, smiling but impatient. "Mr. Rockwell? You're just in time. We're closing the flight now. May I see your boarding pass?"

Lloyd fumbled in his bag. He found the pass and gave it to the woman. She tore off the stub and handed it back. "Enjoy your flight to New York."

Lloyd passed through the entrance and onto the pontoon that led to the plane. His heavy steps bounced on the springy flooring.

The fact was, he didn't know Suze. It was impossible to fall in love with someone after one meeting. He'd been indulging in pure fantasy.

Her chest hurt. Hair was flopping in her face. She had taken off her ridiculous high heels at the entrance of the terminal and was now racing and skidding across the floor in her stockinged feet, trying to check the departures information screen as she ran. A red light was winking next to the New York flight, indicating takeoff in five minutes.

Suze headed for the nearest airline desk, bent to put her shoes back on and strode to the head of the queue. "Emergency!" She made her voice bossy and posh. "Urgent message from Ten Downing Street. Let me through." The crowd drew back, impressed.

"Rockwell," she told the official. "Lloyd Rockwell. Has he checked in?"

He eyed her skeptically. She raised her chin. Slowly, methodically, he consulted his records. "Yes, he has. May I ask—?"

"It's imperative that I speak with him. I have an urgent message. Top priority. Can I go through to the gate?"

"Quite impossible, I'm afraid."

"It's very important. I, er, I have security clearance."

"Might I see your identification?"

Suze's confident front crumbled. "Please," she begged.

His eyes moved indifferently beyond her. "Next?"

Tears gathered in her eyes; she brushed them away. She wasn't giving up. Suze turned around, scanning the terminal. "INFORMATION," said a sign. She dashed toward it. She would page him. He would hear her message and he would think . . . Never mind what he would think. She was beyond embarrassment.

She thought of his blue eyes, his warm voice, the energy that had crackled between them. Afterward he could leave, if he still wanted to. First, she wanted to tell him that she loved him.

Lloyd rounded the final curve of the pontoon. There before him was the open aircraft door. A flight attendant stood in its metal jaws. On her breast pocket was a bright red heart.

Lloyd stopped.

What was it Jay had once said? *Love. It's the only thing.* Of course you could fall in love, just like that. No one promised it would be easy.

So what was he doing?

Jay was right.

He had to go back.

"I'm sorry," he shouted. "Go without me!"

Then he turned on his heel and ran back along the springy corridor, through the gate, past the bemused flight attendant, into the waiting room and out into the passage beyond. Here he settled in a steady, uninhibited lope, his misery and his tension dropping away with every step. The dam burst. Emotion flooded his body, warm and welcome and cleansing, foaming through his veins.

Passengers coming in the other direction glanced at him in alarm and moved to clear his path. Lloyd laughed aloud. He didn't care what they thought. He didn't care what anyone thought. He felt powerful, invincible, unstoppable, free. For once, he knew he was doing the right thing.

Suze's expressive face floated before him. Of course he knew her! He had slept in her bed. He had helped her cook dinner. He had listened to her cry. He knew she tore the tops off cereal boxes; he knew which was her underwear drawer; he knew she liked bright colors, Frank Lloyd Wright, canned tomato soup and Simply Red. Well, no one was perfect.

He burst out of the passage and sprinted back the way he'd come, through the almost empty shopping mall. Ahead of him now were the baggage X-ray machines. He made for the metal-detector archway; beyond was Passport Control and the public concourse. He was almost there.

Suddenly something blocked his vision. He felt a thump in the chest. A large, bland-looking official was barring his way. "Now then, young man, what's the hurry?"

Lloyd stopped, panting and bemused. His eyes scanned the terminal as he cast about for an explanation. Then the miracle happened.

On the other side of the passport desk, pacing back and forth, looking furious, was Suze. Lloyd's mouth dropped open; he must be hallucinating. As if aware of his gaze, she looked up and saw him. They stared at each other in shocked delight. Then she grinned and reached into her jacket—*his* jacket—and pulled out something which she dangled high in the air: his keys.

The official repeated his question.

"I forgot something," Lloyd replied, gazing over the man's shoulder into Suze's eyes.

"It must be very important, sir."

She was lit up like a Christmas tree. She was fizzing like a firework. And it was all for him. Lloyd smiled.

"It is."

Acknowledgments

I welcome this opportunity to thank the many people who facilitated the writing of this novel by providing practical help and information; flaws that remain are my own: Mark Baker, Carole Blake, Richard Ehrlich, Deanna Filippo, Tamara Glenny, Lizzie Grubman, Nadine Johnson, Esther Kaposi, George and Marjorie Misiewicz, Christina Oxenberg, Lucy Sisman, Francisca von Walderdorff, Tamie Watters and Jane Wentworth.

Special thanks go to Louise Moore, my editor, for her unfailing loyalty, optimism and professionalism.

My greatest debt, as always, is to my husband Adam, whose generosity of heart and mind is beyond measure.